HOPE FOLDED HER WINGS WITH A DISTURBINGLY LOUD RUSTLE. 'IT'S NOT SAFE FOR ME TO BE HERE.'

'Has anything happened?' Humility asked.

Hope sighed. 'Talk. A great deal of talk. I've tested the waters in the Nearecloud mansion and in the Crescent. Aneisneida, Soderingal, Zin and Emni all say they would support you in a recoup.'

'Anyone in his right mind would support anyone other than Pati.'

'The city remembers *you* – Humility Garden, the first and last *human* Divinarch. A sort of mystique hangs around your memory. Everyone speaks of you with reverence.'

'But not one of them will risk his skin for me.'

Hope's wings fluttered. 'Can you blame them for being afraid? He has the flamens – and not just the flamens – dancing at his fingertips. Pati's got the whole world in his fist!'

Felicity Savage

DELTA CITY

ROC

Published by the Penguin Group
Penguin Books Ltd, 27 Wrights Lane, London W8 5TZ, England
Penguin Books USA Inc., 375 Hudson Street, New York, New York 10014, USA
Penguin Books Australia Ltd, Ringwood, Victoria, Australia
Penguin Books Canada Ltd, 10 Alcorn Avenue, Toronto, Ontario, Canada M4V 3B2
Penguin Books (NZ) Ltd, 182–190 Wairau Road, Auckland 10, New Zealand

Penguin Books Ltd, Registered Offices: Harmondsworth, Middlesex, England

First published in the USA by Roc 1996
Published in Great Britain in Roc 1996
1 3 5 7 9 10 8 6 4 2

 Roc is a trademark of Penguin Books Ltd

Printed in England by Clays Ltd, St Ives plc

This is for all my people who've respected me doing my thing—or who've tried to interfere, thus producing an equal but opposite reaction! Props also to everyone who showed support on the 16th. It meant a lot. In chronological order: James, Margaret, Matthew; Donald Alec, Donald Allen, Ian, Rachel, Roddy, Sharon; Hannah, Saffy, & The Little School in general; Diane; Andrea, Andrew, Ari, Ashish, Brent, Chong, Chris, Cory, Dayone, Ethan, Gary × 2, Greg, Jamil, Jen (my special rid), John, Julian, Julio, Justin, Kara, Kiet, Lawrence, Malik, Matt, Mike, Mina, Miriam, Nathan, Oleg, Ravi & The Rest, Sandhya, Sarah; Joe; and everybody I've left out either accidentally or on purpose.

Contents

1. The Redhead 13

2. Divaring Below...23

3. A Slow Night in Heaven...32

4. Heir...39

5. An Endless Night in the Whorehouse District...........47

6. The Freedom Wheel 54

7. Divine Intervention 66

8. In the Golden Egg...82

9. The Death of Comeliness...91

10. Impatience 101

11. Gossip 113

12. Something Like Normal 123

13. Hope's Folly...133

14. Certain Illusions 138

15. Red and Sable 149

16. Betrayal..164

17. Good-bye to the Lakestones 170

18. In the Sea Garden...179

19. Humility Under Stone...186

20. Inviolate One...188

21. Among Ladies 193

22. Solemnity 201

23. God of the City and of the Heart..............................210

24. Destiny Besieged...220

25. Murder in the Dark..225

26. Gallowsbirds...237

27. Recruit 248

28. Groundswell 261

29. The Wall of the Chrumetown Granary......................268

30. City of Charity 278

31. Conquering Passion 287

32. The Face of Treachery 298

33. Sword-lizard-winter..306

34. The Red Haze 311

35. Slow Time in the Eye of the Tiger.............................320

36. Swordfish 333

37. Victory 336

38. Decent Bones 349

39. Sideshow 353

40. *Elpechim* 364

41. The Return of the Good Things..................................368

42. In Human Country...375

DELTA CITY

THE CHRUME

CLIFFS

The Old Palace

PALACE DISTRICT

Tellury Crescent

The Eft Pool

Antiprophet Square

MARSHTOWN

CHRISTON

House of Larch

TEMERITON

The Rats Den

THE WHARF DISTRICT

SHIMORNING

THE JETTIES

Delights and Diversions

DOXTON

WESTPOINT

THE SALT MARSHES

Sol's Studio

ROYALLANDIC OCEAN

N

THE MAINLAND

"Miracles are according to the ignorance wherein we are by nature, and not according to nature's essence ..."

—Montaigne, *Essays*

The Redhead

Gete and his father returned to Sarberra behind the rest of the fleet. The sun was half-sunk in the ruby glitter of the sea. They tied their boat to its crag, slung the catch on their backs, and started up the path that wound between hillocks of gorse and heather.

Gannelets winged their way home. High overhead, Gete saw the batlike shadow of an early-rising predator. The village clung to the eastern slope of the island. Its stone huts glowed pink in the sunset. Dusk was a relief to eyes that had squinted at the black sparkle of the sea all day, searching for the little disturbances that indicated shoals of surface-feeding swordfish. As they entered the village, Gete and Da avoided waddling geese, bone-thin cats, and dirty, sleepy toddlers. Something was not as usual ... Gete had it! An evening as still and sweet-smelling as this, anyone with a minute to call his own should be taking the air, puffing on heather-stem pipes, mending clothes, repairing friendships.

"Da," he started, but before his weary brain could find the right words, Da had gone ahead down the dark gangway between their home and the Silverfins'.

Gete closed his mouth, plunked the net of barely moving fish he carried in the cold-box out back, and went into the kitchen.

A fug of smoke filled the room. Women and children swarmed, twittering. Gete sensed an air of macabre excitement at someone else's misfortune. But everyone who mattered was here; who could that be? The men sat around the hearth, discoursing with slightly more animation than usual. Heavy boots, heavy smocks, heavy faces.

Nights, Gete generally took his place on the edge of the circle—it wasn't worth offending his elders by going off on his own, might give them the wrong impression, what with him being a redhead and all they'd be quick to think he had a chip on his shoulder; didn't make sense, but that was the way of the world. Amazing to think it wasn't that long ago he'd been drooling with happiness, *one of the men at last!,* drop-jawed like an idiot as he swiveled his face from speaker to speaker.

He'd heard all the conversations there were to have, now—four-hands times each, maybe five-hands. Now while the men talked, his thoughts went to Heaven. It lay on the nearby salt island of Faraxa. He had never been there. But everything Desti said about it made it sound more fascinating. Desti said he'd take Gete there as soon as his *serbalim* gave him permission. Nebulous, cranky beings! Desti wouldn't dream of going against their orders, even though he resented them. They did not like his coming to Sarberra, although they had not expressly forbidden it. Could they really be as sagacious as he painted them?

Desti himself was so ordinary. Smiling and equable, always ready to help caulk a hull or quiet a crying child. Gete's mother insisted on mending his tattered tunic and breeches for him, not seeing that the holes were *decoration,* like the fish and birds she embroidered on her own family's festival smocks.

But back when Desti first started visiting Sarberra, he had been much stranger than he was now, more violent. It had taken him several months just to get used to working in sunlight.

What kind of village could Heaven be, to support such impractical behavior? Gete wondered. Or was it so inhospitable that the gods *had* to indulge in impracticalities, just to keep their heads straight?

Gete wondered so much about Heaven that he knew it could not be good for him. Like right now. Standing here with his mouth open, letting his thoughts drift! Anchor out, boy!

He sidled through the gathering and located Da just as he pushed between two younger fishermen and plopped himself down in the circle. His stool screeched at its misfortune. The smell of sea salt hung around the men like smoke: it permeated their coarse white fur and their hair. Gete breathed deeply, gripping Da's fish-scale–splotched shoulders. He winked at Tience and Rag and Imp and Tim, who all stood behind their own fathers. "I should na say he'll last the night," Godsman Stickleback pronounced with certainty. "Did ye na see the fella's face? He looked ninety and he could not be more than sixty."

"Na," Old Godsman Flamefish interrupted, with the privilege of age. Power gleamed in his cataract-filled eyes. "Na sixty at all, not at all. Old, that man is! Old! Eighty is more like it . . ."

"Na," Godsman Sharquetooth said. "He is not more than fifty-five. Fifty-eight at the outside!"

Gete could feel the tension in his father's shoulders. Da was physically restraining himself from interrupting the exchange. Not even the pigments and gaudy rags he donned for the children's amusement at festival time could make Teous Gullfeather a figure of fun. At times Gete had tried hard, inside his own head, to make Da look pompous; but he just could not do it.

Da cut in respectfully, "Who is this man? What has passed?"

"Eh?" Old Flamefish turned their way, head poking out like a sea turtle's. "Ah, Teous Gullfeather! Tis a flamen who has come! Godsbrother . . ."

"Transcendence," someone supplied.

"Tis so. Has the summer fever, he do, and he's dying. Divinarch preserve us. His leman rowed him from Letherra all by herself. She's na so old, neither, poor little scrap, and does he die, she must take his place here and now . . . we will be responsible . . ."

Gete kissed the top of Da's head, then turned away to see what there was to eat. A flamen was a flamen—even if it seemed strange, almost blasphemous, for one to be doing such an ordinary thing as dying. You'd think he would rejuvenate himself with a miracle. But everything flamens and lemans did was strange—they were far harder to understand than the one god that Gete knew. Wasn't that odd! Gete caught his mother's eye. She disengaged herself from the chattering flock of women and he hugged her in greeting. Her body felt small in his arms; his chin touched the top of her head. He pointed at the cooking hearth. "Eh?"

"How is it ye're so skinny, my son, when all ye think of is food?" She pulled his head down so that she could kiss his cheek. "It'd be disrespectful to lay things out till the flamen's gone, poor man, but ye might as well have some stew. No telling how long he'll cling to this world, and 'twont be as tasty tomorrow. Desti's watching it."

Desti was not only stirring the big turtle-shell pot but minding several babies. His silvery-white wings, as tattered

as his shirt, buzzed behind his shoulders, so fast that Gete
was worried. Once, Desti had opened his wings too suddenly and taken a small child's finger off. After that he had
been more careful. This absentmindedness meant he was
really upset. "What's wrong wit ye?" Gete asked in between mouthfuls of stew that he gulped without chewing.

"He keeps asking to see me. Your Mother Brownfern
hasn't let anyone know. But I can hear him through the
wall."

Gete couldn't hear anything over the noise of voices and
spattering flames, but he knew Desti had faculties that were
more than human.

"I've never seen one of *them* before." Desti cursed in
his own language and yanked a little Sharquetooth girl out
of the hearth. "*Haugthirre* child! How does he know I'm
here? I stayed out of sight! Should I go in to see him, or
would that just be throwing oil on a fire? He won't lie *still*!"

Gete served himself seconds and began to eat. *So* good.
Salt and fresh fish. Coriander and other herbs from his
mother's garden. Autumn was the best time for herbs. He
wished all the world would clear out; after a hard day on
the water, a man deserved peace and quiet—

"You stupid *haugthirre hymanni*! Mannerless!" Desti
cuffed Gete on the back of the head, so hard that Gete
dropped the bowl on a child, who squealed. Gete's teeth
knocked together on the spoon and he swallowed a chip,
the shock made him lose his balance. His head smashed
into the stone wall. Stars exploded between his temples.
Growling, he struggled back, ready to fetch Desti a proper
one, when the god grabbed his wrists with one hand and
his shoulder with the other, holding him immobile. "I'm
sorry! I always *forget*!" And Desti was kissing him, on his
forehead, his cheeks, he was always so contrite—

"And you *oughter* be!" Gete struggled away. "Gods'
blood, what's the *matter* with you?"

Before the god could answer, the door to the inner room
swung open and everyone in the kitchen turned. A half-
naked, scraggy, white-headed apparition staggered out on
the arm of a blond-furred girl. His head swung ponderously.
All the noise in the room drained into silence as he stumbled toward Desti, muttering. Desti sprang to his feet and
flattened himself against the wall, fingers seeking the cracks
as if he were trying to find a door handle. The girl—the

leman—had tear paths on the fur of her cheeks. "Lord . . ." the flamen sighed, coming on. "Lord god . . ."

Mother Brownfern burst out of the inner room. "Godsbrother!" At once reverent and righteously scandalized at her patient's behavior, she grabbed the flamen's arm and dug her heels in.

"Please, Transcendence!" The leman had a thin, young voice. "Please lie down. There's no god here." Fiercely, she gestured at Desti to get out. The translucent lids of Desti's huge silvery eyes flickered up and down. He didn't move.

"How dare you lie to me, leman!" the flamen shouted. His voice boomed like a horn. "I feel him! You cannot know how I feel him! He is like a shining sun on my blindness!" *Gods,* Gete thought.

Belatedly, a couple of women jumped up to help maneuver the flamen backwards. The men hitched themselves around on their stools, mouths dropping open, heads swiveling. After a painfully undignified struggle, the Godsbrother was hauled back once more into the inner room.

Desti's fingers closed on Gete's wrist in an unbreakable grip. "I have to see him." Gete cringed under the eyes of everyone in the room as Desti pulled him toward the inner door. "He can't possibly see me. It's a myth. I must find out. We are not gods, we never have been! That is what the *serbalim* say!" He pulled Gete through the rude plank door of the bedroom, and as it closed behind them, hot smoky firelight gave way to steamy darkness, and the smell of smoke and stew gave way to the pungent smell of boiled herbs. Gamesfoot, to draw out the fever. It didn't seem to be working. Gete's nostrils flared as he detected the smell of death. The leman and Mother Brownfern were kneeling on either side of the pallet, holding the Godsbrother down: they seemed frozen in place, their pale faces turned toward Gete and Desti.

"Lord," muttered the Godsbrother, and he shook them off like unwanted garments. Struggling to his knees, he lowered his forehead to the goatskin coverlet. "My lord god, instruct me. Am I obeying your wishes by continuing in the Archipelago? Or must I return to Delta City? The Divinarch has issued a call to all of us to return. But I feel that I am needed here. But I no longer hear you so clearly in my heart as I did." He stopped, breathing heavily. "On this island alone, two children lie sick. There is a blight

on the mountain flax. These rocks were never meant to
support humanity! I am *needed* here! Lord god, what
must I do?"

"I'm not a *serbali*," Desti said. "I'm not even a *mainraui*.
I'm inferior. I'm *wrchrethre*. Why are you asking me?" His
wings quivered. His voice rose. "All I know is Fresh Spring
Heaven and Sarberra! I know nothing of you and your
cities and Divinarches!"

The leman sobbed. Gete staggered back out of reach of
Desti's wings. "Lord god!" the flamen begged. "Please . . ."
He had been sinking deeper and deeper into his prostration
as he spoke. Now his head turned so that all his weight
rested on one cheek. He let out a whuffling sigh.

Panic gripped Gete. How much worse luck could there
be than to see a flamen dying? He reached for Desti's arm.
"Let's get out of here. Mother Brownfern'll say you did it.
Anything to shift the blame. Dry old bitch—"

Desti swung around. Pale furless face, strained unseeing
silver eyes. Then he pulled away and vanished into thin air.

It hurt Thani almost more than his actual death that
when the Sarberrans laid his corpse out, Transcendence's
mouth settled slowly into a smile. The heat in the inner
room of the hut made him stiffen fast, and as rictus set in,
his smile became more pronounced. He had been gaunt
when he died, and now the skin of the corpse tightened
over the skull so that it looked almost as though he were
laughing; gloating cruelly over the desolation in which he
had abandoned her.

Grief numbed her to the core, so that she fumbled for
words to thank the islanders for their hospitality. Gone. He
was gone. Out of determination to complete her duties as
a leman—not out of any sense of obligation to the ca-
daver—she watched over him all night, resisting the Archipelagans' efforts to coax her away, refusing their offers to
take her place. What did they know about her flamen?
Transcendence had hated these islands. You'd never have
known it, watching him bend his white head to listen to
the fishermen's wives and children, spend energy he didn't
have to work miracles for them; but then again, he had had
nothing against the Archipelagans themselves. They were
just a procession of hungry mouths, injured limbs, and
blighted crops, like any other people. What Transcendence

hated was the dazzling heat, the everlasting smell of fish, the hours they spent sailing from island to island, the breeze that never let up so that after a while it felt like a sandstorm in your face; no, it couldn't have been more different from their beloved Calvarese deserts!

Calvary. At night as they walked the vast empty spaces, stars glittered like the gods' embroidery on the black sky, and Thani scuffed trails in the sand with her feet, and Transcendence's tolling voice instructed her in the stories and religious parables which she would eventually need to pursue their calling.

After their nightmarish stay in Delta City, she had been sure Transcendence would take her back to Calvary. She had done her duty—hadn't she? What more did he want?

But her prophecy had changed the direction of both their lives as utterly as a bend in the bank of a stream. Now that Thani had killed a god (although it hadn't felt as if *she* were doing it: it wasn't *her* bringing the knife down, stabbing him again and again, cutting him to bits where he lay in his pool of white innocent blood ... Now that she had done *that,* even were they to go back to Calvary, it would not be the same. That was what Transcendence had said, closing the subject forever, as they stood on the deck of *K'Fier Diamondback,* while Thani watched Delta City vanish over the horizon.

Three years, and she had shrugged off her bitterness. The decisions and responsibilities of itinerancy left no time for it. She pleaded with Transcendence to go slower, to spare himself. But he obeyed the guidance in his heart, even to the extent of ignoring the call for all flamens to return to Delta City and make obeisance to their new Divinarch—a god who had replaced Thani's very own sister (killed her, they said). Humi, that ambitious and exotic sibling from whom Thani had felt so alienated the last time they met. Even when they were children Thani had not loved her sister, but Humi's memory was disproportionately prominent in her thoughts as she and Transcendence sailed deeper and deeper into the North Reach.

The seas grew stranger: fully half the islands revealed themselves as monumental jewels set in the water, glittering, warning the traveler not to approach any closer if he valued his eyes. Salt islands. Heavens. As they passed them, the sea seemed to rise and fall without moving, like black dunes.

The North Reach islanders clucked at Thani for doing "man's" work; they used Transcendence as a glorified midwife. Most of them had only seen a flamen once, perhaps twice before. Some of them did not even know that the Old One, the seventeenth Divinarch, had died! They had never heard of Thani's sister, or the new Divinarch, the master of the Hands.

Transcendence's body had weakened. His mind, lucid as ever, had chafed against the limitations of the husk that housed it.

Thani rubbed the heels of her hands into her eyes. The candle sputtered. Surely the night must end!

Overtaxed, summer fever, susceptible—

But the fever had not killed him. Wretchedly, she knew *she* had killed him. Four years ago, when she prophesied. That day, they were caught. From then on, their decline had been as inevitable as if they were caught in a river pouring into a gorge and over a cliff.

The murder of a god. It had changed the whole world. Thani's sister had saved Thani and Transcendence from execution for their crime; still, as Delta City shrank in the distance, Thani had been violently on edge, expecting to be killed at any moment, the way she had killed the Heir to the Divinarchy.

But the gods had known they did not have to lift a finger. The Archipelago would do their work for them.

Sails swelled whitely, grew, billowing across the North Reach. Darkness pulsed. She was in a hot, smelly room in a little hut on an island, but it felt like Purgatory. Every time the seal's-fat candle flickered, the corpse's face looked more like a skull. And Thani had a better view of the life ahead of her: a life as limited as death.

She leaned back, resting her head against the wall. Scent of rancid fat and raw-tanned leather. For once, her fair, short hair was tangle-free; the stones caught it up in little fans, as if she were underwater. Her scalp ached as if it were sewn together patchwork with a dozen seams. She stared into the kinetic shadows of the roof.

Harrima was too small to support predators—a mere peak of salt rising out of the water. Godsman Gullfeather

and his redheaded son ferried Thani there in their stinking
fishing boat, with that inexplicable god perching on the
bowsprit to watch out for a cove. The Gullfeathers young
and old had to tie rags over their eyes and she had to
squint through her lashes, but the god's eyes could tolerate
the rainbow glare of the salt with ease.

She felt like crying. She wiped her nose on her sleeve.

There was *Faith,* her and Transcendence's sailboat. Another boy of the village had brought it to Harrima. He
stood waiting on the shore. In silence, the Gullfeathers
helped Thani out. The god looked at her with distrust not
unmixed with fear. She refused to meet his eyes as she
climbed to the shore. The other boy took her place in the
Gullfeathers' boat and the redhead cast off. Soon they
were gone.

Faith bobbed on the swell, a little brown shell tied to a
formation that overhung the cove.

She hated that boat!

Her eyes were aleray starting to hurt. It was time.

She turned on her heel and started up the mountain. She
no longer bothered to squint. Soon she found a flat place
where she could rest and wait.

The delirium took her after two days without food or
water.

*Sand ridges gleam rosy in the dawn. A small tent is
pitched in the gray shadows, in a dry valley between dunes.
The child crouches behind a pile of rocks above it, on the
western slope. She has risen early to watch the kangaroo rats
drinking dew off the cacti. They lick and hop and lick as
the line of day sinks down the hill, hastening to get their fill
before the sun burns the desert to bone.*

Garment by garment, Thani shucked her clothes. They
were nothing but a nuisance to her now. Her fur was darker
on her torso and legs, which had seldom seen the Calvarese
sun; her breasts were the tawny brown hue she'd been all
over as a child.

When she surfaced from another whirlpool of dreams,
she knew taking off her clothes had done no good. If there
was one thing the Archipelago shared with Calvary, it was
heat. In Delta City it was hot too, she remembered confus-
edly as the sun hammered her into the salt. Royalland's
was a sticky heat, soupy with the reek of the marshes. Calvary was dry. Here, the sun was merciless, like a cudgel

embedded with broken glass. It came *through* the formations just as it would through dirty windows, so that there
was no shade anywhere. It burned her to lie down, but she
could not even think about standing up. She lay in the
open, breathing, just breathing. She could not smell anything. The inside of her nose was baked. Would the wind
never rise? Was it true she had once *dreaded* the storm
that would take her vision?

*Another morning, another resting place, and wild juniper
bushes scramble up the hill. A clear spring runs down into
the olive green hollow. Here, beehive huts cluster, stone soap
bubbles which have not burst or multiplied for two thousand
years. Black-furred children rush outdoors, tweeting to each
other. Another child stands with her father lover Godsbrother on top of one of the surrounding hills, looking down
at the oasis then smiling up at him: she is pleased with herself. She timed their approach so that they should arrive here
just at dawn. But of course he cannot see it—*

A cool breath of wind touched her. Memory ripped to
shreds and blew away, like a sail tearing loose from its
shrouds. She groaned. As the sun sank beneath the sea, the
formations began to creak in the rising wind, and the dusk
gave her strength. She struggled to her feet and began to
climb the slope.

Particles of salt borne in the whirling gusts scoured her
body. Salt briars cut her feet. Branches snagged her naked
limbs. Her fur was sticky with blood when she finally
reached the top of the mountain.

The blizzard raced so thickly over the bald crest that she
could see nothing. Sobbing, laughing, bleeding, lightheaded,
she danced. She stumbled, fell, got up again, a pale embodi-
ment of the storm, battering herself farther and farther toward numbness. When the pain reached a certain intensity,
she stepped to one side and looked at herself. A black-
splotched piebald spector with jerking limbs, making herself
a fool for no one to see.

Horrendous! said that self, who had stepped aside. *You
look as though you're having a seizure!*

Then the pain got worse again and dragged her back to
herself. Particles invaded her eye sockets, like swarms of
angry bees. Tears spilled down her cheeks. The wind
howled in delight.

Another gust swirled into her eyes. She winced, in the way one does when stubbing a toe that has gone to sleep. She could not feel anything.

Later she went even farther away.

Divaring Below

"*Delighted* that you could come!"

Serbalu Sugar Bird stood on tiptoe to look into Hope's face, beaming. "Everyone has been asking after you! You never come home anymore!"

Sugar Bird wore no face paint, to show off her porcelain-smooth, coral-colored skin. But her panniered gown, the latest Rimmear fashion, crushed her figure into an hour-glass, forcing her chest up into the semblance of a bosom.

Hope embraced her, then complimented her on her fetching choker of white stones.

"Straight from the jewel shops of Veretry!" Sugar Bird said proudly. "Moonstones! I'm disappointed that my dear little Uali has gone over into the service of the dictator, of course, but since he has chosen to waste his potential in human country, it is just as well that he has the wherewithal to send me souvenirs."

Broken Bird and Bronze Water would not look too kindly if they heard that. "It's stunning, Sugar!"

It was almost certainly quartz not moonstones. Behind Hope the receiving line lengthened, *serbalim* chattering louder in an attempt to broadcast their impatience, fluttering their fans. Hope stepped past Sugar Bird, her tulle skirts bouncing around her ankles. "Shall we sit together at dinner, Sugar?" It was rude even to ask, considering that Sugar was hostess, but Hope was the celebrity here, more so than Broken Bird and Bronze Water (*if* they had come). She might as well make the best of it.

Sugar Bird clicked her tongue with mock impatience. "I have already placed you on my left hand, darling! Naturally!"

"You're such a dear!" Hope kept her voice light as she

said, "You'll have to tell me all about your new little Foundling."

"You have never even *seen* him?" Sugar Bird made a glittery moue at the next *auchresh* in line. "We should make the Maiden promise to attend at least one ball a month, shouldn't we? One is in danger of forgetting that she is a Divaringian at all!"

Bronze and Broken Bird traveled all year, *teth"ing* from Heaven to Heaven with scarcely a holdover; they had started to become something of a fixture. Hope had heard it said (in a whisper, of course) that before you missed them, there they were again. It was affectionate chaffing—the *auchresh* world trusted and respected Bird and Bronze—but Hope was a novelty. She hardly ever, as Sugar had observed, found time to return to the salt anymore. She was more *wrchrethre* than any *iu* had ever been. Even Bird and Bronze's sincerest supporters fell silent when she entered a room—not on purpose, just to stare at her. It was wearying.

There was no longer a prohibition on venturing into human country. But while the political impasse of Pati's fiery dictatorship and Broken Bird and Bronze Water's disarmingly coolheaded influence over the *serbalim* lasted, none was needed. Hope *lived* in human country. But unlike Pati and his Hands, she was welcome back in Heaven whenever she wanted to come. (No *serbali* could refuse to receive the Divinarch when he made his infrequent sallies into the salt; but those visits, replete with marching musicians and corps of Hands, were looked upon more as traveling freak shows than honest efforts to improve diplomatic relations.)

They still called her the Maiden. They still looked at her out of the sides of their eyes. Now she knew how the Incarnations had used to feel in Delta City, in the old days.

She stood between two rows of blank-faced, white-tuniced *triccilim*. She took a deep breath and moved in among the circulating *auchresh*. Everyone greeted her as a familiar. Her cheeks were covered with kisses. Garishly made-up *keres* beamed at her, exaggerating every nod so that their *wrillim* jangled loudly enough to be heard over the roar of conversation. *Iuim,* few in number, pushed their way through their entourages of males to hug and squeal over Hope. Some of the males, too, were cynosures of attention:

garbed in the mesh hose with floor-length coatails that had
become all the rage, they affected a remote, blasé manner.
She felt most kindly toward these.

Auchresh society had started to originate its own fashions. It had to. There were no human fashions anymore.
But the *auchresh* styles were no more practical than those
the Deltan couture houses had used to come up with, and
Hope did not think them very flattering.

Two *keres* were waiting for her to notice them. Power!
What were their names—"Wonderful to see you again,
Pink Claw!" she exclaimed. "Honored, Stami!"

They bobbed their heads and retreated. She looked
around for the next wave. There was none. She must have
greeted just about everyone who was someone. The lower-
status guests—mostly *keres* her own age—stood nervously
at a distance, clattering their jewelry. Somewhere a fountain
played. Voices thundered through the hall. The musicians
were sawing away with all their might to make themselves heard.

One strove so hard for delicacy here, didn't one? But
delicacy was a thing of daylight. Detailed embroidery. Landscaped gardens with bees buzzing over rosebushes. Night
blunted all fine points, it blurred filigreed whorls of meaning, it blended multiple layers of tact. Night evoked vivid
colors, exaggerated forms, outré behavior.

Yet one strove . . with a determination which was, itself,
essentially *auchresh* . . . for delicacy.

The gong boomed hollowly. Hope envisioned supper.
Waiters clad in white to the chin—fearfully impractical.
Dishes hidden by smoky glass covers, so that one must
guess at what one was going to have to stomach. Witty
small talk with strangers.

And no one to hold responsible for the whole hilarious
satire. No one at all.

Except, perhaps, Bronze Water and Broken Bird.

She quelled a surge of anger.

They had better be able to explain themselves!

They had better have come!

One of Pati's more foppish personal Hands, Eyrie, had
sworn they were going to be at Sugar Bird's tonight. But
Hope had not seen nor heard a whisper of them. And if
Eyrie had been wrong she would not know, because she
could not ask. She was not officially in communication with

the *er-serbalim,* and she had no contacts in Divaring Below
to do legwork for her. Even here, she was sealed off from
the salt.

The tide of *auchresh* surged slowly in the direction of
the dining hall. Claws, hands, *urthriccim* caught her sleeves.
"Maiden! I heard that Sugar Bird has roast salt quails for
the first course!"

She curved her lips into an urbane smile and worked
her way across the flow to the edge of the foyer. Ribbed,
transparent walls soared up into a geodesic vault. From the
outside, she remembered, the mansion resembled a bloated
water porcupine rising from the lake. But on the inside, the
ridges provided welcome excuses for little alcoves tucked
between them. She chose one swathed in pale blue curtains.
Mercifully, it was empty. She sank down with a sigh of
relief on the frugetsfur cushions, and lit a pipe. The *serbalim,* influenced by Bird and Bronze, frowned on tobacco
as a human vice. As she smoked, her wings trembled behind the cushioned seat.

Why did I ever build the Folly?

No! For pity's sake don't start on that now!

She rubbed a scratchy lace sleeve across her eyes. She
had to go sit on Sugar Bird's left hand and catch up on the
gossip. If she didn't, Sugar would think she had left the
ball without warning, and she would have to do exactly that
because otherwise things would be so awkward. And when
would she have her next chance to talk to Broken and
Bronze? She could not foresee any time when their paths
might cross again.

The blue frugetsfur was seductively soft.

Never before in her long life had she stood alone in the
world's eye, without someone whom she could love and
look to for direction. Once it had been Pati. Even while
they were parted, in the last days of Humi's Divine Cycle,
while Hope tried vainly to graft herself back onto the world
of Divaring Below, it had been Pati. Right up until he
seized the Throne.

But she could no longer tolerate him. All she had now
was the Folly. And her secrets. She was chained with secrets. Promises she had made, and the principles she could
not discard in order to break those promises. Chains.

If only she could take these brittle costume balls seriously, it would be some small release! Then maybe she

could relearn the art of the essential, sweaty socializing that followed. Maybe she could raise a . . .

She could plainly hear the fountain tinkling. The music had stopped.

With the tip of one golden finger, she ground out her pipe. The hot ash sent waves of pain up her arm. She got up, left the alcove, and went to find the dining hall. When she got there, their voices crashed over her like a wave. They had not yet started the soup.

"I *hope* you have something to say for yourselves!" She rested her hip on the back of a chair and dug her toe talons into the rug. "You're not helping relations between Pati and the *serbalim*! As long as our people are persuaded that humans are inferior creatures we cannot gain by associating with, they won't take anything the *kere* who has proclaimed himself Divinarch over human country says seriously. They refuse even to listen to him. He is humiliated. If he breaks his ties with the salt altogether, it will be all your fault."

"A breakdown in communications is inevitable, I am afraid, Hope." Broken Bird's voice was gentle. "Pati's extremism has placed him on one side of a gulf which I am afraid we must recognize, for better or worse."

Hope sighed in exasperation. Broken Bird perched on the rim of the gold tub in which Bronze Water reclined, massaging the loose skin of his scalp. A scent of peonies rose in the steam. The parlor was chaotic with *teth"ing* boxes that disgorged outfits suitable for every Heaven, from a rural Eithilindre "family" to cosmopolitan Rimmear. The luxury of this guest suite infuriated Hope. Eyrie's information was good, as she had discovered by systematically exploring the mansion (all the other guests had either fallen asleep, *teth"d* home, or reeled off in pairs and threes to continue their reveals in pirvate; as far as Sugar Bird knew, Hope had gone home too) but hardly anyone in the household knew the *er-serbalim* were here. This was a rest stop for them, courtesy of Sugar Bird's *irissi* Tree Seed, a man as reserved as Sugar was gregarious, who took no part in her balls and sociales. Hope felt she might like Tree Seed, if she ever talked to him.

"Why haven't you contacted me, at least?" she said to Broken Bird. "That would have done *something* toward repairing the breakdown of communications! And surely, quite apart from that, I had a right to know that you planned to foment unrest in the Heavens."

"Unrest?" Bronze twisted up to see her, frowning through the steam. "The Heavens are far calmer than they were before Pati's coup."

"*Schism,* then. Young *keres* are slipping off in droves to follow Pati. Your rationales don't satisfy them. Before long the *serbalim* will have to react to the loss of their *triccilim* and Foundlings. They can't turn a blind eye forever."

Broken Bird gripped the rim of the tub with her feet and said in a bright, mean voice, "It will never reach that point, because Pati can't last. When the humans vanquish him, peace will return."

"*If* the humans ever controlled human country—which I think impossible—that still wouldn't be real peace! It would be only a facsimile!" Hope moderated her voice with difficulty. Daylight crept around the edges of the heavy tapestry drapes over the window. She was on a human schedule, like the Hands, and right now she had been awake for twenty-four hours, not counting the hours gained in her *teth*" to Divaring Below. Tiredness and frustration shortened her temper. "In telling the *auchresh* to maroon ourselves in the salt, the way we were before the Wanderer, you're ignoring the last fourteen centuries of history! You claim the word *god* no longer applies to us. You tell *auchresh* not to think of themselves as gods because the word springs from our relations with humanity. But you *must* see that in advocating the pure, uncorrupted *auchresh* way of life, you're assuming that there *is* an *auchresh* way of life. And what I've seen tonight persuades me finally that there is not."

She had them both watching her now.

"You say our race has stopped developing." Broken Bird opened her mouth, but Hope hurried on. "I know, that has been the conventional wisdom for thousands of years. And we do have our biological limitations. But we take pride in our intelligence, and rightly, for once one of us is civilized, he can learn anything. And we've been soaking up changes from humanity for thirteen centuries. Even as we gave them knowledge, they gave us it back, altered. We're *not* a static race, just differently structured from the humans, and if you call the way of life we have here in Divaring Below ecstatic and eternal, then you're wrong. It's no more than a parody of Deltan society before the fall, enacted in darkness."

Bronze rose out of the water like a mountain draped in satin. Broken Bird sprang off his shoulders, flying through the air to land on her feet. She picked up the wet hem of her dress and scrutinized it. "Oh, Hope," she murmured, gazing sadly at the broderie verenaise, "are you trying to say the conclusions Golden Antelope drew about our race were *wrong*?"

"I am! He was a madman!"

"I quite agree. He believed we were inferior to the humans. Bronze and I take the far better considered view that we are *superior*." She pulled her dress off over her head and minced toward Hope, presenting her back to her. Bronze Water toweled himself, his back to the women. Hope helped Broken Bird out of her false-ribs and the moss-green petticoat underneath. The small *iu* walked over to a trunk, stopping on the way to pat Bronze on the back, and pulled a loose salt-flax dress over her head.

"*This* must have come from human country," Hope said, holding up the beribboned petticoat.

"It was a present from little Humility Garden." Broken Bird leaned against Bronze Water. He caressed her with fat, sheeny fingers. Hope tried to recall if they had used to express affection so openly. "We used to like her, didn't we, Bronze? We helped her find her feet. Of all the lords and ladies Pati put an end to, she is the only one I would bring back from the dead, if I could. So you see I do not like to throw the petticoat away."

Hope wondered what Broken Bird would say if she knew Humi was not dead. She would probably be scandalized, and see that matters were put to rights immediately. "Hypocrisy is an easy trap to fall into," she said pointedly.

"You are too impatient, Hope!" Bronze said. "You were ever so." He had dressed in breeches and a dark purple tunic that disguised his paunch. The paunch had enlarged significantly since the last time she saw him; yet he was still not laughable, he possessed a kind of dynamism that gave her the idea that unlike Broken Bird, he meant everything he said. "Nonetheless I have a soft spot for you, Maiden. Let us untangle this tangle." He indicated a scroll-armed couch and quirked an eyebrow at her. Warily, Hope perched on its arm. Bronze Water climbed heavily onto the couch and squatted up so that their eyes were on a level. "Golden Antelope," he enunciated, "was a madman."

"I'm glad we agree on something."

"He glorified in failure. He was ready to sacrifice both human and *auchresh* lives indiscriminately to attain his goal. His goal *was* the wanton sacrifice of lives. Thank the Power, the Divine Balance swung in our favor, not his, and now I feel there is no danger of upheaval within the salt. I cannot say the same for human country."

"Pati has it well under control."

"But the balance between the races is still delicate. That is what we must work on. We must actively craft a peace that can devolve into an isolationism agreed to by both *auchresh* and humans. That's what Broken Bird and I are doing."

"Lulling us into complacency?" Hope muttered. She sat up straight and said more loudly, "But you deal only with the *serbalim*. What an incentive to schism! Aren't you *aware* of the lower classes of *auchresh*?"

"One has status," Bronze said. "One must speak to ears attuned to one's voice."

"And that's not even the point." She stood up. Daylight came in strongly around the drapes, washing the taper flames out. Soon the sun would rise. As she paced, anger pumped through her veins. "The point is that you are *wrong*. There must be change. It can come peacefully, or violently, but we can't return to what we were! Oh, Power, I can't go over it again. I can't make you understand." She slumped against the wall. Daylight flooded along it into her eyes. She was momentarily blind. And they were touching her, their arms slipping around her in that uniquely innocent *auchresh* gesture of comfort. Their body heat warmed her. She felt she had come to a place of safety. She knew that was not the case. "Dear," Broken Bird murmured, "don't you understand? Pati does not represent humanity! There is no *need* for us to deal with·him!"

And Bronze, gently: "Hope, sweetheart, are you *really* an unbiased observer? Think. Pati was your *irissi*. Then your *elpechi*. Now—I don't know what you are to each other. But however things stand, you are not so close as you were. You don't have to tell us. We can see it. It seems to me as if you must feel some ... bitterness. Might *that* not be what's making you obsessed with his role in this?"

He was right. She was a female. And weak. And Pati had been all in all to her.

"No!" She thrust them away. "How much lower can you sink without admitting it to yourselves? We are all *wrechrethre*. Pati is an *auchresh* of our times—and example even *you* will end up following whether you like it or not."

"Hope."

The scent of peonies was cloying. She stepped back against the curtains. "I don't know when we'll meet again. If you want to find me—have someone describe the Folly. Nobody will notice if you come. Status doesn't show on the outside, you know. Not in the city."

She *teth*"*d* away from their protests.

The thrum of Delta City soaked into her skin. Her forearm fell over her face. She lay crumpled on the floor as if there were nothing inside her clothes. It was later in the day in Delta City, of course, a golden midsummer morning. Sun came hotly through the glass. This was her cupola. It gave the Folly a faintly ludicrous silhouette: an upward-thrusting fountain topped by a pimple. None of her servants were allowed up here, even to clean.

Her forearm cast a welcome weight of shade over her eyes. She stared into the deep ocher color, the honeycomb pattern of fine lines. Her skin seemed to ripple like the surface of a stream.

She would sleep for a while. Perhaps later she would go visit Humi. It was always good to be reminded that there was someone in a worse fix than yourself. She could tell Humi for certain, this time, that Broken Bird and Bronze Water thought she was dead. And as usual, she would have to refrain from mentioning Arity. The temptation was always there. But Hope knew better than to say anything, now that Humi seemed to be getting over him. Hope had felt such a rush of relief when Humi finally raised the question of a recoup. Not least because it proved she was consigning her love to the past, focusing on other things. It was better that she forget Arity. They could never meet. And Arity was no longer the *auchresh* he had been. The last time Hope had seen him, he had slung his arm around the ugly young *kere* beside him and told her to go away.

The ceiling rippled. She stood up, gasping in the cool shadows of the roof.

A Slow Night in Heaven

"Eights," Sual said to the hustler, grinning with stained fangs. His right hand drifted over the knife at his thigh. "Saw it come up eights. You can't cheat me, *hymanni-fucker*. I got friends."

Arity hoped Su wasn't relying on him to prove that claim. He had no heart for a fight. The stars glowed brilliantly over the chasm, shining on the broad stone windowsills of the lamplit tavern. Sitting in the eastern window, his bad leg dangling into the chasm, Arity could not help thinking. As a rule, he tried to avoid that activity. *Khath* helped. Transparent distilled *ruiks*blood, it numbed the brain and ruined the body—much the same thing alcohol did for humans. But tonight the glass felt so heavy he thought it might fall from his fingers.

He took a swig and glanced at the stage. The entertainment had not got any better since he and Su came in. A young *ghauthi kere* was making overtures to a chained predator, trying to arouse its sheathed penis. Later on the *auchresh* and the animal would couple, the *haugthule* raking the boy's shoulders with clipped talons, the boy screaming with pain as he was split in this self-abasing acknowledgment of his parentage.

It held the audience spellbound. It had shocked Arity too, the first few times he saw it, but that was a couple of years ago. Nothing had changed since, except the sizes and shapes of the participants. This was a small *haugthule,* no more than Foundling-size, snapping dispiritedly at its handler. The sickly green hue of its wings was probably due to its having been kept out of fresh air too long. Its cupid's-bow mouth drooped at the corner, and as the long lashes fluttered Arity swore he saw tears in its eyes.

But predators did not cry, or at least that was the common wisdom, and Arity would rather not get close enough to find out the truth.

He felt restless tonight. News had filtered down to this honeycomb of streets, this cesspit he called home, where

the dregs of Rimmear washed to and fro: news of a new
predator in Rimmear, this one a man. The Divinarch was
coming. With pomp and splendor and free *khath* for all of
Heaven's hungry poor, he was coming to discuss some matter or other of failed communications with the *serbalim*. It
was quite a momentous occasion. Peach Branch, a fat fuzzy-
headed *serbali* whom Arity had seen once from a distance,
had issued a proclamation. Moreover, the Divinarch was
bringing a fully fledged retinue of Hands: to the *auchresh*
among whom Arity drifted, *they* were the most interesting
part. Even low status *firim* had heard tales of the
wrchrethrim. They spoke of them with mixed awe and
contempt.

But Arity himself could not stop thinking about the
Divinarch.

A shard of his other life, the life he did not think about.
Poking painfully through.

(Sometimes Delta City and all in it seemed only to have
been figments of an encroaching insanity which had rushed
near and enswarmed him in a dripping cloud, while he was
injured maybe, tormenting him with false tastes of happiness before he woke to the unsubtle world.)

On the stage the *haugthule* yowled, a long shriek of misery. The boy scrambled backward, terrified out of his pre-
tense of boredom. Laughter rippled from nearby tables.

Arity gulped the rest of his drink, grateful to have his
thoughts interrupted. He touched Sual's yellow hair. "Let's
get out of here."

Su did not hear. Su was gambling with heart and soul
and complete concentration. Su, or Unusual Day, was the
best distraction Arity had found from memories, with his
laughing eyes and his darting tongue and childish questions.
Did Arity really love him? Was the roof of the chasm made
of glass, or was the sky a picture painted on it? Sual had
never tried to climb higher in the city than the highest
bridge. But ignorance breeds a superficial worldliness that
impresses the overly refined, and when Arity was new and
naked from his illness, he had been completely taken in.
Now he knew the truth, it was too much bother to redefine
their relationship. Not that it ever had been defined, in
words. Su was a good lover: he found Arity's scars erotic.
Also the thorns.

Arity slid down and pressed his face against Su's shoulder. "Hustlers be a Power-damned sight stupider at the Blue Skybird," he said to Su, by way of an opening, and also to flatter this hustler, who was looking dangerous on the other side of the table. "Let's go." He had discovered that he badly wanted to leave before the show started in earnest.

"*Haugthirre* hasn't said I don't owe him no *denear* yet." Under his ragged, billowy shirt, Su was as rigid as the back of his chair. Eyes locked, he and the hustler stared each other down. Rudimentary wings poked high behind their heads, like hackles, like—memories tweaked at Arity's mind. Cats in an alley—

"I said, I want to *go,*" he said loudly, jerking Su up.

Caught off guard, Su stumbled out of his chair, twisting and fighting to keep his eyes locked with the hustler's. After a minute he gave a hiss of despair and threw himself ahead of Arity. Arity staggered on his bad leg. "Damn *idiot* cripple boy." Su reached around and shoved him in the back, right where he must know the worst scar was, because several thorns grew out of it, poking holes in the weave of Arity's shirt. "Find us somewhere that *haugthirre* cheat won't find *me,* then!"

"Is it that serious?" Arity's heart sank: Su was a tricky business proposition at the best of times. Given even partial access to Arity's supply of *denear,* he went wild.

Su laughed. "All I'm sayin is, the dear old Skybird won't save us this time. We're too hot. Less get over to other side an lay hands on Nifi and Red Sedge. Safety in numbers, an that."

They passed through a curtain of swinging himmisfur strips into a chilly, smoke-free passage. Servingmen, naked like overgrown versions of the Foundlings employed by taverns on the top tier, hurried along with pots of *khath.* The passage hiccuped Arity and Su out into the street. Starlight swam down between the eaves of the buildings that teetered over the street. No one was about. Arity thought he heard a disturbance behind in the tavern and wheeled, awkwardly.

Su plucked at him. "Less go. I mean it: I swore em too damn much. I was sure I had that last roll cornered."

"I got it downtier if you want to pay," Arity said. He might as well use Hope's money, if she was determined to give it to him. Better that than get murdered when some *kuiros* found out about his riches.

"Nah. We'll lose em, come on."

They took off uphill at a lope. All of Rimmear's streets sloped upward to the bridges. The Laughing Haugthule Tavern received starlight only because it was on the edge of the chasm; the rest of the tier was buried black under a league and a half of city. Arity felt Rimmear looming like a cliff behind him, humming.

Footsteps echoed on the slick salt in a side alley.

Su glanced sideways and said "Shit." He grabbed Arity's arm, pulling him faster. Sweat broke out on Arity's temples. The thorns stopped him from wiping at it.

Behind them there was a shattering crash. This time Arity could not help spinning in Su's grip. He could see nothing around the corner, but he heard shouts trumpeting like bugles. Most of those with dirty work to do here did it as cleanly as possible, in private: this gave the streets a speciously safe, quiet feel, when in fact anyone who looked like a country boy would not last three corners. Only occasionally did violence spill into the open. Arity cursed the noise for giving the footsteps a chance to work their way around ahead. "Leave me here—" he panted, as much out of a need to stop running as anything else. "You'll outdistance em."

"He'll take it outta you."

"We're only *ghauthijim*."

"But he's a *haugthule*. Come on—"

Ahead of them, the bridge swooped upward like a pale ribbon. They dashed out onto the rusty, ringing expanse. One decrepit guardrail stood up from the edge like a row of spines. The smelly wind of the chasm gusted dangerously from all the points of the compass. The other bridges, above and below, crisscrossing, joining, curved around this bridge in a celestial network that might aeons ago have been crafted to replace the constellations with something better designed. All the bridges were close to empty. *Slow night.*

But here you could tell nothing from the looks of things, just as you could tell everything from the way things looked.

At an intersection, a fat blue-skinned *auchresh* welled up in front of them.

"Shit!" Su yelped.

An ancient, stinking *iu* and her escort of *keres* was waddling along behind Su and Arity. Su nearly knocked them
off the bridge as he dashed back the way they had come.
Arity muttered an apology to the old woman as he followed. The scars in his sides were cutting him in half. He
could not keep up.

"Ailoa . . . !" a voice hailed them from the bridge above.
" 'Ello, nameless low-status! Impoverished cheat! I take it
out o your *skin!"* The hustler from the Laughing Haugthule
swung over the guardrail of the bridge some thirty feet
above and plummeted down to their bridge. The flexible
metal dropped when he hit, them snapped back, tossing
Arity into the air. The old *iu,* who by now had reached the
downslope, gave a croaking screech. Arity struggled to get
to his feet. As the blue-skinned *kuiros* pelted past him,
almost casually he brought a fist the size of a small dog
into the back of Arity's head. "Cripple," Arity heard him
say, and then the world cascaded slowly apart in a waterfall
of white.

There was a fire on the east side of the chasm. The
Laughing Haugthule Tavern was burning. The flammable
salt insulation under its tiles flared yellow and blue. People
were screaming and climbing out on the windowsills. Somebody dropped off, down, down, writhing like a spider. Arity
thought groggily that he should really go do something
about the deaths. Help. Something. Yes.

That was the kind of thing that had got him half-killed
in Delta City, wasn't it? His scruples. A heart, an actual
heart! Sin for an *auchresh!* In Delta City, the only thing
that had saved his face was the Heir's arrogance, which had
kept him aloof and incomprehensible, as much to himself
as to others. Now his scruples were negated by his power-
lessness. Almost always, but not quite often enough.

So he'd reshaped the Heir's arrogance. Remade the cage
into armor. Dull, patchwork stuff, let him blend in nicely
while keeping him clean and dry inside, like a snail in a
garbage heap.

Hadn't done him much good against that *kuiros's* fist
though, had it?

One of his legs was hanging off the edge of the bridge.
With an effort, he locked an elbow around the stump of a

guardrail and pulled himself to safety. He flopped back, shuddering with the effort. Stars filled his eyes. Stars pooled in his brain. An old *auchresh* plodded past, grumbling to himself about corpses on his bridge again. Undoubtedly he had a knife. Arity held still until the muttering died away. Then he steeled himself to get up.

And above him wings flapped, leathery, tired. The wind died around him, blocked off. Claws chinked on metal.

Auchresh could not fly.

It was a predator. Possibly the one from the Laughing Haugthule. It squatted in front of him, running the chain through its wicked little claws, wondering whether Arity was good to eat. It picked its nose. It cocked its head on one side like a winged green Foundling.

Arity shrank back, weaker even than when the leman's knife had bit into his body, when he had felt his blood rushing out of him. This was the living ghost of his ancestors. This was shame alive. He reached carefully for his knife.

Yet there was the fascination that brought countless *auchresh* back to the Laughing Haugthule and taverns like it night after night after night, to turn glasses of *khath* in their hands and stare at the stage, and it held him immobile.

The predator darted its head at him and bit him on the shoulder.

He yelled and struck out with his knife.

It flinched back, snorted through its nostrils, and lifted into the night.

On the edge of the chasm, the tavern subsided into white-hot ashes.

After painstakingly knotting his tunic around his bitten shoulder, Arity got up and shuffled down the bridge. He smelled Sual before he reached him. The hustler and his friends had emptied their bladders on his body. Also they had done worse things. No doubt these particular mutilations were their signature, and they meant the body to stand as some sort of monument to their prowess. Mutilation was a new trend that the *kuirim* had picked up from tales of Delta City which were only just now reaching them. Arity thought it hubristic, and he hated it as he hated all things that reminded him of the city. And for once, he could do something about it. Panting, he heaved the body into the chasm. Let it choke the river along with the rest of Rimmear's waste.

He supposed he should be sorrier for Sual. But they had only been *ghauthijim*. He stretched, feeling each puckered scar on his torso bite deep. How marvelous that he was not compelled to grieve.

He dragged himself home.

Home was a rickety building on the bottommost tier. The skylights were splattered with muck thrown down from the city, but at least there *were* skylights. He paid enough for them. The curtains that one hooked over them during the day were rolled up, thick with salt dust. He never unrolled them. He laid clean clothes on the bed, then stripped off the soiled ones in a method perfected by time and practice, ignoring the ache in his shoulder, eyes shut so that he would not have to see himself before he got the other garments on.

The dawn brightened overhead as he cooked supper. The sunlight in the salt was so remorseless that it would cook your food for you, especially when it came through the flawed panes of glass salt that passed for windows here, but Arity was used to his little stove. Su had won it from the proprietor of a cookhouse for him. He felt a pang only when, unthinking, he laid two plates on the floor.

He finished the food in a daze. Then he lay on his bed, watching the square of cloudy sunlight creep across the floor. The room looked as bright and flat as a chord on an out-of-tune *farader,* but uglier. Every time he drifted part-way into sleep, his heart would thud, and he struggled to open his eyes, desperate to escape the images of bat wings and mindless gold eyes, and clawed hands playing with a broken chain.

When he finally did sleep, of course, there was Pati.

Heir

Because Gete's mother had taken the dying flamen in, his leman had become the responsibility of the Gullfeather family.

"Better go get her today!" Godsman Stickleback said to Gete's father. Four dawns had passed since they left the girl on Harrima salt. A breeze ruffled the sea. The eastern sky glowed pink, but night's dark skirts trailed behind Sarberra peak. At the rock harbor, the troop of men and boys separated to their boats.

Gete's father wheeled around. "Why ent *you* get her, Godsman Stickleback?" All along the crags, faces blank with sleep turned toward him, then away, uninterested. Kin Stickleback was the only man ever awake enough to talk in the mornings, and he would as a matter of habit rattle on and on, whether the others listened or not. "We have our dinners to catch!" Gete's Da said. "And my wife owes the hag Brownfern a passel of fish for her help wi' the Godsbrother. Ye go."

"Ye want the girl to die? 'Twill be on yer head, yerself an yer fine redhead son."

"Her own boat is on the island!"

"An let me put my hands on the woodhead whose idea 'twas to take it!" Godsman Stickleback knew it had been Old Flamefish's idea, and that Gete's father would say nothing against the old man. He rested one foot on the prow of his boat and opening his mouth peculiarly wide, cocked his head on one side. Gete's father stamped down into the boat and said, "Let's go." Hypnotized, Gete neglected to let down the centerboard before he untied the boat. They skidded across the wavelets toward Godsman Stickleback's boat, and Gete scrambled to give her a keel. They darted away, reaching across the breeze. Gete's father staggered, caught the tiller, and threw back his head and laughed.

"Right then, boy! We'll go see does that girl still live, and does she, I do guarantee we'll get ourselves a little

miracle by way of thanks!" Da's laugh was infectious. Gete
joined in.

The sun rose. Red spangled wine curled away from the
side of the boat. Gete pulled the jib in tight, then wrapped
the ropes around his fist and leaned back. Sometimes, on
a long reach, you got to thinking that the world had ground
to a stop, that everything in the whole vast machine was
hanging there quivering, waiting for you to break the note
and go about.

But not today. He couldn't stop thinking of Desti. Since
the incident with the flamen, when the old Domesdean man
had sensed Desti through the wall of the kitchen and called
on him for guidance which Desti could not or would not
give, the god had been away from Sarberra. When he came
back, he was rude and uncompanionable. And loath though
Gete was to admit it, that left him at loose ends. When he
was small, he had been good friends with the other boys,
but since they got older, Tience and Rag and the others
had learned that Gete's red hair marked him out as an
object of suspicion. Whenever a goat died or a net was lost,
people looked askance at the redhead. So with increasing
frequency, he fell back on Desti's friendship.

And that marked him out as an object of suspicion, too.

Desti, you turtle, he thought as the sails belled sweetly,
tugging on the ropes. His father sat at the tiller, brows
furrowed; he was probably wondering where the swordfish
shoals were likeliest to be today, and how long they would
have to look for them after picking up the leman. *Desti,
you stupid sea-pig.*

She sat on a salt tree stump, her feet dangling over the
water. Gete saw through the rag he had tied over his eyes
that she was not clothed. He was grateful they weren't close
enough for her to see him go muddy: since his fur was
white to transparent, even whiter than most Archipelagans',
when it stood on end, his dark skin *showed*.

But after all, she could not see anything. Her eyes were
gray and milky like the sky before rain. Behind her, the
salt brush rustled with a deceptively wet sound. She held
onto a transparent sapling and pulled herself upright. Scabs
marred her body from head to toe; one of her large dark
nipples was sliced half off. "By the gods," Gete's father

muttered, and brushed a hand over his heart. "Divinarch in heaven."

Gete just sat with his mouth open, caught between looking at her and showing her disrespect.

"Well, get on with ye!" his father said sharply. "Help her aboard!"

Gete climbed out onto the salt and extended a hand. She shied back like a wild beast. She was horribly thin. As he stood helplessly, she wrinkled her brows, opened her mouth, then closed it, and put her head on one side, appearing to *search* him with cloudly eyes.

His father swore in exasperation. "Dammit, boy, go fetch the little boat. *I'll* see to her!"

Gratefully, Gete obeyed, scrambling away to where *Faith* bobbed against the rocks. To take his mind off the leman's disconcerting behavior, he thought how very hot the salt was. He had never come here before this episode. Twigs, rocks, all burned his bare feet as if he were standing on the hot hearth on a winter's night. He climbed into *Faith* and let down the sail, aware that his father was gentling the girl into their boat. "What's yer name, sweetheart? Ye can tell me. Ye're safe, now." Da's voice carried clearly across the salt.

"Tha—aah," he heard, in a croak that at first he did not identify as a human voice. He ducked under *Faith*'s boom and saw the leman's cropped blond hair flying as she shook her head. Gete's father had given her his shirt to wear, and she clutched it about her throat as she said doubtfully, "Not Thani. Not . . . anymore. Godsister Thankfulness."

Gete's throat closed. Untying the painter, he twisted *Faith's* tiller and she leaped off over the waves.

Several women were waiting by Sarberra bay. They greeted him first with cries of concern and then with disappointment when they realized the flamen wasn't aboard. "Poor little thing." Godsie Tiler squinted out over the waves, brushing fingers over the knot of her head scarf. "She's but a young girl . . ."

They meant to mother her! Gete could not stop himself from smiling as he tied *Faith* to a crag. How long would their good intentions last when they were confronted with that imperious, confused girl whose eyes one could not even meet? No longer than a stone could float!

But when Da sailed up with the girl, she docilely permit-

ted herself to be led off, submitting to criticism of her thin-
ness and plans to feed her up. Gete watched the blond
head bob away up the hill amid the dark ones. It struck
him that she was not a woman in the usual sense of the
word. She had probably been a very good leman.

"There's na one for you to be moonin' over!" his father
said, reaching up from the boat to slap Gete's ankle affectionately. "She's a Godsister. And Domesdean to boot, eh?
Move yerself. We've got the rest of the day to find us a
shoal."

Godsie Gullfeather declared supper communal. So many
of her friends had already invited themselves to gape at the
newmade flamen that Gete understood she could not turn
the rest of the islanders away. Communal meant that everyone brought food; Gete gorged himself on a lip-licking variety of dishes. Afterward the women set to work clearing
up, and Da trudged off to a gathering at Old Flamefish's
hearth. Men only. No boys. Gete played with his little sisters in front of the cook-hearth, not wanting to think about
the fact that since Desti was not here, and wherever the
other boys were they would not welcome his joining them,
he had nothing to do.

While the little girls were absorbed in a picture puzzle
he had drawn them with a stick of charcoal, the flamen
emerged from the inner room. She stood in her bare feet,
in a robe the women had whipped up for her. Precious salt-
flax cloth. How could she repay them? That was a blasphemous thought. He squashed it.

"Regretfulness," she said.

Gete opened his mouth but said nothing. Her cloudy eyes
seemed to look straight into him. Had she really lost all
her sight? Or was it fading slowly, like a sigh going out
from the lungs of a corpse?

"I want you to be my leman," she said. She sat down
beside his sisters and wrapped her arms around her knees.
"Will you?"

He could not speak. She was a creature straight out of
witch stories. Her milky eyes and her sun-bleached fur with
its dark roots repulsed him.

"Answer me!" Her colorless brows drew together. "Are
you there?"

"Do—do I have a choice?"

His sisters watched, round-eyed. One was three, the other six. His mother was watching too, hands on hips, frowning.

"Yes," the flamen said testily. "You are old enough to choose."

"Then—then no!"

And the door swung back and the room was full of men. Tience and Rag and Imp and Tim came behind their fathers, looking scared yet excited. They had fooled him. Da came forward with a smile on his face, his arms held out, and an expression in his eyes that told Gete his heart was breaking. "Blessings of the gods, my son!" He folded Gete in his arms "I pray you'll be happy," he muttered, "I do so—"

Gete wrenched away. He could not think of how to put his refusal so as not to slight the Godsister, but his face must have said it well enough. They were all staring at him. "I can't," he said miserably. "Much too old. Don't know why she wants me. Sorry!" If he stayed in here a moment longer, the very weight of their gazes would squash him into acquiescence. "Sorry!" he yelped.

He swung around and dashed out the yard door, out into the night. The windows of the village winked out one by one as he threw himself up the mountain. Gorse snagged his shirt, depositing prickles in his fur, and more than once he sank a foot in one of the little bog holes that never dried up even in summer. Sweat soaked his body. The nippy breeze chilled him. The stars shone faintly behind scudding clouds. Their glow showed him nothing except the heavy pyramidic blackness of the peak. "Desti!" he shouted. "Desti!"

He clambered higher, up the steep rock faces and knolls. "Desti! Goddamn you!" The wind wuthered in the rocks, bringing a faint perfume of gorse blossoms. *"Desti!"*

The mountain had never felt so inhospitable. It shrugged under him, and he slipped and put his hand in a fresh pile of goat droppings. Cursing, he staggered upward, up to the summit.

In what could have been one hour, or many, he was weeping on his hands and knees. "Gods damn you, I need your help, offal-brain pig god! I have to get away from here! They've tricked me!"

Silence.

"Desti!"

Some way down the hill, there was the scuffle of a fox making a kill. A rabbit's shriek.

The truth hit him like a sharp knife, taking his breath away.

Desti was a god. He ought to be able to hear Gete's prayers. Maybe he could hear. But even so, he was not coming to answer them.

Beaten, Gete dragged himself home. He washed off in the hen trough and came dripping into the kitchen. It felt very late. The flamen sat alone by the fire, her chin in her hands, staring at the scattering of embers in the banked fire.

She raised her head when he entered. Her face wore an expression of blank exhaustion. It made her look young and vulnerable.

" 'S me. *Sorry.* I acted like a child." He advanced. Then he heaved a sigh and stopped to speak to her. "I'll come with you, so."

She took his hand and pressed it to her cheek. It was an awkward moment. Gete felt a drop of hotness on his hand. Quickly, he withdrew.

"Come," he said. "Let's find you a pallet to sleep on."

They left next morning before the fishermen. Gete said his good-byes to his family with a strange sense that they were making a to-do about nothing. He kept forgetting that he was not going out to the shoals with Da, and that he would not return with him at sunset.

The entire population of Sarberra, even Godsman Sharquetooth's crippled son Arden, carried in his mother's arms, came sleepy-eyed to see them off. *Faith* wallowed under the weight of so many provisions that Gete finally had to call a halt to the gifts, for it was clear that the Godsister was not going to. When somebody lowered a basket into the boat, she just moved her feet to make room for it, smiling vaguely. "All set! We're wanting to drop anchor at Riethella tonight an make Taramia tomorrow. This's all we need."

Brave words, but he had never even been to Taramia. His heart was pounding. For the first time in years, his friends threw their arms around him. Even the girls of the village, who as a rule would not let a boy anywhere near them, hugged him. It came to him that they were all look-

ing at him with awe. Bitter triumph. Strangely enough,
when he embraced his parents and sisters he did not feel
the crippling emotion he had expected.

The only thing that reached deep inside and twisted his
heart was the knowledge that now his father had no sons.
There was no excuse for that betrayal: not even Da's
avowal of pride. "Do well, me son. Wear your name as if
it fits you." Da squeezed Gete tightly and let go. Gete
could not meet his eyes. He swallowed. Redhead or not,
he was Da's only heir . . .

Better not think on that! He stood up to cast off.

But the Godsister was getting to her feet. *Faith* rocked.
The Godsister had no feel for the sea, though she held
ropes better than any other girl he knew. "I have to—"

"What?" he snarled softly.

"I've to pay them back. It's a rule. If I don't do it now"—
she was standing precariously in the stern of the boat; people gaped at her—"I'll never—"

Abruptly time seemed to grind to a halt. The sea stopped
lapping against the rocks. A crying baby fell silent, or
rather it was still crying, but the sound hung protracted in
the frozen air. *Like being on a reach,* Gete thought, or tried
to think. *That feeling*—but his brain had gone as heavy as
wet sand. Moments did not exist in this heightened, brightened, hardened version of the world. But if they had, the
phenomenon would have lasted a moment, just long
enough for everyone to recognize it for what it was

and *twitch*—

the sun bounced up as if it were on a spring. Pink gold
rays arrowed over the sea.

Everyone's limbs seemed to loosen, laughter broke forth
as if some danger had passed, and above their voices, Gete
heard little Arden's shriek: *"Mum!* Lemme down!"

He scrambled to the ground and jumped up and down,
screaming with joy.

Well, well, Maybe the girl had no timing—but she was
the real thing. Gete could not help grinning. Then he struck
his forehead with the heel of his hand: this was their
chance. Quickly, he cast off and brought *Faith* about. "Sit
now," he hissed at Thankfulness, and she collapsed into the
stern. He swung the boat's nose away from the wind.
"Good-bye!" he shouted to the crowd. Her voice echoed
his thinly. "Good-bye . . . good-bye . . ."

Before *Faith* rounded the point, he saw the fishing fleet scattering out from the coast, their patched sails puffing in the wind.

Thankfulness laughed. She ran out of breath fast, and held her side. "I forgot the circle. Damn, I forgot everything. I've helped Transcendence with it a thousand times, too."

Gete was rather taken aback by her sudden familiarity. He said stiffly, "Only natural. Yer first time, an all."

"Ah, but it wasn't my first time. I had to work a miracle on myself to keep myself alive, on that island."

"Thought you couldn't work miracles on yourself," Gete said.

"Never again."

"Why? Is't a rule or somethin?"

"Yes. There are a great many rules. Nothing arcane, for that comes naturally: but the dictates of proper conduct." Now she was speaking formally. "You will learn them all in Delta City."

"That's where we're going?"

"Yes. As fast as we may."

"To the Divinarch?"

"At his behest."

Gete nodded. He did not know exactly what she meant, but he got the gist. A traitorous excitement was surging through him. He had consented to leave his home in a fit of fatalism, when he had felt sure that there were no such things as honesty or loyalty in the world. Now, all at once, he realized that there were, and that he was leaving them behind. Instead he was taking on a kind of bondage, a loyalty he did not feel. That ought to weigh like a stone around his neck.

But he had seldom felt so exhilarated. *Faith*'s prow sliced the waves into dancing white curls.

Delta City!

If only he could tell Desti!

An Endless Night in the Whorehouse District

Summer was over. Humi could feel it in the wind coming through the high windows of Hem's living room. Now came cold, and the children would fret because they could not go outside, and the foxglove on her windowsill would die. Her eyes might not be good for anything else anymore, but they could still fill with tears, and did so at the slightest provocation. *You can't cry now!* she told herself, as she always did. *You have sewing to do!*

And Ensi was pulling at her. "Auntie Humi, play with me! I'm bored!"

Five years old, and not allowed outside, it was small wonder the child was bored. In fact, her patience had lasted an amazingly long time. Humi just wished she had been able to amuse herself until Godsie Woodlock's petticoat was finished.

"Please!" Ensi's hard little head butted against Humi's thigh. "Please please please—"

"Just a few more minutes. Try to hold out." Stab, stab, stab, tiny whipstitches. This was the only way she could even partially repay Hem and Leasa for their kindness. It was a good thing she was already blind, she thought with black humor, because if she wasn't she would have lost her sight from doing fine work. There were few jobs to be had in a city where hundreds of women who had once prided themselves on their idleness must now work to help keep their families. Apart from prostitution, to which she had not sunk, and would not, sewing was the only employment open to a blind woman who had still not learned to think of the world in terms of sounds and smells and sharp corners, whose eyes they told her were still as black as ever.

A woman who had been Divinarch.

She should not even *think* along those lines, in case the Hands could somehow—she smiled at her foolishness—read her thoughts.

But they were so good at sniffing out anyone who had been an atheist. Anyone they disliked for any reason at all. Most of the atheists she had known in the old days were gone now, saving only those whom Pati had spared for his own, unfathomable purposes. The merchants were calling themselves *Godsie* and *Godsman* now. But quick reconversions seldom fooled the Hands. They said they took those they arrested to Purgatory, but as they said it they laughed nastily, and Humi knew better than anyone else in the city that *Purgatory* was no more than a code word made up by Pati for the thing that most people called Heaven.

So she must not make a single move that might draw attention to the house of a humble Temeriton shopkeeper.

And she *must* get this petticoat finished.

Swoop and stab and measure the distance to the edge of the cloth by feel.

"All right, En. All done!"

Working at her own speed, pretending not to hear the little girl's joyous cries, she folded the dress and put it in the basket. Then she slid off the sofa to the floor, patting the air. Her hands encountered nothing. "You'd better stay still, you know ... I can hear you if you move so much as a hair ..." She concentrated on picking Ensi's excited breath out of the weave of background noise. The ting of the shop bell, Leasa's gentle voice talking to a customer, a drunkard reeling up the alley, his smell overpowering the autumn scent on the wind, the rattle of sedan wheels in the concourse ... *Ah.* Humi flattened herself to the floor like a stalking beast, curling her lip for the benefit of the child whom she knew was watching, hypnotized like a bird before a snake. *"Gotcha!"*

But Ensi had darted out of her hands. Humi heard high, hysterical laughter and the patter of little feet on the stairs.

She sat back on her heels. "You're getting bratty."

"I'm coming down," Ensi answered, but stayed on the stairs.

Humi pushed her hair out of her eyes. Now that she no longer dyed it, it had returned to its natural texture, so nappy it would not stay in a braid. Probably as good a disguise as anything that Humility Garden, ghostier, had ever come up with. The Divinarch, she remembered, had used to have an immaculately arranged coiffure.

"Here I come, Auntie!" With a squeak of varnished

wood, En catapulted off the banister into Humi's lap. Taken off guard, Humi toppled backward and banged her elbow on the low table.

"You brat!" Pain blurred her judgment. She slapped at Ensi and felt her palm connect.

"Aaaaah!" Ensi blubbered. "Me going to Mama—"

Humi caught her as she staggered to her feet. "*No*. We have to let Mama alone. She's very busy." *And right now, one customer could make the difference between covering costs and borrowing to pay the rent.* Hope had not visited the Lakestones' house since the very beginning of the summer, and so the money they counted on from her had left a gaping hole in *Delights and Diversions'* finances. In these times of tightened belts, it was impossible, Hem had explained, to make such a venture as a curiosity shop show a profit. Yet it would be too risky to branch out in a new direction. They might lose everything.

Humi knew, though Hem did not say it, that the danger was not of losing money, but of Humi's being uncovered. The family were like rabbits frozen in an open field, unable to move an ear in case the circling predators spotted them.

She felt wretched, yet there was nothing she could do except silently try to show her gratitude.

Ensi was still crying. Frenziedly, Humi rocked her in her arms, wrung by the peculiar desperation to comfort her which came of that occasion, more than four years ago, when she had almost sacrificed Ensi to Erene. The family had probably forgotten the incident, but Humi still felt as if she had to make up for her lapse of feeling. She felt as if they were looking over her shoulder every minute to make sure she wasn't doing uncouth ghostier things to the child. "Let's go out to the alley and play with the kitties!" she suggested. Never mind the chills: if she could only get Ensi to quiet down—

"I dowanna!"

"I think Sharque's sitting on the back doorstep waiting for you. I think he's thinking, 'Where could Ensi be today?'" Inwardly, she winced. But Ensi wiped her face. Humi could hear her scrubbing her fur.

"All right."

Thanking the gods, Humi led her out to the hall and fumbled for the latch of the back door. Ensi pushed her aside, muttered "Lemme," and catapulted outside.

Cold wind licked Humi's fur. Cats, dogs, pigs, peacocks, and other semidomestic beasts could always be found combing Temeriton's back alleys in search of food. They were Ensi's only playmates, at least since the Whitehills, the last neighboring family with small children, had moved to the mainland. "Better starve than be arrested and have my sons thrown into the gutter," Servat Whitehill had asserted. There were not enough ferries to carry all Delta City's would-be émigrés to the mainland, and not enough work to keep them alive once they got there. The Hands had finally declared that to cross the Chrume or board any ship bound for another Royalland port, one needed a passport costing fifty shillings. People had started fleeing overseas instead, but they were dribbling away more slowly.

Ensi had finally got the cat she called Sharque to stay still. She struck up a one-sided conversation with it. From the high, frantic tone of her voice, it was clear that she was getting sick. *I'm a bad caretaker,* Humi thought. "Stay away from that old man!" she called, remembering the drunkard, who usually spent his days in the alley, dozing. Ensi made an absent yes noise.

Humi lowered herself to the doorstep. The smells of boiling lentils and mangy cat and drunk beggar did not bother her. She imagined the pale gray expanses of sky visible between the roofs. She tasted the salt in the wind that washed past her face. It gave her a sensation of freedom otherwise lacking in her days: a sensation of delicious danger. Perhaps it would rain.

Rain was one of the good things about autumn, especially after a summer such as they had had, sixday after sixday of dust and parched throats. If it *did* rain, she would go out and stand in the middle of the alley. She would get soaked, like the cats, like the squawking seagulls. Leasa would scold her when she came inside—for risking illness, for risking being seen—but she would not repent. She would not care if she got ill.

It did not rain.

When eight o'clock came and Leasa locked up the shop and Hem came back from the junk merchants, and the wind coming in the windows was still dry, Humi made up her mind not to be disappointed. It was a small thing, after all. But at the dinner table, she was struck by an uncontrollable

wave of misery. Unable to hold it back, she fled upstairs to
the tiny room Hem had partitioned off from the children's
bedroom for her, and soaked both her sleeves with bitter
tears.

She recovered in time to say good night to Hem and
Leasa. *Sorry, sorry, sorry,* she thought helplessly. The softness in Leasa's voice told her that her face betrayed her.
But they all knew about her crying fits. How could they
not?

When they were asleep, she had the run of the house.
She poured herself a glass of cheap Riestasis and entered
the shop. She paced between the racks, noting Hem's new
purchase of some little brass prayer bells, brushing her fingers over the statuettes of Hands that lined the shelves.
Wood, with limbs defined by their drapery. These were
selling faster than anything except the paintings of Pati. She
pressed her face to the door, listening to the outside.
Lockreed Concourse was not what it had been before the
fall, of course—but it was still the first place Deltans came
to forget their troubles. And people had enough of *those*
to keep any number of watering places and women's estab-
lishments in business. Doors thunked, releasing bursts of
noise. Sedans tinkled up and down the street.

Humi sighed, dunked her wineglass in the kitchen wash-
bucket, and wandered upstairs.

She had a secret.

The box under her bed overflowed with brushes and pigments. Ziniquel and Emni had brought them to her. She
did not know why they had bothered; wasn't it obvious to
them that a blind woman could not paint? But when she
realized what she *could* do, the first ray of hope had penetrated the blackness in which she lived.

She stood her latest ghost on her bed and unwrapped it,
sucking her fingers from time to time to warm them. A
seagull: Meri, the Lakestones' son, had caught it for her.
Any apprentice would muddy with shame to practice on
such a creature. But she was not *painting* it, as an apprentice would have. Rather, she was coloring it with more emotion than she had used on some humans in her days as
senior ghostier, but the only pigment she had used was a
matte white wash. She was *carving* it with the ghostier's
chisels, all different sizes, with which one traditionally

chipped at ghosts to make a hand hold a book, or define locks of hair from a mass. She had *willed* the legendary blind man's sensitivity into her fingers—as she had done for the cat and the pigeon and the rat ghosts under her bed. She had carved its feathers into an exaggerated sheath of knives. She had made its tail a spiked, inlaid fan with different textures telling the picture story of a lovers' tryst. She was shaping its face into what she hoped was a realistic human scowl.

Meri told her it was a realistic scowl.

She awaited the judgment of a more sophisticated audience.

Would her crude, wood-chiseler's approach work as well as paint? Would the textures she had created seize the eye and pull the viewer into the seagull's cold, to touch it and experience its all too human frustration with its imprisonment in this body?

Did such a sophisticated audience still exist?

Would she ever have the chance to show it to them, or was she torturing herself with false hope?

She rubbed her eyes with her fingers.

Outside, a cat was being eaten alive by a pig, or possibly a predator.

On the other side of the partition, Meri and Ensi breathed heavily.

She raised her face in the dark, teeth bared, shivering.

At first she had thought that Hem and Leasa kept the shutters closed for fear the sunlight would hurt her. She had railed at them to open the windows in the name of the gods, in the name of the Divinarch, on pain of torture.

They had closed the door and left her.

It was the wisest thing they could have done. Alone, she had to come face-to-face, so to speak, with the horrifying truth inside her head.

The blackness around her was neither the result of closed windows nor a side-effect of Pati's poison, soon to wear off. The rushed, impromptu nature of the miracle Godsbrother Joyfulness had worked on her had left her alive, but blind.

At first it had been like living in a safe box, locked away from all human contact. Hem and Leasa tiptoed around her as if she were a wounded predator. Ensi and Meri had been frightened to stay in the same room with her. Then she had realized that *she* had to hold out her hand first. Little by little, they reciprocated her overtures, and the four rooms behind the shop became habitable again. At the same time, figures from her old life started to seep into her new one. The débacle at Godsbrother Puritanism's had left few survivors, and those who remained were only voices (footsteps, rustling hems, annoyingly audible little habits that she'd never noticed before).

They would not tell her anything they thought might offend her. It was startling, and funny, to realize most of them were still afraid of her.

But—she reasoned—if Aneisneida and Soderingal Nearecloud, Gold Dagger, and the Hangman still feared her, then she must still bear *some* resemblance to the woman she had been.

One night as she lay in bed weak with holding back the tears for him, exhausted with trying not to sleep so that she might not dream of him, she came face to face with the implication of her own continuing survival. It burned like a fire, lighting up her mind. In later months, it would prove a freedom wheel such as children lit at midwinter. It spun off possibilities like sparks, and each spark died. But that first night, she only felt it as a burning, consuming thing, like a new infatuation, a chimera that took her mind off her tears.

Revenge.

She was still Humility Garden, Divinarch of Royalland, Calvary, Veretry, Pirady, Iceland, the sundry isles of the Archipelago, and Domesdys et al. Nothing had changed. Pati's coup had wreaked havoc on the world, and damaged her badly. She was not a fool, to deny that. But his poison had broadened her vision even as it ruined it.

It had been an incident. One that had passed.

It was her bounden duty and heart's desire to repair the damage it had done.

Revenge.

Someday, she would have her realm back or die in the trying. And until then she would carve seagulls.

The Freedom Wheel

Arity missed Sual more than he had expected to. He wondered, when a large enough dose of *khath* opened some of the closed doors in his mind, whether the year in Delta City might not have rendered him *incapable* of that utterly superficial passion that was central to *auchresh* nature. Or maybe he had been born like this. There had not been anyone before Pati, had there? No. And there had not been anyone in the years between Pati and *her*. (Not even numb with *khath* did he allow himself to think her name.) No one except for a few of *lesh kervayim* who had practically thrust themselves down his throat, not to put too fine a point on it. After he rejected them as *ghauthijim,* the consensus had gone around that the Heir was cold and a little strange. Uppity, but too weak to back up his dramatics.

That was what they had thought of him.

On the first count, at least, they had been wrong.

Weak.

He shuffled up the creaking stairs of his building, gripping the saltwood banister. His head felt disconnected from his feet. The night was only half over, but he was sick of the taverns. Down here, there seemed always to be a kind of alcoholic slop washing around the floors, as if the river had overflowed its crumbling banks. (The river. Ridiculous that after living here more than two years, he still did not know that river's name, or if it had one.) Down here, the ancient servingboys grinned with blackened fangs and pressed themselves against you when they poured your *khath*. They were serving two drinks for the *denear* of one in honor of the Divinarch's arrival, and Arity had foolishly taken advantage of the offer. *You revolt me,* he thought to himself. Extraordinary what a falloff in quality there was between the tier where Sual had lived, where the Laughing Haugthule had stood, and the bottommost tier of all, where he lived.

He reached the landing and hung over the newel post. He vomited into the stairwell, great retches that left him sagging over the post, his eyes watering, listening to his puke splatter on the floor of the hall far below. If the thorns had grown on his stomach, the spot pressures might have injured something inside him; but like a porcupine's prickles, they grew only on his back and throat, through his hair, and on the backs of his arms, with a few scattered on his chest.

The lingering effects of the *khath* allowed him to think about them, too.

His head was much clearer now. He would sleep for a while, and then go out again.

Down here, just as on the topmost tiers where the *serbalim* lived, some bars stayed open even through the day. It was considered fashionable. The hypocrisy.

His door sagged open on its one hinge. "Charity"—he murmured in mortal, to which he reverted when he was alone—"your brain is rotting. Even if the lock doesn't work, you could *close* the *door.*"

Shaking his head, he went in.

Pati sat on the bed. He was a pale shade in the starlight drifting from the skylights. His eyes burned with an inner light, one blue and one brown.

Just as he had sat waiting in his suite in Wind Gully Heaven, those first nights when terrified, yet honored beyond speech, Arity had crept through the passages to receive the mainraui's *favor.*

Dumb with terror, Arity stumbled back against the doorway, clutching his throat as if he could somehow enable himself to speak.

"Oh, in the name of the Power." Pati spoke in mortal. He got up and pulled Arity bodily into the room, then kicked the door shut. "Collect yourself, man! I'm not a shade. You're not hallucinating."

How long since Arity had heard someone else speak in this language?

"I didn't think I was hallucinating."

Pati did not notice that he had been insulted. "I thought it would be best to wait for you. I know where you spend every moment of your wretched existence: I could have come and grabbed you out of one of your repulsive little haunts. But I didn't want to embarrass you by recognizing you down there." He narrowed his eyes. "Ari, you look terrible."

Arity gestured around the bare little room. "Why do you think I don't have any tapers? If you want to admire my thorns, you should come back during the day."

"Are you inviting me?" Pati licked his lips, grinning wickedly.

"Pah." Arity turned away. "I'm not quite that desperate. I've heard things. You and all the Hands live like humans. You even live with humans. A case of the ruler and subject pigging in together. Your most trusted servants are flamens and lemans."

"Just who have you been talking to? I was not aware such slander was on the streets."

"Hope." Then Arity cursed himself as Pati's face darkened and he swore in *auchraug*.

"Damned *iu*! She works against me every opportunity she gets!"

Arity smiled, this time in pure pleasure. He could get one up on Pati and at the same time give him a filthier, more correct picture of the man he himself had become. "What makes you think those things prejudiced me *against* you?"

There was a pause. Then Pati grinned, showing his white fangs. Closing his hand on Arity's wrist, he dragged Arity over to the bed and sat him down. "So you *do* miss Delta City."

"I wouldn't go back there for the world."

"That doesn't mean you don't miss it."

"Not the place. Just the people."

"Oh? Who?"

Damn! He must still be drunk. He was falling into all Pati's traps. "Never you mind."

Pati arched a pale eyebrow. "Are you sure?" He paused. *"Irissi . . ."*

Irissi! The memories were rushing back. He could not fend them off. *The door creaks and he turns. The muscles in his neck ripple. I am mute with awe, waiting for him to laugh and order me out because I have not brought the gherry he requested. But instead, after a minute, he smiles. His smile is like the sun that is creeping around the curtains of his room.*

My fear is a valid memory, the nervousness of a boy going to his first lover, but the cruelty and vanity in that smile were superimposed by later years. This Pati isn't the Striver. He's young and sincere. He gets up, tilts his head, and kisses me.

Arity shook his head. Fear thrilled through him. "Get out of my room!"

"You don't want to remember, do you?"

"Remember *what*?"

"There's nothing like reprising an experience to bring it back."

"Leave me alone!"

Pati settled more comfortably on the bed. Arity became aware that the Divinarch smelled of expensive perfume, and a second later, he realized he had thought of Pati for the first time in his official capacity. Like dunking his head in cold water, he remembered who Pati was. Such a gap. He was speaking to the *Divinarch*. The man's first blow had found a chink in his armor and cut all the way to the bone. But it was not too late to undo the damage. All he had to do was invoke reality.

He retreated, on his feet. "They'll be looking for you. You must have been missed."

"Oh, not to worry. I scheduled this in." Pati glanced up at the skylight. "I have another couple of hours yet."

For some reason this cut deeper than anything else. Arity heard his voice rising like a child's. "You fitted me into your *schedule* as if I was any *serbali*?"

"What else could I have done? I am Divinarch! All of those common *serbalim,* as you call them, have claims on me."

"And you rank me with them. You grubbing, sycophantic diplomat. Your memory is shorter than a Foundling's cock. Why are you in Rimmear then?" Arity did not know why he felt cheated. "A matter of failed communication?"

"In a manner of speaking."

"If I were to *teth*" right now, you would never see me again. *There's* a failure of communication for you." His mind was made up now. He glanced at his cookstove, his clothes chest, his dusty curtains, mentally saying good-bye to them. The Ugly Iu Tavern? Or the Sadui's Rest? Which was likeliest to be empty at this hour?

"Ah." Pati laughed. "But you are not *going* to *teth*", are you?"

The moment stretched.

Arity lifted his hands, palms out. The city throbbed outside, softly, like blood in his ears. "What do you want of me?" His voice sounded strange to him.

"I want you to come back to Delta City."

"For my health? The air here may smell bad, but I am assured it is an excellent physic for weariness." *Of life.*

"You will die before long if you keep on like this. One cannot expect to consume enough *khath* every night to fill the Chrume and survive. But that is hardly the point. I want you for *my* sake, not yours."

Arity folded his arms. "At least you're honest."

"I owe you nothing Ari, whereas you owe *me* your life."

So *that* was it! Arity waggled a finger in the air, grinning. All was solved. So cold-blooded! "You think you had anything to do with it, *ruthyali*? I owe my life to Hope. She nursed me back to health. And I've thanked her many times, I believe. Now get out."

"The last time she came to visit, you had some ugly yellow-haired *ghauthi kere* in your arms. You turned her away."

"She *told* you that?"

Pati's mouth twisted. "*There's* an *iu* who ought to watch her step. She feeds me crumbs of information from time to time. You ought to be careful with her. But to her credit, she would never tell me something she believed important to you."

It would not have been important before Sual died. None of this would have been important before Sual died. "His name was Unusual Day," he told Pati, shrugging. "I loved him."

Pati sat forward. "Was?" he prodded.

"I killed him. I gave him more *denear* than he could handle. He went wild."

"What did you expect him to do? You're lucky you haven't yet been killed yourself, if you're running around throwing money at every *kere* with sex appeal. You weren't made to live in Rimmear."

Arity laughed. He flung around the room, kicking the cookstove, shoving the pillows off the bed, slamming the door. Splintery dents appeared in the walls where he punched them. His scars stung unbearably. Breathing hard, he rammed both hands up against the skylight, almost cracking it. The city towered on one side, like a giant curtain caught in the act of sweeping across the stars. "Shut up, damn your eyes! Shut up! I love it here!"

"Forever," Pati whispered obscurely. His arms went around Arity from behind. Arity's hands broke apart. A knife entered his bitten shoulder but he hardly noticed. Pati was kissing his neck, mouthing one of the thorns. The soft rings of flesh at the bases were exquisitely sensitive. Arity froze.

"Do it again," Sual hissed. *They stood in a curve of the corridor at the Green Jewel Saloon, pressed against each other in the shadows. "Do it, damn you, cripple—"*

Arity obliged. He didn't know how he had ever had the courage to come on to Sual. The kere's *breath was redolent of spices and his hair shone like the sun. He touched several of Arity's thorns, working them back and forth, laughing when he felt Arity stiffen. "Power, these're funny! Never seen em before! You can feel that, uh? Oh, cripple boy—"*

His hands were buried in the dusty salt-fabric folds of the curtains. Pati moved closer, rubbing against his back, almost dancing against him. The thorns on Arity's shoulder blades were piercing both their shirts, drawing blood from Pati's torso. Pati's breath came shallowly. Arity felt his erection hot against his buttocks. He almost lost control then, but memories were still cascading through his mind. By that thin skin of abstraction, his armor held.

"You're scarcely more than a Foundling, aren't you?" Pati held Arity off to look at him. Arity shivered and tried to bury his head in Pati's armpit. *"Whose were you?"*

"Win-Winding Stream's—"

"He's raised you to be a beautiful auchresh.*"* Pati kissed him.

"I love you, mainraui," Arity whispered.

"Pati. My name is Pati. I have a virtue name, just like you."

A few minutes later Pati guided the boy toward the bed. The braced platform gave a little when Arity flopped back on it. The sunlight coming around the edges of the curtains lit up the colors in the coverlet. "Don't hold on to me," Pati scolded. "I want to show you the best of this, and I can only do that if you trust me enough to lie still."

But overtaken by boldness, Arity pulled him down on top of him. He kissed him again and again, his eyes wide. A white strip of sunlight twisted across Pati's shoulders as he

writhed, plucking at the laces of Arity's breeches. "Ah—you
wicked little Foundling—"

And starlight poured down over them as Arity turned
and kissed Pati. He brushed his tongue over Pati's lips, and
at the threat of intimacy, in an automatic reflex, the armor
drew tighter around him, stifling him for a moment, like a
second, impermeable skin. He panicked.

And then it was gone. He was free: sensuously free. Yet
he was protected. The armor had melded with his own skin.
He could no longer feel it. It *was* his skin, *was* his scars.

He did not trust Pati. That was ... a given ...

But it would be a crime, a weakness, to stay away from
him merely because he feared him. A crime likewise to kiss
this way, to run his hands down the perfumed body of the
Divinarch, but who cared? Sual was dead. And no one
cared. Not even Arity. For with this surrender to the past,
he escaped Sual's death, escaped the misery and boredom
of his existence. And he made up for leaving Sual alone by
giving himself body and soul to Death itself, in the form
of an *auchresh* with bicolored eyes and iridescent wings.

The foxglove on the windowsill was dead. Its leaves stuck
to the fur of Humi's leg, when she sat there above the alley.
Cold air licked around her, inside her nightgown. Autumn
rode on it: the stink of the decaying marshes. She knew it
was as dark outside her head as it was inside, but that made
no difference.

Knot and pull, split the thread, stitch stitch stitch.

She had finished her ghost of the seagull. Now she expected to stay up the whole night sewing. Since her days as
twentieth councillor, when she had kept a double schedule,
socializing with the Antiprophet Square set in the daytime
and the *auchresh* after sundown, she had needed less than
no sleep.

Behind her, she felt a hot gust of sulfur. Someone stumbled over the seagull that Humi had left on the floor, and
hissed a curse.

Humi twisted around. "Hope?"

"What's this on the floor?" Humi recognized Hope's
voice, though the *auchresh* moderated it down to a whisper.
"It's not a ghost, is it?"

Humi muddied violently. She prayed Hope could not see
well enough in the dark to make out the hue of her face.

"It *is*! I thought you couldn't—"

"I can't. It's not a real ghost." She swallowed, and qualified, "It's a technique I invented. Different from painting."

"A-a-ahhh." Hope must be clutching the seagull to her breast. Humi slid off the windowsill and sat down on her bed, biting her lip. She heard Hope's heel talons clicking on the floor. "Humi, this is ... it's ... So ... so much *grief ...*"

"Give it to me!"

Hope laid the ghost on the coverlet. Humi located it by its aura of cold, scooped it up, and stowed it under the bed.

"Why haven't you shown it to Ziniquel and Emni? Or Mory and Tris? We could probably find those two if we tried."

"It's too much of me."

"That never used to worry you."

Humi would have been delighted that Hope had come, if she would only leave it alone! Tears were gathering in her nose. Oh, gods. "I ..." Unable to help it, she sniffed loudly.

"*Oh.*" The *auchresh* hopped up on the bed, careful not to make the planks creak, and hugged Humi. She rocked her back and forth, crooning. "I'm sorry ... I'm sorry ... it's my fault ..." The heat of her body was magic. Almost involuntarily, curled there, Humi relaxed. Hope smelled of soot and sea breeze. She must have come straight from the Old Palace.

Why had she come at this hour?

Had she discovered something?

The instinct awoke in Humi, questing.

She pushed the *auchresh* away and sat up. She wiped her face. "I am just so glad to see you." Her voice still trembled. "I was convinced you weren't coming again."

"Humi, the day I don't crave sight of you is the day I am dead. "Hope folded her wings with a disturbingly loud rustle. She touched Humi's nightgowned knee. "But it's not safe for me to be here. And I am so hellishly busy. I have been promising myself that I would come since the middle of the summer. But it hasn't happened. I'm sorry."

"Has *anything* happened?" Humi held her breath.

"Talk." Hope sighed. "A great deal of talk. It is something. The subject is out in the open, at least. I have tested the waters in the Nearecloud mansion and in the Crescent.

Aneisneida, Soderingal, Zin, and Emni all say they would support you in a recoup."

"Anyone in his right mind would support anyone other than Pati!"

"Have you forgotten that you are Humility Garden? The city remembers you. The first and last human Divinarch. A sort of mystique hangs around your memory. Even those few who know you are alive speak of you with reverence."

"But not one of them will risk his skin for me."

"Can *I* help it if they are afraid? Can you blame them for *being* afraid?"

Humi sighed. "The city is a Freedom wheel," she said. "Giving off sparks. But none of them ever catch. So much wet, dead wood." She paused, and said ironically, "But there is always this. If we give Pati enough rope, perhaps he will hang himself."

Hope made a curious little sound. "And strangle the whole city in the process! He's clever! And he has charisma! It won't happen. He has got the flamens—and not just the flamens, either—dancing at his fingertips. He's got the whole world in his fist."

"Well, then, what can we do against him?"

Hope's wings fluttered, snapping. Humi felt their gusts in her face. "Sometimes I think we can do nothing."

"Stop it. You'll wake the children."

"And the secrets. Humi, I am cursed with secrets."

She stiffened. "What are you keeping from me?"

"I cannot tell you! I am sorry!"

In the alley, a herd of feral pigs grunted, scraping through the garbage with their trotters.

Pati held up a set of Hand's clothes—shirt and breeches of fawn silk. "This?" The torch in the closet flickered, casting his hooknosed shadow onto the wall. "Or this?" A mortal man's clothes. "Or this?" *Auchresh* clothes, with a Kithrilindic look to the cutouts. "You can't continue in those rags, anyhow. It would reflect badly on me."

How quickly he had asserted control! Arity's first instinct was to reach for the human clothes. But as his hand went out, he thought better of it and took the Hand's outfit. A smile creased Pati's face. "Good. You haven't forgotten how humans' minds work after all, have you?"

Arity turned his back, stripped, and pulled on the new clothes.

"You'll have to start clipping your thorns again, too." Pati's voice came unhurriedly, as casual as the blow the blue-skinned *kuiros* had dealt Arity on the head. "There's nothing to be done about your scars. But really, you can't live as a member of the ruling class of Delta City while you look like a hedgehog."

"I do *not* look like a hedgehog."

"A rosebush, then."

Arity turned around, tugging the shirt down. It had caught on a thorn in back, and he felt it rip. "You brought me back here to stand beside the Throne looking exactly the way you want me to, so that everyone knows I have succumbed to you. This is what I want to know. Do you want me—or do you want my head on a pike?"

Pati stood in the door of the closet. The torchlight blackened the room behind him. "I want *you*. To alter yourself as much as I ask you to. I want to adorn you, beautiful one. Won't you let me?" His voice took on a cajoling tone. "Don't you remember Wind Gully Heaven, how you would steal one of my garments, and roll it up and pin it to your sleeve, so everyone knew we were lovers?" His voice was seductive as sweet cream.

"Power." Arity could not bear it. What had he gotten into? Snatching the torch off its bracket, ignoring Pati's cry, he dashed it into one of the racks of clothes. They were salt-fiber fabric, so flameproof. The flame sputtered and went out.

In the other room, there was the creak of a door opening. A sleepy *auchresh* voice called, "Pati? Are you back?"

Pati spun. "Melin! Go away!"

"Cujali! I knew it was you! You just cried out, didn't you?" Footsteps. "Is something wrong?"

"No!" Pati lifted on tiptoe and shouted, *"Hands!"* His voice boomed as if his lungs were a pair of brazen bells. Even Arity clapped his hands to his ears. *"Hands!* Take him! Take him to Westpoint!" He strode forward and pulled Arity's hands down. A brief struggle erupted in the other room. Pati held Arity close. The Divinarch's heart was pounding. When all was quiet, he lèt go.

"Who was that? Your lover?" Arity had not realized that Pati's physical strength was superior to his own. His eyes watered. "And you're throwing him over for me. Well, well, well. All right. I'll cut my thorns. I'll hold my head high. Anything for you, Divinarch. I am your servant."

"Then stand at the right hand of my throne, Arity. Be my Heir."

"No!"

"You said you would do anything."

"Anything but that!"

"Be a Hand, then. My Inviolate One." Pati wrapped his arms around Arity. Endearments tumbled from his lips. Far below, the sea crashed against the cliffs. Pati kissed the tears out of Arity's eyes.

"Who was that I saw as we *teth"d* in?" Arity whispered. "Not your *cujali*. Before that. A small, winged one. He *teth"d*."

Pati gripped him tighter. "No one knows we are here. The city believes the Palace to be empty but for a few servants and Hands. But when we return *next* from Uarech, everyone will see you, for you shall stand on my Throne. Heir or no Heir. All my Hands attend me from time to time. And if you will have it that way, you shall be no exception."

"Yes," Arity whispered. "That's all I ask, milord Divinarch. That's all I have ever asked."

Downstairs, Humi prepared bitter chocolate and poured it into two pottery cuplets. They stood in the shop to drink it, talking desultorily of trade and Deltans they both knew: who had been arrested, who had left the city. Presumably, Hope was watching the last of the nightlife dribbling along the street. Humi watched the blackness inside her head. The mobiles hanging from the ceiling tinkled every time Hope shifted her wings.

Aneisneida's baby Fiamorina had just celebrated her second birthday. "When I look at her, it seems to have been a hundred years since the fall," Hope said. "One realizes how little politics matter, in the grand scheme of things."

Humi laughed. "How beautiful, Hope. But politics matter more than anything. Without politics, there wouldn't be a world for Fiamorina to grow up in."

Hope did not answer. Humi hated that the *auchresh* kept secrets from her. She supposed Hope had a good reason;

yet it saddened her. Would they drink chocolate and talk of nothing forever, while the city atrophied in Pati's iron grip?

But Humi could not risk alienating the only real friend she had. No matter how useless Hope believed it was, she would keep on proselytizing on Humi's behalf. That would not change. Hope was loyal. Unlike Zin and Emni, Aneisneida and Soderingal. They had all disappointed Humi. She had not seen any of them in more than a year.

Hope stretched, setting the mobiles jangling, and said, "I must go." Humi accepted her empty chocolate cup and a kiss on each cheek. "Oh," Hope said, "I almost forgot this." She took Humi's hand and closed it around a lumpy weight.

Humi felt the shapes of coins inside a leather bag. "Oh, you don't have to," she said automatically, but the words stuck in her throat. In order for *Delights and Diversions* to survive, Hope did have to. And Hope knew that. "We'll pay you back as soon as the shop starts making a profit," she said awkwardly. "Hem hates taking loans."

"Tell him to consider it a gift," Hope said firmly. "As always."

Humi bounced the little bag in her palm. At least five hundred shillings, if it was silver. She swallowed. "Hope, do you have any idea when I shall see you—"

Sulfur gusted around her face. She choked on the second half of her sentence.

Once again she was alone in the shop.

The air seemed colder now the *auchresh* was gone. Humi breathed deeply, once, twice, sticking her fingers in the corners of her eyes, and went back behind the counter.

Power, Hope thought as her feet hit the floor of her bedroom. *Why couldn't I tell her? Why couldn't I?* "She must have thought it odd beyond comprehension!" She flopped back onto her sumptuous bed. The springs accommodated her wings. She lay still, feeling the tension drain out of her great shoulder muscles. *If Ari is returning to the city, she will have to know sometime, and better that she find out from me—* "Why on earth would I come in the middle of the night, rattle on about her ghost for several minutes, and then talk of nothing, unless I was cracked?"

"Milady Hope?" A candle appeared around the door at the far end of the long room, casting a yellow glow on the polished floor and the elaborately carved oak bureaus on either side of the door. Above it hung the wrinkled face of Hope's favorite human servant, Godsie Grenworth. "Is all well, milady?"

"Yes, Godsie. Go to bed. No need to send Shari—I can undress by myself."

"Ah, yes. Not as if you was one of them ladies as used to be, any'ow, with dozens of different buttons ..." The old woman withdrew. Hope valued her, though she was sometimes overbearing. It was hard enough to get any servants: few Deltans, be they pious or atheistic, would agree to serve Hope as if she were just anybody. Harder yet to get them to call her *Milady*, though she thought it the most innocuous title out of those she had to choose from. Certainly, she could no longer style herself a god. That would lump her along with the Hands.

She laced her hands behind her head. Drawing her feet up onto the bed, she stared at the midnight sky she had had painted on the ceiling. *Power, Arity,* she thought, *have you no self-respect? None at all?*

Divine Intervention

Qalma was twice as large an island as Sarberra. A stone town straggled uphill from the docks, vanishing around a ridge that was scattered with trees. Gete could not keep from staring as he jumped out of *Faith* and made her fast. He had never seen a tree before, except on salt Harrima, and those hadn't been real.

He stooped, found Thankfulness's hand, and jerked her up onto the dock. Without reproaching him for his clumsiness, she straightened, turning her head as if she could still see, biting her lip. She stared with salt-crystalled eyes toward the town, the brown bundles sitting in the sun, the doll-sized figures working on the terraces to the east, the blue cone of the peak above. Gete grabbed the rucksack that held their possessions from her and hefted it over his shoulder.

"Gete ..." she said in that trailing way she had.

"Godsister."

"This place feels god touched."

He said nothing. Over the six days of their traveling, he had learned to keep his mouth shut. It was less frustrating than receiving such answers as, "Because the gods will it so." Or that penetrating, milky stare of hers. Impossible to tell what was passing through the mind behind those blind eyes with their glitter-studded irises. She just stared, and said nothing, and Gete cringed like a bird being eyed by a cat.

"What is this place called?" she asked abruptly.

"Qalma, Godsister."

"Ah, yes. I was here with Transcendence once, I believe. 'Heavy Water'—I think that is what that word meant, in the beginning of time, before the Archipelagan language was melded with the outside tongues. I think Transcendence told me so." She started to blink, then stopped. Gete remembered she had said that blinking scratched the insides of her eyelids to blood. Eventually the lids would grow back into the orbital hollows, making room for the crystals. "The eighth house on the left. I think that is where we will find him."

"Who?"

She stared at him as if she could not believe he had to ask. Finally, she said, "The god."

Faith bobbed alongside the granite pier. All the other boats must be out at sea. Gete hoped he hadn't tied up in anyone's prized berth. But even if he *had*—well, a leman could commandeer anything his flamen needed, couldn't he? Thankfulness's foot slipped on old fish scales, and she grabbed his arm for balance. Woodenly, correctly, he set her on her feet.

"Ah ... aaaah. Hold on to me, leman ... please."

He did as he was commanded. Slowly, they progressed along the pier and started up the broad bedrock slope of the road. Gete looked back and saw evenly spaced splotches on the pier shining in the afternoon glare. The marks of fish piling. In parts of the Reach where the nets did not lure swordfish, but the bigger, poison-tailed coelakates, you could not carry the catch up from the boat—it would twist around and sting you. Coelakates could stay alive out of water for hours, and their stings had caused deaths even on Sarberra, which was really too far north for their shoals. So Mid-Reach fishermen must leave their catch on the dock overnight to die.

Thankfulness drew a sharp breath, and stumbled.

"What's wrong, Godsister?"

"No ..."—she was breathing hard—"... thing. It is just the heat. You remember that ... I was not very well yesterday."

It seemed that with her, unwellness was perpetual. Maybe it had to do with the salt crystals' throbbing incipience, or her incomplete recovery from her ordeal on Harrima. She was still thin. In the shadows of her cowl, her collarbone stuck up, razor-sharp as a ridge of rock sticking out of a hillside. But then again, maybe all flamens were like her. He hadn't encountered many of them, had he? And that wasn't just because Sarberra was so far out of the way of the world—it had to do with the new Divinarch, and the fact that many flamens (Thani had told Gete) were forsaking his service. Maybe, as a result, the remaining ones had to draw more on the strength of their own bodies. Thankfulness constantly complained of headaches and weakness. And although guilt whispered at him, Gete could not help resenting her for it.

The mirage of Delta City had receded far into the future, superseded by the specter of his loyalty to her. For the gods' sakes, it was like being *married*! Except he didn't even *like* her!

She shuffled beside him toward the eighth house. Her shoes were falling apart. In the few weeks they had known each other, he had already had to get her one pair of new shoes and two new robes; he had no idea how she managed to wear things out so fast.

"Tis an old man sitting by the door," he said. "And a little babe asleep with him."

"I know."

"You—what?"

"I—I—" She made an anguished little sound. "Gods' greeting, venerable Godsman!" she sputtered. "I am Godsister Thankfulness! I am only just come from ..."

"Shettara," Gete murmured. "From Shettara! Would I be correct in assuming that you harbor a god in your home? I should like to do him honor—"

"God? Easter? Ah, he's out to the fishing." The old man squinted at Thankfulness and Gete. "Gods' greeting to ye,

flamen. He'll na be back for 'nother few hours, does the
sunshine hold. But ye—ye must be sent from the Divinarch
himself. We have sore need of ye in this house." He stood
up, laying the baby on the bench, and bowed his gray head
to Thankfulness. "Me only son is dying."

The god Easter was an unhuman looking creature with
ragged scraps of wings on his shoulders and muscle-bound
arms that reached nearly to the ground. Nothing like slim,
handsome Desti. The lines on his face made him look about
Gete's father's age, but Gete knew he was probably much
older. His full name was Warm Easterly. Gete did not get
a chance to speak to him before supper, nor did Thankfulness get a chance to make her obeisances to him. In fact,
Gete wondered if she even *knew* the god had arrived back
in Qalma with the rest of the men: in order to find out
whether she really could sense these things, he had not
told her.

He looked out the door of the Finspine house and saw
the god gutting yesterday's catch with the other fishermen,
on the scale-covered stones around the well at the top of
Qalma town. They must have carried the catch up the hill
early this morning.

On Sarberra, gutting would be women's work. But here,
the women had not yet got back from the terrace gardens,
and so the men finished with the coelakates and dispersed
to their houses to cook up the supper their wives had prepared in the morning, affectionately chaffing each other in
a way that made Gete's heart ache.

All except Hasti Finspine. He lay ill in an inner room
with only his old mother to tend him. Some days ago he
had been stung in the face by a coelakate: his fever had
developed complications and he breathed painfully, with a
bubbling deep in his lungs. The room smelled of the nox-
ious fluid he coughed up. A purple blister had cracked one
cheek open like an overcooked loaf of bread.

Eventually Godsie Finspine returned from the terraces
with her four children, all of them covered in dirt. The
bustle of the family dinner was subdued. Thankfulness startled when Gete finally described Easter's entrance, but she
said nothing. Perhaps she was saving herself for the work
she had to do later on.

It was imperative that Hasti Finspine return to health.

Qalma might look prosperous, but in truth, Godsie Finspine whispered, standing by Gete as Thankfulness knelt at Hasti's head, their margin of survival was as thin as a starved cat. Gete knew the story. He'd grown up with it! As he hauled his first net out of the water at age six, in the spring sunshine, the winter gales had howled in the back of his mind. He'd seen the storms behind the approval in his father's eyes. All Archipelagans had eyes the color of night. (Except Gete, whose were blue.) The loss of one able body could diminish the season's returns enough that not all the islanders would live through the winter. Of course Warm Easterly could take the Finspines' boat out, Godsie Finspine said, but one god could not do *everything*! Could he?

She asked Gete this last question as if Warm Easterly were a volatile, unknown quantity, a cause for dire apprehension. It served only to remind Gete that this was *her husband* lying on the pallet.

"I will heal him." Under her fur, Thankfulness's face bore lines of strain. "Owing to the conditions, I must dispense with the ritual, but I *will* have silence. Out, all of you." She nodded stiffly to Warm Easterly. "Even you, milord god."

Obediently, the gathered islanders, and one god, shuffled toward the door. At that moment, there was a flash in the shadows. Gete smelled brimstone, and he saw a slight yellow-clad figure—silver wings—owlish eyes—

Desti saw him, too, and knocked Qalmans out of the way as he dived for the door. Gete went after him. Warm Easterly tried to intervene, shouting in that incredibly loud voice that Desti had sometimes lapsed into, too. But the children were in the way, and Thankfulness cried piercingly, "Leman! Leman . . . ! What is it? *Where are you?*" Her voice was panicky.

The tail of Desti's tunic whisked around the outer door. Gete plunged after him. A noisy rain was falling from the twilight sky. Rivers streamed down the street. Gete sneezed water out of his nose as he pursued Desti up the street, across the open square with the well, and onto the ridge. The ground was much lumpier than it had looked from a distance. He had trouble keeping the god in sight as they clambered over hummocks and little ravines. Why didn't Desti vanish? Gete wondered blurrily. Then Gete would have no chance of catching him! But again and again he glimpsed the yellow tunic. Grass flattened to mud under his feet. He slipped and cursed, pushing wet hair out of his eyes.

Ahead, Desti vanished through a line of trees. Gete arrived panting at the rustling, wet barrier. For some absurd reason he hesitated. Then he shut his eyes and pushed through, half-jumping, half-falling over a stone wall into a muddy ditch sheltered from the rain.

Goats sniggered in alarm and scrambled away.

Desti stood barefoot in the mud, his wings bedraggled, both palms up in a gesture of surrender such as children make to end a game of tag.

"Why didn't you vanish?" Gete panted. "I never woulda caught you!"

"I would have lost you if I wanted to."

"You feared of anyone seeing us talking? You want me to say I never found you?"

Desti looked at his feet. Water droplets flew off one wing as it snapped out, then folded in again.

"Well, if that's how tis, you damn well better have something worth sàyin' to say," Gete said viciously. He scuffled a clear place in the goats' droppings on the side of the ditch, sat down, and glared at Desti.

After a moment the god came and sat down beside him, leaning against the stone wall, his feet drawn up. The rain thundered on the leaves overhead. Now and then, a fat drop splatted on the earth. For a long time neither of them spoke. A stealthy sense of lassitude crept over Gete. He remembered the Dividay afternoons they had spent on the mountain, taking advantage of the holy day to eat wild bayberries and watch the clouds go by. Sometimes cloudbursts made them shelter under crags. Leaning against each other's backs—Desti's wings were surprisingly comfortable—they would stare at the raindrops plummeting past the mouth of the little cave. They seldom needed to talk.

Now, sitting in the mud on Qalma, Gete did not want to talk to Desti any more than he had back then. But he *had* to. He had to know why Desti had scarcely returned to Sarberra after Godsbrother Transcendence's arrival.

That probably meant asking about Heaven and the *serbalim*. The part of Desti's life which had nothing to do with Gete—which evidently included Qalma. The thought of re-

ducing Desti's comfortable mystery to cold reality saddened
Gete. Nonetheless, he said, "Have you been back to Sarberra since?"

Desti shook his head. The god's hands, twisting between
his knees, were longer and slimmer than Gete had ever
noticed before. The nails were shaped like chicken claws,
clipped off short at the ends of his fingers. "My *serbalim*
forbade me to go back."

"You and your *serbalim*."

"They said they would banish me from Heaven if I ever
visited human country again."

"So what are you doing here?"

"I'm coming to that." Desti looked at Gete. "They never
liked me visiting Sarberra in the first place. You know that.
And then, sea-pig that I am, I let them find out about the
flamen's recognizing me. That was enough for Briar Finger
and Sweet Tornmouth. They said I was violating *er-serbali*
law. Easter tells me they were lying—the *er-serbalim*
haven't prohibited us from going into human country. But
since we're so far away from anywhere, Briar and Sweet
Tornmouth can do whatever they like."

"But what're you doing here *now*?"

Desti licked his lips. "I came to see Easter."

"What's he doing here? Is he from your Heaven, too?"

"He's been expelled. He wouldn't obey the *serbalim*, and
they took away his *ruthyali* status. He lives here. I think—
I think I have been expelled, too."

The rain hissed down on the leaves. Gete swallowed. His
grudge against Desti suddenly seemed to have lost all its
meaning. "You and me're in the same boat, then," he said.
"Me elders told me to shove off. I'm not living on Sarberra now."

"What? Why are you—then what are *you* here for? I
thought it was a fishing trip or something—"

Gete laughed. "Haven't cast a net in ten sixdays." As
briefly as possible, he told the story of his having been
press-ganged into lemanhood.

"Oh." Desti shuddered. "I'm sorry."

"I am, too!"

"It isn't that bad, is it?"

Gete did not answer. Some goats ventured back into the
ditch and chomped at the leaves on the top of the wall,
bringing a shower of raindrops down on Gete and Desti.

After a time Gete said, "But it was *your* fault, as much as 'twas anyone's."

"What?" Desti twisted around and looked at him. "What did *I* do?"

"Ye didn't answer my prayers. I thought you were a god like the flamen said ye were. And I wanted you to come take me away, or change their minds—or something!"

"I can't hear prayers! You *know* that!"

"Yeah. I know now. Now it's too late!"

The goats tossed their heads and climbed back up into the rain. The water in the bottom of the ditch was becoming a small river. Desti slid his foot down and splashed in it. "Power . . . I really do owe you one!"

"You don't owe me anything. Don't give me any easy rides."

"Well, I want to tell you anyway." Desti splashed harder in the water. "First of all, my people have a name which isn't gods. We call ourselves *auchresh*."

"What? *What*-esh?"

"We're predators, really. Predators' children. Our Heavens are built near predator lairs, so we can keep our numbers up. There's a lair on salt Fulima—that's where I was born. It came time for my *breideii* White Oakenroot to take a Foundling, so he *teth"d* over to Fulima and found me living on the water's edge, on raw fish, trying to keep myself hidden from the predators. They would've eaten me, even though one of them gave birth to me. I was about your age, I think. I don't remember, but that's how Oak says it was. He brought me back to Faraxa—"

"Wait," Gete said. "Predators gave *birth* to you?"

"Haven't I just told you so?"

Predators? The winged, fanged beasts that lived on salt islands and flew across the seas at night to prey on humans' homes and holdings? They were *animals*! Imagination could conjure up no creatures bloodier or more cunning. What could predators have to do with the gods?

Desti seemed to be saying that the gods weren't gods at all, but *descendants* of those beasts. But—but if he was telling the truth—if there were no real gods—then what of Transcendence's vision?

Gete asked a question at random out of the dozens filling his mind? "Your brei—whatever—he's your father? He adopted you? Then you're just like us?"

"Yes." Desti bit his lip. "Yes and no ..." He stopped speaking. His head came up. "Oh, Power. Curses." A half-guilty, half-frightened look came over his face, as if he had been caught nicking someone else's catch. Gete followed his stare to the place where the stone wall curved into the night. There did not seem to be anything wrong. But Desti had those faculties, that extraordinarily powerful hearing—*not* human—ears like a predator's—

"Thank the Power I've found you!" Warm Easterly hurried along the ditch, knocking down a rain shower of droplets with his massive head and shoulders. "Desti, what have you been telling the boy?"

"Nothing." Desti's wings whirred. "Nothing."

"You have. I can see it on his face."

"Gete, I'm sorry! It was all lies!" Desti flickered, and vanished.

Easter shouted something unintelligible, in an impossibly loud voice, and grabbed vainly at the shrinking hole in the air.

Gete flattened himself against the wall. Divine retribution appeared to be visiting itself on him for having entertained the notion that Desti's people might possibly be something other than gods. *Please go away—it wasn't me—*

Easter squatted down in the bottom of the ditch. "Desti didn't handle that very well! Don't blame him for it. He's young. He doesn't know how to manage relations with your people yet."

Gete knuckled his eyes. "But was it—was it *true*? All that about"—he gulped—"predators?"

Easter's big fists rested on the ground, like those of the Veretrean apes Gete had once seen painted on a plate that had come all the way from K'Fier. This god was not handsome. Not like Desti, whom some of the girls had sighed over. *If only 'tweren't for his wings—*

"Desti is forty." Easter's eyes crinkled. His skin was pale in the dark. "By our standards, he is scarcely into his teens. Younger than you."

Gete gripped a wet, licheny stone that protruded from the wall. "I don't understand."

"You don't need to. Just forgive him. You'll probably never see him again. There's nothing to be gained by *not* forgiving him."

"But—but—" *But what should I forgive him for? In the*

turmoil of his incomprehension, Gete had lost sight of the reason he had been angry with Desti in the first place.

"I won't punish him. Don't worry about that. But there's a lesson it is high time for him to learn; one that *firim* all over the world have learned: your people find it easier not to understand things. Since you are comfortable living with paradoxes, why should we make things more complicated by explaining them to you?" Easter's face became grave. "And of course, there is the danger of the Hands for those who know too much. And the disapproval of the *serbalim*. Both for you and for us. In light of *that*, it may be a long time before we can share all of the truth as we understand it with you." Easter rocked to and fro on his heels. "For now, it is enough that we share meat and hard work."

He looked straight at Gete. The rain was coming down harder, plopping through the trees. "Why aren't you with your Godsister?"

Thankfulness.

Oh, no.

Guilt drove everything else out of Gete's head. He sprang to his feet. "Oh, gods!" For the last couple of hours, he had forgotten her as completely as you can forget anyone. *What kind of leman am I?* "Oh, gods—"

"Your best move is to get back to her quickly, I think." Easter boosted himself to his feet and wrapped those long arms around Gete. He was drenched with rain, yet he still smelled of salt, the way Desti had whenever he arrived on Sarberra. But *this* was the salt of the sea, of nets and sun and sails, not the flowery vaguely good-to-eat scent of the transparent islands—

Blackness cut off Gete's breath. His pulse. His nerves. All his links to himself. Panic came in a flood. But since he had no body, it seemed queerly distant from him. *Did he knife me? Am I dying?*

His brain flopped like a fish out of water as his feet hit the wet rock of the village street. Silver piles of coelakates gleamed way down on the quay. Rain roared. Gete's teeth chattered. "What did ye *do*?"

The god laughed. He stood a little way uphill, with his hand on the door of another house. "Go to your flamen, boy. Do your duty."

"What about you?"

"I have more than one house here." Easter smiled again, lifted the latch, and went in.

In the ordinary way.

Gete's eyeballs hurt. So did his whole body, in subtle, unfamilar places. His spine and the roots of his hair ached. Grown boy though he was, his eyes stung with tears. His hands shook as he lifted the latch and went inside.

She was not there. The hearth at the end of the room glowed sullenly. The room was filled with trembling shadows. All the supper pans hung neatly on the walls. The table was pushed against the downhill wall. Barrels and packages of foodstuffs lined the wall between the table and the hearth.

Gete wiped his eyes. He put his ear to the inner door and then opened it a crack, letting a wedge of dim firelight into the inner room. He counted the figures on the various pallets. The four Finspine children. Hasti's younger brother, Refu Finspine, and his wife. Their three children. The grandparents. On the farthest pallet, Nali and Hasti Finspine lay curled together, although the atmosphere in the room was warm to stifling. Godsie Finspine's round arm clasped her husband's shoulders. Her fur shone pale in the darkness.

The room smelled of burned herbs. Gete recognized the reek of fumigation.

So Thani had done her miracle.

Gods, gods, and I wasn't here!

He might not like her very much, but his failure to do his duty stung him into an agony. He closed the door carefully and rested his head on the planks. What kind of leman was he? What kind of man failed at the only task life had given him?

He was no more use than a fish on dry land. Flapping around ineffectually like one of those damn coelakates. Helpless as a girl in a boat.

But there was *one* girl who could handle a boat.

He would not have acted like this back on Sarberra!

But then, back on Sarberra, he had never had his entire religion infused with doubt in the course of a single evening. Back on Sarberra, he had never had decisions like this to make. He had never had to be so strong, the sole crutch of this sickly, frail girl who was nonetheless so heavy to bear up—

"Gete," she said in a voice like a feather drifting across the floor.

He started upright, dashing the tears away. *"Godsister?"*

In the shadows of the barrels, in a nook beside the hearth, her eyes shone like opaque red jewels. She must have been sleeping. Her breath was so faint he could not hear it over the whisper of the rain outside.

He rushed to kneel at her side. "Can you forgive me? I'll try harder, I'll do better by you—"

"I—I'm all right. Really."

Her hair was matted. Tenderly he lifted her up, laying her head on his knees so that he could comb out the tangles. "Tell me if it pulls." Each sleeve of her robe hung in two pieces, and the seam around the hood was frayed, too, trailing threads over her shoulders. " 'S *that* how you wear out your clothes so fast? The miracles?"

"I think so. I don't know why, though." Her voice was so soft he could hardly hear her. "Regretfulness, I am so tired. I don't think I am doing this right. It shouldn't be so hard to work miracles—and I can't think of any possible reason why they should spill over into my *hair* and my *clothes*."

"Things're different than they were," Gete reminded her.

"They are! They are! Sometimes, when I work a miracle I feel as if I am balancing the whole world on my shoulders, and taking a terrible risk with it—that I am only just holding it, and that if I drop it the Divine Balance itself will shatter—"

Gete shivered. "Idle dreams," he said firmly.

"All our lives are idle dreams." Her chuckle was fainter even than her voice. Gete worked at a tangle on her nape, lifting her a little to reach it. The knobs of her spine protruded, all the way up to the base of her neck. She was naked under the disintegrating robe, having taken off the shift dress she wore under it during the day. He laid her back on his knees and massaged her forehead. "That feels good." A spasm of pain made her clench her teeth, but she knotted her jaw. "Go on," she said.

She was stoic and brave. Bending down, Gete dropped a kiss on her forehead. Then he came to his senses and straightened up. "Sorry!" he whispered, and yanked at the tangles.

She had gone very still. Now she frowned. "You're hurting me, Gete."

"I'm sorry. I said I was sorry." Was that a sparkle on her lashes? Could she still cry?

"I mean you're hurting me in . . . hurting me. If you hate me, then just tell me so, don't pull my hair like that. I'll put you away from me and take another leman right here on Qalma."

"Godsister, how can you say such a thing?"

"You put a good face on it, but I can tell. I made the wrong choice. Well, none of us is infallible. I'll just choose again." She shrugged, her eyes still closed.

He did not know how to reassure her. Frantically, he scooped her up in his arms. She was as light as a small child. How did you tell a girl you had suddenly realized that you loved her? Was this normal? Or was it like incest? No—everyone knew that flamens and lemans—it was all right!

He kissed her. Messily, because he had started crying again. "Godsister, don't put me away. I'll stay with you as long as you'll have me. I beg of you. Keep me by you."

Tears spilled from her eyes. She wrapped her arms around his neck and pressed her lips to his mouth. She had small, crooked teeth. How could someone so thin and ill-kempt be so pretty? He didn't know. He only knew she *was* pretty, even beautiful, with her milky globes of eyelids and the blood trickling out from under them onto her cheeks. His hands moved not of his own will, but according to some deeper instinct (it *must* be instinct, for he certainly did not know what to do with a girl) as he stripped the robe away. She had big joints and wide angular hips. He remembered his first sight of her, before flamenhood set in. She had been a sturdy girl. *And will be again. She will be again!*

Her face contorted in anguish when he finally penetrated her. There was no resistance, only a torrent of pleasure that swept him away faster than he had expected. Her thin fingers gripped his back and she hissed between her teeth, wordlessly, as his thrusts shook her.

It culminated.

A moment afterward, catching him completely off guard, came the wash of tenderness.

"I talked to Desti tonight," he whispered.

"Don't want to know." She snuggled her head into his armpit.

"What happened?" Gete said.

"Whah?"

"You useta be as cold as a raw fish. Now you're all cuddly."

A whisper of laughter. "I suppose . . . I made the right choice, after all."

"How can you tell, just from . . . that? From what we did?" Funny, ironic, that he should be the one doubting their bond, after that violent joining!

"If we were another man and woman, what we did wouldn't mean much," she said. "You of all people should know that." Her milky, granulated orbs were red in the dying firelight, like a dead fish's. "But since we are flamen and leman . . . well, I believe it's triggered something."

"What?"

"The flamen-leman bond. Don't you feel it?"

The rain pattered on the roof. Gete shut his eyes and tried to find his way deep inside himself. He could not find anything mystical, or any new thing at all apart from his desire for her. He said so.

She gave a relieved peal of laughter.

"Oh!" He shut his mouth.

"But it's broader than that, too. There's a . . . responsibility that you will come to feel, the way I felt responsible for Transcendence. Almost as if I was the adult and he the child. It's like looking back through a flawed window, but I can remember. Your task is to safeguard the world, by safeguarding me. If that doesn't rest lightly on your shoulders, well, it *shouldn't*! But as long as you accept the responsibility, we'll do well."

He shivered. Then he pulled her over and kissed her. "I accept *you*."

She whispered wonderingly into his mouth, "I always did wonder what it felt like from the other side."

"Thankfulness . . . Thani?"

"Mmm. I was almost asleep."

The fire had nearly gone out. Strings of vegetables hung

from the ceiling, undulating in the shadows, like vines dangling from the tree cover of a forest Gete had never seen. That primeval Veretrean forest, perhaps, where apes like Warm Easterly swung from limb to limb of gargantuan celery stalks.

"Why did you choose me in the first place? I was so useless, for so long. Why didn't you choose someone ... easier? Younger?"

Thani sighed. She sounded wide-awake now as she said, "It's not like picking the prime billy out of the flock, Gete. I chose you because I didn't think you were born to live on Sarberra. If *I* hadn't been a leman, I would have been perfectly happy growing up in the Domesdys saltside, marrying one of my cousins, working the fields, bearing babies. I wouldn't want to do to another child what was done to me. The pain of separation from one's destiny is intense, although short-lived. But wherever *your* destiny lies, I was, and am, pretty sure it's not on Sarberra."

"But how could you tell ... how did you know ..." A shudder passed over Gete's scalp as he remembered salt Harrima. She had stared at him. It had almost been as if she had recognized him, without being able to see him.

"I knew it when I saw you."

"Could you still *see*? After your ordeal?"

She chuckled. "In a way. I was half delirious. I knew my sight was going to go soon, and I had already lost my ability to distinguish shapes. The salt undergrowth was a blur. But when you stepped out of the boat, I saw your hair, and I knew it would be a long time before I lost my ability to see *that*. It's like carrots—I don't suppose you have those in the Archipelago."

Gete extracted a lock of his hair from under her head and stared at it. "Nope."

"Or like those flowers your people plant in front of your houses. Witch's wands. I was absolutely terrified of not being able to see my own leman, and for that reason, I decided to choose you. Later, as I listened to your mother and the other Sarberrans talking, I realized my instincts had been right. You were different. So I told your father I wanted you. And he said they would meet to decide whether they could spare you."

"But ..." This seemed to fly in the face of everything she had said before. "Was it completely random, then? If

I had black hair, you'd never have noticed me, and I'd still be on Sarberra?"

"It's all tied up. Your beauty, your destiny. The surface is inseparable from the essence. The surface *is* the essence."

She paused.

"No one makes ghosts anymore. I had a sister who was a ghostier—a maker of ghosts. She's dead. Maybe her friends still ply their trade, but the flamens no longer choose ghosts from the continents. The Divinarch chooses his own now, without asking our advice, and there are no beauticians, no presentations, no viewings in Delta City. But if there *were,* I'm convinced you would already have been chosen. You are so lovely."

Gete had never been called lovely before. He did not know whether to take her seriously.

"Your path leads to Delta City. It would have led you there whether I came to Sarberra or not. But thank the gods, I was right when I perceived qualities in you beyond mere beauty, that would be useful to me now, in a different age, when different things are required of us."

Gete silently thanked the gods in his turn that times had changed. He did not want to die as a ghost. He wanted to live. Delta City seemed unimportant now, no more than a crystallization of his future with Thani.

"How much can you see now?" he asked. "Can you still see my hair?"

She shook her head. "Everything is blurred into a kind of eternal twilight. In the sun, there are rainbows. I can see movement, if it's fast."

He winced.

She must have felt his distaste. Her voice rang suddenly clear. "And I pray, leman, for the day when even those remaining impurities vanish from my perception, when I will thank the gods that I no longer need to falsify myself to my people!"

"Sorry!" Gete pulled her close, trying to restore the sense of ease between them. He could not stop forgetting this other side of her, the side that made him doubt everything Desti had told him about the gods. But it seemed that only one or the other, could exist at a time in her bony, overworked frame.

In the Golden Egg

Leaves and branches filtered out the noise of Rimmear. Limping as fast as he could in the middle of a column of Hands, beside an Eithilindrian who grinned all the time, along a tunnel of salt trees pruned to concavity, Arity's sense of displacement was heightened. He felt as if he were back in human country, in one of the gardens on the Royallandic mainland that she had shown him, when they had *teth"d* after—

Best not to think.

Rose Eye, *serbali* of Rimmear, lived high on this landscaped hillside above the chasm. None of the edifices up here, pastiches of Delta City's Antiprophet Square mansions for the most part, were more than a couple of hundred years old. Mazelike gardens showcased them to advantage. Each seemed cocooned from the next, propounding an illusion of rambling parklands on what was actually a steep mountainside. Here, deep in Rose Eye's quiet garden, Arity was acutely aware of the multitudes of shades that made Rimmear's atmosphere so stifling. Their whispers crept down his back like fingers.

Rimmear, like most Heavens, traced its roots back to the dawn of *auchresh* civilization, to the time before Heavens were called Heavens. Delta City was nowhere near as old. When Arity and Pati returned to Rimmear after their flying visit to Delta City, the weight of the city's history had dropped on him like a stone. He had actually cried out, and Pati had put his arms around him.

Best not to think!

Rimmear's legendarians asserted that the city had taken root on the banks of the river of the chasm. It had been a tiny, prehistoric Heaven of houses built to look like the spiky *treikos* formations that prevailed in the bottomlands. Most of those ancient dwellings were now taverns, walled in by gimcrack salt-wood buildings. Arity remembered getting drunk in one of them, staggering away, puking as he ran, from a would-be *ghauthiji* who had got him trapped between two of the spikes sticking out around the back door. The ancient *auchresh* had armored their homes not just for camouflage, but to protect them from attacks by the predators who had regularly, so the legends said, besieged Heaven. Back then, they had been an active menace to Rimmear, as well as the source of its children. Not chained pets whose lust voyeurs used to arouse their sagging penises.

Down in the depths where there are no Foundlings.

The lower tiers got their children from the upper tiers. Everyone in Rimmear cycled slowly downward. It was a law of nature. A law of status. Of course, some *wrchrethre* souls whose status outweighed that of everyone else in Rimmear deliberately buried themselves on the bottom tiers, to meld themselves to the honeycomb structure of the city in a final act of self-abnegation.

But Pati had rescued him.

This visit to Rose Eye was the last of Pati's diplomatic missions that the Divinarch, in his unscheduled dalliance with Arity, had postponed.

The Hands tramped along between curving salt hedgerows that Rose Eye had had imported from Recharabhy.

"Just a courtesy visit," Pati said yesterday as they lay in sunshine in the diplomatic hotel. "Half an hour. Can't *not* visit any of the *serbalim,* they'd put their noses in the air and then spread rumors about me. Which I do *not* need! Most of them only have status because their *breideii* was a *serbali*: they haven't done anything to merit it, and they do nothing with it besides throw parties. Huneyash, Green Feather, and Dessica mainly control Rimmear. And I've failed to make any impact on *them* this time round. We might as well go home." He had thought for a minute, playing with Arity's hair. "Rose Eye is not completely to be disregarded, though."

Hearing a new note in his voice, Arity looked around. His heart sank. "He's more of a blusterer than anything else, but he's highly unpredictable. And because he has the favor of those thrice damned *er-serbalim* who were once your and my *saduim,* ashamed though I am to remember it ... he has some influence. In fact, I think the *er-serbalim* may even be in Rimmear now. They don't advertise their travels much anymore. But then again, I had that from Blushing Cat, and she is notorious for spreading gossip."

Above the trees a perfect golden egg rose, standing on end, glittering in the night. It was Rose Eye's mansion. The hedges gave way to a steep slope, scattered with trees, and out of these a high fence of laced-together salt beeches rose around the egg, enclosing an inner lawn. Under an arch that passed for a gateway in the fence, Foundlings stood sentinel in a yellow glare of torchlight.

The Eithilindrian Hand beside Arity, a lanky green spider of a fellow (they had been paired off by skin tone), gaped unselfconsciously at the mansion beyond. He dug Arity in the ribs. "Eh. See those shines? Them're *windows!*"

Arity's eyes widened. The edifice was monstrous, and farther off than he had thought.

The Hands started to move again. Arity saw that they were leaving half the column behind. The banner bearers and "Way!" criers sprawled under the trees, already engaged in their off-hours pastimes of teasing the Foundlings and digging their toes into the grass.

Everything about serving the Divinarch seemed to be tedious, dangerous, pointless, or some combination of the three. Arity's post since they had returned from Delta City had been at the inmost door of Pati's lodgings. He was, as he had requested, in the regular rotation.

The mansion was a vast chunk of rock salt hauled somehow from the tumbled crest of the mountain, shoddily carved. Up close, the egg shape was vastly imperfect. Arity reached out to touch the salt as they filed into a dark opening at the bottom. The rock was splintery.

The passage led into a hacked-out vault filled with the lazy rumble of *auchresh* voices. A huge bonfire shone at either end. The hands broke formation and milled around, greeting Rose Eye's servants, swaggering, patently aware of their superiority to these *salthirre* folk. Blue Kestrel, the only real friend Arity had managed to make among the Hands, told him that Pati taught the Hands that status was a bad guide to value. Pati did not allow them to turn up their noses at mixing with lower-status *auchresh*. But most, particularly the *ex-mainrauim* and *ex-serbalim,* could not be broken of lifelong habits.

A knot of Hands bore down on Arity like a heavy beast charging its prey. Before he could move, he was absorbed. "Couldn't face this without *you*," Pati said, grinning, wrapping pale fingers around his arm. "Cheer up! Why so gloomy? Not enough intellectual stimulation among the rank and file? That's what *I'm* good for—"

Shoddily decorated staircases and halls and corridors passed around them like illusions.

They must have ascended very high in the egg by the time they finally stopped. The Hands ushered Arity and Pati toward a lacquered door. Pati had Arity's wrist securely in his grip. A servant in a ribboned bonnet snapped to attention. "The Divinarch!" he trumpeted.

"Shut up, Boli!" someone bellowed from within. "He's not coming until dawn! Tell whoever it is to go away! I'm busy!"

Pati shoved the *kere* aside. "This could be interesting." He thrust the door open. The room was an antechamber with one wall completely made of windows and the others draped with tapestries. Rose Eye sat blobbily on a pile of cushions, mouth open in shock. Broken Bird and Bronze Water—they *were* here?—sat on an overstuffed loveseat. A small, miserable-looking *auchresh* in Uarechi clothing stood in the middle of the room, wringing his hands.

The door slammed. Broken Bird and Bronze Water stared at Pati, not bothering to hide their astonishment, as he lowered himself deliberately into a high-backed chair. Arity took up his stance behind it.

"Oh, Heir," Bronze Water said. His face went slowly soft with pain. Arity had been wrong: the *er-serbalim* were not astonished to see Pati, but *him*. "Has he caught you, too?"

Broken Bird elbowed him. "In the Power's *name*! We are conducting business! Please go outside and wait, both of you. Pati, it was too bad of you to bring him here," she added in a lower voice. She turned her head away. A sea of wrinkles lapped around her neck. Arity's heart twisted. He looked away from her, at the spectacular view of the chasm which filled the wall like a mural. Lights winked all the way down the west side of the ravine, giving the impression of a waterfall sliding downward more slowly than any water could. Above the ridge, the sky was the charcoal gray of waves on a cloudy day.

Pati stirred, and Arity knew he was itching to remind Broken Bird that he was not to be ordered around like some Foundling. He said smoothly, "My dear Rose Eye, I believe there has been a misunderstanding. I do apologize.

This is the hour we agreed on. But finish your business; I shall not disturb you."

As if suddenly unfrozen, the little *kere* in country clothes whirled around, dropped at Pati's feet, and said in a rush, "Please, Divinarch, grant me lenience! The *serbali* Rose Eye, grace guard his step, won't. Please. I've *teth*"d all the way from the eastern saltside in skips and hops. I know my *serbalim* back in Heaven will pardon me if *you* tell them—"

"What is this?" Pati said, at the same time as Rose Eye said, "Shush, *khrithi*!"

Pati pressed on, "Why do you need my lenience? Have you killed someone? I do not pardon wanton violence—"

The little man laughed bitterly. "No, most respected Divinarch, I haven't killed a *kere* in my life, for all I was *main-raui* when I was younger! All I did was pay a few visits to a human Heaven." He said the word in mortal, sending a thrill through Arity. "A *village*. In the Uarechi saltside— Ruhaab is its name—"

"The scum is lying," Bronze Water broke in. "He has moved out of his Heaven. He *lives* in this human village. We have it on authority from his *serbalu*."

"Faint Starbreath has recently become enamored of the honored *er-serbalim* Bronze Water and Broken Bird's thinking," the *auchresh* said. "She declared in front of all of us that it was no longer permissible to leave the salt. Then she expelled me from Heaven. My question is, must I suffer for something she has decided? Divinarch, I beg you—"

Broken Bird laughed derisively. "Hear him lie outright now, Pati! The truth is that he first visited this human hole, this Ruhaab, *after* the *serbalu* made her decision. We have this on authority from his accomplices in crime. Several of them, after they heard our teachings from the *serbalu*, became curious about the human lands. They walked to the edge of the salt, and there encountered their first humans. Bronze and I take full responsibility for this." Her voice hardened. "But it is upon this *kere's* own head that he flaunted his misdeeds until his *serbalu* had no choice but to banish him from Heaven. He is trying to have the best of both worlds."

The little *auchresh's* gaze flickered from one of them to the other. Arity saw that he was not stupid, but that he was at his wits' end. He had cast his stone, made his appeal to Pati, and been caught out in his lie. Now he could only await his fate.

But Pati's eyes gleamed maliciously, and Arity knew what he was going to say before he said it. "I believe him. The *serbalu* must have lied to bolster her reputation." He turned to the *kere*. "I grant you lenience."

Rose Eye hissed.

"Pati," Bronze Water said in mortal, "beware! Your relationships in Uarech have never been better than shaky. You cannot afford to have it noised about that you slandered a *serbalu*, even one as obscure as this fat fool."

"But Divinarch, it's plain that the fellow is lying!" Rose Eye exploded. Arity saw that he was too dense to understand that Bronze Water had been speaking another language, or that he himself was dancing to Pati's tune. He positively bubbled with vitriol. "Not only has he lied to your face, but he has cast dust on the teachings of the *er-serbalim* themselves!" He made a devoted obeisance to Broken Bird and Bronze Water's couch. "What other evidence do you need? You must deny him lenience!"

Pati smiled imperturbably down at the little *kere*. "Go out and tell my Hands that I have revoked your punishment. They will issue you a Divine Seal, which you can take home to your *serbalu*."

"This is *my* affair!" Rose Eye frothed. "This is my *khrithi*. Divinarch, I am sorry to inform you that in the salt, and particularly in Uarech, your Divine Seals are worth no more than the stone they are made of!"

Pati leaned back in his chair and steepled his fingers. Arity saw that lethal glitter in his eyes which appeared when he was at his most dangerous and his most vulnerable. But people were always too busy being afraid of him to take advantage of his weakness. Arity himself was no exception. Pati said in a calm tone calculated to provoke, "But I am Divinarch all over the world, my dear *tith"ahi*. I may do what I like." Broken Bird and Bronze Water expostulated in horror. Rose Eye let loose a landslide of objections. Pati ignored them. He leaned forward and said to the little *kere*, "Go home, my friend. Just *teth"*. I'll send one of my Hands after you. Oh, and don't forget to tell the Ruhaab humans that it is by the grace of the Divinarch you are still free to visit them."

The *kere* scrambled to his feet, face shining. Arity felt

sick. To him, each outburst seemed like a badly penned
step in a rather plodding stage play. Pati was the playwright, a ruthless manipulator who did not care if his situa-
tions were predictable, or ugly, as long as the actors went
through the motions.

"Don't get carried away, Rose Eye," Broken Bird
wailed. "He's using you to wipe his feet."

Pati sat up and bared his teeth.

But Rose Eye shouted at the little *kere*, "You will not
leave this room without my permission!" When the other
tried it anyway, Rose Eye plunged on him, preventing him
from vanishing, and bore him to the floor. Fangs flashed.
The door burst open: the Hands poured in like a pack
of silken-coated hounds. The trumpeter added his voice to
the confusion.

Arity stepped farther back. Pati pulled his feet up out of
the way and sat cross-legged, watching avidly.

Arity turned to stare out of the window. The chalky
dawn sat heavily on the glimmering city. All of the lights
were still slipping downward, or so it appeared to Arity's
eyes, one by one by one.

The furor quieted. As it became manageable to the
senses, it twanged back into his consciousness. The smell
of fresh blood stung his nostrils. A pair of Fists bundled
the nameless *kere* efficiently into a salt-fiber sack. Of course
the one who did not count had died. His death meant nothing in the grand circles where Pati, Broken Bird, and
Bronze Water trod. Just another light winking out.

And he had been a liar and an opportunist, anyway.

All the extra people who had rushed in stood about awkwardly while Rose Eye cleaned his hands in a basin someone held. Pati folded his mouth into a severe line. Broken
Bird threw him a furious glance, then shook her skirts out
over the white splotch on the carpet. "Are you, perhaps,
going to offer us *morothe*, Rose Eye dear?" she asked
sweetly. But her eyes flicked to Arity. "I *am* fond of a
small sip of something when the night wears on and on
like this."

Arity had no chance to flee to the servants' cavern. He
found himself lining up with the other Hands along one
wall of the *morothe* cavern. The interminable conventions
of the courtesy call set in, like winter. Even such a one as

Pati, who had fastened an empire together with blood, was neutralized by etiquette. In accordance with the Uarechi *morothe* tradition, the big, high-windowed cavern was empty but for a stone table and chairs. Pati sat across from Rose Eye, feet up, gulping his fifth glass of cool green liquid, discussing local politics. They did not touch on anything dangerous. All hatred must be veiled, all social gaffes smoothed over. The outbreak of animosity that had caused the death of the little *kere* had to be forgotten for the sake of peace in the salt.

But Arity guessed he would hear more of the incident from Pati. The incident was an outrageous crystallization of a rumor that had recently filtered down to the bottom tiers: the fertilization of mortal properties with *auchresh* ingenuity. When he first heard the rumors, he had thought them too outrageous to be true. *Auchresh* living in saltside villages in Calvary, Pirady, Veretry, Domesdys, Iceland? On human-inhabited islands of the Archipelago? In Royalland? *Auchresh* finding *acceptance* among humans? That was impossible!

And yet tonight he had seen it confirmed or at least asserted.

Broken Bird and Bronze Water got up from the table. They stood by the arched windows that looked out over the torch-lit lawn. At last they put down their glasses and drifted behind the line of Hands. Arity steeled himself. Right on cue, he felt a touch on his shoulder. He spun around, facing the two *er-serbalim*. Hopefully, Rose Eye and Pati were too busy smiling and despising each other to notice. "Come away!" Broken Bird moderated her voice to a whisper. Her little blue face puckered. "Please don't let yourself get caught up in this! Just come with us, Arity— we'll take you somewhere safe! We have friends in every continent—"

Sooner or later, the Hands would have to know who he had been. He spoke in clear, articulate mortal without worrying what they would think. He could shrug off the structures of *auchraug* as easily as he had shrugged off the false slum accent that he had affected in the lower tiers. "Bird, I have no wish to become involved in your cause instead of Pati's."

"We have no cause," Bronze Water said in *auchraug*. "Causes are un-*auchresh*. We only preach sanity."

They believed that, he thought. "I need no one's help. Leave me alone."

"Where did he find you?" Bronze Water said. "Have you been in Rimmear all this time? Hope would not tell us."

Broken Bird raised herself on tiptoe, peering into Arity's face. She was so close that he could feel her body heat and smell the dry, salty scent of age. "What did he *do*? How did he catch you like this?"

"I chose to come here. I was sick of spending my nights drunk and my days dreaming."

"You chose . . . this?" Bird waved her hand at the line of Hands: exotic mutates polished and uniformed like shiny toys.

"Bird, you don't know anything about making choices. And that is because you don't know what free will is. You have always worked as the agent of past traditions; you know no other way to operate. The only difference is that now, the traditions are twisted to your purposes, instead of the other way round."

Her face screwed up like a rag. "That is what you would say," she hissed. "*Hymanni* lover."

Don't—no—don't remember—

"Pati is bound by tradition too, Arity," Bronze Water said. "Do you think you are the banner-bearer of some new, free-thinking breed of *auchresh*? We are *all* the tools of tradition."

"Pati only propounds certain of our traditions because he *believes* in them," Arity said. "That is the mystery of Pati: how devoutly, under all the flair and egotism, he believes. I don't know exactly. I don't think anyone knows. But I'm not talking about Pati. I'm talking about me. I think I am the only person in this room who knows what free will really is."

Broken Bird's nose wrinkled cynically.

Arity's heart beat fast. He hissed in a low voice, "Free will is not pretentious cause flaunting. It is being one of the masses. Being absorbed. Being willing to do whatever you are told, and *liking* it that way. *Not caring. That* is free will."

Broken Bird looked frightened. "Being a slave?"

"If you will!"

Bronze Water, staring at Arity, pulled her away. She held onto his arms, her claws sewing his sleeves. Arity felt like shouting. He had won. He was free now to do exactly what he wanted. "Come away," Bronze Water muttered. "There's nothing we can do for him. Maybe after the glamour has worn off—"

"But he's in love with him," Broken Bird said, picking holes in Bronze Water's sleeve. "He always has been. *That's* why he sees this as—as a *noble surrender*. What a monster, what a *haugthirre*, what a throwback—" Methodically, she continued stringing insults together, switching to mortal when she ran out of *auchraug* epithets for Pati.

Arity spun on one heel talon and faced front again. His neighbors poked him in the ribs. One of them unbent so far as to hiss, "What was *that* about? Didn't know you'd learned mortal already!"

"Tell you later," he murmured.

Better if he told them himself. Several of the Hands back in Delta City had been *lesh kervayim*, and he could not avoid them forever. Quite apart from them, there must be others left in the city who would recognize him. He would just have to trust his new peers not to revile him.

At the table, Pati and Rose Eye roared with false jocosity over some anecdote Pati had related. In the shadows, Broken Bird continued her whispered defamation of Pati's sexuality, private habits, and ancestry. Arity had not known there were so many foul words in the two tongues. The sun was about to rise from behind the ridge, striking through the salt trees, turning trunks and leaves transparent. Already the gardens were bleaching to the gray that preceded clarity.

The Death of Comeliness

Sol Southwind leaned out the window of his lodgings, thinking about his twin sister. Beneath, a brace of porkers snuffled about on the tunnel roof of Dock Street. Someone had thrown them a bucket of waste. Amazing how although there were no guardrails, the pigs slithered about the roofs on their trotters, snorting up the slops, and managed not to fall off. It was the middle of the day. A hazy chill day.

Westpoint was no less damp than Marshtown in autumn, even though it was higher above the marshes.

All the way across the city, he could feel her.

He closed his eyes. What would she be doing at this time of day? Gliding to and fro in the stone kitchen of the Chalice, tying an apron over the outmoded gown that was the only outward sign of her nostalgia for the old days, helping Algia and Eterneli wash up after lunch? No, that didn't quite work. Was she in Melthirr House, with her family? Emni, Zin, and their baby were the core of the decimated *imrchim*. It had been a dark day for the ghostiers when they were reduced to a family! Or perhaps Emni was in the workshop they had made out of Erene and Humi's old apartment, instructing one of her new apprentices. *But what will they do with their craft, Em?* Sol thought with a flash of anger. *Why are you bothering?* The image dissolved as frustration overtook him. Why were she and Ziniquel troubling themselves to train a new generation of ghostiers? He wondered for the thousandth time. The apprentices would never have a venue for their art, unless they allied themselves with the Marshtown devotees—and all of *those,* just because of where they lived, had apostatic leanings. An alliance with Marshtown might well be the thing that would resolve the Divinarch to bring his thumb down on Tellury Crescent.

Emni and Zin insisted their imperative was to keep the *imrchim* together. They said they wanted to preserve the traditions. Chalice, Eftpool, excursions every Dividay to hear sermons, and so forth and so on. Sol could have—and on the day he moved out of Tellury Crescent, *had*—told them they had already failed. Who was left? Mory and Tris were gone. Algia remained. Eterneli. Zin. Emni. The baby, Lighte. The apprentices Emni and Zin had recruited—Tan, Suret, and Yste. Tan was a flamboyant youth from Christon with a tendency toward old-fashioned atheism, who relied on ghostier immunity to keep him safe from the Hands. Zin had found Suret on a visit to Riestasis in Veretry. She was dark and compact, with smoldering eyes that belied her gentle nature. Yste was a Calvarese-Deltan boy, about twelve years old, the most talented of the three, but odious.

And *Sol* was the only one the Divinarch patronized. That left the others stranded. Had they realized before, how heavily they had come to depend on the noble court? Humi and Erene had systematically cut the *imrchim's* ties to the Divinarchy. Now they were foundering.

Emni and Ziniquel had two options. Apostasy, or the Divinarch-worship Sol had chosen, which he would be the first to admit was superficial nonsense. The Divinarch's pet flamens called Pati the Only God, Practitioner of Divine Power. The Hands were his Inviolate Servants. No one with a mind of his own could believe such stuff. Sol could not explain how the flamens did. But had anyone ever understood the flamens? They sang Pati's praises, and he starved the city by arresting its nobles, merchants, craftsmen, and shipwrights on charges of atheism. Then there were the murders. Whenever Sol left his lodgings, he came across bodies lying ostracized in the streets, or bundled into corners, splotched with their own black blood, daymoths buzzing around their orifices. People attended sermons these days because they knew that the murder victims had mostly shown symptoms of atheism. And Deltans, wisely, valued survival over integrity.

At the beginning of the tyranny, the imrchim Mory and Tris had rushed off into Marshtown to follow the apostates—those few flamens who had refused to swear allegiance to a cruel, unjust, and possibly mad god. The last Sol had heard, there were prices on their heads. Emni and Zin were too cowardly to follow them—though they reviled Sol to his face for truckling to Pati.

Sol had his own reasons for staying in the Divinarch's good books. Emni would thank him in the end.

And anyhow, he entertained real doubts about the apostates. From time to time, Mory and Tris's ghosts surfaced in the Westpoint markets. Powerful pieces painted in dark colors, they were contorted with the cruelty inherent in Mory's work, which she had passed on to Tris. Sol had bought a few because of their curiosity value, but had had to put them away in closets. Even he, who was not deluded as to the value of ruthlessness, was sickened by them.

Ruthlessness had its uses. It had helped him kill Beisa. And it would have helped him kill Emni, too, if his resolve had not been weakened by that streak of softheartedness he despised in both her and himself, which caused him to level off the spoonful of green amaranth. He had left the thing to chance rather than making it certain. And that had ruined his chances at the post of senior ghostier.

When he held the tenth seat on the Ellipse, he'd been a
better ghostier than any of the others would admit. And
his ruthlessness was also the reason Pati patronized him.
None of the others would do the work he did. It was necessary for him to keep cruelty to the fore. The boys and girls
he ghosted on his own initiative, now that he had all day
and all night to work, were dreadfully beautiful—but the
subjects the Divinarch commissioned were transcendent.
He dreaded making them. After he finished each one, he
sent it to the Palace as quickly as possible.

Over *those* emotions (wild dogs straining at their chains,
tussling whirlwinds) he needed only to paint a gloss of his
own interpretation. Over those flamboyant colors, which
lingered even after being turned into diamondine, he
needed only to paint a gloss of pigment.

He shook himself in the cold air. Something ran over his
feet. He started back with an oath. Would those damn rats
never leave him alone! It leaped on his bed and clashed its
teeth at him. His hand closed on a silver mirror that hung
by the window, and he hurled it, smashing the rat against
the wall. It kicked feebly on the counterpane.

He would throw it to the pigs. They were used to such
largesse. He plucked at his shirt, trying to circulate air into
his fur. His lodgings still had an atmosphere of having been
closed up for decades. He had shifted all the furniture into
this room in order to empty out the workshop, so it was
crammed to the ceiling with modish, shoddy statuary and
ornaments that Sol's landlord had appropriated when some
minor atheist was arrested, but which he had never found
a buyer for. Ingrained dirt colored the walls a medium
shade of sewage. Sol sometimes wondered how he had
borne this place for two and a half years. The view was the
only part he liked. Since this was one of the tallest buildings
on the "stern" of the island—and the waist of the city
dipped lower before the ground started to rise again at the
end of the wharves—on a clear day, one could see straight
over the slums of Westpoint and Temeriton, over the
ridged acres of roofs that were Doxton, over the domes
and peaks of Christon, to the edge of Marshtown, which
sprawled toward him down the slope of the island. At this
distance, the roofs blurred into a slate-colored haze.

Today, the cold sepia haze obscured everything beyond
the first few streets.

Yet he could feel her.

Emni.

I know where you are.

But he could not find her. He had tried the Chalice and Albien House; he tried again. She was not there.

A sharp, rotten stench of sulfur hit his nose. He wheeled. A Hand stood at the door, his delicate yellow nostrils flared.

"Greetings, Godsman Southwind, master ghostier," he said in a dull voice. "I bring a message from the Divinarch. Are you occupied?"

Another one.

Gods. I had thought there wouldn't be another. It's been so long since the last. Six months?

Remembering himself, he bowed. "I am the Divinarch's servant, revered one. I am never occupied when he needs me."

No wings sprouted from the Hand's shoulders. He was almost human-looking—like most of the messengers the Divinarch sent Sol—but plain to the point of ugliness, with that snub nose and sunflower-yellow skin. He had been crying, and made no effort to hide it. Sol tried not to look at the puffy eyelids as he waited to hear the familiar message.

But standing at the door, twisting his head like a bird looking around a new cage, the Hand said, "I see no ghosts. Do you really live here, Godsman?"

Sol concealed his surprise. All the others had come out and told him why they were here, and then had spoken no more. The first time, Sol had been nervous to the point of embarrassing both himself and the Hand. Gods never reached that point where they were beyond embarrassment. But by now, he had enough confidence to bend and twist their limbs as if they were mannequins with rotating joints. They were astonishingly obedient. Or maybe they didn't feel pain the same way mortals did. There was no way to know.

"Would the Inviolate One like to see my workshop?"

The Hand pulled a face, then nodded. He followed Sol between the bureaus, and harpsichord stools, and reclining chairs, and empty picture frames, and ghost pedestals, to the kitchen door. "Are these things your ... props?" he asked, eyeing a giant set of needlepoint fire tongs.

Sol laughed. He kicked a pile of gold-leaf hatboxes. "Gods, no! I've been trying to make the landlord take the whole lot away for two years. I think pretty soon, I'll just chuck it all out of the window."

The Hand was not paying any attention. On his face was a curious, sour look as though he were trying to absorb himself in Sol's speech—trying so hard that he was absorbed in the trying.

Sol led the Hand down the tiny, gallery-like kitchen and into the workshop. It was blessedly bare. Had he not been afraid of spoiling the atmosphere, he would have spent all day here. Chisels and paintbrushes stood beside the sink at the far end of the room. The partly finished ghost of a five-year-old Deltan girl stood under the window.

The Hand looked up, down, and around, pale eyelashes beating. "Is everything you need to make a ghost in here?"

Sol's head came up proudly. "I could make a ghost with my bare hands."

"But of course." The Hand essayed a smile. Then it twisted into something else. "Like Pati, you need no tool but yourself. I did not realize."

"Our faith is our tool, Inviolate One."

The Hand shook his head in annoyance. "What is your name, ghostier? I mean, what do your friends call you?"

The empty floor lay between them. The Hand shone like a piece cut out from an Archipelagan summer. Bright, breezy days in the South Reach ... out in the boat with Dadda ... thousands upon thousands of silver wrigglers in the net. Honeyfish. He and Emni had both grown strong on that sweet, floury flesh.

"I have no friends, revered one. But when I did have one—she called me Sol."

The Hand nodded sharply. More and more, despite his pug face, he reminded Sol of a bird. "And my name is Melin. That was not always my name, though. I started my civilized life as Flying Warbler, in a small Heaven in Carelastre named Rainbow Gorge. When the Divinarch started to take an interest in me, he renamed me for what he perceived as my primary virtue."

"Comeliness."

"How did you know?"

"It's a common name, Inviolate One."

"Yes ... I suppose so. But as common as that ..." The Hand rubbed the bridge of his nose. "I thought I was more than a *ghauthiji* to him. I knew there were *ghauthijim* before me; I knew there would be *ghauthijim* after me. But I didn't think he would bring a new boy to our suite so soon! Power grant that the new one sees his true nature faster than I did!" He smiled lopsidedly. "I'm a wastrel by nature, Sol. A stupid wastrel. That's why I left Rainbow Gorge. I was no good to anyone, not being strong enough for a *mainraui*, nor talented at any craft, nor especially interested in stories—except when they had humans in them. So I left. My *breideim* wept that they would never see me again. How was I to know they would be right? Must one always listen to warnings? And if one does—what then of life?"

Sol had already heard more than he wanted. He sensed that whether he responded or not, Melin was going to go on. "Sometimes I wish someone had warned *me*."

The Hand laughed. He rolled up a sleeve. "This is what I got for not listening." It was a half-healed burn, deep and meandering. "And this." He shook hair back from his neck, revealing deeply bruised tooth marks. Sol flashed back to his worst days with Emni. "But the worst marks are *here*." Melin tapped his temple. "I did the arm myself, when I could get away, and I smuggled in a friend to do the neck. There's worse under my breeches."

Sol would have to do it quickly now. Before he lost his nerve. He looked past the Hand, at the wall cupboard that held the syringes and poisons. "Your ghost will be different from the others," he said. "I shan't be able to help putting this into my interpretation." *It will be like a threat*—"Pati will know what you've said to me."

"Good! Let him know! Let him worry that the whole city is whispering about his private life!"

"I shan't tell anyone." Sol rubbed his eyes. "How do you think I've survived this long? By spreading rumors? But what if he decides I am a danger to him? I think I shall have to make you so beautiful"—*exaggerate* the threatening aspect, burlesque it to make it harmless, but dignify it with a touch of the tragic—"that I become indispensable to him. I can do that—"

The Hand's face went suddenly kind. "Don't worry.

There are thousands of rumors. They don't hurt him. He's vulnerable, but not where you'd think."

And there was that touch of the tragic in the living flesh. Sol would hardly have to work at all.

"And *you're* not in any danger until you find out where that vulnerability is. As I did. Don't ever flatter yourself that you're indispensable! He won *my* allegiance from a thousand miles off without knowing I was alive. He can do the same with anyone he chooses. He doesn't need you."

Sol inhaled sharply. Now it was undeniable. He had always known, in the back of his mind, why all the subjects the Divinarch commissioned looked alike. The apostates said one thing of him; the flamens whose services Sol attended said another. Now he *knew*. There could be no more doubts about the nature of the thing he served.

Yet he could not stop serving. And *that* was the bond that let him and this Hand understand each other, which would allow him to paint his ghost with stunning verisimilitude, although their lives had touched only as two precipices crunch together over a chasm.

From beneath the window of the workshop, far down in the side alley, came the regular hiss of air. It was the bellows of the Hasper brothers' forge, which they only operated at night in the summer and autumn months. Muted hammers beat a tattoo on stone. The smell of burning metal curled up.

Sol was used to both the noise and the smell. It took the scream of a predator, swooping in over Westpoint, to wake him. By the time he swam up into a swooning, drifting consciousness, he had forgotten what startled him out of sleep.

Humid air filled his lungs like wool. In the starlight, he could see the ghost of Melin standing, faintly luminescent, in the middle of the floor. Drowsy pride suffused him. *Isn't it a miracle,* he thought, *how death can redeem not just the ugly—for ugliness is nothing but a matter of viewpoint, after all—but the indifferent?* This god was indifferent, if anyone ever was.

He had stuffed the indifferent out the window to the pigs. Most of it should be gone by now.

Abruptly he was wide awake. The thought of Melin scattered half eaten over the roofs turned his stomach. The hunger pangs waking in his belly seemed a cruel grace note to his nausea.

A *toothy* noise came from the direction of the front room. Chewing? Of course not. His imagination had been working overtime, and now it was creating something from nothing—child's play, after creating something from a material as hard to grasp as death.

He sat up.

There was the hunger of the body, and then there was the hunger of the soul.

It seemed that Dividay mornings had always been sunny and breezy. Pockets of cloud clung in the hollows of the land as all the inhabitants of Gelska climbed to the flat, open summit of the island and knelt in a circle. Even the toddlers knew not to speak. The horizon of the sea was at once a perfect circle and a straight line, encompassing the world. The solid blue block of the sky, pricked by the peaks of distant islands, held down the sea.

Gelska's own flamen, Godsister Honesty, stood tall in the center of the circle. Beside Sol, Emni fidgeted, skinny as a foam sprite, moving her mouth silently while the rest of the islanders lifted their voices in harmonized devotions. For once in his childish life, Sol was not aware of her. He thrust his small, earnest voice up, thanking the gods for blueness, and summer, and honeyfish for breakfast, and the knowledge that everything would stay the same forever.

Fuzzy memories were the storms in the Eftpool, and the steam-bath warmth on a winter's afternoon, and on a summer's day, his breath frosting under the dome. Silver ripples on the circle of black water. The swimmy kaleidoscope of colors in which a hundred generations of ghostiers had read something—or nothing.

He had not visited the Eftpool since he made his first ghost of a god. He was terrified of what he might find. Nothing—or *something*? Each ghostier's efts came only to that ghostier's call. So his secret was safe, as long as he stayed away.

The end justifies the means. The end justifies the means. *The end—*

Someday he would have Tellury Crescent for his own. Only Emni stood in his way—and Zin, to a lesser extent, because Sol had no scruples about offing *him* if it became politic to do so. When Pati finally decided to bring them

down, Sol would be there. He would be their chosen suc-
cessor. He *knew* it. He would bring in new apprentices,
revitalize the whole organization, reshaping it for this age
in which Emni and Zin's traditions simply were not viable.
He would ask for pardons for Mory and Tris, and in gratitude they would come back and help him. Their tempera-
ments would not prevent them from allying themselves with
a traitor. And Pati would be so impressed that he'd return
all of their Ellipse seats, and then—and *then*—Sol would
be well on his way to making the ghostiers a power such
as they had been for thirteen centuries.

Such as they would be again.

The end justifies—

"Gods," he said aloud.

He got to his feet. His muscles were as stiff as knots
in wood.

That was *definitely* the noise of champing coming from
the other room.

He slipped silently through the kitchen. Detecting no
movement in the maze of furniture, he skirted the room
and approached the window from one side.

There it was, perched on the roof of the street tunnel
below. Folded wings shielded its back. It had a child's body,
toes gripping the ridgepole, knees up on either side of its
ears. Its face was small, human, heart-shaped. It stuffed
pieces of Melin's carcass into its mouth with dreadful speed.
Its fangs glittered in the starlight.

Sol choked off a noise of disgust.

Fair curls flopped in the starlight as the predator scooped
another fistful of meat out of the corpse's face.

*Gods, Em. I need you! Need you . . .! Remember how we
used to come together after one of us made a ghost? I know
I sometimes pushed you away—just to prove that you would
come back—but all the time, I loved you for caring—*

And intuition leaped, death-defying, earth-repudiating,
across the city, and found her. She had been in Thaumagery
House all along. Now her lover and baby lay with her,
sleeping in the great, sunken bed. *Why did she go to Thaumagery? To be alone. Why must they come and plague her?*

Sol had hated living alone in that dusty bat cave after
Owen died. Emni went there now mostly, he thought, to
make him feel guilty. On one of his visits to the Crescent,
she had told him it brought back memories of Beisa.

I do not need to be reminded of *you,* she said, which keeps me from making proper use of the place. You come here far too often. What do you want of me? Do you expect me to tell you where Humi lives?

Gods' blood. She covered her mouth.

"Oh, sweetheart," Ziniquel said, shaking his head, "that's torn it."

Now in Thaumagery House, Zin snored faintly, one arm thrown over her stomach. The sheet lapped like white water to the edges of the bed. Emni stared up into the darkness, playing with her long black braid.

I haven't been well Sol felt her think. *But I can't afford to be unwell. The imrchim need me. Zin says I got up too soon after having Lighte. Or could it be Sol doing it to me poisoning me again?* Hatred flared briefly, like an ember bursting into flame. *I would suspect him if he were on the other side of the world not just in Westpoint. But I'll kill him first I'll kill him before he takes me away from them*

Sol wrenched away. Breaking his hands off the windowsill, he crouched down low, shuddering.

Impatience

"Can you not quiet her?" Aneisneida did not want to think about how nervous she felt. It was absurd! She was only going to see the Divinarch. Her father would have been ashamed of her.

But he had always been ashamed of her anyhow.

She frowned at the scared young nurse who was jogging Fiamorina up and down. The smell of wet commoners thickened the air. Apart from Fiamorina's crying, the hall was silent. Aneisneida had been the only supplicant with the temerity to bring a fractious toddler to an audience with the Divinarch. But she had not planned to queue behind hundreds of nobodies! She had assumed that she would receive special treatment, as she had every previous time Pati summoned her to his presence.

Instead she found herself turned away from the great oaken doors, back to the end of the line. At Pati's pleasure, she supposed. To keep her on her toes. Anger bubbled. She would dress him down properly for that! She would . . . she would . . .

If only she dared!

This time she would speak to him the way her father would have, whether Pati was sitting on the Throne or a wooden bench: not as a god, but as an equal.

"Do you think I employ you to hold her while she cries?" she snapped at the nurse. "I employ you to make her fit to be my daughter—or at least look like it in public. People are *watching.*"

"She's hungry, milady," the nurse said. "Shhhh, love. Where is Milord, Lady Nearecloud?"

"I believe he went to find refreshments." *A mug of ale,* Aneisneida thought with rising frustration, *at some unspeakable Marshtown tavern, where he will be as happy as a cockle in the mud, swapping smut with the regulars.*

She glanced ahead. "We're almost there."

Only five or so drab petitioners waited ahead of them. Two Hands stood tall at the great doors, smooth-skinned and impassive. Twisty horns grew from the temples of one; crimson wings jutted behind the shoulders of the other. In the old days they would have been called Divine Guards. Pati's main change when he took over had been to instruct the Hands not to expel troublemakers, but just to knife them.

This new practice made for distinctly quieter queues.

With a throb of longing that was almost pain, Aneisneida remembered the old days. As a child she had occasionally glimpsed the petitioners as her father hustled her to the Throne Room to take up some issue with the Divinarch which he had not resolved to his satisfaction in Ellipse. Once—*once*—they had had to wait outside. Aneisneida had been about ten. A little girl accompanying her parents— mossy-furred commoners, all three of them—had stared at her. Aneisneida stared right back. Something was strange: *she* had fixed her gaze on the other's snubby face, but the girl kept looking a little lower, no matter how Aneisneida wriggled out from under her gaze. At last the girl put out her hand and fingered the embroidery on Aneisneida's bodice.

Aneisneida squealed and scrambled around Belstem.

From behind the safety of her father's bulk, she hissed vituperatively at the other girl.

For all she knew, that girl could be standing behind her now, fallen on hard times, silently criticizing Aneisneida's ability to keep her child quiet. Aneisneida wanted to sink into the floor.

"Can you not—" she started to say to the nurse.

But at that moment a rank hessian smell blew into her face, and a gaggle of Deltans pushed around her as they emerged from the Throne Room. Without noticing, she had reached the head of the line. The Hands nodded, simultaneously—*they must practice that,* she thought—and desperately, *Where is Soderingal?*

Gathering up nurse and child, she swept in

Now she faces her lord, small and daunted as a pale-furred mouse, fascinated.

Where are you, Soderingal?

The chandeliers in the Throne Room are not lit, probably to conserve tallow. Her lord has forced economies on the people and the Palace alike which are oddly conceived, to say the least. Aneisneida's father would have laughed in the face of anyone who suggested that perhaps it was not necessary to keep all the rooms in the Summer mansion lit, all night. Aneisneida's father believed in the good life. She no longer dares to live anything approximating the good life. Aneisneida's father did not believe in the gods. He would have sneezed, sans handkerchief, at anyone who suggested he bow down to one of them. Aneisneida does not dare not to bow down to them.

Especially this one.

The only illumination in the room comes from him. His pale hands and pale face shine like more jewels on the Throne—that massive conglomeration of trinkets, glued together with black age. His stillness is hypnotic. Aneisneida feels her heart slowing. Even Fiamorina, at the back of the Throne Room, has stopped crying. It is as if time has ground to a halt.

"Report," he says, in his unmoderated divine voice, and the word vibrates through her bones. Her back straightens. All her limbs dangle inside the silk casings of her court dress, her fine atheistic dress, like the limbs of a marionette whose strings are wound around the puppeteer's finger. Words bub-

ble in her throat. Everything she knows... even about Humi...

And then another voice exclaims from the Throne, "Name of the Power. That's the Summer girl! Pati, I thought—Hope told me—they were all dead!"

Pati growls with annoyance.

Aneisneida shakes her head.

"I keep this one alive," Pati says. "For my pleasure." The voice is loud as ten trumpets, but Aneisneida can bear it. It is no longer divine.

She takes a breath of relief. Father, I haven't let you down—

The doors swing open, screeching faintly. They never used to screech. Oil must be another of Pati's ludicrous economies. Soderingal comes in past the sentinels, striding easily, just drunk enough to tip his feathered hat insolently to the Divinarch. His court clothes are soaked black with rain. Aneisneida rushes to him, weak, wanting support.

But as usual, she ended up supporting him, holding him up as his initial show of confidence gave way to drunken staggering. She felt furious with him for leaving her in the lurch. But she recognized that he had saved her. She had been on the brink of blacking out. It had happened before, and it was hard to forget afterward, very hard to dismiss the whole thing as a dizzy spell, because afterward Hands would come and taunt her with things she had told Pati. Just little things. She was usually able to break the spell before she revealed anything important, by thinking hard about her father, but there was always the possibility that she would not be able to. And so she was abjectly grateful to Soder.

"How many have you had?" she whispered.

"Where's Fia?" Shaking his hair like a wet dog, he wiped the rain from his brows, and searched the Throne Room with narrowed eyes. "Eh, Anei? Where's me peridot doll baby?"

Aneisneida pointed at the nurse, who had retreated into a corner. But Soderingal did not follow her indication. His mouth had dropped open. He was staring at the throne. "Suck me," he whispered with his habitual crudeness. "If that ain't the 'Eir. *Look!*"

She looked.

And gasped.

Smaller than the other Hands in the twilight, he stood in a niche halfway around the lefthand crag of the Throne. It was unquestionably Arity. Smaller? No, just hunched. His hair was clipped close to his head. His expression was withdrawn, distant.

Feeling their stares, he seemed to wince and shrink into himself.

"Look 'ow 'e stands all lopsided," Soderingal whispered. "There's something wrong with 'im."

"I'm not surprised." Aneisneida kept her voice steady by an act of will. "Don't you remember what that leman *did* to him?"

"Wasn't there. But I 'eard. By all rights 'e ought to be dead."

"No one could have survived so much damage! But of course he lives because he is a god, and immortal." The easy answer that issued from her lips horrified her. One picked up doctrine so quickly when one was forced to socialize with the pious, for lack of anyone better.

The trouble was that she had never quite understood that part of her father's lessons. If they were not gods, what were they?

All she knew was that she must be obedient to the letter of her own, faithless faith. "I suppose ... I suppose they recuperate faster than we do. Or their bodies are different."

"It's a miracle," Soderingal whispered, staring.

"There are no miracles! The flamens are shams!"

Soderingal shook his head mutely. Aneisneida whirled. The Divinarch leaned forward in his seat, chin on hand, watching them confer with an amused smile in his face.

Soder sidled back from the Throne.

The dog, Aneisneida thought.

"Milord!" She dipped her head gracefully. With an effort, she put Arity to the back of her mind. She would deal with him when she had time to think. Obviously, Humi had to know he was alive. Like Pati, Humi could convince you of anything she chose—for instance, that a recoup was possible. But when you left her presence, the fire went out of your belly. For fear of having a longer-lasting conviction instilled in her, Aneisneida had avoided Temeriton for a good year. Now she would have to go back. Humi had to know about *this*.

But she should not think about Humi now. In Humi's archenemy's presence, that was somehow, obscurely, dangerous.

In the corner, Soderingal cooed to Fiamorina. Aneisneida ground her teeth and curtseyed to the Throne. "I do apologize for our rudeness!" She dimpled. "Family troubles!"

"I quite see. Is it not delightful to live in proximity to those who are dear to you?" the Divinarch said ironically.

Aneisneida tittered obligingly.

"I know I enjoy it." He smiled. His eyes flickered sideways. Then he beckoned, and Arity clambered around, stepping on the projecting bits of the Throne, and laid his head on Pati's shoulder. Pati wrapped his arm about Arity's waist and kissed the cropped brown hair, smiling over his head at Aneisneida the whole time. Aneisneida gaped. Pati let go and Arity returned to his pedestal, his fingers drifting over the places Pati had touched: a faint smile hovered on his mouth. Aneisneida felt certain they were lovers.

But why was Arity standing on the wrong side of the Throne? He was the Heir!

She let her confusion show on her face. At least a year ago, she had realized that the best way to keep the life which Pati had so inexplicably granted her (out of contempt? pity? awareness that she was powerless?) was to let everything show. Fear, eagerness to please, revulsion. In short, she acted like a monkey. She was not sure if the capacity for keeping secrets she had discovered in herself shortly afterward was a result of her deliberately exaggerated vapidity—a new layer of personality growing underneath, so to speak, as the old rose to the surface and molted—or if it had been there all along, and only now showed itself. Sometimes she thought that she had not come alive until after her father died.

Sometimes she castigated herself for entertaining such thoughts for a minute.

The Divinarch was watching her, bicolored eyes narrowed, fingers steepled. Belatedly, she realized he could see her thinking.

She turned a cartwheel and threw a few balls into the air. "I am afraid not much of note has passed since we last spoke, milord. Godsie Shafteel, the wife of Pie Shafteel, the pious governor of Christon, you know, has a gorgeous new evening dress. I know there is no longer any call for us to wear such things ... but ... I am thinking of having one made to a similar pattern. Would you allow me such an indulgence?"

He was smiling. "What pattern is it?"

She illustrated with her hands. "Big satiny panniers. *And* a bustle. Underneath, lace skirts, ruched up to show a colorful underskirt of some heavier fabric." The dress she wore now was of Veretrean silk, in the style that compressed one's torso to a slender stem. Aneisneida prided herself on her figure, especially after having borne a child, which was why she had worn this gown rather than any of the dozens of others she had no occasion to put on anymore. Its ruffles cascaded from a dropped yoke to the floor. It was more than three years old. The seams were starting to weaken. Aneisneida's mouth watered as she described Inali Shafteel's gown. "I believe she dreamed the design up herself. She is most awfully clever in that way."

"No doubt." The Divinarch nodded. "I give you permission to have it made."

"Thank you!" Quick, before he changed his mind, what else was there to tell? "Oh, yes, and Essne Stockold has given birth to an adorable little son—"

But he had leaned back. He was shaking his head, fingers in front of his mouth hiding a smile like a pale V in the dark. "Now, Aneisneida. You are cleverer than this. You know I don't really wish to hear about dresses. Who has turned apostate, who has died, who has fled abroad, who has gone to the mainland? You are my most reliable informant." The smile vanished. "How is the city holding?"

She drew a deep, shaky breath. Now she dared not do anything other than tell the truth. He had multitudes of other human informants whose reports he would trust over hers at the drop of a feather.

"No one has vanished in the last weeks except those you know of." That was the most delicate way of saying *those whom the Hands have abducted.* "And there are not so many of those anymore, because"—how to put it?—"there are very few atheists left in government and business. Very few. Soderingal and I are the only ones who used to move in high society." She could not help reaffirming, "And you give us permission to keep our titles, don't you, Divinarch?"

"I do, indeed."

"And as for the secular governments of the districts, they have reached a concentration of pious men and women that the city has not seen since before Antiprophet's days." She decided she ought to qualify that poetic statement. "I don't think."

The Divinarch laughed out loud. "Go on."

"The council of Temeriton, for example, used to be entirely atheistic, but now it has no members left from before. Many of the merchants who have gained seats are newly pious—but one bends where the wind is blowing. Does one not?" Quickly, she qualified that, too. "They worship your name." *He keeps me for my atheism.* She must not lapse into the pious idiom. "Unlike me. But then, I am not a councillor, not anymore, milord. No disrespect, milord."

She gabbled on, playing her part. When her report was over, she retreated to Soderingal and the nurse, her mouth empty and tasteless from talking too much. What was this drag in her step? She was *limping!* Twisted, like Arity on the Throne, by her own ignoble role—

Nonsense. She dismissed those fancies.

A sudden rush of blood to her temples reminded her that she had not had anything to eat since morning. Taverns served black bread and fish. Vile stuff. But she would stomach it in the service of her *real* Divinarch. Humi. Aneisneida hated Pati with her blood and bones! And whatever Humi's shortcomings, Aneisneida felt proud to serve her. Visiting her made Aneisneida feel a little better about toadying to a god.

She straightened her back inside her corset.

And it would be delightful to have a resurrection, rather than a death, to report. Even if the resurrected party was the Heir—a god whose ambivalence had always confused Aneisneida at best, and intimidated her at worst. Humi had to know. He had been her lover. She would *have* to do something, now that Arity seemed to belong to Pati. Such an unheard-of alliance simply could not last.

"Take Fia home," Aneisneida said to the nurse. "Our sedans are waiting at the Fewpole Gate. You can find your way back there." She turned to Soder, smiling brightly. "Dearest, how near is the tavern where you got that ale?"

* * *

In the middle of a fisherman's plea for money to repair
his shark-ravaged boat, Pati let loose a jaw-splitting yawn.
"Audiences are over!" He stretched his arms in the air,
smiling like a cat. "Clear the room, my *firim*."

Several Hands leaped eagerly off the Throne, grabbed
the old man, and marched him to the doors. When he qua-
vered in protest, they punched him in the face. Black blood
trailed across the floor. When the doors slammed behind
them, Arity heard their loud, glad voices echoing down the
hall: "Go home! You've missed your chance, all of you!
Come back next sixday! Go home! Go home!" And several
thin screams.

"Get out of here," Pati said to the Hands that were left.
"Cut it."

Iole blurted, "But, *perich"hi*—" and bit it off.

"What? Get out!" Pati half-turned to look at Arity. With
a different note in his voice, he said, "Not you!"

"Very well, *perich"hi*," Arity said.

One by one, the Hands *teth"d*, glancing at him. They
knew he was the favored one. They did not envy him;
rather, they were glad that Pati finally had someone whom
he would not tire of. Arity was grateful to them for understanding that he did not want special treatment, even if he
was not sure he wanted to learn the details of Pati's liaisons
with Melin and other favored Hands, which they had promised to reveal to him.

He gripped a protruberance on the Throne to keep from
swaying. He did not have the endurance of the others, and
standing immobile all day had taken a toll on him. Perhaps
if he moved, his blood would start flowing again. He
jumped clumsily to the ground and began to pace. Now
that the room was empty, he did not try to disguise his
ugly, rolling gait; he swung his arms over his head, and
blood rushed into tense muscles. Outside, night had fallen.
Indoors, it had been twilight all day. The *auchresh* could
see perfectly. The petitioners had been at a distinct disadvantage. Arity had seen Aneisneida Summer blink and
move her hands about in front of her face long before she
or her husband saw him.

Aneisneida. That was that, now, of course. Rumors
would fly throughout the city. Not that it mattered: the city
Arity had loved, which he would never have let see him in

this condition, was dead. (What did Aneisneida *do* with herself all day?)

Today, Arity had seen what Delta City had been reduced to. Pati *must* realize how his tyranny had impoverished and cowed the people! Petitioners ... endless petitioners who asked no more than food.

"How can you justify it?" he said aloud. "How can anyone justify such a miserable mess?"

Pati slumped low in the Throne, wings hunched up behind his ears. "The purge is part of the cure. We should turn the corner in a matter of months."

"I saw no signs of that today."

"Didn't you hear Aneisneida? Atheism is almost eradicated."

Arity said impatiently, "It seems to me that the city was a good deal more prosperous when the nobles were in control."

"But we were decaying inside. That's why I keep Aneisneida and Soderingal around—they're specimens of a vanishing species. Every time I see them, they remind me why I did away with the others of their kind. They embody everything that sickens me. An absence of understanding. Self-serving frivolity. *You* saw it. And people like them were engulfing the world."

The lifestyle of the nobles might have been self-serving. But weren't humans at heart self-serving? The small indulgences one had permitted oneself in such an atmosphere, the freedom to love whom one wanted and laugh at the others, the silly innocent giddiness of Delta City society in those days had compensated—hadn't it?—for the stupid individuals one did sometimes encounter.

Pati said, "If I hadn't done something about it, I would have been shirking my responsibility."

Arity's heart sank. "You're not still talking about *divine responsibility,* are you?"

"Divinity exists," said Pati, hooding his head with his wings.

Arity coughed disgustedly. "The humans have seen us fall on our faces too often now to believe in us. Piety is just a behavior. I'll tell you what they do believe: that the flamens hold the key to their survival, and they know you control the flamens; that the Hands will kill anyone who gets out of line, and you control the Hands. That's power! Why can't you settle for that?"

"My being able to kill people doesn't justify what you saw today." Pati's voice was cold, withdrawn. "After all, your little human *irissu* used to control the flamens, and the crime lords, which was more or less the same thing. If that were all, I could have left things in *her* hands."

The swell of grief at hearing *your little human* irissu was delayed, but inevitable. Arity shut his teeth and waited for it to pass. "Then—why—didn't you?"

"She was incompetent. But that's not the point." Pati leaned forward in the Throne. His face and hands glowed in the twilight. "There is nothing respect-worthy or even properly thought out in atheism. It's flawed in its conception. Humans are incapable of understanding us as their equals—supposing that we *were* their equals—and to me, their inability to understand proves they are our inferiors. I've seen it time and time again. They cannot *help* worshipping us." Contempt hardened his voice. "They used to say openly that they didn't believe we were divine, yet even in those days, none of them could ever speak to us without quivering."

"And you wanted to make sure it stayed that way." Arity hated Pati's reasoned, intractable self-delusion. He hated it because *he* could not understand it. A hard, grainy crystal of misery lodged in his lungs. "You love people to be afraid of you. That's why you have all the flamens in the world come and swear vows to you. If you didn't have to spend your time making sure of the flamens, you could hold more audiences, but no. You love seeing them grovel before you. Concern for the human race!" He swore in *auchraug*, reusing some of the expletives he had heard Broken Bird employ in Rimmear. "You want them securely in your fist. There's no more to it than that."

"Isn't there?"

Arity had been staring blurrily at the base of the Throne, his eyes dark with tears. The new note in Pati's voice brought his head up. Pati was standing in the Throne. His wings fanned out behind his head. High over his head, the prisms in the chandeliers tinkled as the wind from his wings knocked them together. He seemed larger than natural. His voice split into thousands of echoes. "Isn't there?"

"*Power,* Pati. Stop showing off!"

Like a paper figure folding, Pati collapsed into the Throne. He grinned impishly.

"Why the hell?"

"Now do you see why I am convinced the humans are stupid?" His eyes still burned palely, but he was the right size again. His wings were folded at his back, his arms curled lazily along the ornate arms of his seat. "Go on! Argue with me, Wind Gully Foundling!"

Rainbows drifted around Arity's head. He hated to admit it, but Pati's tricks were not completely wasted on him. He should have saved the whole business for later—kept it inside his head, to ponder when Pati slept and Arity lay on his back beside him, drifting through multicolored layers of insomnia. He should never have spoken, rather than have to go through the pain and humiliation of dropping the issue now.

"Did I frighten it, then?" Pati jumped off the Throne and kissed Arity's nose. "Ohhh."

"Power, Pati." Arity moved away. "I'm close to eighty years old. Not a Foundling. I'm civilized. Leave it."

But Pati hugged him from behind, kissing the back of his neck. "Can't leave you. Can't do without you, *irissi.* Not again. Not anymore." All the laughter was gone from his voice.

Thrills ran through Arity like ripples of sound from the fingers of a *farader* maestro. He was malleable in Pati's hands and he thought, *I'm losing my pride. Have to lose something, I suppose, to be free.* Divine, *auchresh,* predator, human, what did it matter? This was Pati. Arity could touch him and be touched by him, unencumbered by the armor which had sealed him off from Sual. He turned and kissed him.

"Let's go to bed." Pati's thin hot body folded around Arity's. Nothingness abolished them simultaneously. Arity's sense of proportion vanished, redly, with the dark Throne Room, dissolving in preparation to change into something else altogether.

Gossip

It proved unnecessary for Aneisneida to sacrifice her gastric sensibilities. Soderingal reminded her that it would be suicide to visit *Delights and Diversions* wearing her court dress. She had to go home first and change into commoner's clothes. Hateful garments! The skirt and blouse rubbed her fur the wrong way wherever they touched her. But it was unreasonable not to have a plate of cold supper while she was at home. She ate in the brightly lit dining room at one end of the table, watched by a bevy of flaking ghosts, while upstairs Fia screamed as the nurse put her to bed. Then the steward, Sailoner, informed Aneisneida that she had promised to visit Godsie Stockold—she of the newborn son. Essne had to be put off by courier, and Aneisneida's whole calendar—a humbler roster of names than it had once been, but still crowded, for she was the greatest lady in the city—rearranged.

It was the middle of the night before she and Soderingal reached Temeriton.

They left their sedan on the Lockreed Concourse. Revelers of all descriptions swaggered and sidled past. All the doors on the street stood open, spilling torchlight and women's husky laughter. Aneisneida knew that if she stayed long enough, she would see most of her male acquaintances, and possibly some of the female ones; she had already glimpsed a pair of Hands entering the Silver Fountain brothel. Their taste for human whores was well-documented.

But for all the merriment, an air of dreary timelessness hung over the street. Every foot of cobbles had been trod before. A lady did not linger here, if she valued her reputation.

Soderingal's head was bobbing to the pipe music trickling from the nearest open door: a slow, breathy melody that meandered up and down, up and down, as if it could go on forever.

Aneisneida dragged him away. Not for the first time, she

reflected that their marriage had started as that favorite
scenario of farceurs—the swashbuckling social climber and
the gullible heiress. But it had changed slowly but drasti-
cally until she did not know what a playwright would make
of it now. A tragicomedy? Just tragedy?

She had to drag him about to get him to accomplish
anything. And he was pigheaded about the most ridiculous
little things. But had he always been like this? Or had he
once been sensitive and flattering? Had he always drunk
too much? Or had it gotten worse since the coup? She
could not remember properly, because like all the foolish
girls in the farces, she had been blindly in love with him.
She sometimes wondered whether he had ever loved her,
or only the mug and bottle, and her father's money.

If *that* were the truth, what a horrible shock it must have
been when Pati's Hands killed Belstem and stripped Aneisneida of nine-tenths of her newly inherited estate!

Soder had coped rather well, she thought. There was still
something admirable there, under the unkempt mien and
the perpetual stink of booze. If only she could lay her finger
on it.

The street gleamed with the rain that had passed. They
left the torchlight as they stepped into the back alley.
Clouds hid the stars in the narrow slit of sky overhead.
Soderingal caught Aneisneida's arm, preventing her from
treading on a hideously alive heap of rags. He knocked on
the door.

Humi opened it, hovering in the shadows, one finger to
her lips. She frowned uncomprehendingly. "Hello . . . ?"

"It's me, Humi," Aneisneida said. "And Soder."

"Oh . . . Oh, gods! What are you doing here? I—I mean,
I'm delighted to see you! I knew you must come soon. We
have much to talk of. My plans are progressing beautifully.
Sssh. Don't wake the family." She smiled beautifully with
her mouth and stood aside. She wore plain green, like pious
but not desperately poor women. Her hair was twisted into
a Rivapirl coil, with only one big wave that she had missed
hanging loose in the back. *As if,* Aneisneida thought, *she
really* was *expecting us.*

Or maybe she never sleeps.

She shivered.

"It has been a long time. Why, if I may come to the

point, do I have the pleasure of seeing you at such an unusual hour?"

"Oh—oh, well, actually . . ." Aneisneida trailed off. Somehow she could not deliver her news. It would be as if she had come to poke sticks at the caged lionet. Cruel.

"Well," Humi said after a pause. "At any rate, I am looking forward to hearing how you have progressed with gathering public support for us. I am so isolated here! But Hope tells me that the city chafes under Pati, and that any rumor of a recoup is well received." She led them into the small, sparsely furnished living room and showed them to the sofa. She fumbled with the candle bracket by the door for a moment, and turned back to them, her smile self-mocking. "Soderingal, could I trouble you to light the candles? I *cannot* master that task."

Soderingal looked her up and down appreciatively as he took the flint and steel. "Amazing 'ow you look after yourself, all things considered."

"Thank you."

"But I'm afraid I 'aven't got much news from the public-support province. Can't do nothing without mentioning your name. Still set on keeping it secret?"

"I think it would be most unwise to reveal myself at this point." Carefully, Humi suggested, "The Summer name would do."

"Oh, no," Soderingal said instantly. "Not come hell an' high water. We're only *alive* on suff'rance from Pati—sorry, milady Divinarch! We're Nearecloud now, an' even *speaking* the Summer name ud be the death of us—"

He sounded impassioned. Yet all the time he spoke, he was staring at Humi's undusted, sleek bosom. Aneisneida broke in. "The heart of the matter is that we need to rouse the people's hearts. They are cowed. And unless, Humi, you are willing to let it be noised that you are still alive, I do not see how we are to manage it."

"Because not one of you," Humi said gently, "not you nor Soderingal nor any of the ghostiers, is willing to risk his own name for the cause of liberty for the world."

"Well," Soderingal protested, "that doesn't seem 'xactly *fair* when it's *your*—"

"I know. I know. It is my throne at stake. The last thing I wish is to strain your loyalty, my friends!" She sighed. "I think eventually I shall leave this house and travel the city, perhaps even the continent, drumming up support. Numbers are essential. We must crush Pati as he crushed us, with force of arms."

The obstacle to that course of action was salient. Reflections of the candle flames lay on Humi's eyes like appliqués. Neither Aneisneida nor Soderingal spoke.

"Yet perhaps there is a better course of action. Perhaps we will see it after we have a glass to drink." She crouched down, displaying the tawny down on her nape and the gentle slope of her shoulders, to burrow in a wall cupboard.

"Everything goes better with a swallow of wine," Soderingal said approvingly.

Humi rose to her feet, holding a half-empty bottle of second-grade rye liquor. Even in the wavering candlelight, Aneisneida could see how muddy her face was.

Trust Soder! Aneisneida leaped into the breach. "My *favorite!* Do pour out, Humi! Or would you rather that I—"

"I can do *this* quite well." Humi's head turned blindly, seemingly at random, as she knelt by the low table and uncorked the bottle. "But thank you." Whenever her stare swung across Aneisneida's gaze, her features looked momentarily, frighteningly, expressionless. She seemed to be concentrating on something within herself. Perhaps her humiliating blindness. Perhaps her poverty. Her name, Aneisneida thought, had finally become appropriate.

She put that thought out of her mind. The idea of seeing Humi at a disadvantage frightened her so deep inside that she could not even identify the thing that made her think to herself, defiantly, *What if she is blind? She is still Humi. The recoup will go forward. And maybe—now here's an idea—maybe she will even win Arity over, so that we have an agent in the Palace! I think that is quite a wonderful thought!*

The liquid in Soderingal's goblet rose to within a finger's width of the rim. Humi righted the bottle and asked Aneisneida whether she too would partake.

"Of course," Aneisneida said warmly.

"She 'ad her pinky finger crooked over the rim all the time, so she could feel the wine rising," Soderingal murmured under his breath. "Not so clever as all that, eh?" He chuckled.

"How has little Fiamorina been since we talked last?"

Humi asked composedly as she tipped the bottle for the second time.

"Oh! Her fur's thickening like grass in spring." Soder grinned, diverted. "She's a real beauty. Pale green. Like that."

He pointed at Humi's dress. Humi looked blank.

Gods! Aneisneida took a deep breath. "Humi, we came because we have some news for you. Someone is alive whom we thought was dead. I'm sure you will be delighted to hear that Arity is living." She paused. Humi did not seem to have understood the significance of the statement. Aneisneida elaborated. "You must recall. Charity. The Heir. A god. He is unchanged—well, almost—he appears to have a limp, and he has cut his hair—and he is living as the Divinarch's lover. At least that is what Soderingal and I think. We saw them embrace, in the Throne Room. We did not speak to him—"

Something splashed her knee. She jerked back, and gasped. Rye liquor flooded the table, gleaming in the candlelight, dripping onto the floor. Humi knelt stiff and still as one of her ghosts. Her arm appeared to be frozen, tilting the bottle over the glass. The last of the liquor flowed out with a series of glugs. "Oh, gods," Aneisneida gasped, and clung to Soderingal.

"Think p'r'aps we'd better be going, Divinarch." Soderingal pulled Aneisneida to her feet. He reached down, rescued the brimming glass, and took a swig. "Nice t' see you—"

"Oh, come *on*," Aneisneida whispered. "Come *on*!" Soderingal paused in the door of the living room, chewing his lip. *I am going to cry,* she thought, appalled at herself. She felt like an indulged child whose father has slapped her.

The bottle dropped out of Humi's hand, chinked on the floorboards, rolled under the settee. Then Humi lifted the corners of her mouth. "I agree, Lord Nearecloud," she said, wheezing a little. "This is one visit perhaps better cut short." Like an afterthought, she added, "You *were* telling the truth—just now—weren't you? He is alive? He is Pati's lover again?"

Again? Aneisneida thought. *What?*

Soderingal's grip tightened on Aneisneida's arm. "We was telling true. And 'ow I wish we 'adn't been."

Humi gave a laugh, like the bark of a dog. "So do I."

Soderingal pulled Aneisneida stumbling out into the little dark hall. The back door took an age to open: the latch was cranky. But Humi was there, pushing them aside, working the latch. Her face was blank. But the hand that rested on Aneisneida's arm shook like a rickety house in a gale.

The Neareclouds could not escape over the threshold fast enough. The door closed behind them and the latch dropped. They stumbled down the alley. It had started raining again—but not heavily. Aneisneida would not be able to disguise it if she cried. She took a shuddering breath.

The Lockreed Concourse had gone quiet. The only doors still open lay closer to the center of town, where they had left their sedan. The glistening street, humped like a snake so that the water ran off into the side gutters, was nearly deserted. The lanterns over the brothel signs glowed red. Soderingal crossed the street, pulling Aneisneida from pool to pool of light. Then she heard a faint sound braided into the city's hum.

The chink of heel talons on cobbles.

A Hand.

No.

And she *recognized* the smaller of the two approaching figures, *recognized* the slim, incongruously breeched silhouette. Recognized the one god in Delta City who had such high-set, sweeping wings.

They came face to face.

In the dark, it would have been possible to mutter "Excuse me," and pass on. Aneisneida had done it before. Hope's companion was a Veretrean in the prime of life: a sailor, from the cut of his clothes. From the smell of him he was also as drunk as a bat in daylight. He grinned at them, showing perfect teeth. He did not realize the situation. Did not realize that he *was* the situation.

It was still possible to make the best of things. Aneisneida lowered her face and made to go around the pair.

"What in the merry hell you doin 'ere, Hope?" Soderingal exclaimed with awful jollity.

Hope put one hand to her face. She pulled her companion up into the middle of the concourse.

"What the *fuck!* We need t' talk, Hope!" Soderingal bellowed. "We've been to see Humi. She's in a bad way—"

The ex-Maiden wheeled. Her mouth was a thin golden line.

"Oh, Hope," Aneisneida sobbed, "we told her Arity is still alive, and she spilled the rye liquor—"

"Dog's piss—"

"—on the floor, and we left, and I don't know how she is taking it." It took a tremendous effort for Aneisneida not to fall to her knees in front of Hope. She had never seen Humi lose control before—not even when the entire Ellipse combined to force her to abdicate. Now Hope was all Aneisneida had left to place her trust in. Not because she was a god, but because of her serenity, her seeming invulnerability to change. She was timeless. She was an insider everywhere. "I'm sorry, Hope!" For once, it was easy, not distasteful, to apologize. "I shouldn't have told her—I didn't know what I was doing—"

"Lords and ladies, may I present Aneisneida and Soderingal Nearecloud," Hope said acidly, tiredly, "unable to leave well enough alone. What on earth did you tell her for?"

"She's drunk," Soderingal whispered to Aneisneida. "The gods can hold barrels of liquor, but *I* can tell . . ."

"We thought she'd be overjoyed," Aneisneida wailed. "We thought—" *The recoup—clearing the air in preparation for the storm—*

"Are you stupider than you look? Overjoyed!" Hope snorted unsympathetically. "Your skirt's in the gutter, Aneisneida!"

"It's only cotton." Aneisneida gathered her dress out of the filth. She wiped her nose. Her hand smelled like the sewer. "I can afford a hundred of them. Oh, *Hope*—"

"She'll be all right, I tell you." Hope turned her face away from them. Over the Veretrean's shoulder, she said, "She's resilient. She's recovered from things before."

The Veretrean sailor placed a host of small, sloppy kisses in the hollow of her neck. Her wings quivered as she arched against him. Overhead, a torch flame, caught in the vortex created by the movement of her wings, bent in half and went out. As the darkness swept down, Hope pulled away from the man. "She had to know sometime," she said. "I was putting it off as long as I could. Thank you, I suppose, for relieving me of the responsibility."

"Wait. You *knew* 'e was alive?" Soderingal said. " 'Ow? You weren't there today—"

"Where do you think he's been these past three years?

Of course I knew. *And* I knew he had come to Delta City—
I saw them arriving myself. I was on a reconnaissance mis-
sion in the Old Palace. That was more than a sixday ago.
They left again right after that—but now they're back for
good." She shrugged. "Far be it from me to guess how Pati
has gained such power over him."

Aneisneida bit her knuckles. She had a feeling she knew.
The Veretrean lurched in front of Hope, gathered her in,
and kissed her mouth. "Let's go," he mumbled with
drunken arrogance. "You're comin' back to *Gefiya* with
me, my wingy beauty—"

"But does this mean anything's changed?" Soderingal
persisted, drowning out the Veretrean's cajolements. "Is
Pati gonna change 'is policies? Is Arity gonna be Heir
again? Why's he come back, if not? Just to fuck the
Divinarch?"

"I think that is quite possible!" Hope called from the
darkness. "I doubt anything will ever change! That is the
state of affairs we are in, now! But you saw them this afternoon. You can judge—"

"But I thought you were close to Pati," Aneisneida said.
"I thought you knew everything!"

Hope laughed. "Well, now you know differently, don't
you?"

And the mist-shrouded, barnacled semblance of a world,
that hulk of reality of whose slippery hull Aneisneida main-
tained a precarious foothold, where she had balanced since
it capsized two years ago, stood on its beam ends. With a
tremor that shook her through and through, it settled
deeper into the sands. A mist of uncertainty enveloped her.
Hope could not be trusted. Neither could Humi. They were
vulnerable—*just like her*—Hope was embracing her lover,
but she had forgotten her strength. The Veretrean's back
arched the wrong way, and his arms flew out. Just before
his spine must shatter, Hope let go, hissing. The man shook
his head as if to get rid of water in his ears, and pulled her
back to him.

"Fuckin' 'ell," Soderingal exploded, staring at the dark.
A purple bright diamond burned there, shrinking to nothing. "Fuck it! Anei—"

"Keep it to ourselves," she whispered. "Soder, we
can't—can't let anyone know—"

"What?" He glanced sharply at her. "Are you crazy, Anei? Let anyone know?"

Her teeth chattered. They were alone in the silence of the uneasily sleeping city. The rain grew a little heavier, stippling the waters of the gutter. Far up the street, she could see their porter sitting between the shafts of his sedan, twirling his hat.

The gods are human. The gods are vulnerable. The gods are not.

Years of atheism had not brought it home to her as finally as tonight had.

But Hope had taken her disgusting drunkenness away with her: Aneisneida no longer had to see what she did not want to. After the first shock abated, interpretations slipped into place with the ease of familiar prostheses. It was true after all, it had always been true, it was still true, that the gods could not lose their cool even if they tried. The Veretrean sailor had not been a sign of weakness on Hope's part. He had been a manifestation of her power over the city.

Aneisneida did not feel so alone nor so responsible when she knew that *someone* was watching over her, weighing everything that could possibly happen, choosing each outcome for the best.

She leaned back into Soderingal's arms, pleating the wet cotton of her dress in her fingers. "Don't move, Soder," she said. "Please."

"Well, well." He wrapped his arms around her waist. She heard a smile in his voice, though what he found to smile about, she did not know. " 'Aven't 'eard *that* for a while."

"That doesn't mean I am giving you license to take liberties! Hold me. Only hold me still." Reality had just been redeemed from the edge of the quicksands: she needed a few minutes to solidify it in her mind. It was not yet safe to walk on.

Ari.

Humi lay in perpetual darkness. Her fingers crept like dazed mice through her hair. The night mist came in through the aperture in the wall, sewer-scented, kissing her with cold, ethereal lips. It protected her. It would continue to protect her for another couple of hours yet. After that—

Her body did not feel like her own. It was molten: it had

no bones or tendons, only heavy, insensate flesh. She could not re-create the chills and glorious climaxes he had sent through it. She could not feel anything at all.

She could not even re-create *him* in her memory. She thought of herself as a moderate to inept blind person, but perhaps she had sunk farther into the darkness than she had realized. She had stopped thinking of people in terms of faces. And on top of that, in fending off the memories of him—*all* the memories, sight and sound and silly little pledges of devotion—for three years, she had reduced them to shadows.

One swam near, suffusing her with a fleeting sense of victory.

He had had purplish-brown hair, soft and loose to his shoulders.

He *still had* purplish-brown hair.

Fresh tears oozed from the corner of one eye. They trickled over her cheekbone to join the crust of dried salt water at her hairline. Her fingers plucked erratically, freeing one strand after another from the tangles produced by her tossing and turning.

But of course there can be nothing between us anymore. He belongs to Pati now. He has always belonged to Pati.

Why couldn't she muster very much grief? Time. Blindness. Numbness. As first-time lovers are wont to, she had loved him without qualification or restraint, scarcely realizing how deep into their union she had sunk until she had given a good half of herself over to him. She had not just loved, but adored him. Until Thani, her misguided little sister, intervened.

And now her devotion had atrophied.

But according to Aneisneida and Soderingal, Thani had never actually accomplished her task. The question gnawed at Humi. If Arity had not been dead, where had he been for three years? In Wind Gully Heaven? Some other Heaven? Then why had he not come to her? Had Pati had him all along?

She wanted to know the logistics of his disappearance—but emotionally, she felt nothing. No longing. No desire. The tears did not bleed from any sort of wound, but from her old friend the hollowness.

Her inability to act. The pointlessness of talking over the recoup with Aneisneida and Soderingal. Emni and Zin's

absence. Hope's devoutly and repeatedly pledged loyalty
that Humi suspected to be increasingly based on guilt. They
emptied her of emotion. The emptiness leaked salt water
as regularly as a cracked pipe. She filled her time with rats
and seagulls. Had she not been ghosting, she would have
been in bed when Anei and Soderingal arrived, and she
might have avoided hearing the awful news. She would
have had at least another whole day.

But the news was just another wedge in the crack. Just
another crack. Whether Arity was alive or not, whether he
was still the Ari she had known or not, nothing could ever
be the same again between them. The most she could hope
for was maybe, one day, to come face to face with him and
ask a few questions.

She took a deep breath. She forced herself to think of
possible ways around the problem of her blindness in the
matter of rallying the masses that were not there.

Something Like Normal

Erene derived a sense of accomplishment from weaving that
was *fuller,* somehow, and less bittersweet, than any pleasure
she had ever got from ghosting. In weaving, one created
something from nothing. Ghosting had never given her that
feeling. Whenever she used to ghost, she had known in her
heart she was reducing a human being to an object of cold,
dead permanence. She could not think of it as anything but
a process of reduction, now that Tellury Crescent and all the
ghosts she and Elicit had made were half a world away, not
close enough to chill her with the beauty that had taken shape
under her hands. She remembered only the deaths.

But not any more often than she had to.

She sat at the tall floor loom Elicit had made, shuttle
nosing from side to side of the warp, gazing out of the
window. When spring came, bulbs would sprout from the
muddy patch in front of the house. How satisfying it was
to struggle for one's daily bread! She and Elicit had the
jewels they had brought from Delta City—but they prided
themselves that they hadn't yet had to sell them.

The west coast was one of the most underpopulated regions in the continent of Pirady. Here, they had discovered that though they represented themselves as coming from Grussels, they were still mistrusted as foreigners. Thick with hardy forest from which only backbreaking labor could extract arable land, the coast was battered winter and summer by the sea, which stretched to the ends of the world. It was home to widely feared but timid barammoths that left footprints the size of buckets around the house. People huddled in tiny, incestuous clusters. Shikorn town, around whose huts the ground had, over millennia, been plowed into submission, lay three days inland through the forest.

No one lived closer to the Paeans except Shine, in the little hut he and Elicit had built this spring. Erene loved Shine. Yet she often felt a guilty sense of relief that he was not living with them anymore. They had taken him in a year and a half ago, when he stumbled ragged out of the trees, lost and starving in the bountiful forest because he had no idea what was not poisonous. He had hit it off right away with Artle and Xib. But they were *Erene's* babies. Not his. And Elicit assured her that she had not been wrong, as winter storms beat in from the sea and they were cooped up for days on end, to worry that Artle, the elder, was growing to look on Shine, if not as a second father, as a partisan elder brother who gave piggyback rides and played games even when Mama had given strict orders that the house was to be tidied.

But Elicit had not broken the news that Shine would have to move out just to appease Erene's maternal jealousy. Remnants of the piety with which he had been raised still clung to him. Personally, Erene did not understand how *anyone* could believe in the gods after living with Shine for a year, and listening to him make love to Keef by the fire, on the nights when Keef visited from Shulage; but the pious were a mystery to her at the best of times. Even her husband. Elicit had insisted that it would hamper Xib and Artle's development for them to grow up with a god for a brother. In Delta City, they had never lived so close beside the gods—or *auchresh*. He insisted it was unnatural.

Erene knew he was using the children's wellbeing as an excuse to allay his own discomfort. But what of it? Was this strain inevitable between human and *auchresh*—or should Elicit try harder to get over it? They knew little more about Shine now than they had when they first stumbled across him. And the children did not even know that he was different from themselves! Living as they did in the wilderness, neither of them was learning conventional social skills. *That* wasn't Shine's fault.

Still, Elicit said stubbornly, the fur around his mouth twitching as he suppressed his emotions. Better for Shine to maintain some distance.

And Erene had kissed him and assured him that anything he decided was right.

It gave her a thrill to submit to her husband. An ordeal of responsibility such as she had gone through in Delta City did not easily let her forget how onerous it was to have to make decisions.

And every day she gave thanks, to whatever power there might be, that after three years of marriage she and Elicit were still in love with each other. An easy, undemanding love. As parents, they balanced each other perfectly. Erene's natural stiffness—the impulse that told her she had to discipline the children, or they would grow up soft— canceled out Elicit's tendency to overdo everything. His excesses of love, which had helped both of his apprentices turn out disastrously, were carefully monitored by her when it came to Xib and Artle.

But unlike Erene's apprentices, *Elicit's* (according to the last carrier pigeon to arrive from Tellury Crescent) were still alive!

The first Hand who had ever visited Shikorn, two and a half years ago, had stood in the middle of the muddy town square and announced that Erene's apprentice was dead, her short Divine Cycle "terminated" by the god whom Erene had known as the Striver.

Poor Humi. Infected with the ambition that had stretched Erene thin. Distance did not soften Erene's grief, or ease her guilt.

She blinked. Here the children were back.

"Mama!" Artle dashed across the patch of mud in front of the house. Where was Xib? Shine must have him. "Keef here!" Artle stopped outside the door to wipe her shoes. Warmth spread through Erene. Barely three, but she knew her responsibility to help Mama and set an example for the gray fuzzball one-year-old in the arms of the tall god striding out of the trees.

Erene swung around on the weaving stool and held out her arms as the door opened, letting in the cold scent of pines. Her daughter flew across the floor. "Keef ee here! Can we go to the sea? Keef said he—"

"Darling. It's too cold. Keef and Shine have special, hot blood, so they may be able to swim, but *you* can't." Erene lifted Artle onto her lap and rubbed her cheek in the tumble of soft silver hair. "You can help me finish this length of cloth. Mm? And if you're good. I'll let you be taster when I make supper. We'll bake honey buns to honor Keef."

"Wanna," Artle murmured, fumbling with Erene's dress. Erene wondered what was passing through her mind. Was she thinking of the shingle beach at the bottom of the cliffs, where Shine had *teth"d* the children on calm days in summer? Or was she thinking of the promised honey buns? Or had she completely forgotten the conversation when infant memories recurred to her, making her remember that this was where she had sat to nurse? It had been hard on her to cede the breast to Xib. Childrens' minds were even less comprehensible than *auchresh's*. All one could do with either was look after them and hope for the best.

Shine ducked under the lintel, carrying Xib. Tall, winged, pinkish-blue of skin, he gave a beaming smile. "Errie! Guess who's here?"

"I *told* her," Artle squealed, starting up in Erene's lap, at the same moment as a square-bodied, brown-skinned *auchresh* dressed in the uniform of the Hands came in the door. Together he and Shine seemed to fill the room, with their white, glowing teeth and huge cat's eyes tipped nearly on end in their pointy faces. Xib sang a wordless baby song, bouncing in Shine's grip. Erene stood up, letting Artle slide to the ground. "Welcome," Erene said, smiling, and closed her teeth as Keef took her in his arms and squeezed.

After supper, Keef lit a pipe, put his feet up on the kitchen table, and told them the news from Shulage, the provincial capital. Elicit argued with everything—not for the sake of argument, but in an effort to open a serious debate on theology and politics, such as he often held with Shine. Keef deliberately ignored these gambits, rambling on about cattle markets and apostate flamens, blowing smoke rings.

The fire diminished slowly in the hearth. Candles flickered among the piled dishes on the table. Outside, trees

moaned and knocked their branches together in the dark.
The sea grumbled softly, far away. Erene stroked Xib's hair
where he slept on her lap and watched Elicit get more and
more incensed. Keef had a self-important turn of character,
but Erene was usually pleased to give him the attention he
craved, for he possessed both humor and kindness. Occasionally he was cruel without noticing—that was the effect
of spending every day parading around Shulage intimidat-
ing people—but she trusted him with the children, as Elicit
did not, for she could see him guarding his every word and
gesture, like a barammoth tiptoeing around on its huge feet.

Shine's kindness was instinctive; Keef's was studied. But
he ought to be congratulated, in Erene's opinion, for study-
ing. Once he had brought a couple of other Hands here.
They had refused Erene's offers of drinks and chairs. They
had refused Elicit's attempts at conversation. They had
stood back to back by the mantelpiece, profoundly uneasy,
fingering the crescent knives at their hips. When Artle
made a sally at them, wooden doll in hand, they started
simultaneously, knocking the mantelpiece off its supports
and breaking several ornaments. Artle ran and hid in the
bedroom, crying, and Xib crumpled into wails. Keef and
his friends left almost immediately.

Yet Keef was always at ease, clean of that dangerous
edginess. Erene wondered how he managed it. When Elicit
had temporarily talked himself into the ground, she mentioned it.

Keef seemed pleased to have another opportunity to ex-
pand. "It has everything to do with one's mental state. Either one absorbs the atmosphere at headquarters—or one
doesn't, in which case one can shake it off at will. It gets
harder and harder to think my own thoughts instead of my
captain's. But I think I'll be all right, as long as I keep
coming to see you and Elicit." He chuckled fruitily. "Your
family is a palliative! You keep me balanced! That's why
Yellow Spruce Heaven welcomes me and Shining Stone
whenever we want to go home, not that you ever do, Shine.
We're still something like normal. Whereas the fellows
from Long Waterfall tell me their *ruthyalim* have chucked
them out for joining the Hands."

Shine smiled, holding Artle as casually as a mother might.
He sipped from his wineglass, but said nothing. Alcohol generally quieted him—"until," Keef had confided to Erene once,

shocking her, "we get into bed. Damn, he's hot! Why d'you think I keep you supplied with the best Riestasis?"

Elicit leaned forward, hands flat on the table. "That's nonsense, Keef. There's got to be another reason your *serbalim* didn't throw you out. How could it have anything to do with us? Erene and I and the children are humans, just as much as the people you and the rest of the Hands herd around in Shulage."

"Ah. Erhmm. You got me." Keef frowned at his pipe, making a to-do out of tamping down a new bowlful of tobacco. "Actually, it doesn't have anything to do with you. I was just flattering you. If you'd been *auchresh*, it would have worked!"

"Enough flattery, then! What's the truth?" Elicit pursued. "How do you and Shine reconcile two different worlds?"

Keef sighed. "The fact is, Elicit, Shine and I come from a very rural Heaven. In larger Heavens, they feel compelled to speak of the earth as 'two different worlds'—as you just did. And they find many different ways of dealing with the dichotomy." Erene stared at him. This serious, intelligent tone was a world away from his usual pompous jesting. The fire and the candles, casting their ruddy gleams one on either side of his face, deepened the lines around his vast jewel-like eyes. "The *serbali* of Long Waterfall Heaven, Weeping Beetle, has been influenced by ideas bigger than his little Heaven needs. As I said, he has prohibited his *firim* from going anywhere near human country, and outcast the ones who defied him. By contrast, our *serbali*, Moss-choked Gully, is wise in his stupidity. He doesn't object to humans at all, because he knows nothing about them except what Weeping Beetle told him. And Beetle is Moss's enemy, so Moss is convinced everything he says must be untrue. It's marvelous!"

"But what did this Beetle tell him?" Elicit asked impatiently.

Keef gestured to Shine.

Shine drew breath. "Did either of you ever hear of Broken Bird and Bronze Water?"

"Oh!" Erene said. The men all looked at her. "We were councillors with them both in Delta City," she explained, suppressing an urge to laugh. "They kept to themselves. Of course, we attributed their reticence to their being gods. But now I think that they were silent because they believed there was no point in arguing anything. They supported the then-Divinarch, Golden Antelope, who asserted that there was a single fate in store for the *auchresh* no matter what they did. I think I see what you're getting at, Keef! According to Golden Antelope, we mortals were the greatest race, the *auchresh* were not gods, and you had no place in our affairs." Elicit made an incoherent noise. She said, "It's what he told me."

"Yes, and Broken Bird and Bronze Water's views are a derivation of that philosophy!" Keef said. "In their view, you humans are beneath our contempt. *Wrchrethre auchresh* are scarcely any better. The *er-serbalim* tolerate the current Divinarch only because they have to. And Weeping Beetle, like so many others, has embraced their views wholeheartedly! But Moss-choked Gully rejected them simply because he heard them from Weeping Beetle! When Shine and I chose to leave our Heaven, it scandalized Weeping Beetle no end, and Moss was delighted!"

Shine shook his head. "Only out here could he get away with an eccentricity like that. We are a *very* rural Heaven. But there are a great many Heavens like us. The world isn't made up of Divaring Belows and Tearkas and Rimmears. There are thousands of Heavens where Bronze Water and Broken Bird's message has only come by word of mouth, and garbled at that. Before the *er-serbalim* started touring the Heavens, most of us didn't know humans existed; but now tales of humans are reaching every Heaven, either by way of the *er-serbalim* or recruiters for the Hands, and more and more *auchresh* are leaving for one reason or another, and Moss-choked Gully cannot be the only *serbali* in the world who doesn't condemn our departure. Power knows how it will all end."

"Why did *you* leave, though, Shine?" Erene asked. "You're not a Hand. I've always wondered what brought you here. But I never felt quite right about asking."

Shine rocked gently back and forth, holding Artle. "It was Keef, of course." He looked at his lover as if begging permission. Keef nodded. "Keef heard the Divinarch's message through Esult, who was then a recruiter trying to start a troop of Hands in Shulage. Characteristically, Moss-choked Gully welcomed Esult to our Heaven and feted him like a *mainraui.* The glory of the occasion went straight to Keef's mercenary little heart, which had always wanted to shine, and knew it never would, not as one *mainraui* among many *mainrauim* in a backwater Heaven in Fewarauw."

"Ouch!" Keef said. He blew out his cheeks and grinned.

Shine did not so much as look at him. "Several weeks later, Keef walked into Shulage—*walked,* for since no one from our Heaven had ever been to human country, he had no way of knowing where to *teth*"—and presented himself to Esult. Four *mainrauim* from Long Waterfall Heaven had already come, and they told Keef about the reception they had got when they tried to go home—ostracized, deprived of their *mainraui* status. So Keef decided not to risk the humiliation. He never came back.

"But just before he got the idea to be a Hand, he and I had pledged *irissim.* We were young. I decided to walk after him and see what had happened. But once I left the salt, I got hopelessly lost. I wandered for weeks without seeing an *auchresh* or a human being. Eventually, I ended up here. And after a few months, as you remember, I met Keef in Shikorn village."

"And all was right with the world again." Keef grinned. "Oh, Power, oh, Power! Uh-*uh!* Shine, I'll always remember when I realized how much I'd missed you."

Elicit's face was hard as metal in the light of the guttering candles. "It seems to me you've set a dangerous example, Shine."

Shine finished his wine. "To whom? I suppose that's a stupid answer. Well, you can blame Esult, not me."

"Blame Broken Bird and Bronze Water," Keef said. "If it weren't for their influence—even though it was a *reverse* influence—Esult would never have been allowed into our Heaven! And besides, isolationism is so damned unproductive!" He waved his hands. "If it wasn't for the isolationists, all the salt would support the Divinarch!"

Shine frowned. "If it wasn't for the isolationists, all the salt would support the Divinarch!"

Erene shivered.

Elicit persisted, "Esult seems to be like the kind of god who would be happy to jump on the Divine Balance and send any one of us to Hell."

"I have to put in a good word for him," Keef said. "He's my captain, and he's one of the most virtuous *auchresh* I have ever known."

"Virtuous?" Shine said. "You mean fanatic." He turned to Elicit. "*I've* met Esult, too. He's the kind who never seems to show their true colors until they've reached positions of power. His kind would make us a dangerous race, if the isolationists and the Hands could ever reconcile their differences! He's a true son of his forebears."

"Nonsense!" Keef said. "Esult is perfectly sane! He worships the Divinarch like a god!"

"As would you, if you were a proper Hand," Shine said furiously. "You really ought to be sitting on the table while Erene and Elicit sit on the floor. You ought to make them lick your feet clean. And why didn't you force them to cook one of their adorable little children for supper?"

Erene cried out.

"Enough!" Elicit thundered and rose to his feet. "This is my home! You will have to account for me before you drag my family into your spats! I demand an apology."

Neither *auchresh* moved. They stared at him, mouths slightly open. *Oh, Elicit!* Erene thought, her heart aching for her husband. She was perhaps the only person present, including him, who understood: all evening he been trying, and failing, to trap the *auchresh* into saying something that would confirm them as gods in his mind. Now, at last, their petty catfight over Esult's character, and their drawing him into their argument, had pushed his understanding of them to the point where he could no longer bear to participate in the demolishing of the wall between *auchresh* and mortal.

Xib's crying was the only sound apart from the trees scraping in the wind outside. Erene remembered herself and held the baby to her breast. He latched on thirstily.

"Give me my daughter," Elicit demanded, his voice breaking. After a second's delay, Shine lifted the sleeping child and deposited her in her father's arms. Elicit looked down at her as if scrutinizing her for signs that she was god-touched. "I think that you should both go home. This is one of the least productive arguments I have ever taken part in and it has gone on long enough. I will not allow you to slander my wife and children as you did, Shine. If you cannot apologize, you will have to leave."

Incredibly, both *auchresh* rose to their feet.

"Stop!" Erene said. " 'Lici. This isn't going to help you stay pious. How are you going to worship someone you have bested?"

Keef laughed. "Bested?" he yelped, rather hysterically. "I could teach you a thing or two, Godsman Paean! I could—"

Elicit shook his head as if trying to clear his mind of a lingering dream. "Get out." He stood up and carried Artle

out through the weaving room, into the bedroom, leaving
Erene alone with their guests.

Shifting Xib into one arm, she opened the back door. A
gust of cold black wind whirled in, bringing droplets of rain.

Keef made a face. "Ugh."

"I think you *had* better go," Erene said. "I was afraid
for a moment there—but the storm has broken. Come back
in a couple of days, Shine." She smiled tiredly. "Everything
should have blown over by then. He is too intelligent not
to want ever to see you anymore."

Keef glanced at Shine. "Do you want to *teth*"? I'm a
little drunk: you'll have to take us."

"No." Shine's eyes were closed, his face tipped to the
storm, the globular lids fluttering. "Winter's here. I should
like to walk."

"We'll be drenched!"

Shine opened his eyes. The luminous black pupils reflected Erene and Keef, like little pale statues. "This is why
I stayed in human country after I found you, *irissi*. Share
it with me."

"Now I know why they say renegades are too strange to
live." Keef shook his head. "All right. I can savor life with
the best of them." He turned to Erene. "Thank you," he
said at the same time as Shine. They laughed at themselves,
remembered the gravity of the situation, and gulped it back.

Erene smiled with tears in her eyes. "Oh, you two," she
said, almost crying. "Love each other. Don't let—these
things—get between you!"

Shine said, "I *hope* you're right that Elicit won't hold it
against us, Erene. We argue between ourselves, too. Over the
same things. We weren't trying to snipe at him—or anything."

"Yes," Keef said. "Really. You should hear us sometimes. Your friend Shine is secretly a rabid factionalist,
Erene! Next thing you know, he'll be bringing *ruthyalim* to
tea and forming them into a renegade army!"

The two were outside. The darkness swallowed all of
Keef except his eyes, but Shine glimmered like a branch of
phosphorus. "See you soon!" he called, blowing a kiss, his
hair already wild in the wind.

And Keef's voice, laughing, "As good a night to you as
ours is going to be, Erene!"

The whole front of her body was wet from standing on
the threshold. Moving clumsily, she shut the door, dropped

the latch, and wiped Xib's little gray head with the tail of his wrap. Incredibly, he was still sleeping.

"Come to bed," Elicit said, softly, from the other room.

She woke in the night to find him with his back turned to her, weeping. She raised herself on one elbow and leaned over him, wiping his face with her fingers. "I love you," she whispered.

He did not answer. His silent sobs shook the bed. The children slept peacefully in their cot, and Erene gave thanks for that—nothing is worse for a child than to see its parent cry. Eventually she whispered, "Did you—did you prove something to yourself, tonight?" She did not mean it as a subtle I-told-you-so, but as a you-can-confess-if-you-want, and she knew he would understand that.

But his voice was even more broken than she had anticipated. "Gods . . . ! It's gone! Gone . . . What am I going to do, Errie?"

She bit her lip, caressing him.

"The children—how will they grow—gods! How can I teach them something I don't believe myself?"

A tear trickled out of her eye. His emotions were hers. But now he needed comfort. "Don't worry," she whispered. "They *will* grow up. And that's what matters. They don't need faith. And it would be false to teach it to them if we have none. Everyone around them loves them. What do beliefs matter, if they have love?"

He turned over and grabbed her to him, holding her so tight it hurt. She kissed his tearstained fur and whispered, "Don't worry, don't worry," thinking, *Now I am a mother in body and soul I am not the same anymore. I have fallen into the habit of soothing even him with optimism that I do not feel.*

Hope's Folly

Hope sat on the edge of the narrow bunk, legs awkwardly splayed, watching the frame of torchlight around the cabin door move up and down. The effect might have been the same if *Gefiya* were rocking in high seas. The ship was lashed close in her berth in the Delta City docks, but Hope herself was rocking, quivering like a door assailed by a battering ram: the Veretrean sailor knelt between her legs, thrusting into her with the vindictive violence that had characterized all his lovemaking of late, whether their trysts were planned, or, like this one, as sudden and inconvenient as assassinations. His fists bundled the tender leather of her wings, holding her in place. In an effort to erode her self-awareness, she let her head flop in circles on her neck. She felt alone and detached up here, with his shaggy black head next to her shoulder, and the onslaught down below having no more effect than a series of not particularly well-placed blows.

"What's wrong with you, eh?" Ders grunted, and Hope murmured "Oh, *ohhhh* . . ." and stirred herself, moving with his thrusts, trying to find that spontaneous rhythm that visited them on their best nights and transformed ordinary friction into fantasy. But it did not come. He finished and slumped over her, breathing like a beached nightsharque. She supported herself on her hands, gazing at the underside of the top bunk. This was the end of their assignations. Tomorrow morning, *Gefiya* sailed to Port Teligne with her cargo of Chrumecountry fruits. And the thing that troubled Hope was that she could not have cared less.

Humi, she thought. *I should have gone to see Humi.*

"Fuck. Ahhhh." Ders stood up and groped in the clothes sack hanging on the wall. The light coming through the crack of the door illuminated a stripe of sleek brown fur on his back. The cabin smelled of male sweat, and salt, and moldy cheese: six sailors shared it, and Hope had deduced from fragments of overheard ribaldry that they took turns having it to themselves, to be alone with the women they brought back to the ship. Ders did not tell her so, but she was sure she was not the only woman *he* brought here, either. The first time she came, she had got lice from his quilt. The night after that, she had tried taking him to the Folly, but he had glowered with embarrassment at having the social gulf between them pointed up so baldly, and bruised her green and blue in his lovemaking. So they had gone back to dark, cramped trysts on board the ship.

Pulling on a shirt and a pair of clean breeches, he spoke. "You'd better leave."

Hope sighed. "Ders. I'd just like to know ... what do you feel for me? Anything?"

He wheeled around. "I haven't got time for this kind of talk, milady. Get out of here. And don't get seen, neither. Go in a flash. Some of the boys are pretty pious, and if they saw you, I could be drummed out of me situation."

"Do you love me?" Hope said. "I love you," she added, to encourage him to reply.

"Gods." His face twisted, and as if he could not restrain himself, he spat on the floor. Wiping the back of his hand across his mouth, he started to speak, then shook his head. "How can you ask me that?"

Hope cocked her head on one side. "Do you despise me for letting you have your way?"

He leaned against the wall and folded his arms. "I gotta get my beauty sleep, milady. We're sailing at dawn."

"Do you mean you're just going to end it like this?" She endeavored to put a quaver into her voice, desperately trying to drum up a scene. "Is it because I'm not a good enough lover that you despise me?"

"There ain't nothing wrong with you, Wingy. You're no different from any other woman. 'Ow's *that*?"

"Aha! So that's it!" She bounced to her feet. "No different from any other woman! You were expecting *divine ecstasy*, weren't you? And I disappointed you. So you're punishing me with ending it without so much as a word of affection."

"I never said I was ending nothing!" Ders protested.

A shadow obscured the crack at the bottom of the door. She raised her voice. Whoever was listening might as well get the full benefit. "Well, I'm *not* any different from any other woman! How does that feel? It's all a hoax! The closest anyone can ever come to divine ecstasy is a whorehouse in Heaven!" It wasn't working. Her emotions were still comatose. She felt nothing. However, one did not get angry and then break it off for no reason. "I!" she said, and then realized she had lost her train of thought.

It seemed she had succeeded in one respect, though. Ders took a step toward her, his fists clenched. "You bitch. You fucking *begged* for it. I fucked you once and you begged for more! Crawled on your *knees* for it!"

She retreated, feeling excited.

"I used to be pious, too," he said thickly. "And you

fucked *that* up nicely! I'm never gonna be able to look at a god again without remembering what it was like to fuck you! Never mind praying!" He hawked and spat, sloppily, missing her. "And it wasn't even worth it. I've had better whores than you." With a shock, Hope realized he was almost crying. "Better *dog bitches*—"

"Woooooooah." From the passage came the sound of ironic applause. "Finish her *off*, Ders—"

Ders wheeled toward the door, making a superhuman effort not to cry.

Hope sobbed.

She lay on her back on the ground, under a rhododendron. The waxy leaves slithered over each other, hiding the stars. It must have rained while she was on board *Gefiya*. The stink of leaf mold filled her nostrils, and her wings flattened it into a concavity under her back. Already her shoulder muscles were jittering with discomfort. This was why she had ordered featherbeds for her Folly into which she could sink like a piece of flotsam. No process of evolution had shaped her to lie on her back. No process of evolution had shaped her at all. Living as an *auchresh* was living with a handicap that nature had intended to kill you, and which you had daily to overcome with grit and will.

Or not.

I was too strong for him. I was a spice that became a poison. I was using him for my own ends. And all the time I was destroying his beliefs, just by being what I am. It's a god's responsibility not to let her subjects get close to her, no matter how foolhardily they flutter to the flame! It's a god's responsibility, for the Power's sake, not to beckon them closer!

If I returned to the salt I would no longer be a god ...

Arity had stayed in Rimmear for this very reason: so that he would no longer have to endure being the object of the mortals' obsession. But he had come back to Delta City. Not to be Heir, but to be Pati's plaything. He had taken the easy way out, the common cure for the meaninglessness of a life that was the object of no one's obsession.

Hope did not have the hook of love to hold her here. Nor the hook of godhood, for her status as a god was crumbling fast, will-she nill-she, through acts like taking Ders as a lover, and her all-too-visible ineffectuality. All she had was her Folly. But she could not contemplate leaving. Not even for a little while, as Arity had. *We are both* wrchrethrim, she thought. *We can't stay, can't stay away.*

The fatigue of her position ground her into the wet earth. She wasn't wearing anything apart from the shell of her wings. She shivered and twisted on her side.

Visible between the lower branches, the Folly towered in fantastic silhouette against the sky. The grounds occupied all of what had once been Antiprophet Square, and the surrounding mansions' gardens. Pati had razed them as a lesson to the city, but Hope had appropriated the site, and built the Folly using money she made from selling her estates in Divaring Below. She had asserted herself as a power in the city, in those first months when she had been flushed with her conviction that a recoup was inevitable. But she and Humi had let the iron cool—in themselves, and in the hearts of the allies whose support would be necessary in any campaign. Now it seemed that the city was resigned to wearing its new master's yoke. Some people were even starting to believe that Pati *was* the One God, as he insisted. And what Delta City felt, the rest of the world reflected.

The Folly stood like a waterfall frozen before it had leaped to its full height. A shadow bird-netted in wood and steel.

Did Humi know the recoup was never going to happen?

Hope had not visited Lockreed Concourse since she tried to deliver the news of Arity's return, and guilt ate at her for her negligence. Aneisneida and Soderingal, by their own report, had half killed Humi by dropping the news on her out of a clear sky. How had she handled it? Had she survived?

Hope rolled on her face, plunging her fingers into the leaf mold. Worms wriggled around her talons. *Breathe. Stay alive. All you can possibly hope, Hope, to do is . . .*

"I can't bear it," she said aloud.

The night did not answer.

"I can't bear it!"

She hurled herself out from under the rhododendrons, gripping her head with her talons, shaking it back and forth, shrieking softly. "*Do* something!"

Starlight bathed the shrubs. The shadows of the taller trees dappled the grasses. Blood inched down her neck from the burning places on her scalp, down between the roots of her wings.

She clenched her fists. A garbled sound came from her throat. She couldn't stop shaking. She was frightening herself.

She was not completely powerless! There were still a few things she could do. Her own heart might be frostbitten beyond cure, but there were others who could be healed, who could resume their love where it had broken off. And who knew if love might not lead to something more solid!

She, Hope, had merely to do the honors. She still had her secrets, each one a jewel in its own little coffer, and now it was time to start spending them.

Certain Illusions

Arity had the night shift at the Dog Gate of the Old Palace. Pati had offered to exempt him; but Arity had refused, as he refused every time Pati tried to treat him differently from the other Hands. Pati, it turned out, had wanted Arity to himself tonight. They quarreled. Ordinarily, Arity would have dissolved into shaking ecstasies and flung himself at Pati's feet—but tonight he said, "I'm sorry, I have my duties." He did not know where he got the strength. Pati stared at him. Arity *teth*"*d* to the guardhouse, sat down, and accepted a mug of ale from Blue Kestrel.

"Didn't expect to see *you* tonight," Kestrel said by way of a greeting.

Arity took a gulp of ale before answering, "Neither did I."

Perhaps I knew I needed time to myself, he thought, not without conscious irony, as the alcohol warmed his stomach. *In order to maintain an obsession you must leave space between the two of you for delusion. Not reduce it all to bodily contact. Because that has limits, where the other does not.* He wasn't afraid that he might go the way of Melin and the others. But he knew he must be the one to give the flame air, for Pati would not.

After half an hour he was on duty. He went out of the

guardhouse and took up his position. Dog Gate opened out
of the lowest level of the great courtyard, on a street that
had once been bustling and well-to-do. Most of the houses
were boarded up now. The silence of an empty beach—
stones, darkness, waves silently eating at the sand—hung
over the whole palace district. How different from Rimmear. What had it taken to make a human city seem older
than an *auchresh* city?

Arity stood loose and relaxed, like Mosquito Ruby on
the other side of the gate, flicking his gaze over the street,
up the wall towering above him, down to the cobbles. The
sentinels were not decorations, but safeguards against attacks from unknown malcontents which Pati still feared,
though most of the Hands had long dismissed the likeli-
hood of any resistance to the Divinarchy.

It was bitterly cold. Soon Arity's eyeballs were the only
part of him that could still move. The houses across the
street were a chiaroscuro in black and white.

Sulfur burned a hole in the night. The smell of an actinic
teth "tach ching gusted into Arity's face. Mosquito uttered
an oath and drew his crescent knife. Arity was a half second
behind, poised to stab or throw.

Hope popped out of the firework, striking the cobbles
lightly. She was wearing a lacy dress that reeked of cam-
phor. "Ari!" She grabbed Arity's arm. "You're coming
with me! We're going to pay a visit to someone whom you
haven't seen in far too long. Hello, there!" she said to
Mosquito. "Don't raise the alarm, will you? He'll be back
before anyone knows he's gone."

"Who is it?" Arity muttered. "Hope! Who?" He was
captivated: he forgot to struggle. He could only think of
one person he hadn't seen in far too long, and *that* could
not be. He tried to pull away.

"Don't!" she said. "I have to concentrate—"

"I don't know where she *is,*" Hope whispered worriedly.
They were climbing the stairs that zigzagged upward
through the attic of the house in Temeriton. Her talons dug
into the back of Arity's hand. "She never leaves the house!
It would be dangerous for her to come up here—and she
doesn't take risks!"

Arity said nothing. He could do nothing except follow.
He did not dare voice his suspicions, in case she laughed

at him. The certainty of a horrible anticlimax petrified him. Yet he dared not *teth*" back to Pati and report Hope's attempt to subvert his loyalty, even though that was what he ought to do, because it *might* be—

It could not be.

But *could* it be? When he saw Hope glowing with this almost treacherous fervor, in her dress with its loops of rotting lace, when she *teth*"d him to this tumbledown house in the brothel district, he'd seen that she had made some sort of decision, and was determined to carry it out, even if she were forced to resort to underhanded means. He had seen this ashamed yet determined sneakiness in her before, on the occasions when she had resolved to defy Pati.

Dust blossomed from their footfalls.

But it can't be! She's dead!

"Power," Hope gulped as they rounded a worm-eaten partition. The stairs doubled back on themselves, slanting straight up to an open hatch in the roof. A silver sea swirled and lapped at its lip. The dust stirred by their climb, lit by the rectangle of starlight coming in the hatch, resembled foamy, crashing waves. The sky in the hatch, by contrast, was tarry.

"They wouldn't leave it open, not in autumn. This means she's up here." In one leap, Hope was out of the hatch. Her skirt and hair and wings blew out, a tumult of silvery veils. She drew breath—and then froze, beckoning Arity.

He had thought that his courage would fail. But he found himself beside Hope, gazing down a slope of damaged tiles at a gutter as wide as a small river, set on top of the wall that faced the back alley. In the gutter knelt a slim, lithe woman, gazing down into the alley, fair hair tousled in the wind.

Moments of catharsis pass like shocks of pain, with undertones of pleasure. Eagerly sought, or dreaded; dwelt upon before and after the fact with morbid intensity. Yet all Arity remembered feeling at the time was the wind striking through his shirt, chilling him so fiercely that his teeth clattered together.

There could be no doubt that it was her.

No trick of the wind could have duplicated her voice. ("I have never been up here before, you know," she was saying in a pleasant tone, apparently to nobody at all.) No trick

of the starlight could have mimicked the grace that almost
hid the trembling tension in her poise.

"Our time together has been most pleasurable," she was
saying, and Arity believed three years had not passed.
"Even if I do not see my way clear to accepting your kind
offer—well, I have gained a new spot to idle away my leisure hours! It is nice up here! Also, I think I smell house-
monkeys; do you?"

"Yesss, milady." Her companion rose to her feet. Arity
gasped. The other woman's robe had let her blend into the
night—she could have been a flamen, except that the robe
was black. She tossed her head, and her hood fell back to
reveal a small, androgynous face. "I smell them. What of
it?" Soundlessly, she moved up behind the younger woman,
shaking back her voluminous sleeves, flexing her hands.

"I use a variety of small animals in my work," Humi
said. "Rats, seagulls, cats—even a dray dog whose master
could no longer afford to keep it. But the possibilities of
those are limited. A new species to work with is a delightful
boon. I do hope I can catch one. Perhaps you could help
me!"

The Hangman—it could be no one else—bent from the
waist, placing her head a few feet left of Humi's. "If I have
granted you sssuch a boon, will you not repay it by accepting my offer?" She straightened up.

Humi turned her face left. Her voice was strained and
sad. "I dare not. I am too vulnerable. My allies have all
fallen away from me."

Beside Arity, Hope was chewing the tips of her fingers.

"Without more support, I dare not commit myself to a
campaign such as you propose. I am sorry."

"I never thought I would hear the Divinarch say *I dare
not.*" This time, the Hangman did not bend down to speak.
Humi twisted, her hands coming up to shield her face. "Or
I am sorry." The Hangman's hands closed on her shoulders.

"I dare!" Hope shrieked. "I dare!" Down in the gutter
in a flash, she tossed the Hangman against the roof like a
baby. The woman's head cracked against the tiles. Hope
pulled Humi to her feet and hugged her. "*Humi!* What is
she doing here? I thought we had decided that we wouldn't
involve the underworld without agreeing on it together—
what did she offer you?"

"Gods! Hope! Well, how do you expect me to get your

consent when you don't show up for two months straight?
I—" Humi pulled away. She cocked her head as if to listen.
She wore a plain dress that hung perfectly on her slim
figure, showing her bare shoulders under the tangled cloud
of hair. "Who is with you? Who is it?"

Arity stood up. In a voice that came out jerky and
strained, he said, "*Irissu,* it's me."

"You thickhead," Hope wailed, "she can't *see* you—"

"I know who it is." Humi's voice turned disconcertingly
hard. "What did you bring him here for? He's Pati's plaything. I haven't anything to say to him."

How had she found out? Hope must have told her! Behind him, a housemonkey, maybe two, waked by the noise,
jittered in annoyance. He gripped the side of the hatch.
Without knowing that he had *teth"d,* he found himself shaking her violently by the shoulders. *For three years I tried to
kill myself to be with you—wherever it is that we can be
together without anyone noticing—and you haven't anything
to say to me? I'll give you "haven't anything"!* Yet the
words that came from his lips were defensive rather than
aggressive. "You were alive. And you hid here for three
years, and never once thought to let me know you hadn't
been killed. You might have spared me that!"

She struggled mechanically, like a hare that has been in
a trap for hours. But her face was not in it. Her eyes darted
randomly from here to there.

And he knew. He let go of her as if she were red hot,
coughing with a helpless nausea. Everything he had meant
to say bubbled up and stuck in his throat. *It's the shock. It
doesn't make any difference—not really! It's the shock—*

"Sickening, isn't it?" she said. "I must say, yours is the
most dramatic reaction I've had yet. But then, no one else
was quite as familiar with the old me as you—were they?"

"How—Power! How did you—"

"Gods!" She moved her head impatiently. "You know
what happened here! Think!"

Pati. Of course. Part of him rebelled against Pati for concealing the fact that his poison had only blinded her, not
killed her. Then he realized that of course, Pati did not
know either. "I thought you were dead! Has Hope known
all along? Oh, Hope! I thought—" He stopped.

"What difference does it make? I might as *well* be dead.
But I *am* glad we've met again. Ari, I want to know"—her

voice sharpened—"how could you become his lover? That's one of the things that intrigues me most about the whole business. How could you give yourself to him? You used to be so independent. Was that real? Or was the *auchresh* I knew always an illusion? Did you always love him first and foremost?"

He shook his head. "What do you really want to know?"

"How could you do it?" Did she feel pain? Or was this just the dispassionate needling of an interrogator? "I don't understand."

Two realities warred in Arity's head: one that he saw before him, and one that he had accepted for three years. The conflict between senses' testimony and disbelief made his vision blur and his head ache. A strange exhaustion—the nervous system's response to overstimulation—weighted his limbs down. He fought to think. Humi's face and voice, her very presence, had thrown him back three years into a world of shimmery fabrics and ghosts and bells. His memories of that place were fresh and timeless. He could not deny their existence: not to himself, nor to her, not to her face.

And yet he must be honest—he would be nothing at all if he were not honest—there was Pati. She knew all about it. He could not deny it, and more important did not want to. He floundered. "Before I knew you, I loved him. I suppose ... I—I suppose it seemed most natural. You know. After you were gone—"

That wasn't true. After he learned Humi was dead, *nothing* had seemed natural, not eating, or breathing, or blinking. But how to explain that the only one who could possibly have replaced her, in any measure, was the one who had already replaced her? In Rimmear, it had made sense in a visceral way. Self-immolation. It still made sense, although less clearly. He had to struggle now to remember how he had felt that night when he and Pati sealed the bargain with kisses.

"I love you." So difficult to explain. "But when you were gone—you don't understand how hard it was—"

"Is it true, Hope?" Humi did not turn her head, only raised her voice. "He says he loved Pati before he loved me. Is that true?"

"That's *not* what I said!" Arity spun around to plead his case with Hope—and fell silent. She crouched in a rain puddle a little way along the gutter, her hands over her ears, beside the unconscious body of the Hangman, shaking.

But Humi could not see that Hope was not listening. Arity cringed as she continued, confidently, as if she were speaking to an attentive audience. "Think back, Hope. When he came to Delta City, twenty years ago, when he discovered Pati had left him for you, how did he act? Before the fall he told me that he realized then that his affair with Pati was only a youthful infatuation. But I always suspected he was lying." She paused. There was no answer. She rubbed her forehead with her hand, an admission of vulnerability. "What am I *saying*, Hope? Why am I wasting my breath trying to resuscitate a dead love affair, when we have political concerns to deal with? Hope ... Hope?" She turned her head, squinting as if she could see. "Where are you?"

For a moment, with her guard down, she was her old self. Arity stepped forward, meaning to take her in his arms. But before he reached her Pati's face billowed up before him, a cobweb with two burning holes. It clung to his hands and face, stopping him as effectively as if he had waded into quicksand. The left eye, the blue one, smeared itself over his cheek like a streak of luminous paint. When he tried to look straight at the face, it was invisible, a blast of heat roaring out of nowhere. He could not force his way against it.

Humi rubbed the bridge of her nose. "But really, the middle of the night is not the best time to discuss these things."

The wind gusted between them, great downy puffs of cold. Arity did not go to her. He had stopped trying. Excitement heated his blood so that he did not feel the cold. Pati held him spellbound: it was almost as if he had reached out from the Palace and tapped him on the shoulder. He felt like weeping or falling to his knees.

Humi lifted her face, blotched with dark patches in the starlight. "I know you're still here. Go away. I haven't anything else to say to you—and I expect the sentiment is mutual."

Arity drew a deep, shuddering breath. "Humi. Let's be civilized, shall we? Let's remember that love is not the only, or the most important, thing in the world."

She appeared to be listening.

"I'm not your enemy. I might be able to give you more help with whatever it is you're planning than *she* can." He jerked a shoulder at the unconscious Hangman. "Why can't we talk as equals?" Pause. "Allies?"

She gave a tinkling laugh. "Are you mad? You'd betray me."

"All right. You may not trust me. But does that mean we can't be pleasant to each other? I'd thought better of you."

Her face brightened, became a social mask. "Of course I can tell you about the Hangman!"

That had done it. Arity experienced a bitter exultation. Seductive, like sugar in the blood; chilly, smooth.

"It's nothing a man would find particularly interesting! There's *no* political alliance between us. We were friends before the fall. Ever since she told me she was a woman, and she came from Domesdys, we've had a lot in common. Our mutual friends—our mutual goals." She shrugged. "We both have a sense of nostalgia for the city as it used to be. We talk of the past."

"Oh, yes," Arity said. "Well." His mind was working fast. *Nothing political?* Her ambition was so obvious it was in poor taste. She aspired, of course, to regain the Throne.

But that was nothing new. Was it? In Rimmear, recovering from his near-fatal injuries, before he knew she was dead, he had dreamed of a laughing, tawny-haired girl who walked beside him through a salt forest and yielded to his kisses, but who faded before he could taste her, like all dream things. The starlight thinned her to a wisp of mist and she disintegrated. The dreams had threatened him during his waking hours, too, after he learned she was dead, when he sat in the bottom-tier taverns during the day. Laughing at nothing—running away to Veretry for a couple of hours, to pretend there was no such thing as other people—drinking chocolate in her Antiprophet Square apartments as dawn came up over the marshes . . .

But that girl had never existed. She was the invention of a *khath*-inflamed brain.

(Pati whispered to his mind, deadening the nerve ends.)

There had been nothing more than a physical attraction, and now that too was gone. Humi had always been the hard-edged, knife-faced woman she was now. He did not see how he had ever loved her.

He stretched, feeling the chill of the wind once again, calm and collected. It was as if a huge weight had vanished off his shoulders. "Well, we have a great deal to talk about, you and I—but I think we should put it off until another day. Easier than dragging things out tonight." He took care to put a smile in his voice. "Don't you agree?"

She started. She seemed to have fallen into a reverie of her own. "Oh, yes. Have I told you all you wanted to know? My life is rather dull now—there is no other way to put it."

He nodded his head.

"Yes. I suppose—yes. It has been a true delight. Thank you for coming, Ari." She half-smiled. "I see the past in a quite different light now."

"So do I." He saw a possibility of consolidating his victory over her, and himself. "Listen—if there's anything I can do to help—"

"Perhaps there will be. You mean . . . ?" She cocked her head on one side.

"Yes." Arity calculated his hesitation. "Why don't we speak plainly? You want to regain the Throne. Pati wants me to be his Heir. So far I have refused, but I don't know how long I can keep on refusing. I would rather see you become Divinarch than me. So perhaps we can come to an understanding."

"You mean—" She sighed. "Pati."

"Exactly."

"You want me to spare his life, when I regain the Throne. In return for your not telling him about my intentions."

"Yes."

"Well, frankly, I think that's rather premature of you." She touched her cheekbones with the same self-mocking gesture she had used when talking to the Hangman, earlier. "Like this, I cannot see how I shall ever come to have power over him."

Her ambition was a cold flame, then, not a hot one. It made no difference of course, but something prompted him to play with her. "What I meant was that perhaps, with my help, it wouldn't be so remote a possibility. The same thing must have occurred to many people—we'd have to be very careful—but supposing you were to succeed, with my help, we would have to have an agreement along the lines I am suggesting. What I want . . ." *is to have things the way they used to be* . . . Impossible! "What I mean is that if we collaborate, I'm sure we can work things out without anyone's getting hurt. I love Pati—but I think it would be best for everyone if he wasn't Divinarch. All the odds are against him. You do see what I mean."

"You're incurable!" Humi said. "Ari the peacemaker! For starters, I could not trust you that far, and even *if* I ever succeeded, I would—" She stopped. Quick as a viper, she said, "This isn't a ploy to make me speak treason, is it? You're not going to betray me—are you?"

"Do you think I would do that?"

"No," she said mistrustfully.

He smiled. "Then we've already reached an understanding."

Over the whistling of the wind, a sob reached his ears. He turned. Hope curled in the bottom of the gutter, weeping with anger. "No use . . . no use . . ." Her dress floated on the rain puddle. The wind had frozen the wet lace into stiff curves that crackled as she stood. "You *can't* just let everything you used to have slip away! Don't you see how *false* this is, Humi? You know you're just being polite, so as not to make this too painful for both of you. But you *do* love each other! If you would just admit it, Humi, maybe we could win him back. Maybe we could win his *heart* back. But oh, no, you have your *pride*—"

Humi said in a voice stiff as ice, "I do have my pride." Her back formed a razor-straight line. "But I am also honest with myself. And with others."

Hope laughed rather wildly.

"Honest is the last thing you'll ever be, senior ghostier!"

"I am no longer senior ghostier. And I am no longer attached to Charity. He and I understand that the past is the past. Why don't you see that the only way to make *any* future is to stop trying to re-create it?"

"You two were my last hope," Hope sobbed. The Hangman stirred and sat up. Hope wheeled and pointed. "And if you trust this *haugthirre* woman rather than Ari, Humi, you're blinder than I thought you were!"

"I'm going," the Hangman said thickly. She stumbled at the slopes of the roof. Quite dexterously, almost as if she could see, Humi caught her, pulled her close, and whispered. The Hangman sat down heavily.

"Well, don't ask me to do anything more for you and your damned recoup." Hope was crying. "That's all I have to say, Humi! Don't count on me!"

Arity stepped toward Hope and pulled her close. He felt competent now, and hugely successful. "I'll take you home. You're all worked up about this—though I can't see why. Humi and I have behaved with perfect amicability toward one another, considering the circumstances under which we meet."

Hope wept inconsolably. "Listen to you. Just *listen* to you!"

Arity turned to Humi. "We'll talk again, then?"

She smiled thinly. "Can I lay it on you to visit me, not the other way round? I am not able to get out and about with any great efficiency."

By this time his loyalty to Pati had sunk so deep that he had almost forgotten he was going to betray her. She was right, it *had* all been a ploy—a perfectly conscious manipulation of the past that lay between them. But all was fair between lovers, was it not?

"I'm taking you back to the Folly," he said to Hope, meaning to get her out of the way before he returned to Pati to break the news. This might not be an advantageous place to be in the next few hours.

"I'm too tired to *teth*"," Hope moaned.

He kissed her on the nose. "Then describe it. I've never been there, you know."

Through fitful tears, she did so. The Hangman and Humi stood together—one watching, the other seeming to. The last sight he saw before nothingness was their faces side by side—bony, fair, inscrutable. At that moment they were nearly identical. It shook him. His destination wavered in his mind, and instead of emerging in Hope's second-floor ghost parlor, they slipped down through the floor, and tumbled through thick, scented steam for what seemed like minutes before crashing into Hope's swimming pool.

The water was green, hot, and tasted of incense. They surfaced, gasping. Arity's hair was short now, so it wasn't plastered to his eyes like Hope's. After the initial shock, he realized that the water felt delicious. Succumbing momentarily, he dived, turned a somersault, and came up paddling. It had been too long since he swam. Not since the Divine Guards. He and Humi—

Slam the doors, lock them, ram a chair under the knob! Delicious!

Blue tiles lined the pool. A glass dome, lit from above by torches, could be seen as an opaque, multi-sunned sky overhead. On the walls, murals of salt cats and trulles curvetted through salt forests. "How often do you use this place, Hope?"

"Not very." Her eyes were wide in the steam. "Mostly for relaxing."

"But you keep it heated all the time?"

"I sold my mansion in Divaring." She was swimming with her spread wings. They chopped the water like huge golden paddles. "I have plenty of money!"

Arity knew why she had built this little ocean, hidden away, here whenever she needed it. It was for the same reason there had been a pool in the Divine Guards' quarters—a luxury today's Hands were not afforded—the illusion that it gave. It was the reason all *auchresh* liked to live near water.

"Power, Hope!" Pity suffused him. "You're a worse hypocrite than I am!"

In his and Pati's private suite, there was no water. Only the honesty of nakedness.

He yearned for it.

He breaststroked fast for the side, anticipating what Pati would say when he told him everything that had happened tonight. Humi was nothing to him. And Hope—well, Hope, floating on the undulating sheet of her wings, tears trickling from the corners of her eyes, would just get what was coming to her. That would teach her to interfere.

Red and Sable

Night had not yet fallen on the K'Fier wharves. But the light would go soon. Even through his tiredness, Gete felt frantic energy sparking the air, a pressing awareness that the day's business had yet to be completed. The warves bustled with ship's crews and warehousemen, loading and unloading, quarreling and dealing and trading. The noise

was unbelievable. It grated on the brain, impossible to rele-
gate to the background.

He lashed *Faith's* painter around a convenient bollard
and straightened up, rubbing his back.

The family they had stayed with a sixday ago, the
Grimeses of Cithamma, had told him to sail as far down
the wharves as possible before tying up. Now he saw why.
This small pier was evidently reserved for flamens' boats:
the gappy line of two-man craft, scarcely larger than din-
ghies, clean of fishing nets and the nacreous scales of the
lobefish they netted in the Inner Archipelago, told a plain
story. But Macul Grimes hadn't mentioned the nerve-rack-
ing ordeal of sailing through the shipping, trying not to get
crushed by boats the size of small islands which plowed
constantly in and out of the calm passages between the
stone piers, looming above *Faith's* sails like sudden penin-
sulas. Eight-foot waves reared on either side of their bows,
furrowing the sea into deep troughs. More than once *Faith*
had heeled right over.

Gete scowled with indignation, and knelt to help Thani
out of the boat. Her cold little paw closed gratefully around
his. She did not let go even when he had hoisted her up
to the lumpy stone wharf. A stab of familiar anxiety pierced
him: sweat glistened on the fur of her brow, even though,
here, hundreds of leagues south from the North Reach, the
claws of winter had already closed tight and the wind was
icy. He had known her a whole season now, early autumn
to early winter, and she had never once looked completely well.

"How're ye feeling?" he shouted. The racket behind
them disguised the fear in his voice.

"A little tired. I'll be all right once I'm beside a warm
hearth. That last hour was grueling, wasn't it?" She smiled.

"I'll say!"

"That family. The Cornwells." Her fingers tightened
around his. "Do they live near?"

"Didn't say. But I want to get ye there soon's possible."
Macul Grimes had given Gete a string of complex directions, which he was afraid to hold in his head much longer
in case they became distorted. "Here, gimme the bag."

This pier, unlike the others, was nearly deserted. A group
of scruffy children loitered around the gates that led to the
town. Gete paid them no mind, supposing them to be the

offspring of wharf-hands, amusing themselves while their parents worked. But as he and Thani approached, they formed an uneven barricade across the gates, and whining voices reached his ears. "Alms . ... please ... Tuppence for meat, Godsister, o' yer mercy ... Heal me ... heal me!" Gete shuddered with distaste. He could not help feeling sorry for them—but gods! "Out of the way. Go home to your mothers!" One boy was naked but for a shirt. "Get some clothes on! Have ye no decency?"

But they paid no attention. As he pulled Thani between them, they actually tugged her robe. "Heal me ..." pleaded a tiny fellow with one arm strapped to his side. His fur was gray with dirt. "Please, Godsister ... please ..."

Accosting a flamen! Why didn't the city governors do something about them? But Thani had stopped dead. *Oh, no,* Gete thought. She tucked the edge of her hood behind her ear—a gesture left over from her days of half-sight— and held up her hand. "What are you doing here?"

An older boy shoved past the little one with the broken arm, his hands cupped as if to catch rain. He smelled terrible—feces and fish. "Alms ... Godsister, leman, o' yer kindness!"

"*I* been here longest," a girl shrilled, catching Gete's coat. "I ain't eat in two days, waitin' here for a flamen t' show. I'm hungry!"

Gete shook her off, barely controlling revulsion. "Godsister! Come on."

But Thani had stretched out her hands, feeling the children's bare shoulders and ragged heads, and they thrust themselves under her touch like cats eager to be stroked, pitiful hope on their faces. Gete swallowed protests. "Have you no homes to go to?" Thani asked, her voice soft. "Where are your parents? The last time I came through K'Fier, I was not met by a reception like this!"

"Mum and Da been arrested ..."

"Ain't no livin' for Da no more, this's me little sister Ura, she's hungry ..."

"Hands took me whole family, Godsister, I got nowhere to go. Nobody'll take us in."

Thani turned to Gete. Her face was stiff with horror. She hissed, "These are *atheists'* children, Regretfulness. What kind of pass has K'Fier come to, that they must beg from *flamens?*"

"I don't know. Maybe the Cornwells can tell us. Let's get out of here." His own feelings were mixed; he could not cope with the scene before him.

But Thani stood still, sweeping the children with her glittering blind gaze. After a moment they fell uncomfortably silent. Quietly, she asked, "Which of you was really here first?"

The silence deepened. Gradually, the children fell away, and the small boy with the broken arm shuffled up to Thani. With a convulsion, he threw his good arm around her legs, butted his head into her stomach, and broke into sobs.

Gete knew what had to come next. He held her shoulders, their foreheads touching, the child's icy little body sandwiched between them. The other children spread into an impromptu circle that stretched across the pier. Thani breathed deeply, gathering her strength, and healed the boy. It took a bare moment. His teeth gleamed, cleansed of filth and decay, as he ripped his splint off, shrieking with delight.

He had time to leap up and down on the hard stone before the other children closed in on Thani again, desperate now, their faces hard and almost cruel, like sharquettes at the sight of blood.

Before Gete finally got her through the gates into K'Fier, Thani had given away all the clothes in their backpack, the backpack itself, the few coins she had on her person, and the remnants of their food supply. Gete shook his head in despair.

Citizens and foreign sailors alike gave them a wide berth of respect as they made their way down the street; men touched their foreheads, women dropped rudimental curtseys. (Kierish folks were apparently, in these days of the new Divinarch, far more pious than they had ever been before.) "Thani, what'm I going to do with you?"

She was trembling with cold, having given away the wrap she wore under her robe. As they sailed south, Gete's smocks and breeches had become inadequate, as had Thani's shift dresses; families they stayed with had supplemented their clothes pack with cozy wool undergarments, and one sheep raiser had even given Gete a shearling coat. But he was shivering nonetheless. Winter lowered yellow and sullen over the peaked slate roofs. "*I'll* have to beg, now, to get clothes for you so you don't die o' cold!"

"They needed it," she said.

"But you couldn't help them all. And there's three more, over there, begging from people who go by. There's a little boy—looks as if he's been beaten. There's a girl, maybe eleven, holding a baby—"

"I won't lie to you, Gete. I have never encountered anything like this. In Delta City, when I was there last, people tried to cheat us, atheistic commoners tried to get Transcendence to change farthings into crowns, men disrespected us in the street without apology. There were paupers on every corner. But never any children! No children without *any* kind of home! The Deltans have that measure of decency, at least!"

Gete prickled. " 'S nothing to do with the Archipelago. We're better than this."

"I didn't mean that." She grasped Gete's hand and pressed it to her cheek. "If K'Fier is like this, what must Delta City have come to? How have people's hearts changed so dreadfully?"

It's because the children are atheists' brats, Gete thought. From the gods who lived on islands near K'Fier, he had heard of the Hands' habit of arresting atheistic families in sudden, swooping raids. Any children who hid, or ran away, would not be worth returning for. And who would help the children of the merchant who had oppressed you every day of his life? You might even get a certain satisfaction out of seeing them starve, as you starved.

But the answer might be more sinister than that. People *were* dropping alms in the children's hands. Nobody ignored them. Some turned their purses upside down to show they had nothing. Was the misery a result of a city's hardheartedness—or its *poverty*?

Since leaving home, he had learned a lot about poverty. Sarberra had always hovered on the brink of starvation, kept from the edge by backbreaking work and rare miracles. He had thought it normal—now he knew they had been desperately poor. Yet it had been share and share alike, and orphaned children were welcome in a dozen homes. Here, things must be so much worse that people were no longer *able* to help each other.

He did not think, however, that he would have liked the

city even in its better days. The messes that the food sellers
along the street were cooking up smelled like tanned
leather. The stalls that sold jewelry, trinkets, and sundries
seemed to be full of trash. Foreign sailors predominated
among the customers of every shop. Unsurprisingly, perhaps, Gete saw that the native Kierish demonstrated every
sign of deference every time one of these great men hove
near, swaggering and blowing smoke from both nostrils;
white-furred (but grubby) Archipelagan women hung in
doorways, pouting and showing their thighs. For some time,
Gete could not figure out why they stood there. When he
saw one of them approached and fondled by a sailor, he
realized with a shock what they were selling.

Shouldn't—*that*—be kept off the main street of the city?
Confined to the night hours?

"A flamen is walking on the other side of the street,
Thani. His leman is a boy of about ten. He has seen us.
Both of them bow to you." Gete swept a bow, and winked
at the little boy, who grinned back across the street, en-
tranced by this sign of fellowship. Thani murmured urgently, as she curtseyed: "Gete. Tell me of his eyes. The
flamen's. Am I imagining it, or is there something—"

"Salt crystals," Gete said, puzzled. The Godsbrother
looked perfectly ordinary: hurrying about his business, with
no time to cross the street and talk.

"No. Something else!" Thani relaxed. "Never mind.
They have gone."

It was quite extraordinary how she could tell where other
holy beings were in relation to herself. After traveling with
her for a season, and seeing her meet various "renegade"
gods and a couple of other flamens, any doubts he might
have entertained about the authenticity of her "sensing"
power had vanished. It was not infallible but it definitely
existed. He had almost forgotten the tales of the gods' private lives (true? or not?) that Desti had hysterically spilled
out to him on Qalma. And even if he could not *quite* dismiss the feeling that he was missing something, that the
gods Thani prayed to and the gods who fished, herded, and
played with Archipelagan children were just not the same—
the paradox did not demand his attention. He had too
much else to think about.

Thani was looking tired, breathing hard. Her salt crystals
started out of her eyes like baby teeth. They were passing

in front of a low stone wall behind which shrubs and waving grasses partially hid a red-trimmed mansion set back twenty feet from the street—an oasis in the succession of shop fronts and town houses. Bronze catlike beasts supported the portico, and squares of red-dyed glass filled the upstairs windows. This was right, this was a landmark. What came next? He glanced around for a side street on the right, with a blue-roofed building on the corner—and spotted it, with a sinking heart, halfway up the hill. It looked a league off.

"Let's sit down for a bit," he said, making a quick decision. Flamens were not supposed to impose their needs on laity who also had to make their living—but surely this was a fair exception. Across the street he had glimpsed a tea bar, doors closed against the cold, steam and smoke puffing from vents over the windows. "You need some soup, and some meat."

"Gods, Gete. I don't think I could swallow flesh."

"Right. Bread then. I'm not letting you get away without eating today."

She straightened her back. Her posture was so perfect when she wanted. She seemed like a lady. "You're more than I deserve, Gete. I believe I am spent for today. If the Cornwells have pressing need of us"—she smiled painfully—"they will have to wait."

"Indeed!" Gete guided her out into the street at a appropriately stately pace, forcing a donkey cart and a convoy of wheeled travoises to stop and allow them past. He pushed open the door of the tea bar. Warmth eclipsed them. Half an hour later, sitting at a window table with several emptied dishes between them, he felt comfortable enough to remark on something that had swum to the top of his mind. "Funny how there don't seem to be any gods here. And we've scarcely visited an island without one since Qalma."

She started. She even gave the appearance of glancing around—a sign she was really perturbed. "Gods, Regretfulness, keep your mouth shut!"

"Nobody's listening," Gete said. *He* was the one who could see. And he saw that the tea bar was crowded with customers, well-to-do for the most part, who once they had acknowledged Thani's presence had become absorbed once more in their own conversations. The quiet hum of voices was pleasant after the racket of the docks and the streets.

The scent of mulling wine pervaded the place. "Lady Tea," as the proprietress called herself, had offered Thani whatever she wanted, but the woman had class enough not to dance attendance on them. "Anyhow," Gete said, "the gods don't exactly keep their existence a secret."

"Not on the islands. But it's high time you learned about cities, Gete. The difference in population between a city and an island community can be small, but feelings run differently on streets than they do on mountain paths. Deception plays a large role. I think"—she paused, and swallowed—"I have talked to some of the renegades, and I think—well, in cities, you know, there are Hands. And the Hands do not want to know their country cousins exist. So in order to keep the peace, our friends oblige them. If there are renegades living here, they are not walking the streets like you and me. Red Picarge, whom you will recall we met on Arlanga, said—very philosophically, I think—that it is a small sacrifice they make, to avoid the wrath of the Divinarch."

Gete had stopped listening. She had *talked* to the renegades? He blinked. He had thought—

He muddied with shame. Gods, it had been patronizing, one could not call it anything else, to think she was only capable of falling to her knees in front of them! He had underestimated her.

"They're all gods, after all," she said defensively, as if she were aware of his surprise. "All part of the divine entity of which the Divinarch is the living symbol. The Hands and the renegades and the others that we do not see, those who live in the salt. Their affairs are all scripted by the Divine Balance, and in this Divine Cycle they are playing them out here among us to give us an insight into their ways. We are very lucky to live under such a philanthropic Divinarch! A chance to understand the inner workings of the divine! It would be a sin to shut our ears to it!"

Gete felt a rush of love. His Thani was not all flamen yet, not all marble. He seized one of her hands and kissed it. She giggled, pushing at his head. "Stop! Leman, I command you!" He paid no attention, licking her wrist, tasting the salt in her fur. Her laughter turned to hiccups.

Then without warning, she went silent. Gete knew it was not a ploy. He dropped her hand.

"Outside the window," she whispered. "Other side of the

street. Describe him to me, leman!" Her face was a mask of longing.

Even before he looked up, Gete knew it was a Hand.

"He's a head taller than the rest of the people," he said slowly. "Their respect for him is great. They circle widely around him. He walks in a bubble of dangerous silence, swaggering like a lord, as if he owns the stones he walks on."

Other poeple in the bar turned to look out the window. A hush fell.

"His face is"—like something badly carved out of clay— "round and simple. His skin is greenish-black. He gazes into nothing. His back is swollen and rounded, but he carries the deformity carelessly. He wears a loose shirt and breeches—it is like a uniform—"

"It *is* their uniform," someone muttered.

"—of scarlet silk. He has a crescent knife in a sheath on his hip." The figure stopped at the gate in the low stone wall, glanced up at the mansion, then, expressionless, let himself in. Gete let out his breath. "He's gone."

Thani sank back in her seat. "Ahhh," she breathed, as if she had just had a sublime experience. Then her face wrinkled. "Gete, do you see any more of them? In the street?"

The patrons of the tea bar were resuming their conversations. Gete found that he was shaking. "No."

"But there must be. I can *feel* them." Her voice rose a little, slightly hysterical; then she remembered herself, and leaned across the table, hands flat on the rough-chiseled stone. "Maybe they're in the next street, then. Behind those houses." She gestured vaguely. "Four or five of them."

Gete did not know what to say. He knew she was always right about these things. "There's something else coming," he said, trying to distract her. "A carriage. Pulling up at the gate of the large house across the street. Oh, now *this* is beauty, Thani!" The four huge, black dogs that drew the carriage frothed and whined, biting at their harness: beautiful restive beasts, as full of energy as sailboats in a high wind. "Red reins on the dogs, and red trim on the carriage—which is a low, boxy bit with a canopied roof—to match the red trim on the house. And there're little cats holding up the corners of the carriage roof, just like the ones holding up the entry of the mansion!"

"Red, did you say?" Thani said in an oddly constrained voice. "Sables?"

"Cats?"

"Sables. Red and sable are the Salmoney colors. The richest atheist family in K'Fier. Is *that* where we are? Why didn't you tell me? I know this place! Last time I was here, with Transcendence, the Salmoneys' gate boy spat at us. I would never have chosen to rest within view of such a place!"

Gete blinked. "Well. I suppose that's them getting out of the carriage now. There's a girl wearing a red dress . . ." Pretty. A translucent-furred elfin face, and masses of black hair. "And a boy with her, holding her arm. Her brother? No, her betrothed I think. He's not wearing half so many frills. He must be from a poorer family."

"There are not many atheist families left in K'Fier with eligible sons, I should imagine."

"And now her parents are getting out. A plump older lady, with her hair in a pile—a fine figure of a man, with thick white fur—"

"Lord and Lady Salmoney. Gods!" Thani exclaimed. "Oh, gods!"

"What have you felt?" He looked around but could not see anything wrong. "What is it?"

Outside the window, the street was completely empty but for the Salmoneys. Ironic, that even in these days of a forced increase in piety, the Kierish should show more respect for their atheistic lords than the Hands of the Divinarch. The Salmoneys appeared to merit an entire street to themselves. It had been some time, traveling through the Middle Archipelago, since Gete had seen a family as affectionate as this appeared to be: their arms were constantly around each other, and when Lord Salmoney laughed, which was frequently, his voice rang out, coming through the window of the tea bar. The liveried servants did not stand stiffly behind the carriage, as Gete would have expected them to, but lounged around with the family. The fiancé picked a pale green flower from a tree overhanging the wall and offered it to the mother of his sweetheart.

The tea bar had gone uncannily silent. Everyone stared at the Salmoneys. Thani looked as if she were staring, too, but he knew from long experience that she was concentrating. "Describe it to me, Gete," she hissed.

And the Hands appeared out of the air, one after another, like a life-size magic trick, and surrounded the Salmoneys and their servants where they stood, shoving the suitor away from the wall, shouldering all eight or nine humans into a tight, frightened pack. Confusion roiled for a moment as the servants were subdued. The Hands' voices belled out and their knives glimmered in the sullen twilight. "In the name of the Divinarch, I arrest you . . ."

"That's it," someone inside the tea bar muttered, and everyone sagged. Wine and tea was slurped.

"Knew they couldn't last much longer."

"They knew it too. Look at them."

A man near Thani and Gete made a righteous show of spitting on the floor. "But they're scared, aren't they? Scared as sheep."

The Hands postured around the little bunch of prisoners. Six of them, all different in face and form, their variations minimized by the loose, bright uniforms they all wore. The greenish-black-skinned one who had gone into the mansion earlier was rolling off what sounded like a list of charges, knife held high over Lord Salmoney's head, like a statue in a battle-ready pose.

No one inside the tea bar was even trying to hear. They were complaining in low, half-guilty voices about the catastrophic blow that the commandeering of the Salmoney estates would deal to K'Fier's merchants. "Bought half the cloth my man weaves, they did!" said one woman.

"Rab the china shop's gonna have to close up a cause a this, you mark me."

"What about the men in their employ? How many of them d'you think the Hands will take?"

Only Thani was silent, trembling. "*Gete,*" she hissed, plucking at him, "*there are more!*"

Gete twisted in his seat, staring at the arrest. What was she talking about? Nothing had changed.

Then the dull, regular harmony of the Hands' litany was altered, shattered, by voices in a new counterpoint. More gods popped out of nowhere, exclaiming with indignation. From their expensive tasseled and piped clothes, and their outrage, Gete could tell they were on the side of the humans.

The argument was fast and loud. It might have been in another language for all he understood—it probably *was*.

He deduced what was happening only by the behavior of
the humans. Outside, the Salmoneys had got behind their
dog carriage. He glimpsed them furtively helping each
other over the wall into the garden. Inside, for the first
time the customers of the tea bar were showing real alarm.
Many hàd filtered out the back exit, and the rest cowered
against the wall, as far as possible from the windows and
the door. Lady Tea crouched behind the counter, only her
eyes showing, froglike, emitting helpless little bleats of protest. Belatedly, Gete grabbed Thani and hustled her away
with the rest. His voice flowed along smoothly, almost without his help, describing the scene. Thani's brow furrowed
as she concentrated on his every word. He was her only
link, her lifeline.

All the Salmoneys, men, women, and servants, had vanished into the greenery. None of their captors seemed to
have noticed. In ones and twos, more renegade gods stumbled out of the house, clustering behind their leader. There
was something dangerous in the air, an uncontrolled aspect
to the confrontation, a volatility. "*Gods,*" a man next to
Gete breathed. "They're legless, every man jack of them."

That was it. The man chewed his fingers, muttering, "I
told Ruth he ought not to supply their smokewort for free.
Gods or no gods, it's nothing but a temptation to excess.
Now look what's happening. I told him. I *told*—"

"Smokewort?" Thani barked.

The man jumped like a startled rabbit. "Local specialty,
Godsister! The gods can hold their wort better than any
man alive, but even they have limits, may they forgive me
for my impertinence." He touched his forehead and added
piously, "Divinarch keep them! And forgive my misguided brother!"

"The gods are their own masters, Godsman," Thani said.
"Anyone flatters himself who thinks he can corrupt them."
She sounded both angry and afraid. The glass in the windows shook as the blue-skinned god shouted with unintelligible passion at the greenish-black-skinned hunchback.
When the Hand did not react, the blue-skinned god shoved
him in the chest and turned away, spurning the dispute—
and behind him, the hunchback slid slowly into his fellows'
arms, white blood spreading down his scarlet shirt. The
renegade grinned at his fellows, exposing his back to the
Hands, quite deliberately Gete thought, in a show of con-

tempt. A wet stiletto gleamed between his fingers. He
twirled it, showing it off.

A girl's scream spiraled from the undergrowth, a delayed
reaction to the stabbing. As if in response, the renegade
raised his eyebrows and opened his mouth. Gracefully, he
knelt, dropping his face to the cobblestones. A tooth-tipped
crescent knife had filleted him like a fish, laying him open
from shoulder to sternum. The dogs whined, tossing their
heads.

Gete did not see much of what happened after that. His
eyes refused to show him gods fighting and killing each
other, any more than his tongue would describe the carnage. All he could tell Thani, rather uselessly, was that
although gods on both sides were falling at a horrible rate,
the number of combatants seemed to be growing. Soon he
saw why. The Salmoneys had emerged from hiding and
seized knives from the dead to defend their allies, the renegades. People poured out of the shops and houses on both
sides of the stret, turning the combat into a free-for-all,
crowding to get near the Hands and work out old
grievances.

The Hands were fatally outnumbered. Yet as far as Gete
could see, only one of them lost courage and *teth"d.* The
rest fought, and died. In a very short time, the remaining
renegades stood alone in the street, dripping, their faces
twitching with the first twinges of sobriety.

The humans, nobles and commoners alike, were falling
away from the edges of the melee, disappearing into doorways and side streets. All the bodies, too, were gone, carried off by relatives or worshippers. The lack of set dressing
gave the street a dreamlike feel, as if the massacre had not
really happened. The dogs and dog carriage had disappeared too. Kierish were as much opportunists as anyone.

A cold wind blew into the tea bar. The doors swung
creaking on their hinges. Except for Lady Tea, gibbering
behind her pastries, Gete and Thani were alone: sequestered from the scene, just as they were sequestered from
all the lives they passed through. Gete did not feel they
were in any danger. The renegades, four of them now,
stood empty-handed, looking stunned.

"Forgive them for their sins," Thani said at last. Her
voice wavered. "Gods—gods?" She made a noise like
laughter. "*Someone* forgive them for what they have done

here! I see ... I see ..." She gulped. "They have started more than they have ended. Death ... more death ... and disillusionment—"

"Kierish are going to come looking for you in a minute," Gete said. It seemed to bring her back down to earth. "A good many of them were wounded."

"Well, they will have to look elsewhere." Her salt crystals seemed to glow for a minute, then she sagged against him. Her temples pulsed under the fur. "This is all I can do. I hope they will forgive me."

Outside, thunder growled, and an icy winter rain teemed out of the sky, hissing on the cobbles, slicking down the gods' hair. The blood was soon gone from the street, the gutter cloudy only with dirt as it chuckled down toward the wharves.

She would not allow him to unravel the knots her rain-miracle had embedded in her hair. Late at night, she sat naked on the window seat of the room the Cornwells had given them, alternately picking at her hair and sinking into immobility. Gete could see her attempts were doomed. Her hair had grown longer. He would have to cut some of the tangles off, if she would only let him.

The brazier at the foot of the bed burned like a miniature furnace. A crucible of scented water was attached to the top of its frame: the water steamed constantly, just off the boil. Condensation ran down the slick folds of the curtains and the bed canopies. Outside, the stairs creaked, and whispering voices passed the door in the blackness. The Cornwells were going to bed. "I can't manage," Thani said at last, in a high, strangled voice. "Come here, leman. I need you." Then she jerked her legs up and hid her face in her knees and began to sob.

Looking at her starved, bruised body, with its pale fur sticking up in whorls, Gete felt impatient. Who did she think she was, to command him?

She's your flamen, you son of a turtle!

But his loyalty was sorely strained. The Kierish who'd been involved in the massacre had sidled up to ask for her help, both men and gods, asking her to heal them—and he had had to refuse for her, over and over. Later, her silence had given way to rudeness directed at the bewildered Cornwells. More than once, during the lavish dinner the family had laid on for their guests, Gete had wanted to apologize for her—or crawl under the table himself. Had she been doing it deliberately, out of evenhandedness? Or just out of blind self-absorption?

He'd never known her so sharp-tongued and edgy. What could be wrong?

Then, suddenly, he *did* know.

Horror froze him. He shivered in the hot room.

You've lost faith, haven't you, Thani? You've lost that deep-down faith you never questioned before, not even when Transcendence died. I felt it coming when you told me you had questioned Red Picarge! I should have understood earlier! Ever since we saw the gods killing each other, you've been wandering on a strange island populated by strange beasts. No wonder you made defensive noises when we tried to approach you.

"Gods!" He darted to her, hugging her, kissing her. What could he do? How could he help her now? "I shouldn't have let you sit through dinner! I should have made excuses! I should have—"

"Gete," she said in a choked voice, "oh, Gete. Help me. Convince me that . . ." Her words were lost in tears. But he heard a difference. The rage was gone from her voice. All that was left was a terrible sadness. The urge to protect her swelled in him, like a lump in the throat all over his body, and he carried her to the bed.

After the first few minutes, she responded with violent passion. It was what she needed.

It felt good to be naked in the hot, damp room. They lay side by side on top of the coverlet. She tucked her head into the hollow between his arm and shoulder. "How are you feeling?" Gete whispered. "Are you more . . . comfortable now?"

She kissed his underarm. "You always make me feel better. You know that."

So another piece of her sight was gone.

"What about the Salmoneys? What d'you think'll become of them?"

"Oh, we need not trouble over that," she said comfortably. "A larger, better destined delegation of Hands will be dispatched to take care of them. The Divinarch will not let them get away with any more insubordination such as we witnessed today." She wriggled against his side. "They are unworthy of our attention."

"Do you remember what *really* happened?" Gete said, rather recklessly. "How the Hands arrested them without provocation, and how they died? Or is there a process in your mind that alters your memories to fit in with your idea of proper, pious behavior?"

For a moment she went quite still. Then she shook herself and said, "Do stop. I'm tired. And we have to get up early tomorrow to find a ship to Delta City."

He said no more. But he felt a sense of victory. He would humor her. The matter had yet to be resolved; perhaps Delta City held the answers. Perhaps there, he would find a god willing to answer the questions he had not asked since he last saw Desti. (Qalma seemed very far off now. Soon it would be even farther.) Delta City. He grimaced with distaste. K'Fier had sickened him. How much more deprived of joy must the world's greatest city be? How much uglier? How much filthier?

And to think he had once rejoiced—so naively—at the thought of going there!

He concentrated on stillness. Don't move a muscle. Don't disturb her.

Gradually, dizzily, he melted into the featherbed, spinning slowly around and around. Thani's body nestled close to his. She was asleep. The condensation coated the insides of his lungs.

Betrayal

Arity took a salt grape from the miniature tree on the tray beside him and crossed one ankle over his knee, trying to get comfortable. He hated these jewel-inlaid chairs. The walls of the royal anteroom were lined with ghosts—as if an invisible audience were witnessing every word they spoke. The ghosts of *auchresh*, Pati's previous lovers. Dreadfully morbid.

Pati himself was not sitting on gold and tourmalines. He curled in his special leather armchair, legs tucked under

him, like a gangly child. His fingers were steepled before
his nose and his different-colored eyes shone. "So where
did Hope take you? All Mosquito Ruby told me was that
she appeared wearing a dress from the depraved times and
commanded you to come." His tone became a mixture of
accusation and hurt—"And you went with her voluntarily."

"I went with her because she used to be a friend of
ours," Arity said. "But apart from that—" He felt delighted
that Pati had worried so much about his whereabouts that
he had covered him with kisses instead of demanding to
hear his story right away. When his return was announced,
the Divinarch had been in an unscheduled Ellipse meeting,
but he had dismissed the Hands and flamens who constituted the other twenty twenty-firsts of the Ellipse and
swooped on Arity, who was loitering with his heart in his
mouth in the royal suite.

"She *teth*"d me to Temeriton." Arity plucked another
grape and spit the seeds into his palm. They were exactly
the same color as the razor-smooth circles in the hollows
of his body that would grow into thorns if he let them. He
deposited them in the corner of the tray. "We climbed to
the top of a six-story town house. Hope promised me I
would thank her for having brought me."

"I confess I'm lost. She didn't steal you just to make me
tear my hair out. So why?"

"Well, you'll never guess who I met." Never mind the
formalities. Arity had no patience for them. His heart was
pounding. "An old enemy of ours."

Pati's smile went as hard and cold as frozen fish. Slowly,
his fingers slid together until his hands were locked into
one oversized fist. To himself, he murmured, "I should have
known she wouldn't die so easily. I do not think she has
ever given up a fight in her life."

Arity gaped, deprived of his revelation. Pati obviously
knew who they were talking about. But why should he have
guesed so readily!

"She's not fighting anymore!" Arity said. "She's blind.
Your poison blinded her. She'd be better off dead. I just
thought you might find it amusing to hear what she has
come to."

The fingers worked. "I find it highly disturbing. I hope
you memorized the location of the house. We shall have to
surround it. If she's blind, she'll smell any *teth*"*ing,* so we'll

approach on foot. I should think twenty Hands will be enough." He paused. "Hope knew where she was. They're probably all in it together. How far can the rot extend? Humi is blind ... She drank every drop that was in the glass. Either she has the constitution of a sharque, or it was a miracle. Before she dies, I hope I can extract the name of the Godsbrother or Godsister who did it from her. I will toast them over a furnace. But in any case, it means Hope is the ringleader. I shouldn't have let that cursed *iu* have the run of the city! Dammit!" Pati pounded the arm of the chair—a wildly uncharacteristic gesture that showed Arity just how shaken he was. His wineglass fell off and rolled onto the floor, bleeding maroon into the runnels between the floor slabs. "How am I going to pin them down?" He looked at Arity again. "Tonight the Hands gave me reports of unrest in several foreign cities. I had thought I would concentrate my forces abroad. I've ordered a slew of arrests. Now I find I must turn my attention closer to home!"

Arity did not answer. Pati stopped and peered at him more closely. Then he gave a rather crooked smile. "You see what an impossible task mine is. One day, you will thank me that I groomed you for the Throne."

"When I was younger, I was prepared to take the Throne, even if it wasn't a position I particularly relished," Arity said. "Now things have changed. I've changed." The inevitable consequences of his betraying her—he must have known this would happen—He barked, "Don't kill her!" and his voice sounded to him not desperate but menacing.

Pati peered at him, his eyes hooded and vaguely red. "Are you trying to blackmail me?"

And once Pati had said it, Arity knew that was exactly what had been in the back of his mind. The contorted, terrible faces of the ghosts spun around him like a circle of silently jeering onlookers. They goaded him into speech. "I will not be Heir."

Pati stared at him. "You're not ... You're in it, too. With her. Did you go to see her because—Was it planned? What trickery is this?"

"Power! That was not, not, *not* what I meant! I wouldn't have anything to do with their sordid little plot if they paid me!"

But Pati had got hold of something now. His beaked face advanced toward Arity, swimming in the dimly candlelit air the way it had rippled in the night on top of the Temeriton town house. "You love her. That's it, isn't it. You'd do things for love that you wouldn't do for status. You weakling."

Arity shrank into his chair. A moment ago he had been ready to stand up to Pati even at the cost of bearing his anger. Now, fear hollowed him out like a cold wind in his belly. His limbs went to quicksalt. Pati's wings buzzed, making rainbows out of the candle flames.

"You've always loved her. You little liar."

"Have sense, Pati! Would I have betrayed her to you if I still cared for her?"

"I don't know what your plan was. But there are certain things I can read as clearly as the look on your face!"

"I don't love her. I have no feelings whatsoever toward her. She's as redundant to me as she is to you."

But the wind blew keen and hollow in him, smelling of salt. He was in the wrong, he was lying, and Pati knew it.

And Pati was all he had now. Humi had thrust him away. *He's Pati's plaything. I have nothing to say to him.* And *Arity and I understand that the past is the past* ... The past was the past! The present was Pati! For the same reason he had clung to Pati ever since Rimmear, he had to cling to him now.

"I *love* you." He seized Pati's hands off the armrests of his chair, kissing them. "You're all there is for me!" If he went on in this vein a little longer, ecstasy would come. Even now he could feel himself starting to shake. A branch of the miniature grape tree showed in sharp silhouette on one of the haloed candle flames. "I *love* you—"

"Liar." Pati wrenched his hands away, one thumbnail scoring Arity's upper lip. Arity tasted blood.

Patience. His whole body quivered. "She means nothing to me. I'll prove it. I'll show you the house tonight. We'll *teth*" to the roof where I talked to her, and you'll identify the street, and we'll go back in the morning with troops."

Knuckles rattled on the door, and a Hand burst in without waiting to be asked. His step faltered when he saw the overturned wineglass and the blood on Arity's face, but then he blurted, "Lord Divinarch! In K'Fier! Five Hands killed!"

The atmosphere ebbed out of the antechamber like water flowing out of a lock. Arity took a breath.

"Is that anything unprecedented, Vori? Calm down." Arity never ceased to be astonished by Pati's theatrical ability. Pati's face smoothened. His voice was flowing olive oil. "We won't learn who did it. There are never any witnesses. The humans will say the Hands were struck by lightning."

"But lord Divinarch, this time it's different! One of them fled when he saw there was no hope. He *teth*'d back here. *They* did it—the r-r—" The Hand's voice failed him, and he gulped. "The renegades."

In the ensuing pause Arity heard the sea growl, far below, as if it could not abide all the fights and acrimonious accusations it was forced to witness.

Even before Pati's rise to the Throne, Arity had known it would come to this sometime. With the *auchresh* race polarizing into *wrchrethrim* and *salthirre,* it had had to come to this. *Auchresh* killing *auchresh.* Cause for instant execution in any Heaven.

Pati said, "I grant them anonymity and they kill my Hands! Are they trying to force me to respond to their subversive activities? How? They are the *serbalim's* responsibility, not mine. Where is—" He broke off. Too softly for Vori to hear, he whispered, "Where is my liaison with the *serbalim?* Plotting against me." Arity winced. Pati raised his voice. "Where is the *kere* who returned?"

"He—he's wounded. Delirious." Vori hopped up and down with urgency. "Lord Divinarch, with due respect, the Hands ask me to convey a request to you! They want permission to kill the *haugthules!*"

"Fire-bellied young *mainrauim.* Deny them it. Get me Sepia. Get me Glass Mountain. Get Silver Moon. Get Val." Arity cringed. These particular *keres,* the ex-*kervayim,* made him feel weak and ashamed. Their calm authoritarianism masked elitism, and a fiery devotion to Pati. The other Hands were far more tolerant of Arity's status as Pati's lover. *But what am I now? He won't just let it drop.* The invasion of outside concerns seemed annoying, superficial, like a wrong note in a song. *I've never seen him this angry.*

The *kervayim teth*'d into the anteroom, knocking over the side table that held the miniature grape tree. A tumble of silk-clad limbs seemed to bulge out of the room. None of them took seats.

"I beg you, Pati, let us punish them!"

"We've pretended we don't know what's going on in the Archipelago long enough. And it's not just the Archipelago, either," Val said. "Although these K'Fierish fops are

the worst of the bunch. If they weren't ready for a nasty
surprise a year ago, they really *are* stupid."

"In my view," Glass Mountain rumbled, "it would be as
well to crush them before this happens again."

Pati gazed at them in what could have been surprise. "So
it is to be a diplomatic embassy, my councillors," he said
ironically, and one side of his mouth curled. "I approve."

"Their very existence thumbs its nose at your divinity."
Silver Moon watched Pati's face avidly for signs of approval. "And everywhere they go, they spread atheism of
a far more subversive stamp than Antiprophet's. They are
a threat to your godhead."

"Yes." Pati said. "I am with you there."

"They must die!"

"We will treat them like any other blasphemers!"

"We'll crush them," Val said, shaking back his sleeve, "like
this," and he slowly closed his fist. There was laughter.

"Have any of you thought about what you're doing?"
Arity said, standing. *"Auchresh* killing *auchresh.* There's no
precedent for it. And do you know why?" They were all
staring at him. "Because it's *suicide* for our race. Suicide!
We can't *afford* to kill each other, when the humans are
doing it for us every day!"

"Well, well," Val said. "Loverboy has turned military
authority."

The buzz of talk continued as if nothing had been said.
Could they let that *pass?*

*I was Heir! I was leagues above all of you! Have I sunk
so low in your esteem that you insult me as you please?*

A voice cut through the noise. Arity's heart leaped, but
it was only Coiled Rainbow. "As for a precedent, Arity,"
he said pityingly, "there is a very clear one. *They* started
the killing, late this afternoon."

"Yes," Val said. "They started it. Are you disposed to
argue with the facts?"

Pati was talking to Glass Mountain. He did not look at Arity.

The room was loud with plans. A hundred Hands were
to go. No, a dozen. No, two hundred. Fists. New recruits.
The councillors would go themselves. No, they shouldn't.
The Divinarch ought not, with all respects, to go either.

"I shall go," Pati said. "But none of you will. Together,
you are as valuable as I am. In the event of my death, you
are needed here."

All Arity heard was that the *ex-kervayim* were not going to go, and Pati was. Perhaps he could somehow prove himself to Pati! He raised his voice. "Count me in. I'll go."

Pati swung around. His gaze was like a crack of sky glimpsed from the bottom of a shaft: too bright to bear.

"You. I'd forgotten you were there."

Oh, no, you hadn't. Arity's breath came slowly, painfully, as if the air were sand. He felt himself bending at the knees.

"Sepia." Pati beckoned with one finger, still staring at Arity. "This . . . traitor." Pati pointed. Arity didn't understand. He felt as though he were drowning. "Take him to Westpoint. Immediately, if you please. I do not want him to escape. I do not want him here when I return from crushing the upstarts."

For one moment their reaction deafened Arity. He nearly blacked out. Then Pati turned furiously on them.

And *lesh kervayim,* that cabal of smoke-stained *wrchrethrim* who had matched their steps with the Striver's on the long march from the salt, taken responsibility for gathering his army of Hands, and now counted themselves privileged to look down their noses at each other: *khath* and *morothe* addicts, as possessive of their gem-encrusted suites in the Palace as they had once been of their lovers: these golden *mainrauim* whom long exposure to each other's company had rendered as alike as deformed fledglings in a lair fell silent at the sight of their Divinarch's face.

Sepia took hold of Arity's arm.

Then he understood.

Good-bye to the Lakestones

Humi threw her belongings blindly into a bag made of the Hangman's robe. She wrapped her ghosts in her clothes and packed the chinks with the few ornaments and jewels Ziniquel and Ensi had brought her, things from her old life. "Help me with this," she said to the Hangman, and together they dragged the dray dog ghost out from under the bed and stood it on its feet. It filled most of the floor space.

Humi heard the Hangman sucking her fingers to warm them up. "Could *never* of weighed that much when it was alive. My hands're frostbitten! There must be seven ghosts in that bag! You gonna be able to carry it?"

"Of course," Humi whispered, and hefted the knotted robe over her shoulder. She heard the fabric straining and put it down quickly. It was even odds whether her shoulder or the robe would have broken first.

In the end she only took one ghost. The seagull, the last one she had completed. The rest they arranged on the bed, mice and rats and cats and birds all perched on top of each other. "Are they painted?" the Hangman said as they stood back. "No? *Really?* I am something of a connoisseur, milady, but I have not seen this technique before. I am absorbed."

Humi did not intend to show the Hangman how little impact her flattery made. She said, "I'm leaving them for the Lakestones, in partial payment of the debt I owe them. But when I am in a position to make more"—she smiled; the Hangman had moved out into the children's bedroom and Humi lowered her voice so as not to wake Meri and Ensi—"I shall craft you one of my best."

"Ulp," the Hangman said. A second later, Humi felt another presence. From the warmth, and the silence with which he had approached, she knew it was Hem.

"You are leaving us," he stated.

"Hem"—she moved toward him—"I was going to wake you." But she had judged the distance wrong, and she fetched up without warning against his broad warm chest. His heartbeat muffled through his flannel nightshirt. It took a huge effort not to lay her cheek on his chest. She stepped away. "You must eradicate every sign that I was here. The Divinarch will search the house tomorrow. If I were you I'd get the children out on some pretext, just to be quite safe. But if there's nothing to implicate you, you won't need to worry." *Beyond Ari's word.* She swallowed. "I've left some ghosts for you."

"Ghosts?" He seized her shoulders. "Humi, what have you been up to? I thought that you—"

"Hide them under that stack of junk in the cellar. I doubt even the Hands will look there. Then, in a month or so, you can sell them. You ought to get more than enough to cover the costs of anything the Hands may break in their search." The things were probably good enough for that, anyhow.

"One moment, Humi. Why are you leaving? Do you realize what we would have thought if we had woken and found you gone?"

"I told you. I was going to wake you!" For a minute, tears threatened as it all weighed down on her. Arity alive. Arity her enemy. It was all gone, their bond, the one thing in her life that she had thought change could not take from her. Now she no longer had even her memories. He had contaminated them. "I'm sorry," she said, her voice breaking.

"*Gods,*" the Hangman muttered in disgust.

Humi flung her head back. What was she thinking? Nothing had been taken from her but a burden. She was free.

"To cut a long story short," she said, "one of the Hands has found out where I am. He used to be a friend of mine and he tried to convince me that he would not betray me—but he has forgotten how well I know him. I could hear in his voice that he was lying. I played along so that he would not suspect I knew, hoping to earn more time to get away. But I don't know how well I succeeded. They may be here any minute."

Hem was silent for a minute. When he spoke, he asked only: "How did . . . this Hand . . . find out where you were?"

"It was Hope's idea." Humi winced as she remembered the Maiden's tears of anger. It was the first time she had ever heard Hope cry. For *her* sake, she wished the encounter had been a success. "She was here too. I hope she does not suffer on my account."

"I cannot think of anything more foolhardy she could have done," the Hangman said waspishly. "Everyone knows Ar—"

Humi interrupted her before Hem could hear the name. "That is all, I think. The ghosts are there. Give my love to Leasa and the children." Their even breathing came from the beds behind her. It was astonishing how soundly children could sleep. Turning, she made her way to the heads of the beds and dropped light kisses on their hair. "Don't forget to take down the partition," she reminded Hem. She thought he understood without her telling him, that if she ever returned, it would not be in her old capacity as child

minder and occasional seamstress. "You don't want even
the suggestion that someone lived here."

"Your *room*," Hem said with unexpected feeling. "Ha.
Closet. Humi, I have leased another room from the Brundels upstairs. One that receives the morning sun. We were
going to give it to you for midwinter."

"Oh, Hem." *I'll kill myself if the Hands arrest you,* she
thought.

"*Really,* milady!" the Hangman called. She was walking
downstairs with deliberate emphasis on each step. "I think
we should *leave* before the Hands arrest *us!*"

"I'll put the ghosts in the shop," Hem said. "Where better to hide them? And tomorrow morning, I'll send Meri
to Tellury Crescent to warn Ziniquel that they must say
they made them, if the Hands make inquiries. Or are *you*
going to Tellury Crescent?" His voice was hesitant. She
could tell he did not want to know anything dangerous.

"No." Her eyes stung. "I'm not." And she fled downstairs. As she pushed through the jingling door of the shop,
her load bumped against her back. The seagull's cold came
through its wrappings.

Nothing assailed Humi and the Hangman before they
reached Shimorning, except a drizzle. As they made their
way through the palace district, the damp stuck their
clothes to their fur. Humi did not possess a cloak, or indeed
anything heavier than the dress she wore. She had never
needed one. This was the first time she had been off
Lockreed Concourse in three years.

Yet despite the rain and the silence, and the Hangman's
sharp nails digging into her palm, dragging her along to the
place she had promised was safer than anywhere else on
the island but which she would not describe, she was not
afraid.

She felt alive. Alive.

She had forgotten how it felt.

The Hangman did her the favor of telling her when they
came to the Folly, before she could become nervous at
their deviation from the routes she remembered. "Your
lady god friend tore down all five councillors' mansions to
build her Folly. You have not seen it."

"No," Humi said. "Describe it to me."

"You are not a flamen, milady . . ."

"But you are at my command," Humi said mildly. "By the terms of the proposal you put to me earlier this evening, you are bound to obey me. Treachery will be punished."

She was gambling. The Hangman had *real* power over her.

"And are we bound by those terms, milady?"

"*You* are."

The Hangman did not answer. Had Humi won? Could the old Divinarch glamour still be working?

Earlier, she had been unnerved at the prospect of throwing in her lot with the Hangman and her scrofulous crowd. But now she could not see why she had hesitated. If the Hangman was not to be trusted—and if Humi could still control her—she would make all the better an ally. The temperamental hound often wins the race.

She knew what the Folly looked like, though Evita had not told her. She saw it floating above her, rising shadowy from the trees, though by now they had surely left it behind. Had Hope ever described it to her? It shimmered in her mind, half concept and half image, like a memory of Wind Gully Heaven. *Her* Folly. The image in her mind was probably very different from the building around whose park they scuttled on damp streets. But that did not matter. For the first time in months, she had imagined something new in terms of a visual image.

It fascinated her, both as a symbol and a solecism, wrenched from the salt to Delta City.

The noise of Shimorning stretched its tentacles out and gathered them in.

The blackness flickered with stars of gray. Humi tripped over her feet as they threaded a complex path along the gutter. Her wet clothes slapped against drunk pedestrians. Everyone seemed to know the Hangman, and hailed her loudly. She replied in a mumble, almost a grunt, as if she feared being caught out in an indiscretion. But no one else was so circumspect. It seemed as if the night freed tongues ordinarily guarded for fear of the Hands. And that made no sense, for the gods' traditional hunting time was the night. The world was upside-down.

People laughed freely here in a way they did not in Temeriton, Delta City's pulsing vein of shame. From the tones of the voices and the smells as Humi brushed past each person, she could tell how he or she had spent his night. She wanted to be out, too, drinking, making love, *doing*. How had she *lived*? She almost dragged at the Hangman's shirt and told her to stop, go into a tavern, accost one of the thousand Shimorningers she seemed to know and ask which dive was buzzing ... but then Evita plunged down a side street, came to an abrupt halt, and said, "Here we are, milady." She scratched on a plank door with her fingernails.

"Our biggest problem, milady," Gold Dagger said, " 's that the tyrant knows you're alive. If it is as you say. 'Ow much time does that give us? Not much, I betcha. Not enough to get the troops together. We got to find some way to throw 'im off the scent."

"No one saw us coming here," the Hangman said. "I can guarantee that." Even without seeing their expressions, Humi could feel the tension between the crime lords. The Hangman was tense, like a cat walking on her neighbor's territory; Gold Dagger sounded even more jovial than usual. To distract them from each other, Humi made a production out of sipping her brandy. "*Exactly* how much Pati knows is unclear." They had put her in the best chair, but to them the best was the oldest: it was saggy, the jewels on the armrests scratched, and it smelled of mold.

"Everything depends on how strong a hold he has over Arity." Instinctively, she gritted her teeth, but the pain didn't come. She was free of the burden of loving him.

"You mean 'e might not 'ave ratted after all?" Gold Dagger said skeptically.

"Oh, no. I am quite convinced he did. What I mean is that he may not have thought to tell Pati about my incipient alliance with Evita. In which case, Pati will not scent danger beyond my survival, and provided that I can stay out of sight, we have as much time as we need."

"Well"—Gold Dagger cleared his throat skeptically—"I 'ave less faith in the Heir than you, milady. Betcha he told him everything 'e knew. Question is, 'ow much did 'e *hear*?"

"If I remember correctly, when he and Hope arrived, I was refusing Evita's offer." Better to forget that last, confused minute on the edge of the roof. That minute, anyhow, might have been what saved her from the grayish oblivion of the hollowness.

"Did they show themselves right off? Or was they there before?" Gold Dagger challenged the Hangman.

There was a short silence. Finally the Hangman said, "I have no idea."

"You're supposed to be—" Gold Dagger said, starting to froth with indignation, and stopped. A moment passed. Humi wished she could see their faces. Then Gold Dagger cleared his throat. She heard him removing his boots from the table with a precipitous clatter. "You *need* me, Hangman! Without me, you're nothin' but an assassin. It's through *me* you 'ave this chance to hit it big. It's *me* who owns half the men in this city. Not you, Evita. If I'd gone straight, I could of been an atheist councillor. As it is, I have more power than any other mortal in this city."

Humi felt her blood heating. Without hesitating, for that would have been fatal, she reached for their hands. Gold's was patchy-furred, beringed, meaty; the Hangman's was a furry skeleton. Humi said, "Gold, I think you are in danger of forgetting that *you* need *me*. Without me, you and Evita will both sit quarreling underground until Pati has crushed the city, and you, to death."

Neither of them moved for a minute. Gold was the first to withdraw his hand. "Put us in our places properly, eh, Divinarch?" he said jovially.

The Hangman's fingers jerked, like half-dead things. Humi held on, not tightly, but firmly, so as not to let Gold Dagger see how the Hangman had reacted. *She* was the one who must win this contest. It was the first.

Through her teeth, the Hangman said, "You force me to recognize Gold's strength, Humi. There is no need to force me to recognize your leadership. It is not in question. Much joy I wish you of it."

"Never thought I'd hear it from you, Evvie," Gold Dagger said pleasedly. "After all these years."

Humi knew she could not push the Hangman any farther. Quickly, she took her hands off the table and folded them in her lap. "Now that we have *that* out of the way, let's get down to business. I do not think any of us disagree that what we must create is a war."

"I got the facilities for it," Gold Dagger said.

The air in the cave was ventilated only by the tiny fan in the roof, which drew air from fifty feet above. A child knelt by the wall, working its crank. The fruity scent of the

Shimorning gutters wafted in with the air. The caves that constituted the Rats' Den, Gold Dagger had told Humi, immodest with pride, spread for a league under the streets and could be entered through a dozen different safe houses in Shimorning, Marshtown, and Christon. They housed an army of criminals, all nominally loyal to Gold, always in flux, about whom Humi had known nothing in all her time as Ellipse councillor and Divinarch. If she had not been reasonably sure of Gold and the Hangman at this point, she would have been distinctly worried about whatever else they must be concealing.

Evita was a jealous woman, and dangerous. But the understanding between the underworld and the atheists, the agreement that when the conspiracy seized the throne from the Divinarch, it would be the crime lords who provided the necessary muscle and who in return would receive pardons and titles from the new regime, dated back to the days of Erene, Goquisite, and Belstem, and Humi intended to honor it. All that had kept her from seeking Gold Dagger and the Hangman out and convincing them to fulfill their side of the bargain before was fear. They had real power: all they lacked was a guiding hand. In Temeriton (it always seemed years ago) their visits had filled her with repugnance and a dread of illness—physical and otherwise. Now she relished the stink of gutters, and the smell of hot steel. Somebody was working at a forge. The rock walls and plush door curtain of the chamber reduced the sound of hammering to a tinkle, as of water, but Humi was privileged with the blind woman's comprehension of sounds that are just background noise to the sighted. She had that advantage over Gold Dagger and the Hangman, slender though it might be.

As they debated the technicalities of various weapons, and estimated the numbers of troops each crime lord could rely on, the cave took on the feel of a council room, tense and serious.

Someone thumped a steel-butted spear on the rock outside the door. It was so sharp a sound even the fan child squeaked.

"Who the fuck is it?" Gold Dagger thundered in annoyance.

"Get out of my way, gutterspawn," Humi heard, and the curtain swished aside.

She knew that voice. She could not keep from smiling as she shoved her chair back and hurried to the entrance. "Mory!"

Her *imrchu* whom she had thought gone forever. Mory's familiar grip on Humi's wrists sent dizzying thrills of gladness through her. With difficulty, she kept from casting herself into Mory's arms. "Who else is here?"

"I am," Tris said, in a deeper, more confident voice than Humi remembered from the days when the Calvarese boy had been the youngest Ellipse councillor. She exclaimed with delight. He embraced her, kissed her on both cheeks. He smelled of fish scales—a scent belonging to dawn, when the night fishermen returned to Marshtown's jetties with their catch tanks full—and he was taller and better muscled than he had been three years ago.

Mory Carmine and Trisizim Sepal; the least politically active of the ghostiers. Humi had always suspected that the only reason they had been present in Godsbrother Puritanism's parlor when Goquisite and Belstem forced her to resign her throne was because the rest of the ghostiers had all agreed to join the denunciation. Only because Mory and Tris were committed to tradition, determined that the ghostiers should present a unified front to the world, had they been there when Pati and his rabid band of *auchresh* burst in and massacred atheists and flamens alike.

She had always assumed that after that, Mory and Tris had gone underground, out of communication. Ziniquel and Emni had never hinted anything to the contrary.

"What're you doing here?" Gold Dagger said possessively to Mory from behind Humi. She could feel distrust radiating off him. But he did not sound surprised to see Mory and Tris. There was so much Humi did not know!

"And who is *this* you have brought?" the Hangman hissed, apparently in reference to someone else who had come in. "One of your apostate flamen friends, who think that they walk in the light and me and mine walk in the gutter? We are discussing war here, Godsie Carmine! What good will your friends' miracles do when Pati's flamens are prepared to kill and maim for *their* cause?"

It had not been Humi's impression that the apostates were above using their divine powers to kill, but she held her tongue.

"We would not insult our flamen friends by *asking* them to come here with us," Mory said in her prickliest manner.

"The Godsbrother *volunteered* to accompany us because he is aware, as you do not seem to be, that we must put aside our personal biases if we are to have any chance against the tyrant." Mory was clearly on her mettle, here in enemy territory. She gave Humi's hand a quick squeeze as she joined it with a stranger's. "Humi, this is Godsbrother Phantasm and his leman Avari, here."

"I am, as Mory has said, the delegate from the apostate brotherhood," the Godsbrother said in a pleasant voice with a refined Deltan accent. "I come to offer the services of all Marshtown apostates to the true Divinarch. We support her bid for the Throne, and conjoin with her in secrecy."

Gold Dagger whistled, and laughed softly. "News travels fast!"

But Humi had no ears for him. Gold was more or less a known quantity; he could wait. In her best diplomatic manner she greeted Godsbrother Phantasm, and exerting all the charm she had at her disposal she thanked him and accepted his offer.

Later, when the council finally broke up, she left the chamber arm in arm with Mory and Tris. Both at once, they offered her bits and pieces of information about their life since the coup. Fleeing, hiding, pondering, and always, always making ghosts. Juniper and sand and metal tanged in Humi's nostrils: a whiff of the desert. It made no sense, since according to Mory and Tris, they had not been back to Calvary, but she knew it. It was the stink of fanaticism. It was quite clear Mory would have liked to be a flamen. Tris had been considering apostate lemanhood before he grew too old. Nowadays, both of them devoted their days to their art, turning out dark propaganda for their new faith, the worship of no gods.

In the Sea Garden

Morning sunlight soaked into the floor of Hope's dressing room in the Folly. The glass wall had been swung open and the tall herbs on the balcony glowed green. The scent of thyme breezed into the dressing room, carried by the breeze that caressed the roofs of the city. Far off, Hope could hear the first bells of Dividay tinkling. It was one of those rare, perfect winter days like a diamond.

With quick, frustrated movements, she dried herself off. Her eyes hurt from the perfumes in the swimming pool. Her fingers and toes were spongy, like a human's. She flapped her wings and water shot off, making dark pinpricks on the wall drapes.

She had failed to break the weather. But was that surprising? Could one person, even if she was an *auchresh,* call lightning out of an empty sky? She had only generated energy in herself. And it was the energy of frustration.

Together Arity and Humi, the insider and the outsider, could have tied the city in knots. There *could* have been a revolution. Together they had always been radiant, whether they were decried as a scandal or praised as the rising stars in an unstable court. Together, they canceled out each other's tendencies to self-destruction. Apart, neither of them was completely human.

Human?

"Damned *wrchrethru!*" Hope shook her head.

Drawing a deep breath, she dropped the towel. The chill wind rustled the herbs. Goosebumps roughened her limbs. She pulled on her clothes, a ratty pair of breeches and a shirt Ders had given her before she destroyed him. It had a panel of red-and-blue Veretrean embroidery down the front. Picking up her knife belt and her hairbrush, she opened her mouth to call for her servants, but before she could speak, the air at the other end of the room burst into huge blue polka dots. Eight Hands thumped onto her floor. Two of them looked as though they had been in a fight; the rest appeared to be spoiling for one. The door slammed against the wall and several of her footmen pounded in, yanking gold-trimmed coshes from their belts.

She held up one hand. They fell to a halt, snorting like bulls. In a gesture of pacifism, she dropped her knife belt on the floor, and smiled at the leading Hand. He had been one of the youngest of *lesh kervayim* back when she was Pati's lover. She couldn't remember his name. "What does Pati want of me, my friends? I don't think I've done anything ungodly enough to get myself arrested." She chuckled at her own lie. "Surely he has not quarreled with the *ser-balim* again? I won't help him, you know."

"It's worse than that, milady Hope," the Hand said in *auchraug*. She started. They never spoke in *auchraug;* too much of their business was with things for which it had no words. Then she realized it was so her footmen could not understand. She waved them out of the room. The door closed.

"Now," she said in the mortal tongue. "What has happened?"

"We have no time to put it pleasantly," one of the battle-stained Hands said. It was then she noticed one of his rudimentary wings had been sliced completely off. A bandage covered the stump. "We are at war with the renegades. Pati requests your presence in an advisory capacity."

War, she thought. Her mind tumbled over itself with questions. She said only, "You do not mean those silly Foundlings people are talking about who have decided they belong in human country!" *War?* She had never taken them seriously. She'd attributed most of what she heard about them to rumor. Could she really have been so far off the mark?

"Not silly, milady. Not Foundlings." The first Hand held up his arm to stop her interrupting. "Pati demands to see you."

They had spread into a semicircle in front of her. She felt just a little frightened. She was no human, trapped by her surroundings, but perhaps she'd spent too long in human company, for she was keenly aware of the fragile panels of glass behind her and the two-hundred-foot drop. "What is the *er-serbalim's* position?" she asked, to gain time.

"Milady, we do not yet know." They closed in tighter. "Pati demands your presence in the Sea Garden. Your counsel is valuable to him."

"My counsel . . ." Pati had never been short on stratagems. And what did *she* know about war? She did not trust Pati as far as she could fly. This all sounded too outrageous to be true. Impossible that something should have broken at last! She wouldn't put it past him to have invented it just to get her where he wanted her. Suppose—just *suppose* he had found out about last night? She might finally have outlasted her *iu* immunity.

But maybe it *was* true. The Hands were wounded. She did not think even Pati would take set dressing to such extremes. They jostled closer again. They were going to grab her so that she would not be able to *teth*" without taking one of them with her.

Pati wanted her under guard.

The Power-damned *haugthirre!*

"I may meet with Pati of my own free will. But he is stupider than one perceives if he believes he can *intimidate* me—or trap me." As their talons shot out to grab her arm, she *teth*"d. The destination locked into her mind, a crystal image, instantaneously re-anchoring her in reality. The Hands would think she had *teth*"d far away. She would outfox them.

He was sitting on a ledge in the hollowed-out wall of the Sea Garden, waiting for her. They had spoken truth there, anyhow. He did not seem surprised to see her alone. He smiled and beckoned her to sit down. There were too many teeth in his smile. She realized *she* had been outfoxed: he had reasoned one step further ahead than she, banking on her desire to know the truth. "Oh, you misbegotten old *kuiros*, Pati!" she said, going toward him. Both he and the salt trees looked as though they had been painted with frost. He was wounded on the face: the scabbed blood was the same dull white as the salt shrubs in the Garden.

"They could never satisfy me for long," he says. Speaking of himself, his voice is ironic. Waves lap against the cliffs below. The smell of the water is gamy and bracing. Listening to him, Hope thinks she can see all the way out to sea, all the way over the vague blue horizon, past Domesdys, to the ocean that stretches around the world, featureless and populated by strange slow-moving creatures. "I would use them for a little while, and then use Sol Southwind, the ghostier if you remember, to dispose of them. He thinks it is a mark of favor. I wonder if he sees the filth on his hands." He laughs, but it is not quite a real laugh.

"So you sent Arity the way of the others," Hope says softly. "Out of jealousy. Oh, Pati." Under the sententiousness and the self-flagellation there is something deeper. She wants to hug him—his power is such that he has actually made her feel sorry for him—but the scent of the salt enhances her common sense as well as her compassion. Over their heads, the white hyroses whisper in the breeze snaking down between the high rock walls.

"He was just the same as the others. I thought he would be different, but he was the same. Like them, he wanted to hate me. But he couldn't. Maybe that was why I had him killed." His lip twists.

"That's your curse, isn't it? People always care for you. Hate or love, it doesn't really matter. They rip themselves to shreds over you. But I'm not going to do that. Power knows I'm still fascinated with you. I wouldn't have come, otherwise. But I won't let you destroy me. There needs to be somebody who refuses to throw herself at your feet."

"I know I need you," Pati says softly. *"To protect me from the one other who won't throw herself down for me. You know who I mean."*

The sea makes a glopping splash, as if it is trying to reach them. Hope experiences a sense of hopelessness. She wants to cry, but not for Arity. That is too great a blow; it hasn't yet sunk in. She wants to cry for the city, this dear doomed city poised precariously on an island too small to bear its weight.

The sun rose high in the sky while they sat in the rock bower. The war played out fast as a topic of conversation. Pati had been wounded in K'Fier, it seemed, in an action to destroy the renegades affiliated with a family called Salmoney, who had killed five Hands the day before. It was all retaliation, up to that point. But now Pati proposed to turn retaliation into a full-scale offensive. He had deployed all the Hands he could spare, both out of the Delta City forces and out of the continental guards, to kill all the renegades in the world, wherever they could be found. To Hope, this seemed shortsighted and rash. When did fury ever translate into good politics? But she knew the hopelessness of trying to talk him out of it. One thing Pati *never* did was back down. "We must not allow the spread of atheism," he said—obtusely: weren't they talking about *gods?* "I understand now that I was wrong to concentrate on the cities. It is the country communities that rest on the edges of our Divinarchy. As such, they are in the most danger from untoward influences."

"But, Pati," Hope said, feeling that she was banging her head against a wall, "you're killing *auchresh*. As far as the common people know, these *untoward influences* are *gods!* Doesn't destroying them destroy the people's trust in you?"

"Godhead must be protected at all costs." He shuttered his eyes. "I am godhead."

Hope stared at him. She could not believe that he meant it. She asked more and more questions, both uselessly and not so uselessly, for though she could not get anything out of him regarding his beliefs, she discovered other things.

Arity had betrayed Humi. She had never suspected him of such duplicity. It seemed almost right that he had died for it.

Glancing at the sun, Pati said that Sol Southwind had already done the deed; as soon as the results arrived at the Palace, sometime this afternoon, Pati meant to make a personal raid on the Lakestones' house. Humi, too, would die.

That electrified Hope. She had to get away. There was still something she could do.

But did Pati suspect her? Had Arity mentioned her involvement? *That* could be why Pati had tricked her into coming here. Not for sympathy, or counsel, but to confirm his suspicions. If she left in time to warn Humi, she would be a rebel. A renegade. If she stayed to see Arity's ghost, and exclaim over its realism and power et cetera, Humi would die.

She shivered. The air off the sea was freezing. Pati was staring out to sea. Suddenly he turned and said, "It was always you."

She knew what he meant. It was in his eyes, on his lips. She laughed. "I've been blessedly free of you for three years. I intend to continue that way."

"It was always you."

"Indeed, it wasn't. It was Arity."

"He's not an *iu.*"

"Neither am I, really."

The sun had risen to the middle of the translucent turquoise sky and it was shining on them, bright but without heat. Their heads were in the shadow of the alcove. He hooked his foot around her ankle and drew her against him. The familiar, poisonous fire raced through her, and she could not keep from kissing him. Conjoined, the furnaces of their bodies created a wavering bubble that protected them from the chilly air of the salt garden.

She pulled back. "I mean it, Pati. I'm not getting mixed up with you again."

"I need you, Hope."

"To help with your holy wars? Or to replace Arity?" She felt ready to cry. Suddenly panicky, she kissed him again, and the fire spread through her, consuming her. His hand inside Ders's shirt squeezed her breast, pinching the nipple, releasing a flood of sensation. Just in time she heard the knife rushing through the air toward her back.

She *teth*"*d* aside, the most complicated impromptu *teth*"-*tach ching* she had ever done, having to unmake all her own limbs without taking any of Pati's with her. Cold air was a shock as she landed ten feet away. Pati sat poised, his breech strings loose, rather stupidly holding the crescent blade an inch from his own chest.

"What do you think you're doing?"

He was on his feet, his teeth bared. He took one slow step toward her at a time. A small gnolia shrub stood between them. "You betrayed me. You've been betraying me for three years."

She had not dreamed he had brought her here to kill her. To use her, trick her, but not take her life. She had been so unprepared that she had *teth*"*d* instead of knocking his knife upward into his throat. Now she had no time to think, no weapon.

The cold air ventilated her mind. "What about *your* duplicity?" She put several more bushes between them. "You almost had me! You almost had me believing you meant it! And all the time you were wrapping me in your web."

"I did once love you. That was no lie."

"But the rest of it was. You couldn't even be bothered with making me confess that I helped Humi survive your poison. I hid her. I have been in constant contact with her. You had no way of knowing that, but you were so *sure* you were right that you would have killed me without any thought for the years we spent together, without any thought for the hundred-odd years of my life before that." She was backed up against the cliff. She gripped the rock overhang with a futile desire to somehow fly up, away from him. She spluttered in a desperate attempt to make him see. "Every time you kill, it's *time* that is wasted, precious *time* of which this poor limited world has only so much! Isn't death bad enough on its own? Aren't we destroying ourselves already? We don't have enough time to live, let alone die!"

"You're a traitor, Hope," he said mildly, as if her words had been no more than a fall of tiny stones in his path. He stood before her, one hand on his hip. She watched the knife hanging in his other hand. "There aren't any excuses for treachery, no matter how prettily you make them."

"I'm no traitor." She spat noisily at his feet. "I was never your ally! *You* have been the dupe!"

His face contorted. The knife came at her much faster than she had expected, and she felt it lodge like a searing coal in her collarbone before she slapped her hand over his, wrenched it away, and *teth"d.*

Humility Under Stone

Hope found Humi in the council room of the Rats' Den. It was the sixth place she had tried and she was shaking with the expenditure of operative energy. The litter of wine bottles, coffee cups, and empty trays dusted with sugar on the great beechwood table told her that the conspirators staring at her were at least as tired as she. Gold Dagger. The Hangman, sprawling all over the arm of Humi's chair. The apostate ghostiers Mory Carmine and Trisizim Sepal— what were *they* doing here? An unknown flamen and leman, looking quite at home, and another underworld type with foxy reddish fur. Steadying herself, she bounced Pati's knife in her palm. It was blue steel, with a grip shaped for long, thin *auchresh* hands, and a sapphire embedded in the white-stained blade. The nick on her neck stung. "I have looked all over the city for you!" she said to Humi. "Ari betrayed you. I was sure you were dead. Lockreed Concourse is crawling with Hands."

Humi stiffened in her armchair. When she recognized Hope's voice, her face brightened. She made a movement to rise. "The Lakestones. Are they—"

"As far as I could tell, they are safe. Pati does not know which house you were sheltering in."

"Thank the Power for that, anyway!" Now Humi came toward Hope and embraced her. Hope was taken aback by the confidence with which she moved. She did not blunder into the table; though she stumbled, she caught herself neatly, and you would not have thought she was blind at all.

"I thought you had lost your nerve," Hope said, low.

Humi shuddered. "I had," she whispered, there in front of all the others. "And I might have stayed that way forever, if not for you. Thank you for bringing him. Thank you for showing me what I had become. I guessed he would betray me—that is the first thing I realized when I awakened. That's why I came here." With the urgency of a new convert, she hissed in Hope's ear: "I'm *free!* Hope! Free!"

Hope winced. Tears came to her eyes. "Humi—I have to tell you—I can't let you go on thinking that—Arity. I don't know the intricacies, but Pati's had him ghosted. I'm sorry."

Humi swayed. Then she straightened, and gave a perfect smile. Her hair was a blazing cloud of sand in the light of the candles. "He will die in agony for this." She took Hope by the arm and turned to face the table. "My friends, most of you know Hope. But I may as well do the honors."

Humi gestured carelessly at her new allies as she named them, giving a perfect imitation of a sighted person. The Hangman grinned indolently as Humi pronounced her name. *Evita.* Huh. Hope's hackles stirred. So she was no longer pretending to be a man. All the same, Hope did not trust her as far as she could throw her—not after what she'd witnessed on the rooftop in Temeriton.

"Are you in, Maiden?" the Hangman said.

"I have been *in,* as you put it, since before you were born," Hope said censoriously. "And I should be obliged if you didn't call me Maiden, since we are on a first-name basis."

"My congratulations, milady, on your liberation from the confines of Incarnation worship," the Godsbrother said instantly.

Hope inclined her head. The atmosphere in the room was like a newly painted canvas, stiff enough to stand up on its own.

Gold Dagger, whose head had been resting on his fist, let out a protracted raspberry of a snore.

Almost everyone laughed. In that moment of relieved tension, Humi said quickly, "Now that Hope is here, I think we should all permit ourselves a few hours of rest. We can talk in private," she added to Hope, and her words held a wealth of meaning.

"Why don't you come with me," Hope said. "I know several places, although I can't take you to the Folly. I'm afraid Pati will have it guarded." She envisioned armed Hands in every room, crouched behind the furniture, so that if she *teth*"*d* in she wouldn't see them before they saw her. The enormity of it overwhelmed her. She could never go back. She was a runaway in her own city. She had broken with Pati: they were open enemies now. In memory she saw him gliding toward her like a snake on its tail, knife held high, the jewel the same color as his right eye. She shuddered. The weapon seemed to burn her thigh.

As the conspirators separated, the Hangman slid up to Hope and Humi. She wrapped Humi's hand in her own pale claw. "The Divinarch is a guest in my home. You, too, are most welcome to share my hospitality, Maiden."

Hope was about to refuse, in high dudgeon, when she realized she did not know where the Hangman's house was. If she did not go, she would be unable to *teth*" to Humi. Swallowing her pride (anything for you, my heart's own sister!) she accepted.

They were the last to leave the council cavern. From the door, the messy table looked like a child's game left half-done, the candlelit circle puny in the dark recesses of the cave. Their footsteps echoed under the high roof. The foxy henchman, Ferret, swept back the curtain for them. A gust of fresh air rushed into their faces. Looking down, Hope saw that the little boy turning the fan crank had gone to sleep, slumped over his knees, his blistered fingers in his mouth.

Inviolate One

A featureless roof faced Sol's workshop across the side alley. Individual slates coruscated in the sun, and now and again one struck a splinter of light into his eye, making him toss his head as if to frighten away a wasp.

The labored breathing of the Hand at his feet sounded

louder every minute. Outside, in the streets, lemans' bells tinkled, calling worshippers to the Dividay services. Had this been another day, the beautiful, freezing weather would have brought marketers and loafers out en masse— but it was Dividay, and so Westpoint was preternaturally silent. Sol imagined hundreds of dull-faced, cowed people shuffling along Dock Street, on their way to stand pressed together, watched by Hands, to mouth praises of a god whom none of them really respected.

Cling. Ting. Ting.

He looked down at the god and rubbed his chin in frustration. The fellow had come unwillingly, escorted by another Hand. That was a first. Always, before, they had arrived on their own, proud and prepared to die, no matter how frightened they might be. Could this mean the Divinarch's hold over his lovers was weakening? Sol had wondered, as he bowed and smiled and assured the guardian Hand, that the ghost of this young Hand would be not only striking but ready by late afternoon. He (Pati's latest castoff) reminded him of some god he knew, or had once known. Who? He seemed quite mad in a gentle kind of way, wild-eyed, his lips working. Sol, disgusted with the whole business, felt honor bound to get a decent pose out of him. So he had tried to talk him to his senses. Then the god had fainted.

"Hell!" Sol gave the unconscious figure a kick of disgust. His breakfast sat half-eaten on a cross-legged table under the window. "How dare Pati interfere with me this way! Turning me into a monster, a god-killing monster, over and over again." He picked up a roll and bit into it. He had a new ghost, as yet completely unpainted, a teenaged girl the capture of whom in a Shimorning bar yesterday had been an experience to remember. He had been looking forward to working with her.

Ting.
Ting.
Ting.

A male voice solidified out of the faint chorus of bells. Sol knew its words without having to hear them.

"Might as well get to work," he said wearily. He rolled the young Hand over with his foot.

And he choked on his bread, coughing until he had to swig a glass of water to stop his eyes running.

Now the wild, tragic face lay in repose, the features were recognizable. Smooth, bony, yet more human than those of any other god. The eyelashes were the same purplish-brown as the hair, which had been cropped close to the head. That was one reason Sol had not recognized him. But the first reason was the despair that pervaded Arity's sleep, dragging the hairless brows together, crimping the mouth.

Sol's first reaction was an immobilizing exasperation. Then, as he clenched his fists, he was filled with the purest, strongest, most invigorating anger he had felt in years. He wasn't going to be party to a crime of *this* magnitude!

Something had snapped. His sensibilities, admittedly elastic, had stretched too far. Now they sprang back in his face.

You'll have to find yourself another executioner, Pati!

He squatted down and began to shake the unconscious Arity. It had no effect. He got up, fetched two glassfuls of water, and poured them over the god's head. Arity shivered, sat up, and looked at him with bloodstained but lucid eyes. In a voiceless whisper as if of agony, he murmured, "Ghost me."

"Don't be absurd," Sol barked. "I don't know what has happened to you, my Heir, but even in this state, you aren't expendable." He did not have quite the nerve to say, *And even if you weren't Heir, speaking from a purely aesthetic perspective I don't know that your death would be justified.* The other Hands Pati had sent him had at least been compelling, as all gods were compelling; but Arity, the original of the type Pati's lovers all belonged to, looked too human to possess that ethereal intensity. He was neither, nor. Always had been.

How was he *alive*?

Sol had a hundred questions in his mind. But Arity was plainly in no state to answer any of them. Sol remembered him from the old days: self-contained, aloof, loath to fight anyone's battles. Sol had admired his detachment, both personal and political, at the same time as he was irritated by his failure to make the most of the Heir's position.

Now—

Yet *still*!

"I have my limits," he said. "Neither you nor Pati can force me to violate my art." An excuse—it was an excuse. He hated that. It had been a long time since his ghostier's principles rode runner to political exigencies, instead of cracking the whip that drove him through the days. "I won't ghost you, no matter what I lose by it. Now get up."

Desperation came into Arity's blood-veined eyes. His hands clenched and unclenched, the talons scraping furrows in the wood floor. He croaked, "It's the only way I can ... He commanded it! It's the only way I can ... please him! You can't disobey him! Please! Please! I sound mad, I know, but you are a ghostier, you must have encountered cases like mine before ... *Please.*"

Just like all the others, Sol thought furiously, his resolve strengthening. *They all do it to please him.*

"How did he bring you to this? You were *Heir!* You were—*dead!*"

Arity's eyes closed and he smiled vaguely, like a man in the grip of a pleasant dream. Then the eyes blinked open. "It doesn't matter. All that matters is that I've lost him now, lost the life he gave me back, all through my own stupidity. You must ghost me: it is what he wishes."

"I have never made a ghost of anyone, man or god, in the depths of despair. I'm not about to start now."

"But you must!" Panic came into Arity's eyes. He clutched at Sol's wrist. Sol jerked away. The talons drew black-welling gashes along his hand.

"I used to like you, Arity." Sol pulled the god stumbling to his feet. "It's for your own sake I am refusing. Come on. I won't have anything to do with it. You can find your own way back to the Palace and tell him to send you to Shimorning, if he wants you killed. They like to catch Hands in dark alleys there. I think they've done three so far. You might even get bumped off on the way through Doxton to the Palace, if you're lucky." He dragged Arity into the other room. Birdcages, pictures frames, and vacant ghost pedestals toppled as they stumbled through the maze of furniture. "Tell him Sol Southwind is not his servant anymore!"

What are you doing? an inner, scandalized voice screeched. *You're jeopardizing everything you have! Your ghosts, your reputation, your future, your living, your life!*

He would have to leave these lodgings. That much was obvious. The Divinarch exacted harsh revenges on those (like Arity) who had fallen from his favor. Pushing the god out the door ahead of him, Sol took one last glance around the apartment. It was messy, dusty, and cluttered. It smelled of stale food and pigments. All the chair and table legs, in fact everything remotely edible, was rat-eaten at floor level.

He compressed his lips. A cold draft blew down the stairs from the open skylight. The building was silent. In the quiet, he heard a sound from the street, echoing under the tunnel: *chink, chink, chink,* and a *slllither* as if of cloth on stone.

"Bastards," he whispered.

After an eternity the sound faded.

He drew Arity down the stairs.

As he poked his head out into the tunnel, he glimpsed a Hand disappearing slowly around the corner. The god's heel talons thunked on the cobbles. The body he dragged after him bumped along. It was human: probably the harmless shop boy of one of Westpoint's last major merchants. Pati had enough sense not to kill off all the island's trading class. Delta City did not starve. The Hand would probably go to the Crest and leave his victim strategically positioned as a reminder to other potential blasphemers.

Sol pulled Arity out into the tunnel. The god huddled wretchedly around himself, shivering in the cold air. He was in a bad way. Tears of rage rose in Sol's eyes. "Go on then," he said roughly. "Back to the Palace. And don't forget what I told you to tell the Divinarch! Tell him Sol Southwind sends his regrets but he is no longer his to command. He has taken back his self-respect!"

He stopped as he realized he was shouting.

Arity wavered out into the sunlight. It seemed to confuse him. He tried to rub his eyes, but missed, and rubbed his hair.

Gritting his teeth against the impulse to go and prop him up, Sol strode away in the other direction. He, too, was cold—it had, perhaps, not been wise to leave without any belongings at all! But he would not go back upstairs! And he was not destitute, not in the least. Oh, no. He had his ghostier's talent. And the other, more mundane talents, such as his knack for ingratiating himself. He had not left *everything* in the apartment!

He still had his plans.

He had meant to become senior ghostier by working himself gradually under Pati's skin, until he was indispensable.

Well, what was sauce for the gander might be sauce for the goose.

Emni knew where Humi was hiding. Perhaps she would admire Sol's scruples, when Sol told her how devotion to the onetime Heir had prevented him from ghosting Arity. After all, Humi had been Arity's *amoreuse,* hadn't she? Pity, her throwing herself away like that. A nice-looking girl she had been. She and Sol were almost exactly the same age—twenty-three. He had watched her mature, watched her appear to outdistance him, and not even his hypercritical eye had been able to find anything wrong with the womanly manner she developed. Though of course, unlike most people, unlike even Arity, perhaps, he had always known it was a put-on show.

Of course, she too had probably changed.

He could soon find out if it was for the better or for the worse.

Fanning his long black forelock over his eyes to cut back the glare, he swung along toward Marshtown. He started to whistle. Before long, Arity had faded from his immediate concerns.

Among Ladies

That evening at the hour of first glasses, two women and one *auchresh* slipped through the side door of the Peppered Frog and settled at a table at the edge of the barroom. On the stage at the back, five young boys, stripped nearly naked, swayed to and fro. The applause of the enthusiasts below the stage—some male, some female, all loudly drunken—drowned out the pipe music floating from behind the backdrop.

Hope eyed the dirty-fingered crone who plunked her whiskey in front of her with some revulsion. The servers were all ancient. Maybe the idea was to focus attention on the show, or maybe the Frog catered to customers whose tastes ran that way. She pushed the unwashed mug back. "Would it inconvenience your barkeep too much if I requested a clean glass?"

The Hangman looked at her with surprise. Then her mouth twisted. "Maiden, we mortals exist only to please those greater than us. Another whiskey for the lady, Arva."

Hope wore a long robe to conceal her wings, with a hood to shadow her face, and so did Humi. Everyone knew the Hangman, of course; she owned the tavern. Hope's dirty mug vanished and she was offered a shot glass of amber liquid. The whiskey was bad. She made a face. "I suppose your regular customers are easily satisfied."

"You do not find my little entertainment house satisfactory, Maiden?" The Hangman's voice was as soft as oiled fingers sliding up the spine. Her gaze oozed into Hope's hood, and rested there, speculatively. Hope stared back, seething with anger. The Hangman's were the eyes of a lizard. Under the deceptively sleepy glaze, dislike simmered.

Sooner or later they would confront each other. Hope knew the Hangman meant evil toward Humi, and the Hangman knew she knew it.

She said, "I certainly had not suspected you had interests in the tavern business, Hangman. It does not seem consistent with your primary line of work." Was it possible Humi had no clue what was going on? Her hood was up, but her cloak hung open. She wore a gold-trimmed low-cut dress that showed off her figure to advantage. Not too gaudy for the times, yet expensive enough to show she was a lady and could afford whatever she set her eye on. She tapped her fingers in time to the clapping.

The Hangman cracked a smile. "I invested in the Frog for exactly that reason. The assassination business is risky, and one must provide for eventualities."

Humi appeared to return her attention to the table. "Wise," she said with a trill of laughter. "If I had done the same, I would not now have to depend on my friends' generosity."

"Milady, you are not obliged to me. This is my pleasure."

Hope crooked her finger for another whiskey. Drink did not affect her mental faculties, but enough of it, she had discovered, had a calming effect at times like this, when she felt as if she was sparking with excess energy.

"You drink rather copiously, milady, don't you?" the Hangman said, in the tone of one asking whether Hope was really eating rotten fish.

"I smoke copiously, too," Hope snapped. She got out her tobacco pouch and began to fill a pipe.

"It would ease my lot if you two would try to tolerate each other," Humi said sharply. "The air is thick with unpleasantness. Can't you ignore each other, at the very least?"

Hope wondered whether to reveal her suspicions: the reasons she did not dare ignore the Hangman. When she saw the Hangman's mouth open, she spoke fast: "Humi, you're in danger. She means to do you wrong."

The Hangman hissed in outrage.

"You pride yourself on your perceptiveness. Have you really not noticed? I entreat you to break off your relations with her. Deal with Gold Dagger alone, if you must." Humi's face was unreadable. Hope wondered with paralyzing suddeness if she had lost her trust. "I have no motives besides your interest, Humi. Trust me!"

"What a liar," the Hangman said, "what a liar! Ssshe is jealous of me, milady."

"I care only for my Divinarch's safety!"

People turned to stare. Hope lowered her voice to a hiss, training her gaze on the Hangman.

"Power knows what you will do the next time you get Humi alone. I can see it in your eyes, and I will not permit it!"

Humi's mouth was serious. She turned to the Hangman. "If there is the slightest grain of truth in this—"

"It's not *fair*," the Hangman whispered. She clasped her hands around Humi's arm. "Milady, I offer you my humble allegiance and you will turn it down to let this—this—renegade serve you in my stead. She negates everything we are fighting for! She is the image of decadence! She is a scion of this very regime we strive to overturn! She represents the worst, ugliest degradation of the gods we seek to elevate to their proper places!"

Hope gasped.

"You believe," Humi said in frank astonishment, pulling her arm away. "You are a devotee, Evita! How on earth have you managed to stay faithful in the middle of all this?"

On stage, five girls pranced out and joined the boys. The crowd, which had grown marginally larger, grew much louder. The crooked old servitors scurried from table to

table, their cracked voices shrilling jokes and foolery. The
Hangman took a long swig of her drink. "For the most
part, by keeping it a secret."

Humi gestured around the table. "But then, why are you
here? Why aren't you bowing down to Pati's toy flamens?"

The Hangman's pale greenish eyes glowed with passion.
"So that the gods can continue to be the gods, without
being reduced to squabbling monkeys!"

"Oh, so that's why you hate me?" Hope said. "I have
made myself into a squabbling monkey for your sake. For
all of your silly little human sakes. And you hate me for it."

The Hangman's lips puckered. Hope ducked in time and
the gob of spittle hit the man at the next table. When he
rose, his face waxing dark with anger, the Hangman
snapped her fingers over her head, and several of the old
crones grabbed him and wrestled him toward the door.
"You have betrayed your own divinity," the Hangman
hissed. "For *her* sake. Thus lowering her to your despicable level."

"Hangman," Humi said warningly.

But the conflict between worship and contempt could not
be defused. It was more powerful than a river in flood, for
it pulled the woman's bottommost essence up and swirled
it about. "*I* am the only one who should follow her," the
Hangman spat. "I would praise her with my last breath.
You're just amusing yourself. And it is below your dignity,
below you! Leave us alone! Let us fight your battles for
you, as we have done ever since the Conversion Wars!"

"You are making my point," Hope said. The bewilder-
ment had left her, replaced by an icy anger at the Hangman
for making her personally responsible for the Hangman's
own doubt. "Nothing is beneath my dignity, any more than
it is beneath yours. Our races are not so different. They
never have been."

The Hangman seemed about to come across the table at
her. Humi snatched her arm. "This is beneath *all* of us,"
she said. "Hangman, we must keep our beliefs out of our
dealings with each other. Hope—*please.*"

"You favor her," the Hangman spat. "Favoritism has
been the death of many an alliance. Beware!"

"Hope and I have been friends for years—but I value
you equally. Can we not reconcile, simply because it is nat-

ural for us to do so? We are all women. It would be ludicrous for us to hate each other."

"Don't feed me that pap, milady. Except in bed, I
haven't been a woman in ten years!"

*You, Humi, are perhaps the only one of us with any femi-
ninity left,* Hope thought, *and that is because you hold onto
it with tooth and claw, the way an aging* serbalu *holds onto
her looks.*

But the last thing Hope wanted to do was to agree with
the Hangman. The cold anger buzzed inside her. "I think
I had better leave."

"I won't allow it. I need you, Hope." Humi still gripped
the Hangman's arm. Now she reached out with her other
hand and took Hope's. Her slender arms trembling with
the effort, she brought their hands together until Hope's
scaly golden knuckles pushed against the Hangman's lightly
furred paw. "Neither of you will leave without my
permission."

Hope had never seen an expression so compelling.
Humi's grayish-black eyes seemed to come alive like pools
of cold water when the wind stirs them. Hope felt herself
sliding toward that brink. The cold took her breath away.
The cheering, clapping, and music faded as if she were hurtling at great speed, not down into the water, but out, out,
out into the ocean on a fast boat, lashed by icy spray. Her
mouth tasted of stale tobacco, foul with the sleepless days.

Humi let go of their wrists. The room brightened, spun,
then righted itself. On stage, as the children copulated or
simulated it, the pipe player, a brawny young man with
green Deltan fur, tiptoed with exaggerated care among the
couples, tootling on his instrument and directing exaggerated nods and winks at the audience. The Westpointers
roared with laughter.

"All right, then, Hope." Humi nodded. "You can leave.
I am not relinquishing our alliance. And I wouldn't have
suggested it if you hadn't. But perhaps—for now—it would
be best for everyone."

The Hangman glowed smugly.

Hope knew it. She had to go. Her presence aggravated
dangerous tendencies in the humans—atheists, devotees,
and believers all: understandably, they felt overshadowed.

The Hangman was only one example. They could not cope with the concept of the renegade, as opposed to the god.

Better to leave Humi to the tender mercies of her own kind. If only that didn't mean leaving her in such deadly danger!

At closing time, they were all separated in the confusion. Hope watched Humi snake competently through the crowd. The thought flashed through her: *What am I thinking? She can look after herself! She's not a child!*

When they had been shown to the rooms in the Hangman's Shimorning town house which servants had readied for them, Humi came through the door that connected their bedrooms, floating almost *auchresh*-like over the floor in a wispy silver nightgown. "Here," she said, extending a flimsy piece of parchment to Hope. "Here's where I would like you to go. If you are still intent on going."

"I am."

"Then I hope you didn't expect I was going to ignore the chance to put you to work abroad!" Humi grinned.

"I am *committed* to working on your behalf," Hope said, meaning it. She took the parchment. It was engraved with a line drawing of a house surrounded by trees.

"I am assured the proportions are accurate," Humi said.

In the smoky lamplight, Hope peered at the paper. It gave off a faint scent of human sweat. She guessed that Humi had kept it next to her fur. "I'm supposed to *teth"* from this?"

"Can't you?"

"It will require a leap of the imagination, but perhaps I can." Already, her mind was feathering the sketched-in pines with minty needles.

"I want you to work on Erene and Elicit."

"So far as I know, no one has ever died from *teth"ing* with their destination unclear in their minds." She put a smile in her voice. "The barrier between our world and the myriad of others is too strong, too elastic, to be broken by our puny mistakes."

Humi leaned against the bedpost. The filmy gown clung to her breasts. Shadows played in the corners of the bedroom and undulated in the window curtains. "Hope, what really happened between you and Pati? It wasn't just the news about Arity. It was something violent. To tell you the

truth, I'm surprised you came back at all ... You seem—
sparkling. I can almost see you."

"I broke with him." A worm of grief twisted in her.
Today marked the burial of something that had been dying
for years. But neither the length of the bed watch nor the
irascibility of the patient had lessened the final pain. "We
talked for hours. But I do not believe he said one word
that was true."

"He may have let something slip," Humi suggested.

"For a time, we spoke of godhead."

"Yes?"

She shook her head. "We went around in circles. I asked
him how he could countenance a war against our fellow
auchresh. You do know about all that ... Yes? He insisted
it was to preserve his godhead. As you know, he calls himself the One God. Thus far, outrageous as the concept is,
it holds together; but you see, there is a contradiction between the way he speaks of himself and the way he lives.
He is *wrchrethre.* A humanophile. He is no longer a god
in the sense you humans have always meant it. His efforts
to maintain the Divinarchy have changed it beyond any
hope of returning it to its old self. He *must* see that. But I
do not know how he deals with it in his mind. If we knew,
perhaps we could guess at the strategy he will use to track
us down."

Humi had been listening intently. "The question, it seems
to me, is whether he really believes he is a god."

"Or is it, now, nothing more than a desperate struggle
to hang onto power? I can't tell. I don't think he confides
in anyone."

"Maybe Arity knew," Humi said. A shadow flitted across
her face. "Maybe that is why Pati had him killed."

"I don't think so. I think it was to do with you."

"It's always my fault, isn't it?"

"Oh, Power," Hope said, rising to her knees, "that's not
what I meant, and you know it." She pressed Humi's head
to her breast.

"I'm sorry for *him,*" Humi said, muffled. "He deserved
a nobler end than that." She wriggled a little in Hope's
arms and touched the tender nick on Hope's collarbone.
"Did Pati do this?"

Hope nodded.

"It could have been much worse, couldn't it?"

"He was trying to kill me." Hope took a deep breath. "I *was* lucky." She let go of Humi, then pulled her up onto the bed and sat her up with her legs sticking out like a doll's. Humi's lips pooched out childishly, as if Hope's cutting short the embrace had pushed her to the edge of tears.

"Did you"—Hope had to ask—"did you still love him?"

Humi's nose twitched. Her hands dug into the edge of the bed like claws. Finally she said, "Not anymore. He'd changed too much."

"It was his accident that changed him. Ever since then, he's had that look about him—as if he were waiting for the right moment to finish what the leman girl started."

Humi laughed bitterly, leaning her head on her hand, and said not without some irony, "Hope, you are my staff of strength."

"And I'm leaving."

"You'll come back. You must."

"But what'll I have to show for it?" Hope put the picture of the house down on the coverlet. She wore a light nightgown in which she had ripped holes for her wings. Her knees ripped through it, too, as she leaned forward. "There are many other places I could work on your behalf. We don't know anything about the life Erene and Elicit have built for themselves over the last few years. They are sure not to want to be disturbed. Our business is a thing of the cities. I do not think people in the country know anything about the gods' doings! We're in danger of losing our perspective if we don't remember that."

"I think you're wrong," Humi said seriously. The candlelight danced. "This ... war ... of Pati's started in human country. K'Fier is a hamlet, next to Delta City. And speaking of that, I want you to investigate the renegades for me."

What could she do? She had agreed to go. And Humi sounded so confident.

"And as for Erene and Elicit, you'll simply have to convince them that they owe us their help in return for four years of peace and quiet. They belong here. They can leave Artle and Xib behind if they are worried for their safety."

Shaking her head in resignation, Hope leaned over and kissed the well-groomed forehead. After all these years she still wasn't quite used to the taste of fur. A good thing Humi was blind, so she could not see her wiping her mouth on the back of her hand. "All right!" she said. "But don't have the revolution without me."

Humi's head came up. "No one will move a finger unless I tell them to."

Gazing at her sharp, elegant profile, Hope thought: *She means it. The fool.*

Solemnity

As Sol came down Tellury Crescent that afternoon, he glimpsed a white face in the window of the Chalice. No Hands guarded the street. That was unusual! Nobody at all was outside, in fact, except for a few children, and a girl brushing her doorstep, who automatically curtseyed to him. He rapped on the door of Albien House, silently cursing his nerves.

Yste opened it, his squinched dark face closed. "She's not here."

"Aren't you glad to see me?" Sol said in a hurt voice, and brushed past. Inside, he breathed deeply. Albien House, the oldest of the *imrchim's* three residences, smelled of perfume, and cookery, and pigments, and overwhelmingly of dust—a musty yet curiously invigorating odor. It was good to know that something, at least, had not changed. "If she's not here, where is she?"

"At the Eftpool." The half-breed boy danced in front of him. "You can follow her there, if you want."

For a moment Sol thought he was telling the truth, and his gut clenched. He could not go to the Eftpool. Not without endangering everything he had once believed in, everything that Emni still believed in.

Then his senses returned, and he saw that the repulsive Yste had sidled around to stand between him and the stairs.

Not *very intelligent of you, Em!*

"Out of my way," he said gently, shoving the boy aside. "Run and tell Ziniquel his wife is closeted with her brother." He shouted, "Run!"

Yste darted into the anteroom. As Sol leaped up the stairs, two at a time, he heard the Chalice door slam.

The third floor of Albien House, which had once been Humi and Erene's workshop and private apartments, now comprised one huge glasshouse. Entering from the hall, Sol experienced a shock of terror as light drifted over him, absorbing him, blurring his sense of self. But again, reason came to his aid. The light was almost granular in its cool brilliance—it was like walking through weak syrup. Not a multicolored sea. Not the Pool. As he advanced, gravity seemed to change from a given effect to a tangible force that one could use as one wanted. Enviously, he thought, *One forgets how well they've got this place up. The ghosts they paint here must be transcendent.*

Some parts of the roof were screened, creating solid blocks of shadow on the floor. Heavy reed mats hung in rolls at the other rafters, ready to be cranked across if the sun got too bright. In a far corner of the room, a pale figure hugged the wall.

"Gods," Sol said sadly. "I'm not going to *hurt* you."

She detached herself from the wall. Slowly, she came toward him. Her long hair fell like strips of shiny black cloth over her shoulders; she wore plain working wools. Her hands were pigment-stained, the nails bitten short, as of old. Sol quelled a desperate urge to seize her in his arms. Deliberately, he looked her up and down. "Where's the baby?"

"Lighte. His name is Enlightenment. I should think you would remember that, since he's the only descendant you're likely to have."

"I have bastards in half the households of Westpoint."

"Liar. I know you, Sol." Her nose went thin. "You'd never even *look* at a woman who wasn't me."

Such arrogance. Such beloved arrogance.

He wished he could taunt her with the possibility of Lighte's being his. But it wasn't chronologically possible. Besides, although the baby had Emni's white fur, it had Zin's green hair and green eyes. "Do you really flatter yourself that that's the reason I'm here?"

"No." She seized her cuffs in her hands, raveling their hems. She was as edgy as he. "There's something more you want out of me. There's always something."

He took a deep breath. "I'm on the run. I need your help."

"On the run? Are you making a fool of me? You're the

pet of the Divinarch. He would squash anybody who tried to bag you. Though I don't doubt you've plenty of enemies, being—who you are."

"Em." The room smelled of diamondine: a curiously sharp odor like baking soda. "I tell you, it's *Pati* who wants me. The hunt will be up by tonight. I have to hide."

". . . no. I don't believe it." Emni's lips parted and her brows drew together. "*No*. Sol, don't tell me—*don't* tell me you've gone and allied yourself with Humi—"

"Not yet. But I have to know where she is. She's my only hope." He stepped forward—not too far, not far enough to make her flinch back, just enough to impress his urgency on her. "You know where she is. You've got to tell me, Em."

"Gods! She has a fatal influence over us. I knew I was right not to take the children to see her. First Mory and Tris, now you—is it ever going to be finished?"

Excitement quickened in his chest. "Have Mory and Tris joined her? Where are they?" Maybe *this* was why there were no Hands in the Crescent. Maybe they had all been called to a more urgent posting. "You've given everything away. There's no use in not telling me now."

"Oh—oh, gods! Kill yourself along with them if you want, then! It's not as though I care! It was scarcely an hour ago." Her head tossed as if she were being compelled to speak by the blows of an invisible whip. "A courier pigeon came here from Godsbrother Eternity—an apostate. The message said that a flamen of his, with Mory and Tris, who seem to have worked themselves deep into the apostates' trust, have gone as ambassadors to Humi. She is gathering her allies about her. She means to do something horrible. Sol, don't go!"

For a moment he thought she meant to confide in him. Then the door behind him opened. "Em!" Ziniquel exclaimed. "Thank the gods! You're all right!"

Emni brushed past Sol. He smelled her perfume. She leaned against her husband. "Oh, Zin. I told him about Mory and Tris. I couldn't help it—he always drags these things out of me."

Ziniquel's hands nudged aside the heavy locks of hair as he rubbed her back. "How did he get in, love? I told Yste . . ." His eyes met Sol's.

"You would've had to put a good deal more than that child in my way to keep me out," Sol said.

"Yes. I should have met you myself." Zin's eyes were steady, challenging. "It's my duty to protect my ghostiers."

"Turned the senior ghostier properly, haven't you," Sol jeered. "What a comedown!"

"I never wanted anything more than this," Ziniquel said. Sol felt a queer twitch of perception as he thought, *Our desires are exactly the same, aren't they, Zin? Funny. We're so different.* "I never wanted more than to stop the likes of you from hurting the *imrchim.* Now, get out of my house." He jerked his chin toward the door.

It's my house, too, Sol thought. "Not until you tell me where to find Humi."

Emni flung around, her hair flying, and snarled, "Do you mean to break her heart, too?"

Absurdly, Sol's insides leaped. "Did I break your heart? Em, I never knew that."

"No! I mean—"

"It's all *right.*" Ziniquel pulled her close. "Sol, she's in Shimorning."

Getting an answer so readily was almost a disappointment. It proved how genuinely, and urgently, they wanted to get rid of him.

"She's at the Rats' Den. Do you know where that is?"

"Sounds like a tavern."

"It's not. We never heard of it, either, until this afternoon. It's Gold Dagger's lair. The vermin are gathering now, and they need somewhere to hide. Go down to Reddew Street . . ." He proceeded to give a string of complex directions. Sol memorized them, nodding.

"I'll be off, then." He bowed to Emni and said sarcastically, "Thanks for your hospitality, darling."

"And good riddance," came a clear voice from the other side of the room. Suret, the Veretrean girl apprentice, stood in the far door with her arm around Yste. Tan hovered behind her, his long limbs in perpetual motion.

"Keep your nose out of things that are none of your business, little girl!" Sol called to her.

"If I had been at the door, you would not have got past the first step!" Tan shouted.

"Not that you didn't do a good job, Yste dear," Suret murmured, hugging the smaller boy close.

A sudden pang went through Sol. There had been a time, impossible as it seemed now, when he and Emni had been those apprentices eavesdropping in the doorway. But those had been halcyon days compared to these. He and Emni had not been taught to hate anyone. They had feared nothing except growing up, though they had feared *that* rightly.

Yet Tan, Suret, and Yste's Crescent was the same as the Crescent of Sol's childhood in one respect: it was the only home they knew. Childhood memories (even if, like Tan, you were already adolescent when you were apprenticed) faded faster than dried flowers, when they were exposed to the bright light of the seasons in Delta City. All Sol had now to comfort him was a Dividay circle on the top of a mountain, and the taste of honeyfish.

"Do you remember," he said suddenly to Emni, "when we were little? On Gelska? How we used to run down to the pier in the morning to see the boats off—"

"I remember nothing," Emni snapped. "Get out!" Her eyes were wild behind the tangled strands of black. Age lines circled them. That made Sol wince. *Are we still identical?* He had not looked in a mirror in a long time. There had been a time when looking at her was like watching himself, only slightly exaggerated. But their changing relations had probably changed their faces correspondingly.

"I shan't tolerate these intrusions any longer, Sol!"

"Don't worry. This will be the last time."

She turned her head away. "I hate you."

"You're afraid of me."

"I despise you!"

Maybe, inside, she was worse mended than he was from the dreadful night he had poisoned her. Was such a thing possible? The clear sunlight showed up the dust on the floor, the dust on the ranks of ghosts standing by one wall, an army contorted by sudden plague, frozen where they stood. How many ghosts had they actually made recently? Tan stepped menacingly into the sunlight, thin arms akimbo. "Out!" he ordered in a poor imitation of a Temeriton bouncer's voice.

Sol laughed at the irony of it, and went.

"And so the *imrchim* are reunited!" Tris said. "We are the *real imrchim,* you know. United by our commitment to our art. I don't honor those spineless fools in the Crescent with the title of ghostier anymore." He stood in the middle of his and Mory's small workshop in Marshtown, looking around. "For the first time since you left us in '57, Humi, I feel we are up to strength again."

Humi objected, "You are only three. I acknowledge your flattery, but"—she laughed self-deridingly—"I do not think I really merit the title of master anymore." Her hand strayed along the smooth thigh of a ghost dressed in the costume of a monstrous bird (every feather diamondine, of course) and Sol saw a sensual tic at the corner of her mouth. "Now, I am reduced to merely appreciating your work."

Mory's and Tris's ghosts were everything Sol had anticipated: startling in the sheer intensity of their emotion, yet more powerful than most other ghosts for that same reason. Many of them wore masquerade costumes. Red and dark green predominated.

"But my dear Humi, even if there are only three of us, we are still more numerous than the Crescent!" Mory objected. "Algia and Eterneli are not masters in any sense at all!" She wore a droopy black robe and boots that added to her height by at least four inches. "I trust you have not forgotten that if they paint one ghost a year between them, they consider themselves productive?"

Humi smiled, acknowledging her point. "However, I daresay the Crescent is cleaner than it has been in centuries."

"Actually," Sol put in, "no matter how much those two sweep and dust and polish, those houses still look as though no one has set foot there in years. I remember while I was living in Thaumagery House by myself, four years ago, the place must have slipped back several centuries in time."

"You have not changed in the least, Sol," Mory said, her eyes resting speculatively on him. With an effort, he stopped himself from flinching.

Humi, too, had matured. He had expected her face to bear a record of the trials she had undergone—but she seemed to have transcended them. Perhaps just coming here had done that for her. Her voice was melodious, and her blindness contributed to her gracefulness rather than detracting from it. Long eyelashes swept like fringes over her eyes, hiding the flat black surfaces. She seemed perfectly sure of herself.

Mory and Tris, like everyone else Sol had met in the Rats' Den, seemed to think it was a given that a battle would soon come, and that Humi would prevail. He saw that if he didn't watch his step, he would find himself getting caught up in their plans. He had already agreed to teach Gold Dagger's men the secret ways of the old Palace: he was the only one of the conspiracy (as they were again calling it) familiar with the renovations Pati had made.

But perhaps Humi *could* win. Perhaps Sol had landed on his feet here.

Wait and see, he told himself, fighting for objectivity. *You haven't yet told them about Arity. Or the ghosts of the Hands. Give it twenty to one that no matter how apostate they seem to be, they'll hate you for* that.

Flowers of frost bloomed on the windows of the workshop. Outside, moonflower plants swayed, tall green blurs. The workshop was near the Eftpool: another ancient structure in the middle of a block of Marshtown houses, hidden from the streets, and the eyes of patrolling Hands. It had been used as an outhouse by the tenants until Mory and Tris reclaimed it and broke windows in the thick stone walls. Today seemed to have been one long succession of ghosts—from the silent, crystalline Westpoint morning, through the ghost Sol had not made of Arity, to the apprentices hovering like ineffectual shadows in the doorway of Emni and Zin's workshop, to Humi. Humi, back from the dead, beautiful and corrupted, breathing and hot-blooded. Her dress revealed her sandy-furred shoulders. She had dyed her hair auburn. "Hume," he said, "I don't believe for a minute that you're no longer ghosting. You would never be so sleek if you'd been cut off from your art. Are you going to show us your masterpieces now, or later?"

She turned to him, looking cross. "You sound sure of yourself!"

"Did I spoil the surprise? I do apologize."

"Actually"—she glowed—"I *have* been painting ghosts. Not with pigments, but with chisels. I have been playing with texture, using it in some ways I believe are quite original. I only brought one of my pieces with me from Temeriton, and it is at the Hangman's residence in Shimorning, but I should be delighted if you would give me your opinion on it—all of you."

Mory and Tris were unctuous with compliments, expressing their desire to see everything she had done.

"You can go and buy my other pieces from Hem's shop.

He would be delighted. If you disguise yourselves, he will think you are foreigners, and it will be even nicer."

"What is the piece you have? A rat?" Sol asked.

"No. A seagull."

He took her hand. Twisting it over, he held the palm to the light, examining the myriad scars. "It clawed you pretty badly. Or are these chisel marks? Whichever it is, your new technique is very hard on the hands."

"*Sol,*" she said, pulling away, and said no more. Mory and Tris filled the conversational gap with news of the people Sol and Humi had known in Marshtown. Inevitably, the subject of apostasy came up. They sat down on the floor, which was scrupulously clean, and wrapped blankets around their shoulders against the cold. "Pati's most powerful weapon will be his flamens," Humi said. "They are more powerful than the quickest soldier. And they have no morals. Or only twisted ones."

"Ha," Mory said. "We can best them any day."

"The Godsbrothers and Godsisters have been practicing," Tris said. "Some of them have refined the use of miracles to an art. They use their will much the same way we do when we make ghosts. It is all the same thing. They are conscious of their technique."

The talk segued into a pleasurably esoteric discussion of craft. Tris poured chilled wine. As it took effect, they began to reminisce. Sol found himself moved by his *imrchim's* unspoken acceptance. He had not experienced anything of the sort for so long . . . They seemed to have forgotten how they had once ostracized him. He was one of them again, just by virtue of having come here, to Humi's side. And if they had once criticized him for his excess of zeal . . . well, now murderousness was a qualification, not a crime.

But they did not know the worst of it. He had to remember that. They did not know the facts, nor the end, of his services to Pati.

He and Humi sat with their backs against a pedestal, scarcely speaking. Her face tipped toward the ceiling as if she were drinking in the purple twilight that filtered in through the frost. It spilled down her throat, bruising the downy fur. She said, "I should like to see some of the ghosts *you* have made these past few years, Sol."

"Most of them have sold abroad."

"I should like to see one in particular. I believe it was commissioned by the Divinarch?"

Gods. She knows. He said, "The Divinarch commissioned more than one ghost from me. I'd say over the years, there were dozens."

She sighed, and seemed to sag. *She believes now that I did kill him,* he realized with a pang of guilt.

"You have broken the greatest unwritten law of our calling. Mory and Tris know, too. You have probably sensed that we are all a little in awe of you."

He shrugged. "I'm still alive. That's all that can really be said for it."

She laughed: a low, hoarse giggle. "Sol, I am delighted to have you as an ally. I don't know what to say."

"It's all in the deed, Humi. I had to force my hand every time I did it. The remnants of faith are hard to shake off."

"You are still human, then! That is all!"

"I suppose so . . ."

She trilled with laughter. *Must I tell her?* Sol wondered. *I want her. And if she knows he's still alive . . .* "I didn't kill Arity," he said abruptly. "I sent him back to Pati."

She sat bolt upright. Her face was a dusk-colored mask. She reminded him of Pati, the last time Sol had been summoned to a divine audience, the slim ghost leaning down from the Throne, coruscating with intentness. "I knew. I *knew* that could not be the end of it. I *hoped* . . . but no!" Her hand closed on his shoulder and she bowed her head. She was shuddering. "Why didn't you kill him? Why didn't you? Pati would have been disabled by his loss . . ."

Sol was utterly confused for the space of just one second. Then he lifted her head up by the hair and drove his mouth against hers. Her lips yielded to his tongue with astonishing readiness.

"Quite in awe of you," she murmured. Sol could not determine whether she was jesting or serious, and he didn't like to ask. Instead he kissed her again. Mory and Tris did not appear to have noticed; they sat with their heads together behind a furiously leering ghost in traditional Icelandic costume, discussing politics in soft voices.

They managed to keep from tearing each other's clothes off until they had made their good-byes to Mory and Tris, found their escort of career criminals, and returned by a back route to the Rats' Den. Then, avoiding people who would have accosted Humi, they let themselves into a dark storeroom. They had scarcely spoken a word since leaving the workshop. The air was hardly breathable, the heap of pilfered tapestries an uncomfortable bed, but Humi pulled him close with a fierce passion that aggravated his desire. He plunged into her again and again, thrusting deep as he would have thrust a knife into a living body. Not a word passed between them. Their mouths met with bruising force. She gripped him, increasing the friction until he could not bear it; he gasped as he climaxed. Her fingers grasped his back, slipping. His fur was flat with sweat.

They fell apart, breathing noisily in the bad air.

Outside, far down, steel rang on stone.

A thin rectangle of light limned the door. It was a foot thick, to protect the contents of the storeroom. Humi had a ring of keys Gold Dagger had given her. Sol imagined her and himself as two of the treasures, more precious than the tapestries, the chinaware, or the daggers. He laughed.

"What?" she murmured.

"Nothing." Flinging his arm around her, he pulled her closer, wedging her into the curve of his body, kissing the damp mass of her hair. The flat place below her ribs swelled in and out under his hand.

God of the City and of the Heart

They had reached a crossroads. Gete chewed his lip. Boarded-up storage houses bore metal plates on the doors; not for the first time, he wished he could read. They were probably signs of some sort. The few men and women hurrying along in the street bobbed their heads to Thani, but then scurried past too quickly for Gete to accost them.

And anyhow, he *should* know where he was!

He could not admit to Thani that he was lost. They had said good-bye to their fellow passengers, to whom she had preached several sermons over the course of the voyage, telling them they were going straight to the Divinarch.

Then they had disembarked from the *Foam Rider* with their noses in the air and strode off down the docks.

He looked over at her. She had joined her hands in her sleeves against the cold and pulled her cowl down over her eyes. Any minute she would poke him in the ribs and whisper, *Why have we stopped?* For some reason she did not want people to know they were strangers in the city. She jittered quietly, her teeth chattering.

She had had a bad time in Delta City. He knew that much. Something to do with her sister, the woman who had briefly been Divinarch.

She took her hand out of her pocket and thrust it through his arm. He brought her fingers to his lips and kissed them.

Which way?

He chose a direction at random. From the rise of the ground, he guessed that they were moving parallel to the sea, toward the big river. But the streets grew narrower, and twisted and turned at random. Soon he had lost all sense of which way they were going. Now and again, a knot of Hands crossed their path. Instinctively, Gete recognized the almost amorous way in which they jostled close together. It was battle formation. They did not give him and Thani a second glance.

Storage houses gave way to decrepit tenements. Here, at least, the city seemed more alive. Not so many Hands. Children dashed across the streets; women fed house pigs by doorsteps. Cooking fumes misted in the air. Gete guided Thani around the splashes of dung. As they progressed through the alleys, every last toddler and ancient stopped what he or she was doing to curtsy or bow to her. But the expressions on their faces were not right. Not love and worship; fear and slyness. They gave him the shivers.

The sun glazed the streets coldly. A glass ceiling seemed to tremble over the roofs of the houses, warping everything on the ground. The Deltans' faces were brilliant green, like cracked lacquer. Features wobbled and spread as Gete stared at them. Lips formed prayers—or curses? The solid black shadows of windows and doors shifted, lifting slightly to let tiny green hands and noses squeeze out from underneath. The hands made rude gestures and clasped in attitudes of mock prayer. Gete could never quite catch them when he swung his head.

"What's *wrong?*" Thani whispered.

Gete stared at the ground. They were halted in the end of a cul-de-sac. Lime-colored faces swam in the windows. The smell of something burning drifted from a door. A hawker wandered past the mouth of the road, shrilly touting meat-pies. "I'm lost."

"No. Oh, *Gete.*"

"Why did you think I knew where I was going? *You're* the one who's been here before!"

"It was five years ago. I was a child. Why don't you ask somebody?"

"They're afraid of us." It came out unintentionally.

"Gods. Perhaps we shouldn't have come. I should have struggled on as best I could—"

"Then why did we come?"

"Gete, I—just couldn't go on!"

"It was what happened in K'Fier. Wasn't it?" Gete was sweating in the cold. "You've lost your faith, and we've come here to find it again."

"No! Oh, no!" She made a noise halfway between a sniffle and a sob and wiped her nose. "How could I lose faith? I am a flamen! My miracles have not weakened! I . . ."

He stood stiffly by her side. The houses seemed to list closer and closer together over their heads. The sun slowly decomposed, crumbling down onto the cobbles.

"It seems so many things have gone wrong," Thani murmured. "There has to be a reason. There has to be. Sometimes I think we are just counters, like the pawns in a game of Conversion—all of us just lemans, just children—and the gods don't care whether we stand or fall . . . but I *know* that isn't true. There's a reason for everything! This war serves to illustrate something which we are ready to comprehend, and I'm too stupid to understand what I'm being shown—"

Gete could not stand to hear her putting herself down! Angrily, he burst out, "Would it be so terrible to believe that there *is* no Balance? The gods are at war! Is that so unbelievable? Maybe the scenes we've been looking at for thousands of years have finally been lifted, and we're seeing the squabbles backstage!"

"You frighten me!" Her teeth chattered. She gripped his arm. "We have lost our way, that is all. We have to find our way—have to ask—the Divinarch—"

At that moment, the last thing Gete wanted to do was to go to the Divinarch. The very idea terrified him.

After he had given up trying to understand the world of the gods, Desti's world, he had started trying to *understand* the faith he'd followed all his life, because it was Thani's faith. But what if he had been right in the first place? What if the gods were only a troupe of quarreling play-actors? Worse, what if they were absolutely ordinary—like Desti?

He gazed around helplessly. It was at that moment that he saw the figure curled in the garbage beside a flight of steps.

Thani had not sensed it. What did that mean?

Releasing her with a whispered reassurance, he crossed the cul-de-sac and shook the thin, green-skinned god. The nearly shaved head flopped back. The globular lids were closed. Gete tried again, holding his breath. This time the god's eyes opened and he jumped to his feet.

All around, windows, shutters, doors slammed shut. *Chock chock chock.* Gete retreated across the street.

"Better get out of here," he hissed to Thani. "It's a god. He's mad. Or a renegade—"

"No! A god? How—" She flipped back her cowl. Suddenly, she was all reverent ministry. "Inviolate One!" Her voice carried like a bell. "How can I be of assistance?"

"Not in the Palace," the god muttered. "Thought I got there. Where am I?"

"Doxton," came a sigh from a dozen closed windows. Did Gete detect the gleam of eyes in the cracks of the shutters? No Sarberran would ever be so craven as to leave a flamen to her fate, and *watch!* "Chilte Close," they sighed.

"Miles away!" The god slumped. He seemed to have become suddenly disoriented: as if the substitution of the pungently real Chilte Close for the phantasmic Palace was too much for him. Perhaps his disillusionment made him visible to Thani. She moved unerringly to him and put her arm around his waist. He did not resist. Gete shook himself into action, going to support the god on the other side.

"We can help you to the Palace, Inviolate One," Thani told him. Her excited breath formed tiny ice crystals that fell like sugar. "Can you show us the way?"

"I . . ." the god muttered. "I could not believe the insolence of him. He wouldn't do it. Wouldn't. I pleaded with him . . . threw my pride at his feet . . . what there was left of it . . . and still."

Gete swallowed.

"Go back the way you came," the windows whispered. "Till you reach Doxton Concourse. Then turn left."

"Cross Honey Street."

"Cross Immanence Circle."

"Godsister, 'ave pity on us."

"Go past a distillery called Oakyew Brothers."

"Don't punish us."

"Wait," Gete shouted, squinting upward. "Stop!" He was actively hating the Deltans now, but he had to milk them for what they knew. "Go over it again! From the beginning—"

It seemed that the voices guided them all the way, a host of tiny, timorous currents wafting them along the river of streets. Before long, Gete had to clench his fists to keep from hitting out at some innocent passerby. He wanted badly to hurt someone.

Preferably this Hand. If not for him . . . if not for *him* . . .

Gete and Thani might even now be making their way back to the docks!

The Hand was recovering slowly. His wrists rested on Gete and Thani's arms; now and again he stumbled against one of them. In the faraway eyes, Gete saw something that might be madness, or might be dread so great it came close to approximating peace. What did a god fear that much?

The answer was obvious. Gete found his palms were sweating.

Thani kept up a running flow of talk. It seemed rather pathetic to have to remind a god of his own divinity, his supremacy, his invulnerability; but the stream of doctrine seemed to be doing Thani herself some good. Her salt crystals shot sparks of light and her lips gleamed wetly. Gete's heart swelled with a helpless urge to protect her.

And maybe, after all, she been working a very minor kind of miracle. As they entered a very upscale district, where all market activity ceased, and Thani's voice rang emptily off the walls of the high stone mansions—Gete observed a change in the god. His face took on an actual expression. It might be amusement.

A bell chimed far off. In the silence that ensued, Gete could hear the sea. He caught a salty whiff of it, too, carried on a freak breeze down countless alleys. Quite suddenly, he felt at home here in the silence, where furtive fingers moved behind lace curtains in the few windows that still held glass.

And the Palace reared up within wood-and-stone walls, a forbidding, yet higgledy-piggledy height: it looked rather rundown. At the top of a long wooden ramp, two Hands stood sentinel under a suspended row of dangerous-looking metal teeth.

One of them let out a shout. "Arity! *Firi! Perich"hi!*" His voice held a curious mixture of amazement and horror.

Thani broke off. " *'Arity*," she whispered in a dreamlike tone. "No. It is not possible. It can't be." She spun around, shading her salted eyes at the god. They had mounted the ramp and the Hands were closing with them.

The god named Arity shook himself and sighed. "I suppose you'd better take us to Pati." Gete was astonished by the sheer rationality of his tone.

"At once, *perich"hi!*" the Hand exclaimed. "What do you think we are? He has been searching for your ghost all of yesterday and today! When the ghostier vanished, we thought he had absconded with it! Just think how happy he will be to see you alive!"

The other Hand pushed him aside. "Let me tell the *perich"hi*, you fool. The Divinarch rescinded the order for your death yesterday, the minute he returned from taking his revenge on the K'Fier renegades."

"I don't believe it," Arity murmured. His murmur was still louder than a human exclamation, giving the comment the tone of a desperate avowal of disbelief. "He never changes his mind!"

"He did this time. He sent a delegation to get you back, but the ghostier had gone, leaving no traces. Sepia, the *kervayi-serbali*, swore he had handed you over to him—but Pati killed him anyway, to be sure." One after the other, the Hands embraced Arity. "He wants to take it out of the ghostier, too. We haven't found the rascal yet, but we're still looking—"

"It would be too bad to kill him," Arity said. "He spared me."

This did not fit with the mood of hapless despair in which Gete and Thani had found him. Gete shook his head, and slipped his fingers around Thani's arm. Perhaps if he could just pull her away—would she stand for it?

But it was too late. More Hands had appeared out of nowhere. Their delight was at once infectious and grotesque. Clustering into a knot, they surrounded Thani and Gete and whisked them across the courtyard, into a pair of doors in the Palace like a hole cut into darkness. Torches flared within, illuminating twisting corridors. After a nightmarish few minutes they attained a hall where a seething queue of Deltans, shifting their feet and muttering, extended as far as Gete could see. The humans fell mutinously silent when they saw the Hands.

"I do hate jumping the queue," Arity murmured.

"Don't be absurd!" One of the strangest-looking Hands, whose face and throat were mostly covered by a splotchy blue patch shaped rather like a bird, punched Arity affectionately. "They ought to thank their stars you're alive! The Divinarch is in such a bad mood he's sentenced every petitioner so far to instant death!"

"Gods," Thani whispered, and gulped as if she were about to cry.

For some reason Gete had not credited her with understanding the gods' jabber. He steadied her as the Hands swept them down the length of the hall, past the restless civilians, through another monstrous pair of doors that opened as if by magic.

The Throne Room was dim. The reek of death hung sour in the air. Twelve gods stood on pedestals built into the huge, fantastic throne. But the seat itself was empty.

A pile of bodies lay in the middle of the floor. Black human blood trickled from its base. A slim, pale figure stood beside the gruesome hillock, wiping his fingers on a handkerchief. It was an easy guess that this was the Divinarch of Royalland, Calvary, Veretry, Pirady, Iceland, the sundry isles of the Archipelago, and Domesdys, et al.

When Arity entered the Throne Room at Gete's side, the Divinarch went stiller than any living thing ought to be able to.

Arity swayed toward him, like a sapling in a high wind. Just before he fell, he caught himself and stood upright.

"Go upstairs," Pati whispered hoarsely. "Wait for me."

"No," Arity said. "Say what you have to say before my friends."

"Shall I? *Oh, Arity*—Perhaps I shall." The Divinarch's voice was soft as falling drops of blood. "I thought you were dead, and I did not have so much as your ghost. I—" His eye fell on Gete, and he stopped. Instinctively, Gete cringed back into the knot of Hands who had brought them. "What is this thing with the fiery head? There is another one? Dispatch them. They have heard too much."

"But, milord Divinarch," one of the Hands on the Throne called out respectfully. He was a small god with parchment-brown skin and a luxuriant mop of hair, "It's a flamen and leman. Should you . . ."

"Oh, very well then, I'll deal with them." The Divinarch flicked a glance at Arity like a slow-uncoiling lash of fire. "It will only take a few minutes."

Arity made a face, and then shrugged.

Gete poked Thani. This was her moment. He had brought her this far by hook or by crook; now she was on her own.

She took a step forward. "Milord Divinarch," she began, "I come in humble suppliance."

"I'm sure you do." The Divinarch's voice was honey. He snapped his fingers. In a sharp-smelling flash, he was up on the Throne, among the Hands, leaning down. "Come here."

Thani took one step. Then another. Swaying, blind, she stumbled to the base of the Throne.

Forever afterward, Gete would curse himself for failing to break the ice of fear off his joints, failing to go to her, to clamp his hands over her budding salt crystals, anything that might have saved her.

Her lord is the whole world.

She can see him in the gray confusion where she lives and moves.

See him whole and entire, sharp enough to make her cry for her sacrificed sight.

See the veins on the backs of his hands.

See his white bangs springing down the middle of his forehead.

See the pupils in the centers of his bicolored eyes.

Hear his voice honey-sweet, louder than her ears can stand. Its purity is spoiled by the buzzing in the bones of her skull. She takes her head in her hands, trying to shake

*the interference away, but then she understands what he has
asked and she forgets the discomfort and falls to her knees
on the invisible floor, ready to answer, eager to please.*

"Who do you serve?"

"You. You, milord Divinarch!"

"Why did you come to Delta City?"

*"To learn the tales and parables my Godsbrother did not
teach me." The answers are both rote and heartfelt. "To
learn how to worship you better. To learn how to preach
your worship in the far corners of the world."*

"And what did you find?"

*"That—that ..." With a failing of the heart, she knows
she has to tell the real truth. If she does not, he will know,
and be angry with her. "The city is under martial rule ...
The teachers are gone ... The world-renowned flamens of
Marshtown turned apostate. The people are afraid of their
gods, and their flamens."*

*"Those who are truly devout have nothing to fear from
me. Or you. For not all my flamens have betrayed me. Most,
in fact, have stayed in the fold. And this is not martial rule,
my darling. I am merely keeping the peace. Believe me, it's
harder to keep the peace now than it ever was before! The
forces of Change are at work on the world. I am all that
stands between them and you and your people." He jumps
to the floor beside her and raises her up. His hot smooth
palms completely enclose her hands. "Do not lose faith, little starling."*

Do not lose faith! *He* knows. *He* knows *the torture she
has been undergoing.*

*A marvelous peace enfolds her. After so many months of
unfocused yearning, she has found the truth.*

*It's all a matter of having faith. Why has that been so
difficult for her? It is the easiest thing in the world.* Faith.

*No wonder that when she looked for the old stability, it
was gone. The gods are no longer rulers of a well-ordered,
cyclical existence. All the cycles have come to an end or been
broken. The forces of Change took Godsbrother Transcendence from her; they banished her from Calvary, the land
of her dreams. Only the Divinarch stands between her and
its further ravages.*

It was unfair of me to promise security to Gete the way
Transcendence promised it to me. He cannot look to me,
nor to the world, to give him a whole, unbroken life. He

must look to the Divinarch. The Divinarch is our only hope
against the scourge of destiny. He loves his people so much
that he is fighting time itself for our sakes. With his Hands
he is erecting a dam against the tide.

*She trembles. Comprehension ripples like ecstatic sensa-
tion through her body. Bells and trumpets pound against the
inside of her head. She prays the tremors are not physical.
She is so frail.*

"Divinarch, I will do whatever you ask." *Her voice wa-
vers up and down the scale as if she is not paying attention
to what she is saying. But she is, with all her might.* "I will
keep the faith!"

"My pet. My child. My love."

*He embraces her. He could break her in two with his
strength. He is so gentle.*

*She bites the inside of her cheek. Salty blood trickles onto
her tongue.* "Take me." *She smears it with a trembling finger
on the back of his hand.* "Take my body. Take my soul."

*He kisses her forehead, the tip of her nose. His breath
smells of her blood. His grip is like a vise on her arms.* "Do
my will, my own little flamen. Whatever I say. Whatever any
of the Hands say. They speak for me."

"Anything! I'll do anything! I—"

*But he is gone, leaving her with her arms outstretched,
empty. Shining, he strides around behind the Throne, behind
the fainter shapes of the lesser gods. She can still see him,
but faintly, as if through water.* "Thank the Power that's
over," *he says.* "I hate the taste of fur. Now, Ari—"

*She falls to her knees, sobbing, crying, pleading with him
to come back.* Don't leave me!

*But the Inviolate Ones grab her arms and she is half-
marched, half-dragged out through the great doors into a
sea of humans. Darkness. Noise. Where is Gete? She panics.*

*Gete finds her. He wraps his arms around her. He drags
her out of the way of unseen legs and feet.*

*And little by little she manages to stop weeping. It is then
that she senses the light within her. She gasps, puts her hands
to her chest, imagines she can feel its heat ... at the same
time as she hears a bugle voice calling,* "Chrumecountry ...
first barge," *and Gete replies distractedly.*

She smiles, conscious of nothing except profound relief,

knowing that now, wherever she goes, she is at home. She does not have to doubt any longer. The light will never leave her. She is his, and she will remain his, no one's but his, until the day she dies in his service.

Destiny Besieged

"I was wrong to do it," Pati said. He stood at the glass wall, staring out over the speckled sea. He wore a Kithrilindric bedrobe with spangles that flashed when he moved. "But at the time, I believed I had to. You were making a fool of me, with your human *irissu* and your warped politics!" He turned. "You must see that, Ari. Now you are back, I know there will be no more such incidents."

Contrition. From the warnings of the Hands, this was what Arity had expected. Yet it unnerved him. He could not remember any other time when Pati had acted as he, Arity, expected. And the reason for that, he conjectured, was that he and Pati lived by two entirely different systems—call them the mortal and the *auchresh*, call them what you would. The difference had been there ever since they had come to human country, perhaps all their civilized lives. Pati's path was that of the intellectual, the utterly civilized, unalloyedly rational, and his destiny was where it led: the intertwined mountains and chasms of genius and monstrosity.

Arity had never before seen him speak without thinking, without a plan, without any motive except emotion.

But of course Pati had had a bad scare.

"I regretted it immediately! Didn't the Hands tell you? I reversed my order—"

"And you never, ever reverse orders," Arity said.

"Gods! What has the ghostier done to you?" Pati said. "He's changed you! Has he made you into a ghost after all? No, it can't be! Even a ghost is not as cold as you are!"

"It's not that I don't *feel*," Arity said, nettled. He lowered himself into a splay-legged chair made from the skeletons of dog lizards, and reached out to the remnants of the supper Pati had ordered. He swiped his finger around the kasha bowl and sucked off the goo. "It's that—well, one has to locate a balance. There is such a thing as giving in to one's feelings. As lack of self-control. I had fallen so far into that trap that I touched bottom—because I *decided,* and kept on consciously deciding to relinquish all self-control."

"That makes no sense," Pati said angrily. The lamplight made him glow against the backdrop of the dark windows. The room smelled of an unfamiliar body perfume. Had Pati had another *ghauthiji* up here while he grieved for Arity? Arity wouldn't put it past him.

"Hear me out," Arity said. "Yesterday, all I could think of to do was die. I had lost you. Without you, I had nothing in the world to live for. But Ghostier Southwind refused to indulge me. And I lack the courage to kill myself. I could not die.

"I suppose it was inevitable that I realized my only alternative was to live." Arity laughed. "It was that girl-flamen you brainwashed this afternoon who gave me the first push. She babbled on and on about our greatness and glory—trying to convince herself of it as much as me, I think, your pets are not as certain of themselves as they were—and I was staggering along between her and her leman, you know, scarcely able to walk in a straight line. I could not keep from laughing at the utter absurdity of the whole thing!"

"Absurdity?" Pati said sharply.

"Yes, absurdity! The gulf of reality between our lives and our pretensions to grandeur." Arity ate a finger of marzipan. "I don't know about you, but I can't continue as I was. The hypocrisy is choking. I feel sick."

"I see that you have changed in a way I cannot quite appreciate. Though I am trying." Pati leaned back against the glass, his robe outlining the bones of his hips. The silk hem pooled over his bare feet. Arity caught himself thinking how elegant Pati was, then mentally reproved himself. The aftertaste of the marzipan was bitter, like straight vanilla. "But this philosophizing is a dangerous new pastime, as well as an irksome one. Perhaps you have forgotten that we have started a war. Every minute we waste is a minute lost to the enemy."

Arity said, "I can't go on subjecting myself to you."

That got his attention. The blue eye and the brown blazed. "I never asked you to make yourself my slave!"

"You did! Think back to Wind Gully Heaven, and you'll see what I mean. But that doesn't really matter. Since I came to the city, the only way I've been able to defy you is by subjecting myself to you still further. Refusing to accept special treatment. It didn't work. In a way, I suppose I'm acknowledging you were right." The bones of the chair were digging into his backside. He did not take his eyes off Pati, whose rigid stance, like that of a predator poised on a clifftop, vividly betrayed the intensity of his emotions. "But you were right for all the wrong reasons. You wanted to confer privileges on me, but you still wanted me to be your slave." He paused. "That's the way it has been between us, ever since you were a *mainraui* and I was a Foundling. And it doesn't work."

"You are so *blind,* Ari!" Pati's cry of pain severed the silk of the argument Arity had woven around himself. "You have completely misunderstood me. I knew that—but that doesn't mean I *wanted* it! *You* wanted to relinquish all responsibility for yourself, to wallow in the mindless pleasure—or misery, how should I know which it was?—of being needed. Of being required by somebody else. I let you do it because I love you. But have you really failed to see that ever since we found each other again, all I have wanted is for you to love me back? I don't want another Hand. I want a companion!"

Arity kept blinking. These impassioned words sounded as if they were flooding from Pati's heart—an organ whose existence he had seriously doubted.

He had forgotten about the vortex of need that fueled Pati's intellect. Need beyond erotic desire or even the longing for companionship. Need for the thing most lacking in the whimsical, merciless court he had created: honesty. The need of the whole *auchresh* race for trust, an emotion none of them was really capable of. A gift none of them could give each other.

(A gift that Humi, with her charm and humanity, had fooled Arity into believing she had given him—)

Gone, long gone—

"Power, Pati, I'm sorry!"

"I'm not everything I pretend to be ..." Pati's voice broke. If it was not real, it was extremely convincing. "You are the only person who knows that. That is why I . . . need you."

Arity said deliberately, "You're a god." He had to plumb Pati's mind, now he had the chance. He owed it to the whole world. He was the only one in the world who had the faintest hope of finding out what Pati really thought. That was part of why he had returned. "You don't need anybody. Not me. Or anybody. You embody the Divine Entity. You are completely supreme."

Pati laughed. Not insanely. Normally. "You knew me before we engaged in this masquerade, Arity. A god? There is no theory so ungrounded in possibility as the existence of gods. You disappoint me."

Arity nodded, sadly.

The most flawless conceits were, after all, not strong enough to bridge the gaps in reality. Those gaps had to remain mysterious. (Unless one is a flamen, a little voice said inside Arity.) Belief on its own could not span anything.

Yet it was profoundly embarrassing to hear Pati admit it. And even more embarrassing to see him fold up into a dark hump at the foot of the window. Almost unbearable to hear him panting, like an animal that knows it is fatally wounded.

Arity, despite all his intentions to the contrary, went to him and bent down, taking his head on his lap and kissing the vibrant white hair. "I love you," he murmured.

Pati twisted, revealing his face. He was weeping. The muscles at the bases of his folded wings were as hard as stone.

Of course they stumbled into the bedroom. Of course, half against Arity's will and half not, they made love. Sex was after all the mainstay of their relationship—always had been, even when they were not lovers. How could he have thought *that* might change? Pati writhed and sweated and groaned, but Arity enjoyed the pipe of smokewort they shared afterward more than the act. Pati had brought the wort back from the Archipelago. Killing all the renegades in K'Fier had meant ransacking the town. It was potent stuff.

The transparent bowl of the pipe glowed red in the darkness of the bedroom. They lay propped companionably in the high old bed that had belonged to countless Divinarches before them.

I have to clip my thorns, Arity thought. New ones were sprouting, the old bases pushing up from his skin like miniature tablelands. Pati had welcomed the pain of the scratches the razored edges inflicted on him. Arity had known he had a streak that way: its revelation came as no surprise.

"Do you intend to continue as a Hand?" Pati said at length.

"I'll take the title of Lieutenant," Arity said. "Not Heir. Still not Heir." He had thought this out already. "I'll serve as the twentieth councillor, too. I think that's fitting."

"Nothing could please me more. We'll shuffle all the *kervayim* down one. You may have heard that I disposed of Sepia; I would have had to elect a new councillor anyway, and it goes against the grain to promote Hands from the ranks that high."

Arity sucked on the pipe. The smoke slid down his throat like mint ice. Off the top of a lungful, he said, "I have something I want to ask you."

"Anything you like," Pati said.

"Did your patrols find Humi? Or Hope?"

A long pause.

"No."

Pause. Smoke trickled out of Arity's nostrils, thin milky strands, and he released his breath.

"Nor Southwind. Nor the female crime lord. But I doubt," Pati said, "that it will be very long before they all announce their whereabouts."

"You mean . . ."

"They are all in it together. Yes; we would be stupid not to prepare for the worst." The word entered Arity's being, as potent as the smoke.

"Do you really think that's what she intends? I didn't think she had it in her anymore."

"I know she has."

Arity shrugged. "Perhaps you're right. You and she always understood each other in that way. So you intend to defend yourself by attacking?"

"Exactly."

"Two wars at once!" Arity tried to joke. "Just like ancient times, with the Conversion Wars and the quarrels over our role as gods going on simultaneously in the salt—"

"Except that this time we *auchresh* are in control." Pati corrected him. "We know the mortals' capacity for hysteria, and we will try to involve as few of them as possible, on both fronts. And, should we have to crush insurrections here or in the continents, we are not short of recruits. Broken Bird and Bronze Water, the poor misguided *umanurim,* and their obsolete leadership, drive more young *keres* into my arms every day. We even have a few *iuim;* I've made them honorary captains."

"Excellent," Arity said, but the truth was that he did not think it excellent at all. *War.* He wished to the Power he did not have to play a part in it. There seemed not a doubt that neither Pati's ideological crusade against the renegades nor Humi's rebellion could be kept clear of mortal passions, and mortal lives.

Yet he was committed now, and one saw things out to the grim end. One chose one's fate with one's eyes open.

Pati reached for the pipe. His fingers touched Arity's just long enough to convey intimacy, not long enough to be lascivious. The very delicacy of the caress was predictable. But of course Pati's predictability, like that of anything else, depended on nothing but Arity's own predictions. It was he who had changed. After having death snatched from his throat, everything else naturally seemed predictable by comparison. Didn't it?

"Ahhh." The wort glowed as Pati sucked the stem, reddening the concentrated planes of his face. *He is beautiful in the way that any* auchresh *is beautiful, even more so,* Arity told himself impatiently. *I have a gorgeous lover who happens to be the Divinarch and I have just become the twentieth councillor of the Ellipse. Now why does it feel like I've been here before?*

Murder in the Dark

The killers jimmy the back door with stealthy expertise. They close it behind themselves to cut off the draft, and before you can say "Wait a minute . . . aren't you . . ." they have slipped upstairs. They do not have to look for their victims. Do everyone in the house, they were told. So they climb up to the musty, cavernous attic and work their way down. Another family, the Brundels, inhabits the top three

floors, but the killers don't know that and it would make
no difference if they did. Within three minutes, they've dispatched Grandfather Brundel, Father Brundel, Mother
Brundel, Maiden-aunt Brundel, and the five children over
whose welfare the adults have spent all evening arguing.
The question of whether to send them out to their relatives
in Chrumetown (would the journey be too dangerous? does
the risk of staying in the city justify it?) is moot—at the
same time as it has been definitively answered.

Bruises burst up like tumors through the fur of the Brundels' throats. All three killers favor the garotte as a means
of noiseless, efficient murder. The sound of breath has
stopped: the parents still hold each other but their arms
have been transformed into heavy pieces of meat. The
blood no longer moves through the flesh.

The house dog whines and yips on the landing, sensing
something is wrong, as the trio slithers down the staircase
into the Lakestones' apartment.

"Hist," the leader whispers, and with a muttered profan-
ity, the last man draws his dagger from the sheath in his
boot. It whickers through the dark and pins the little dog
to the floor by one eye. The furry beast flops, fishlike, and
is still.

The killers closed all the windows before they started,
just in case there were screams, but all the same, the winter
seems to seep down after them from the upstairs apartment. It is the mute, intangible cold of the absence of life.
The killers breathe easily in it, all their muscles loose. They
are not natives of this rarefied, potent atmosphere, but they
have been changed by their regular visits to the heights.

The little Lakestone girl and the boy stop breathing without a struggle. The woman, too, slips as quietly out of life
as she slipped through its cracks. The man is another story.
He is already awake. When the killers enter the room he
and his wife share, he is hiding behind the door. When he
sees the first man bending over Leasa, he leaps at the killer
with a howl, huge hands raking his back. The other two
are still behind him, and between them they grab the man
and throttle him, one drawing the noose spitefully tight
while the other grips his massive limbs until they stop
moving.

"Pfuh," says the first killer, dropping the woman on the
bed. "Bleeder got me in the kidneys."

"Yer leakin a bit. But you won't die 'fore we get back."

"Fuck it. Less go."

Spitting one after the other, in a ritualistic fashion, on the threshold of the bedroom, they leave through the front door as softly as they came in.

The wounded house stands immobile, crushed between its neighbors, screaming silently for help. Its eaves tilt upward as if it is trying to squeeze out of the narrow space Temeriton has allotted it. One imagines that when it is able to fly, it will wing ungainly off into the stars, flapping its shutters and doors like stiff little wings.

The red lantern of the brothel across the concourse flickers. Night is winding down toward dawn. *Delights and Diversions'* door swings gently, half-open, scraping along the groove it has worn in the cobbles.

Aneisneida's bodywoman woke her at four in the morning. "Get up! Milady, get up!" She shook Aneisneida roughly through the bedcovers. "Milady, get dressed!"

A shock ran through Aneisneida and she threw the coverlet aside. "What's happened?" Strangely enough, Fiamorina and Soderingal did not spring to her mind. With an uncharacteristic flash of prescience, she saw Humi's face floating in the dark, smiling that faint, bland, superior smile of hers. Petula wrung her hands. Her dress was hooked askew, her petticoat showed, and her hair straggled over her breasts. "It's happened! Milady, they're coming! You must get ready to receive them!"

"*Who* is coming?"

The candle Petula had set on the bed fell over, spilling hot wax onto the embroidery.

Outside the window, the palace district was dark and silent. Aneisneida strained her ears. Nothing.

The bodywoman's hands shook as she struck flint and relighted the candle. "The Inviolate Ones! Oh, milady, you must look your best! Your hair—your clothes—what about your pink gown—the one with the tiered skirts? For them, only the best will do. We must show 'em our importance, or we're lost!"

Aneisneida swung her feet to the floor. She stood rock-still, the coverlet crunched between her hands. Petula forgot herself so far as to tug at her arm.

Aneisneida wrenched away. "Stop it, girl!" She brought

her palms together as loudly as she could. A manservant came to the door. Even in the candlelight he looked frightened. "Go rouse Lord Nearecloud!" Aneisneida told him. "And Nurse. Tell her to wrap the little lady up warmly." He did not move. She shouted, "Go!"

When he had gone, Petula begged, "Milady? Milady, are you out of your mind? *Please* dress!"

"It is *you* who are out of your mind! Receive the Hands? They would slaughter us where we stood." Aneisneida knew without having to think about it that Pati had finally decided to exterminate them. The Neareclouds, along with a few other families, were the last seedlings of a palace district vine that had once tried to strangle him. Had she been in Pati's position, she would have assassinated herself a long time ago.

How long did they have? There weren't many families left. Most of them were squatters, practiced at hiding their movements, in case, by some remote chance, the real owners of their houses should come back from Purgatory and punish them. This house lay at the Christon end of the district, within walking distance of Gremlaw Concourse. If the Hands came on foot, as they seemed to do more and more often now, if they swept west from the Palace, if they were keeping Anei and Soder until last, as a child keeps the biggest cherry until the end of the bowl—the Neareclouds might have enough time to get away.

"When they are roused, they are like beasts," she said to Petula. "They do not think. Even if the Divinarch had ordered them to spare us, it would not guarantee our safety."

Petula nodded. Her eyes spilled over and she snatched her gown to her face.

"Get out of my sight." Contemptuously, Aneisneida gave the girl a shove. Smothering sobs, Petula darted out of the bedroom.

Aneisneida picked up the dead candle.

Wax burned her hand. She smelled singed thread.

Cold wind sighed past the gables.

Far away. Gay, delighted shouts.

Fear shivered through her bones.

Calm. Calm.

She stalked to the wardrobe annex and sorted through her pile of dresses. This one had the most jewels on its cuffs. It was not the prettiest. Nor one of those her father had given her. Before putting it on, she slit the hem and weighted it with jewelry out of her boudoir jewel cases. When she was half hooked up, she heard Soderingal come in behind her. He was carrying Fiamorina. "We're leavin," he said. "Get that stuff off of you."

With a contortion that hurt her shoulder muscles, she fastened the last hooks. "Do you really think I'm going to stay here and greet them in my finery? I am not stupid, Soder." She felt no fear now, only a cold determination to enrage Pati, to get away. Like transmogrified terror. Steel.

She shook her wrists at him and the heavy bands of sapphires flapped. "I'll tell you where we are going. We are going to offer our services to Humi. We are going to commit ourselves to the revolution. And thus, we will eventually gain back everything we are going to lose tonight."

"Fuck that. We're goin to join my father in Shimorning," Soder said. "I've 'ad it with bendin my 'ead to Divinarches, no matter what they call themselves!"

"You pampered son of an idle noblewoman." Anger rose in Aneisneida. "What matters is that we have to choose our lord for ourselves. We didn't, before, or only halfheartedly."

A faint, evil orange was flickering in the top panes of the window.

"We're fuckin well not going to throw our lives away. Shut that crap. Humi's a blind beggar, no more, no less. We're going to Shimorning."

Soderingal had never expressed his opinion of Humi so succinctly before. His eyes were like stones.

And Aneisneida felt herself bending, melting—

She *knew* what she had to do! For once in her life she knew what she had to do! And she—

opened her mouth to give in—

And flames rose above the roofs a mere five or six streets away. Aneisneida and Soderingal spun to the suddenly bright window. Fiamorina wailed in her father's arms. The servants hammered on the door. Lord and Lady Nearecloud glanced at each other, and bounded downstairs.

Not even the nurse would accompany them when she heard they were going "to Temeriton . . . to Shimorning!" The servants stood in a tearful gaggle on the front steps,

trusting and foolish, ready to throw themselves on the
Hands' mercy. Petula begged, "You *can't* leave! All the
tap'stries . . . all the silver . . . all yer lovely dresses, milady—"

The loss of her wardrobe did give Aneisneida a pang,
but it was a pinprick compared to the determination the
Hands aroused in her. If only she could make Soder see!
Throwing themselves on the mercy of a crime lord would
be like jumping from the frying pan into the fire.

If the whole city didn't go up in flames.

As they hurried along the broad streets of the palace
district, in the biting night air, they argued passionately.
Soder seemed to have a childish conviction that her father
would be able to protect them from Pati, even if all the
Hands stormed the Rats' Den at once. Aneisneida told him
over and over that he was wrong. Gold Dagger's army of
followers were in it for the profit. Harboring nobility, a
practice which had long ago proved fatal, could not exactly
be profitable. The Nearclouds, or at least Anei herself,
would be turned over to Pati.

She did not want to be held accountable for her husband's misconceptions! She did not want Fia to be held
accountable!

She did not trust Gold Dagger, not as she trusted Humi.

But her feet began to tire, and Fiamorina, passed constantly back and forth between them, grew heavier and
heavier, and the prospect of walking all the way to Temeriton no longer seemed so plausible. She was stumbling with
tiredness as they entered the alleys that twisted along between the Christon concourses. Her slippers were slowly
cutting her feet into bite-sized pieces. And before she realized where Soder was leading her—before she had consented to anything, before she had given in—they were
cutting across the corner of Marshtown that lay between
Christon and Shimorning.

One of their manservants passed them. The alley they
moved in was narrow and dark, but the fellow scuttled past
as fast as a spider across a floor too large and bare for its
liking. "Hoy!" Soderingal hissed.

The fellow reversed his trajectory and matched his pace
to Aneisneida's. His eyes were large and green as toads'
heads, bulging from his smoke-stained face. "They burned

the mansion, milord! *Burned* it! Everything—the stars gray with smoke. Everything. Few of us got away!"

"Just as I was expecting," Aneisneida said wearily.

The man was drawing ahead again. Soderingal called out, "Raille! One thing more! D'you know how we kin get to the"—he tasted the words carefully before pronouncing them—"the Rats' Den?"

The manservant threw up one hand, clasping his other awkwardly to his side. "You can find it anywhere in Shimorning you look, milord. But you have to know how to look." He laughed breathlessly. "Now good evening, milord, milady! Gods bless!"

And he was gone. Starlight glistened in his wet footprints. He must have been bleeding, Aneisneida realized.

Soderingal shifted Fiamorina to his other arm. "And me 'is *master!*" he ground out, charging along, blind with frustration. Aneisneida understood before long that he had no idea where he was going. But for the haze of tiredness that stilled her mind, she would have been furious.

Windows threw a flickering light on the cobbles. A tavern. The back entrance. She could hear voices and laughter. For the first time since they left their house, the sound did not ring alarm bells in her. "Can we go in?" she begged. "Can we sit down?"

Soderingal glanced at her. "I'll ask directions t' the Rats' Den. We won't stay."

It was a hole-in-the-wall, full of regulars who all knew each other. Aneisneida did not understand any of the remarks they addressed to her; but Soder found himself in his element. Despite his purported good intentions, he did not get around to mentioning the Rats' Den until he had had enough whiskey to weight his tongue and make his lips gleam darkly.

All the Shimorningers exchanged significant glances when they heard "Gold Dagger." But the little green-furred fellow who eventually elected himself as their informant refused to give his name. "Yew don't want t' go down there, milord." He eyed Aneisneida's wrists in a way she did not like. "They be thieves down there. And apostates, now, too. And they do say the Divinarch 'ave hidden there, and tis true there are daggermen at every trapdoor, like as if they 'ad somethin to guard."

The word struck like a sunbeam through the fog in An-

eisneida's mind. "The Divinarch?" she gasped. "Not Pati?
Humi?"

"They do say it be Lady Garden. But I've 'eard stories
like that afore, an I'm not gettin' my 'opes up, not me."

"The Divinarch." Aneisneida looked her husband full in
the face. Smoke curled drunkenly between them. All the
sounds of the tavern seemed to fade away as she savored
her triumph. What an exquisite pleasure to outfox him, and
all the sweeter for having done it accidentally! "*Ha,*" she
said. "Shall we go, milord? I consent with pleasure. What
will you call her now? Even your vaunted father serves her.
Is she a blind beggar, or a *queen*?"

Soderingal said nothing. He stared at her with a mixture
of emotions she could not read.

And Aneisneida dashed her face into Fiamorina's robe,
and as the toddler woke and began to grizzle, she burst
into tears, clutching Fia as if the child could compensate
for the loss of everything she had ever valued. The Summer
name was really gone now. Everything that had been Belstem's was burned to ashes, sprinkled across the city. All
that remained was one name.

Humi.

*Give me back the past. Or at least make it safe for me to
pretend I am there!*

Sol lowered his voice as he ushered Aneisneida and Soderingal down the crooked stone stairs. "I ought to warn
you. She should be sleeping. We can only spare her for a
few hours at a time. But she just found out that some
friends of hers have been killed, so she has come down
here to be alone."

"You did not tell us this!" Aneisneida whispered.
"Should we come back later?"

"No. She wants to see you." Sol's mouth pulled downward at the corners. "Just be aware what she has passed
through. You would never know to look at her that an
hour ago she was raging and weeping in my arms."

So the two were lovers? That was all right. Both of them
were ghostiers, so the involvement was almost proper—far
less scandalous, anyhow, than Humi's most publicized liaison, Aneisneida thought hopefully.

The green moss and lichen on the roof glowed over Sol's
torch as he led them around the last corner. He stepped

aside. Anei and Soder found themselves in a monstrous cavern. A table stood some way into the space, and on it was a ring of candles, flickering in a weary little breeze that must have found its way down from miles above and could not get back out. The small circle of light only emphasized the size of the place. Shadows crouched in the roughnesses of the floor like furry beasts. Water dripped down a distant wall. Aneisneida heard clawed feet in a corner.

She clung to Soderingal's arm. Uncharacteristically, he did not shake her off. They had come down through a complicated maze of stairways and tunnels, a labyrinth whose existence Aneisneida had never guessed: it was humbling to realize you were lady of so much less and so much more than you had thought. She guessed that Soderingal, like herself, felt less confident than usual.

Humi sat at the table, quite composed, with something long and scaly crawling over her arms.

"So it has started." She caressed the creature. It sat on her left hand, its long scarlet tongue leaping. "They have taken the palace district. I expect everything is confusion?"

Sol nodded. "They're jumping like fish on dry land. Two knife gangs are scheduled to mobilize within the hour. We're going to take advantage of the element of surprise and try to pick off as many Hands as possible, while keeping our real strength hidden."

"Have we received any word from Hope?"

"No," Sol said. "Not a thing."

Humi sighed enormously. "Well, I suppose I shall be needed upstairs. But we have a few minutes. Lord Nearecloud—Lady Summer." She nodded. "Will you sit on the table? I should not like to make you stand. You will be doing too much of that in the next few days." When neither of them moved, she said with a hint of irritation, "I mean no insult to your dignity. We have had to put etiquette temporarily in abeyance, here."

Rather awkwardly, Aneisneida hitched herself up on the table, arranging her skirts. Soderingal stood quite still.

"Sol, you'd better stay," Humi said. "I think it best if we have a witness to this little meeting."

Soder's mouth opened in indignation. Aneisneida thought, *Oh no, please be quiet!*

But he had not yet got beyond the first blow Humi had

delivered to his pride. "Wotcha mean calling my wife Summer? She's been Nearecloud for close on five years!"

"Oh." Humi sighed. "I am not implying that your marriage is invalid. Only that if you plan to remain here, on my side, it will be necessary for Aneisneida to reclaim her maiden name. If you conferred it on your daughter, too, that would be even better."

"No child of *mine*—" Soder spluttered.

"Have you ever seen a sword lizard?" Humi asked in a louder-than-necessary voice, drowning his objections. "They live down in these caverns. Historians think them to have been extinct ever since the city covered the island, for Delta Island is the only place in Royalland they ever lived, apart from a few other marshlands. But they did not die. They moved underground. They have gone pale through lack of sun."

The creature she fondled was as white as a ghost coated with base paint. Apart from the slap-slap-slap of its tail on her forearm, silence filled the cavern.

"And they are quite blind. Look at its eyes—aren't they beautiful? Purple. But it can't see—"

Roughly, Soderingal interrupted, "Milady, we didn't come to meet your pets. My father sent us down 'ere for some reason I have yet to comprehend. Apparently not even 'is own *son*—not even the last real lord left in the city—can stay 'ere without yer say-so. Not even in the middle of a war. I need yer *permission*—"

"I think it would be more correct to say *especially* Gold Dagger's son," Humi murmured. "*Especially* the last lord in the city. You have been known, both of you, to provide intelligence to the tyrant."

"Gods' blood! All I want is yer *gracious permission* to stay 'ere an' fight on your *side!*" In Soder's sneer, Aneisneida could hear the pain of Gold Dagger's less-than-wholehearted welcome. "Is that too much t' ask? I can 'elp you get recruits—I have contacts—I'm not exactly penniless, an' nor is my wife—"

"All my followers carry weapons." Humi stroked the sword lizard's skull. "Even the blind ones. Even the flamens and lemans. Even the rich. Are you ready to fight, Soder?"

Aneisneida smothered a gasp. Without trying it seemed, Humi had hit Soderingal's weakest point. The thing for which he had had his bodyguards knock men down. The thing for which she herself could not help despising him.

"What are you accusin' me of? *Cowardice?*"

In the corner of her eye, Anei saw Sol drift closer to the table.

"I merely asked whether you are prepared to fulfill *your* half of the bargain implicit in your arrival. Your offer of recruits is very generous—and I shall take advantage of it—but just because you are noble does not mean you are exempted from other obligations. Please do not feel singled out. This is the means by which I ensure the loyalty of all my followers. A knife in the hand is the greatest temptation, after all, is it not?"

Soder had gone the color of mud. Aneisneida could smell his sweat. She wondered what vague plans he had been harboring. Nothing that involved personal risk, she knew that!

"Let me put it another way," Humi said. "You and Lady Summer are a serious threat to our secrecy. If I take you in, you must assure me that you are not only committed to *your* safety, but to *mine.*"

"But we had nowhere else to go!" Anei pleaded. "Why would we betray you? We would be betraying ourselves!" She and Humi were old friends! They had come to see her in her isolation, when even the ghostiers had shunned her! How ungrateful she was! And when had her voice grown so brittle?

"Aneisneida, I have turned hundreds of men away from my service. Atheists, devotees, apostates. They were, to put it bluntly, out for number one. When we are enthroned once more, we will have the latitude to tolerate self-interest." Her voice hardened. "But for now, all my followers must be fanatics, for that is the only way we can combat the fanaticism of the Hands."

Something stirred in Aneisneida, nudging up through her fear.

The need to trust someone.

"I believe in you, Humi," she whispered, almost meaning it. She looked into the tranquil, tawny face. "I'll carry your knife. And I vouch for my husband." She elbowed Soderingal hard as he was about to speak.

Water dripped, splashing thinly on stone.

In the silence, she heard all of their lungs propelling the bad air in and out, in and out.

The sword lizard moved its razor-edged tail smoothly up and down, narrowly missing Humi's face. A few strands of frizzy hair floated free.

"Thank you, Aneisneida," Humi said. She nodded. She might have been embarrassed by Aneisneida's confession— or she might just have been miles away. "We acknowledge your pledge."

Soderingal puffed out his breath. "What do you want from me, then?" he said with bad grace. "Can't leave. You wouldn't let me, now. A fuckin' signed an' sealed declaration?"

Humi shook her head. She held out her hand. "A brush of the lips. One can tell a great deal about a man from the way he kisses."

Aneisneida felt slightly shocked.

"For Anei and Fia, mind!" Soderingal grumbled. "Wouldn't accept such an insult to m' honor for anythin' less!"

He kissed Humi's hand. Despite everything that had passed, Aneisneida noticed he lingered longer than necessary over it.

"Your father did this for me," Humi said, wiping her hand on her skirt.

"Did 'e," Soderingal said. "You brainwashed 'im into it."

Sol grabbed Soderingal by the neck. He dragged him away from the table and Aneisneida screamed. The knife licked Soderingal's throat, shaving off tufts of green fur, and Sol hissed, "Never a word of that. *Think* before you bandy about terms more appropriate to an audience in the Palace! Here, we fight for *freedom*." With a shove, he released Soder. "Freedom!" The sword lizard jumped off the table and scuttled into the shadows. Soderingal rubbed his throat.

Aneisneida cringed, fully expecting an explosion.

"You're gonna teach me 'ow to do that," Soder said thoughtfully.

She thought Sol would refuse. But Humi said, "Yes. Teach him. That would be good for both of you." She was half standing up now, both her hands pressed into the table. "I am going upstairs, so they will be able to spare *you* for a while, Sol. Conduct Lord Nearecloud to the bouting rooms.

Work out your distrust with wooden blades. You might as well get it over with. We will have little time, once battle is engaged."

Neither of the men noticed when she gasped as if she were about to fall. Without thinking, Aneisneida slid off the table and slid her arm around the other woman. Humi's heart was beating furiously. Her palms were wet.

She stiffened. Aneisneida understood. Abashed, she took her arm away.

"No," Humi whispered, clumsily clutching Aneisneida's shoulder. "It's just that I cannot forget." Her voice was urgent, furtive. "I keep trying to forget. And then remembering—all at once, like that. It was my fault, you know. My fault, for not protecting them better from—from Pati—"

Aneisneida gaped. Shock stopped her from replying. And in that minute of hesitation, she lost Humi's confidence. The Divinarch pulled away and smiled with that artificial blandness which always soured Aneisneida's mouth. "*You,* my dear, look positively exhausted. You and Fia shall stay in the Hangman's house. You may have the room I used to have. The handmaid who served me is quite sweet, and efficient, though she is only two years out of Veretry. I suggest you take an escort there soon. The Rats' Den is no place for a woman, and especially not at night."

She blew out the candles, accurately.

Gallowsbirds

Hope had been in Pirady two sixdays, succumbing to the rhythm of Erene and Elicit's life. Her hope of persuading them to return to Delta City was diminishing. They said that of course they were in favor of ending the tyranny. But they would not commit themselves to the war effort. Furthermore, they insisted that before Hope, or Humi, embarked on any course of action, they must speak with the renegades. What they had in mind was for Hope to meet two *auchresh* friends of theirs, Shine and Keef. It all seemed a little ambiguous to Hope: wasn't *she* an *auchresh,* so wasn't *she* a renegade?

Erene and Elicit seemed to hold her exempt from all such classifications. And they looked at her with kindness that made her want to melt, even as she hardened, and said of course she was different.

She was a trifle surprised that they had *auchresh* friends at all. Elicit, at least, had once been so pious.

But the two renegades did not show up, and did not show up, and Hope decided that whoever they were, they hadn't *really* been Erene and Elicit's friends, they had just been playing with them. It was still Hope's opinion that the whole "renegade" rumor was nonsense. In the country, even in a household headed by two émigrés from the capital, nothing had really changed since a thousand years ago. The goings-on in Delta City were of no more interest to people here than news of a hurricane in Veretry. Nothing ever changed. Hands, taxes, visitors from the past—all passed, and all were insignificant in the context of a Piradean winter that enfolded most of the day in darkness, and had even Hope shivering constantly.

On the first bright day of Hope's visit, about noon, when the sun peeped coyly over the trees and made the snow on the pines gleam white, and Hope was gathering the two children and their coats to go play outside, Elicit said to her: "I'm worried, Hope."

"About who? What?"

"Shine and Keef, of course! I think we should go to Shulage to—to see if they're there."

Ungraciously, she capitulated. It could not hurt to humor him, she supposed, as long as she did not let herself be seen by the Hands. She had already visited Shulage, and decided there was no anti-Divinarchical activity going on there or anywhere else. The incident of the "renegades" in K'Fier had been a freak thing, and Pati, the craven paranoid, was going to scatter his troops to the corners of the world to flail at shadows! In Shulage, as everywhere else, there were only the familiar scenes of Hands bullying and tormenting human townspeople who were too much in awe of them to do anything except take it.

Tomorrow Hope would go home and tell Humi to concentrate every particle of her forces on winning Delta City.

But when she and Elicit arrived by *teth"tach ching* in

Shulage, she realized just how wrong she would have been to do that.

They stood in the shadow of one of the funny, squat wooden houses that lined the market square of Shulage. Elicit, beside her, quivered with wrath. Occasionally their trembling brought them into jolting contact. Hope thought over and over, *I will kill Pati with my bare hands for this.*

In the square with its market stalls, people shopped and gossiped and children played games. A water pump squeaked and splooshed. But the winter sunlight seemed false, with blackness in the brightness—as if the sun were only a huge candle shining in the nothingness of the sky, guttering before it went out. Hope felt light-headed. It seemed that the world had wobbled a little on its path, changed its course slightly to accommodate a new heaviness.

A gibbet of raw tree trunks stood to one side of the square, between a costermonger's stall and a beer seller. Six Hands hung from it, their uniforms flapping in the breeze. Chains looped their bodies. They had been hung while they were still alive. The chains were to keep them from using their strength to break away from their captors. Their faces had decayed quite badly. They must have been hanging for at least a sixday.

Hope leaned against the side of the house. She buried her face in her arms, gasping in the scent of pine logs.

By her side, Elicit was being weakly courteous to a human with a thick Piradean accent. "I'm glad I didn't permit Erene to come into town," he was saying. "She wanted to. It had been a long time since we'd seen Shine or Keef, and we were getting nervous. Rightly so, as it seems . . . ! Can you tell me something of what *happened?* Is Shine—is Keef—"

"No, it would not have done for the lady Paean to come into town, it would not! Hardly a sight for the women and children, though they do enjoy it, 'tis not right," the Piradean said lugubriously. "It's the *auchresh* themselves who are wanting us to take the gallows down. Did you ever hear such strangeness?"

"Which *auchresh*?" Elicit said sharply. "Do you mean there are any left alive?"

" 'Course there are, Godsman Paean! The new ones!

Like your Shine! He's somewhere about . . . I can find him
for you . . ."

Elicit made a distressed noise. "In a moment, Godsman.
I must know what happened."

"Ah, well, to cut a long story short. Twas the Hands that
started it. Going about saying they were at war with all
other *auchresh*. Well, our Kingfisher, who's been living with
the Redforests out of town for a good year now—surprises
me you haven't heard—he feels the barammoth at his back,
doesn't he? Word came he was organizing a rumble, and
our young men was to show up at this-and-that place on
thus-and-so day, and Kingfisher turns up with your Shine
and a score of other gods none of us ever saw before. Fresh
out of the salt, we find out later. And wild!" The Piradean
grinned. "We did the Hands right. Got my knife into one
of them meself. I just thought about all the times he'd made
me crawl through the muck when he walked past—and him
dressed in me own hard-earned furs like as not . . . Felt
good, that did. Anyhow, the new *auchresh* haven't gone
home yet, and I can't say as they've outstayed their welcome at all. Hellish strong lads, and friendly, for all they
can't quite speak right."

Hope turned around, wiping her eyes. "Where are
they?" The Piradean was a plump, dark man in the dress
of a merchant.

"Ay, milady *iu*, my respects! You must be new here, too!
Friend of Godsman Paean's, are you?"

Hope nodded.

The Piradean relaxed. "Then I'll point out our boys for
you." He jabbed a charcoal-furred thumb in the direction
of the eddying mass of dull color in the square. "That's
Rippling Pool. And Red Arrow. And Kingsfisher, with
Godsie Redforest, in the yellow dress."

Finally she managed to make some of them out. They
wore the garb of rural Pirady, accessorized here and there
by a garment from the salt. Most of them wore their hair
long—perhaps to emphasize the difference between them
and the Hands swinging silently overhead. They played
with children, talked shop with foresters, haggled over a
cut of meat with the butcher. One was even behind the
counter of the beer stall, handing out foaming mugs.

It made Hope's head spin.

So *these* were the much-bruited renegades! They existed,

all right—and they were hot-blooded, impetuous country *firim*, most of them probably low-status at home, and so selfish-spirited. Dangerous!

She felt that if she did not keep her eyes on them, they would slither like eddies of colored water into the mud.

She could see that within the space of a few days, they had become *units,* members of the community, in a way that was never possible in the salt. Yet at the same time, they were treasured and looked up to as they had never been at home. The mortals hung on them adoringly.

What a seductive prospect!

"There's Shine, Godsman Paean," the Piradean said. "Go get him, shall I?" Hope saw that he was rather shy of Elicit, in a grudging way, but that at the same time he wanted to impress him. The foreigner. The "man from Grussels."

Elicit started. "Yes. Yes, if you will, Godsman Frotto." When he was gone, Elicit turned to Hope. "I cannot believe it." His eyes were slightly wild.

"The killing. Power." She swallowed, and her eyes went again to the small figures on the gallows, unable to resist their ghastly allure.

Ruthyali against *ruthyali.* Lover against lover. The humans committed sins like this every day, of course, on a lesser scale. But in the context of Hope's cool, philosophical race, the reality of it was insupportable.

"Gods . . ." Elicit's gray fur looked muddy. "It is my curse, Hope, to be just a little bit more intelligent than the people here. Intelligent enough to understand the impossiblity of living with the gods and still worshipping them— but not intelligent enough to resolve the paradox. Did you hear what Frotto told me? It is unbelievable. Some of the Shulage merchants are sending their sons into the salt, to the Heavens where these *auchresh* come from. It's a kind of exchange. A goodwill gesture. Of victory."

"And here we stand uncomprehending, an *auchresh* and a human," she said.

"No need to impress it on me!"

But she knew she could never really understand his horror, because for her, the taboo of the sacred did not exist.

Only one injunction beat at her brain, and it was like a gale.

*Let them do whatever they want to do. Only let there be
no more killing.*

She had to get home to Delta City. The provinces were
vitally important, she knew that now, and Humi must know
too. *Let there be no more killing ... !*

But by all accounts the Hands had been murderers. Had
it been *necessary* for the renegades to kill, that the cruelty
might end?

The gibbet flickered against the pale blue sky, its row of
corpses like gap teeth in the maw of a skull. She lost her
balance and put out her hand to the side of the house,
steadying herself. Mud glopped around her feet.

"All of these *auchresh* will be killed," she said in a low
voice to Elicit, while the chatter and clatter of market day
eddied around them. "Pati will descend in full force to punish them for this. Like he did at K'Fier. And there isn't a
damned thing I can do. How can I tell Humi to send what
few men she has here when the same thing is probably
happening in a hundred other towns? I can't even warn
them. It wouldn't do any good!"

"I know." He gazed down at her. The corners of his eyes
were red.

Godsman Frotto strutted up, puffing, with a young *kere*
in tow. It seemed increasingly unlikely to Hope that the
merchant had actually stuck a knife into one of the Hands,
unless the Hand in question had been dead already. He did
not seem very healthy. Neither did the *auchresh*. Dressed
entirely in human garb, he was tall and fair-skinned.
Bruises of sleeplessness hollowed his eye sockets. His hands
knotted together in a nervous yet listless tic.

The merchant looked at him worriedly.

"I'm all right, Frotto," the *kere* said in fluent mortal.
"You can leave me with Elicit." He flapped one hand. "I
know you have a lot to get on with."

Reluctantly, Frotto backed away, mumbling something to
Elicit about riding out to see the family one of these days.

A bubble of silence seemed to burgeon about the three
of them.

Elicit said, "You look absolutely terrible."

"Yes. I have a bit of a headache. I forgot you didn't
know what had happened." The *kere* seemed to see Hope
for the first time. "Forgive me, *iu serbalu!*"

"None of that!" Hope snapped.

He looked surprised. Then understanding came over his
face. "You must be Hope. It is my honor."

"And you are—" She had forgotten the names. Shine?
What was the other? Which had been the Hand? "Keef!
You are Keef."

Elicit hissed between his teeth.

The *kere* gave a humorless smile and jerked a thumb
over his shoulder. "*That's* Keef. I'm Shining Stone."

"Shine, where have you been sleeping?" Elicit said.
"What have you been doing all this time?" He interrupted
himself. "Never mind. I know Erene will have it out of you
and I would not make you tell it twice."

"I cannot," Shine said.

"Then I will, my lad," Hope said with a firmness she was
far from feeling. She could see this young *firi*—bereft of
the one who had, according to Elicit, been his *irissi*—was
in dire need of firmness. Steeling herself, she looped her
arms around Shine's and Elicit's necks. Shine's skin had
the texture of porcelain. His breath was slow, as if he could
not be bothered with filling and emptying his lungs. Elicit's
grip was powerful, his fur as soft as moss, and she thought
she would rather have hugged him any day. Touching him
reminded her of Ders, but the sights she had witnessed
today had bled that painful episode of its sting, replacing
it with broader implications.

Erene stood in the front door wanting desperately to
hold Shine, to kiss away his despair as she would have
kissed away one of her babies' tantrums. She knew the urge
to be only the mother instinct that told her she could make
everything all right with enough love, that dangerous instinct that makes so many women ineffectual; she did not
give in to it. She did not want to lose Shine. She had not
forgotten losing Hem, or Humi. She might not like Shine
unreservedly, but he was part of their life here in Pirady,
this costly fragile life. Losing him would be like coming
home one day to find that someone had emptied the house
of everything that made it hers.

But she could not say that. And there did not seem to
be anything else to say. He had sat down on the bench
against the front wall, his cheeks in his hands. Elicit
slouched at the other end of the bench, dragging at his
pipe. Hope squatted on the frozen mud, playing with Xib

and Artle. Her wings floated over her, tips raised above
the dirt. She looked like a young girl, the golden skin of
her face still unlined after years of alcohol and tobacco and
Pati. Erene could not suppress a pang of envy. She herself
had started getting fat.

Hope loved the children. When Erene hugged them, fed
them, played with them, scolded them, she would sometimes glance up and see Hope watching with an almost
greedy look on her face. Erene guessed Hope had those
powerful mothering instincts, too, and they were part of
what made her so eager to leave Shulage province. That
slim, girlish body would never bear a child—even if she
were human.

Sorry for her. I'm sorry for her.

And poor, poor Shine!

They are all tortured by needs they cannot fulfill, she
thought. *None of them that I have known are able to take
any kind of affection for granted, and so each friend is a
gift whose snatching away is all the more painful for having
been dreaded so vigorously.*

Poor Shine!

A queenbird tooted in the pines. Erene smelled the
smoke from Elicit's pipe, spreading in the chilly air.

"Hope?" Shine said.

Hope twisted around, letting go of Xib, who tottered a
few steps and then fell. Erene moved outside to scoop
him up.

Shine squinted at Hope. "I think I should like to come
back to Delta City with you."

"Oh, no, no," Hope said. "Not possible. You would be
out of your depth, my friend."

"There's nothing for me here. Don't you need all the
help you can get?"

Erene interrupted, "Shine, that's absurd! You don't have
to leave! You know we would love to have you here. You
have your cabin—you wouldn't want to waste all the work
you put into it—"

"Keef worked just as hard on it as I did. *He's* not here
to enjoy it."

Erene winced. She went on, "And the children would
miss you—"

"It wouldn't be forever."

Hope said, "Well. Well . . . Shine. Have you—are you—

do you know the other *auchresh* who have come to Shulage?"

He pulled a face. "They are mostly my *ruthyalim*. We speak."

"Are you—are you permitted to return to Heaven? Are they? Or would you be ..."

"Reviled? No. The *er-serbalim* don't have much influence around here, *iu*. I could go back"—his face darkened—"if I wanted. But I don't. The war is in Delta City." Plainly, he was eager to put Pirady behind him. Erene understood that. But she did not think Shine understood that he couldn't leave Keef behind in Shulage.

"That is where you're wrong." Hope was shaking her head. "Since seeing the town today I no longer believe the war is in Delta City."

"But, Hope!" Erene objected. "Your war is different from ours. Humi's struggle for the Throne has nothing to do with the renegades. She's fighting for power; they are fighting for freedom—"

"Against a common enemy," Hope said.

Erene closed her eyes.

"Against oppression. Against the rule of the gods."

"I see what you're getting at!" There was a note of enthusiasm in Shine's voice. "If other renegades did ... what we did here ... if enough of them could be coaxed into sticking their necks out ... the Divinarch would have a real imbroglio on his hands! He would be besieged on both sides!"

"Shine," Elicit said. His eyes were closed. His face looked tormented. "Why did you join in? I have attempted to understand." He opened his eyes. "I cannot."

The fair-skinned *auchresh* winced, and shivered.

"You don't have to say anything, Shine," Erene said quickly, but no one noticed.

"I would have stopped it by any means possible if I had known what was going to happen!" Shine's eyes were bloodshot. "I didn't know about the Divinarch's war on us. Kingfisher always has his ear to the ground. He gathered the *ruthyalim*. I tagged along hoping to get to warn Keef. We fell on them in the middle of the afternoon, when they were sleepiest. It turned out that Kingfisher had arranged for the humans to join in, too. It was a massacre." He stopped.

"Why? What did you hope to gain?"

"Just what you saw today, Elicit," Hope said, softly.

"I understand that you wanted to save Keef. But if you had lain low, he would never have been killed!"

Shine shrugged: a jerky movement, like a Piradean glass sculpture breaking. "I told you, it wasn't me, it was my *firim!* Esult had publicly vowed to hang each and every nonaffiliated *auchresh* he found in human country from the gallows. My *ruthyalim* in Yellow Spruce Heaven hadn't seen the Hands in too long. They'd almost forgotten they were their *ruthyalim.* Anyhow, they were concentrating on Esult. He was the outsider. The Kithrilindic. They did horrible things to him before they hanged him."

Erene coughed, tried to find her voice, tried again. "Who killed ..."

"Keef? I don't know. The townsfolk. I don't know which one actually pulled the step out from under him. I wasn't watching."

Erene cursed herself, cursed her whole race for having made this boy's world turn so gray.

"I wasn't watching."

"There's so much hatred," Elicit said bitterly. "Pati doesn't know what a graveful of maggots he has nurtured here. He can't."

"But we can turn them against him," Hope said. "We can give them teeth." She bounced to her feet. "It'll be so easy. All they have to do is cry Humi's name before they attack. I couldn't have thought of a better way of frightening Pati witless if I tried! After this it will be child's play—"

Artle paused in her steady consumption of mud to ask, "Who's Pati, Mama?"

Erene bent to ruffle her hair. Staring straight at Hope, she said, "Someone you don't know, darling."

After several more hours of impassioned discussion, Hope and Shine departed for Loge, the town closest to Shulage to the south, where Shine said he had a friend. The subject of Erene and Elicit's accompanying them was not raised again. Maybe Hope did not want to push her luck. Erene scolded herself for attributing such a calculating mind to the *iu.* Before they left, she had been bubbly and excited, kissing each member of the family half a dozen times more than was necessary.

And Shine seemed, incredibly, to have come back to himself. He was reserved, humorous, now and then gracing the dinner table with one of his beautiful smiles. After they finished eating, he slipped away into the forest at the back of the house.

Erene followed him, skidding and cursing on the slimy slopes, wondering why she was going after him when he clearly wanted solitude. When Shine passed through the fringe of the trees she stopped, peering around a flaky trunk. Shine had come to the cliff. The sea breeze ruffled his fine hair as he advanced across the frosty grass to the edge of the precipice.

From here, she could not tell whether he was contemplating the sunset, which bled spectacularly gilt and mauve across the sky, or suicide. Perhaps he was remembering when he and Keef had *teth"d* Xib and Artle to the bottom of the cliff, to swim off the scrap of stony beach. Or he was thinking about stepping into nothingness.

Would that be possible? she wondered. Or would instinct take over, would his natural abilities land him on his feet at the bottom?

Maybe he'd have to use more direct methods. He had no knife. Hope did, and she was sure to equip him with one, too, but maybe by then the danger would have passed. Maybe.

Deliberately, he turned. Erene saw the sunset sparkling in the tears of his face.

"You can come out now."

Though he flinched back at first, she hugged him, aware of her dowdiness in her spindlespun gown, a painful contrast to the figure of pink light and air with his transparent wings: all her talents forgotten except the talent for love, which she found herself getting better and better at now she had all her days to practice it. She gave him the comfort she had wanted to give earlier, holding him close. "There's something more, isn't there?" she murmured. "Are you telling us everything? You don't have to ... but you can. If you want."

He stayed silent, as if he were really somewhere out there in the sunset, not with her at all.

"I know I have to let you leave. But not like this. Please, not like this, with secrets between us." She smiled weakly up at him. "There were never secrets between us."

"There were always secrets."

She winced.

"But everything has to ..." His voice broke. "Erene, I joined in. I lied when I said I had nothing to do with it. I wanted to end the injustice. I thought Keef would get out in time. I thought he would *teth*". And later we would meet and celebrate the end of his bondage.

"But I saw him fighting. I was in the thick of it, shoving to get closer to the place where a Hand from Yellow Spruce Heaven was being chained up, and I saw Keef using his knife on the humans, trying to kill as many of them as possible before he went under. Shulage lost ten men and half as many women, and I daresay Keef did his share. I saw him. Our eyes met. But I didn't drop my cudgel. I didn't go to him." Gently, his head came to rest on her shoulder.

She squeezed him, stroking his hair with rough fingers, muttering, "It's all right, it's all right, you couldn't have saved him ..."

But he twisted and moaned at the onslaught of untruths. She stopped. On the horizon, the crimson sun melted into the sea. It was not a moment for silence; it was a moment pregnant with things that needed to be said. But they had reached another crescendo of guilt and shame and mistrust in their mutual history, and Erene could not find any words that were keen enough to express her sympathy, yet gentle enough not to draw blood.

Recruit

"Hi! There! Get on!" Merce shouted. "Night's coming, you stupid beasts! Get on!" He brought his stick down with a *thwock* on the nearest sheep. "In!"

The flock danced into the barn, throwing him slanted glances out of their orange eyes. He'd had the gods' own task getting them rounded up off the mountain—they were even more willful than usual, it must be something in the wind. Now that he was worn out and ready to slit their woolly throats, they obeyed him as blithely as might be.

"Get!" He landed a boot on the last shit-caked rump, and pushed the woven-stick doors to. He jammed the bars through their loops and wiped the sweat off his face before the wind could freeze it.

Merce hated sheep with every particle of his being. He couldn't wait until his little sister Asure and Cousin Rety were old enough to take over the task of shepherding. Two could work faster than one, no matter how young and silly they were. Or if only Sion had been here to help him! With his trick of disappearing and reappearing, the god could set sheep's sly stupid brains spinning.

There was something odd in the wind. Merce sniffed. Burning? It blew steadily from the direction of Nece, for which Cousins Brit and Emper had set off yesterday with a load of tubers. Butterfly Cote was probably burning dung.

The dun-colored ridge behind him was barren of everything except the furze that left hundreds of tiny bleeding scratches on one's legs, no matter how thick one's breeches were. A twist of smoke rose from the fire pit in Beaulieu's courtyard below. They were all in the fields. Everyone from Cand, Merce's oldest uncle, to his littlest second cousin Ality, was down the other end of the valley, digging more of the hamlet's precious tubers. The yield was poor this year: not yet Midwinters, and they had had to start turning the third field. What gods had decreed that one had to do the most backbreaking work of the year in winter, when the cold chapped your fingers and turned your eyes red and gave you the sniffles? Merce hated shepherding—but he had an inkling that it was the rest of his family who really had the short end of the stick. If he went down there they'd put him to work, too.

Well, he wouldn't go down! A boy deserved *some* free time! Didn't he?

Squinting up at the sky, he thought, *Still an hour of light. Good enough, Sion'ull bring me home. And everyone'll be happy to see him, so they won't care I got back late.* He started to tramp uphill, the wind buffeting his back. *More'n two sixdays since he was here. Wonder if that fellow from Pirady's come back? I hope so. I wanna hear about the war. I mean,* Pirady! *That's the other side of the world!*

Merce joined his hands under his smock to warm them. The fur on his belly was sticky with dirt—it had been months since he had a bath, and he liked it that way.

Reaching the top of the ridge, he scrambled down into the
next forage valley, where tufts of wool decorated the furze
and the few stunted trees; then up another ridge, north a
bit, and an arm of the salt glowed in the valley below him.
The slippery whispering of leaves on leaves came faintly to
his ears. The vegetation that was so much denser than the
scrub of the saltside undulated under the wind like the
waters of the sea.

He shook his head firmly. You didn't walk through the
salt if you didn't have to—that was just plain stupid. He
circled the head of the inlet, pelted over the slippery brown
slopes of the last ridge, and halted, breathing hard, on the
sloping skirt of grass where hummocks of salt popped up
through the ground. The salt merged into the soil gradually,
as if it had been scattered on the ground like sugar on a
table. The first few salt trees were as stunted as any in
human country, and nothing moved in their branches.

Grinning, he plunged in.

The clouds overhead were thicker than wool. He didn't
need the eye band he kept in his pocket. He followed the
way markers he and Sion had left, heading for Heaven.
He'd give Sion a grand old surprise. A bluish scrap meant
northeast. Off-white, north. In a hollow, a black strip tied
to a bush was being industriously nibbled by a salt squirra-
munk: west. *Sheepshit!* He hoped no more of them had
been eaten. Neither he nor Sion had thought of *that.*

But the next marker, which should have been red, wasn't
anywhere to be seen. And twilight was dropping heavy
from the clouds. Merce felt frightened.

Spitting on his hands, he shinnied up a stone-colored
tree. Smears of blood trailed him up the trunk—when salt
bark flaked, it was *sharp.* But he didn't care. He was terrified of being stranded here for the night. Too dark now to
get all the way back before the predators came out of their
lairs. And even if he escaped the predators' claws, and got
home safely, *Mother* would kill him for disobeying! Joy
liked Sion—but she said she would not have Merce going
near Oakbranch Heaven. Of course, that had never
stopped him.

The top of the tree nodded under his weight. The wind
whipped his hair into his face. But he could see—with a
sudden rush of relief—that he was in a hollow halfway up

the white slope on whose peak Oakbranch Heaven flared
like a frozen fire.

He gripped the tree, balancing, drinking in the sight.
"Stupid," he said aloud. "Young fool." That was what his
father called him. "Whatcha get so skeeted for?"

Heaven stood boldly on the crest of the hill, its strong
walls raised like a finger in the face of weather and predators and enemies. In his mind, he compared it to Beaulieu,
those low frost-eaten sheds crowding together in the deep-
est valley of the saltside. "Halloo! *Tith"ahim!*" he shouted
at the top of his lungs. "It's me! Merce! Somebody come
get me!"

No human could have heard him, not from halfway down
the hill with the wind blowing, but the *auchresh* of Oakbranch Heaven were better than humans. They had special
abilities, some of which—like the vanishing trick—Merce
was determined to learn. If Sion hadn't told him they were
not gods, not really, Merce would most certainly have
been fooled.

He yelled again. Several heads popped out of windows,
dark blots on the creamy walls. Merce waved vigorously.
His fingers were getting numb. But before they let go of
their own accord, one of Sion's freinds, a *mainraui* named
Sedge Runner, popped out of the air at his ear. Grabbing
the tree with one hand, so that it dipped heavily toward
the ground, he fastened Merce in his arms. His grip felt
wonderfully warm. He had probably been asleep. "Sorry!"
Merce shouted contritely over the wind. It was difficult to
remember that the *auchresh,* when they were at home, slept
during the day. While Sion was in Bealieu, he kept scrupulously to the Gardens' schedule.

The sulfur got into Merce's nose. He sneezed.

And the tree vanished out of his hands. There was that
moment of panic. Then his feet hit the floor of Sedge Runner's room in the topmost pinnacle of Heaven.

The window was only a slit—in Heaven having a window
at all was, he had learned, a great privilege—but Merce
was unused to windows in any case, and he was glad it was
no larger, for he liked the feeling of shut-in coziness. The
walls were coated with layers of soft tapestry decorated
with pictures of *auchresh* hunting, harvesting, wrestling, caring for Foundlings. A fire burned under the hood in the
middle of the floor. On the small table was a metal pot.

Merce recognized the tannin scent of the drink the Carelas-trians called "Tearka sludge."

Sion was sitting cross-legged on the bed. Merce grinned happily when he saw Gamefly was sitting there too. *Officer* Gamefly, the *auchresh* from Pirady, or Fewarauw as they called it. He was older than Sion, or he looked it, with his heavy head like a big dog and no wings. They were both staring at Merce. "What are *you* doing here?" Sion asked at last.

Merce shifted, somewhat taken aback. "Felt like coming." With sudden inspiration, he added, "Wanted to get off tater-digging."

Sion smiled with relief. "Slyboots! Merce, you are the laziest boy I ever knew! When you are a man, I think you will live in abject poverty!"

"When I'm a man," Merce said, "my kids 'ull do all the work for me." He relaxed. "Can I have some?" He pointed at the sludge pot.

Gamefly coughed. "Heat it up, Sedge," he said. "I did not know your human friends visited you in Heaven! Surely Fretseeker does not approve? He is a follower of the *er-serbalim,* is he not?"

"Yes. But he doesn't—ah—well, to be honest, Gamefly, he is not in the best of health. *O-serbali* Sivene is running Heaven—and he is one of us younger ones. He has spoken of our making ourselves known in Nece. That's the nearest human town. The Hands have an outpost there."

"Soon all the old ones will die off," Gamefly said rhetorically. "Even the *er-serbalim* will die, eventually. Then we shall run our Heavens just as we please. Human and *auchresh* Foundlings will play side by side."

"I'm not a Foundling," Merce said, stung. "I'm twelve. Foundlings are stupid. My father calls me a fool, but at least I can *talk*—not like those silly bits."

The stranger opened his mouth and an avalanche of laughter roared out. Merce put his hands over his ears. He removed them just in time to hear the *kere* say "—approve! I approve highly!"

Sion beckoned Merce to his side. He whispered, "It's all right for you to stay, I think. Here. Sit down."

But why shouldn't it be all right? Merce wondered, as Sion made room for him on the bed. Something was wrong. Why was Sion so tense?

Sedge Runner squatted by the fire and settled the sludge pot on its tripod with a clank. Then he plunked himself down cross-legged on the floor and wedged his chin into his hands. Something was wrong with him, too. Why had he done a servant's task? Merce was a little afraid of all the *mainraum*—Sedge Runner counted it his right to have Sion (and Merce, when available—he was not particular) wait on him hand and foot—so why was he obeying Gamefly? That time Sedge Runner, Sion, and Gamefly had come to Beaulieu, all of them had pitched in (much to Merce's disgust) and helped the women repair the roofs of the fowl house.

Maybe it was something to do with the war, and Gamefly's being an *officer*.

Merce said, "Gamefly, godsman, you've just come here from Pirady, haven't you? Is there fighting, there? Is there eeroics?"

Gamefly gave him a surprised look. "There haven't been, yet. The war is in its early stages. The battle at Grussels will be the first real test of our mettle. We will be hard put to it, I can tell you! The Hands, of whom there are thousands, are far better trained than our mixed human and *auchresh* troops." His head swung, his gaze sweeping Sion, lingering on Sedge Runner. "That is why we need every *mainraui* we can get."

"I won't have anything to do with it," Sedge Runner said.

"You were Found to be a soldier. So were all *mainraum*, did they but know it. Our traditions date from a time eons past when we were less civilized than we are today."

A war, Merce thought, dazzled. *A real war. It's going on right now.* Visions of challenges and duels, like vastly enlarged versions of the games he played with his sister and cousins, flickered across his vision. Suddenly, he wanted more than anything to be there. The prospect of going back to Beaulieu seemed unbearably empty and gloomy. He felt like a fish that has been kept in a tank for its whole life, and then one day the sides become transparent, and the fish sees the sea lapping on the outside of the glass.

The air in the room had the ill-oxygenated tang of tension.

"Time is different in Fewarauw, Sedge Runner," Gamefly was saying. "We are closer to the sun than you are in Carelastre. When I returned there, I thought I had somehow *teth"d* into tomorrow. It was morning, and I had left in late afternoon. The tents cover the meadows around Grussels city like foam on the sea. The spears are as thick as wheat at harvest time. Everywhere, the name of the Divinarch is whispered, praised, and sung. Humility Garden. She is our Maiden General's idol: she is the one in whose name we fight. Her victory will be the *final* triumph of the new over the old."

"Many recruits?" Sedge Runner said skeptically.

"More every day. When I joined up, in Ekmar Province, the army was a hundredth the size it is now. I am merely one of a thousand recruiters. Humans as well as *auchresh.*"

"You oughta try and recruit saltsiders," Merce said, finding his voice. "Divinarch taxes us, too. Hands bleed us of a third of our tears and sweat and toil. We hate 'em." After the Hands left the last time, in the summer, Merce's uncles had shouted at each other. His skin prickled all over again as he sensed their frustrated fury, only dimly understanding it. He had taken the babies inside to stop them from crying while Joy, Mercy, Reedo, and Indine tried to calm down their menfolk.

He became aware that the moment was stretching out and out.

"Perhaps . . ." Sion said. "Perhaps . . . we should take Merce!"

It was then that Sedge Runner spoke. "Oh, no you don't, Sion. Gamefly has manipulated you into this, and I'm throwing my life after yours—because I love you. But you aren't getting the Foundling. I put my foot down."

"Temperament!" Gamefly murmured.

On the fire, the sludge pot boiled over. Sedge cursed in the *auchraug* language and pulled it off with his bare hands. Merce, his mind bubbling with dim possibilities, smelled burning flesh. The scent was oddly familiar.

Sedge's lean, flat-cheeked face showed no emotion. But the tiny wings on the tops of his shoulders fluttered.

There came a knock on the door. "*Mainraui? Firi?* May I be of assistance? I heard something fall—"

"Damn," Sion whispered.

"You must not tell them!" Gamefly hissed. "Not let them know I am in here! It would delay your departure!"

It was Sedge who wrangled his voice into some sem-

blance of normality. "No, thank you, old one. Go away.
We'll be in the great hall before long."

After a moment, a snort came from outside the door,
and footsteps shuffled off down the hall.

Sweat stood on Gamefly's furrowed forehead. The room
seemed to have gotten hotter. It reeked of burned sludge.
"We must be off. Quickly, before anything else happens."

"What about me?" Merce squeaked.

Sedge said quickly, "Don't worry, Merce. We'll drop you
off at Beaulieu."

"No, I mean, I want to come!" He directed his plea to
Gamefly, aware that all decisions were ultimately up to the
officer. Maybe *that* was what made Sedge so irritable. "I'd
be more use to you than ten *auchresh!* I know how to fight,
I practice a lot—*please!*" His heart was pounding.

"Don't be absurd, Merce," Sedge said. "Even if you are
not a Foundling, you are a child."

"Wait," said Gamefly. The heavy red gaze rested on
Merce, considering him. "Not so hasty, my friend. The boy
could be of use."

Sion dropped to his knees and seized Merce's hands.
"How'd you like that, Merce! How'd you like to be a spear-
man! Damn, your family'd be so *proud*—"

"*No*," Sedge said harshly. He stood in front of the bed,
a knotted blanket over one shoulder, his face as flat as a
slab of rock. His lips scarcely moved; his voice seemed to
emanate from the air. "Hear me on this, my flighty young
irissi. The boy stays. What *possible* help could he give us
that would outweigh his loss to his family? He stays. It is
not his war, whatever you say."

Merce's eyes flowed with boiling tears of embarrassment
and disappointment. He tried desperately to swallow them.
They must not think him a child. He was as able as—as—
well, not as a *mainraui*, but he was *almost* as strong as Sion.
"I want to know what it's like," he pleaded. "I have to
see! I want to help!" He produced his trump card. He never
even let himself remember this unless the situation was
desperate. "The Divinarch, Humi I mean, Humility Garden, is my cousin! Did you know that, Sion? I never knew
she was alive, my family are shamed of her so they never
tell no one she came from us. But I bet she'd like to see
me! I could tell you about the way she is! I could—"

Gamefly's eyes flickered. "The *same* Gardens? Can it be?"

"You young idiot," Sedge said. He came forward and his hands closed on Merce's upper arms.

Then the fire flared in Beaulieu's courtyard, lashed by the wind, and a tumult of voices sent Merce staggering against a bench.

The whole family was gathered in the courtyard. The trestle tables still stood against the walls: nobody had cooked the least slop of dinner. That, to Merce's mind, was unthinkable. It meant either famine or domestic disaster.

Brit and Emper were the center of the disturbance. They were telling a story at the tops of their lungs, even more hoarsely than usual. Merce pushed himself up off the bench and shoved into the crowd. His mother took hold of him and said distractedly, "Oh, Merce. Thank the gods you're home. I was afraid the sheep were lost and you'd gone chasing after . . ."

From beyond Grand-uncle Cand and Grand-aunt Prudence, Merce heard the word "dead."

"You smell funny," squealed Asure. "Ave you been in the salt?"

Merce clipped her on the ear to shut her up. He wished he'd never told her about his visits to Oakbranch Heaven—she was too little to keep a secret! "What happened to Brit and Emper?" he asked, stooping.

"They went to Nece!" she squeaked.

"I know that!"

"There was a fire!"

From a couple of relations away, Uth, Merce's father, shot out an arm and pulled Merce to his side. He tipped Merce's face upward and said quietly, "Son, there's been a disturbance in Nece. People turned on the Hands—burned their guard station. People were killed. The town is in chaos, people stealing from each other, neighbors arguing and killing each other over it. Port Taite'll be down on the whole region. There was a god involved. Not a Hand. It would have been better if Sion was here, then we could have vouched for him, I am afraid we'll lose his help—"

"It wasn't him!" Merce said with relief. "I was with him!"

"That's something." Uth's grip relaxed a little.

"And they *won't* come down on us!" Merce was bursting with his news. "You don't know this but the Divinarch 'as declared war on the other gods! The Hands won't have time for *us* cause they're all in Pirady fighting the Maiden General!"

"The war, yes," Uth said. "They knew in Nece already. Brit and Emper just found out."

Merce gulped. It was his cousin's war. Did Father realize that, or had he blocked Cousin Humi completely out of his memory? Humi's war—it was Merce's war!

Brit's and Emper's clothes were blackened with soot. Emper had a great gash on his arm, which his wife Indine was futilely trying to bandage. "Would that we could stamp out every last one of them!" Emper was shouting. "Would that we were our own men again, as we were in the days of the old Divinarch!"

Over the scent of unwashed bodies and soot came a stink of sulfur. Gamefly appeared by the fire. Merce could just see him. He was flanked by Sion, and Sedge Runner, who after dropping Merce off must have worked his way unseen around the walls of the courtyard.

"I am Gamefly of Durenesse hamlet in Ekmar Province, Pirady," he said by way of introduction. "A friend of Sion's. Godsman Garden, your desire to pay the Hands back for the injustices they have done you is heard and understood. It is shared by thousands. In Pirady, an army of humans and gods is preparing to take Grussels from the Divinarch. Our strategists say battle will be engaged next sixday."

Emper shook Indine off. "Inviolate One, are you by any chance here to find volunteers?"

"If so, you've got yourself two!" Brit said.

Merce's other uncle, Gent, stepped out of the crowd, his face muddy. "Three!" The men faced the *auchresh* across the flaring fire pit. Red light glowed on scaly skin and fur alike, giving them all a terrifying aspect. Merce gripped his father's arm. Uth quivered; Merce knew he was debating whether to step forward, too. *No, Father!* he thought. *Don't! It's* me *they're taking!*

"We welcome you with joy," Gamefly said in a sonorous voice that made Merce's bones vibrate.

Grand-uncle Cand coughed. "No. My grandsons, I cannot permit it. We need you here. This is madness."

"Thank you, Godsman," Sedge Runner said quietly. "Godsmen, stay here. This is not your war."

"Yes, it is, friend *auchresh*," Emper said. He narrowed his eyes at Sedge Runner. Merce could not believe they were all on the same side. This felt too much like a confrontation, where justice and reason bowed low before strength. Passion trembled in Emper's voice. "They burned our town. Our granary. For all we know, they have burned every town in Domesdys."

Uncle Reng, Cand's brother, spoke for the first time. He was younger than Cand but he wielded more authority over the hamlet. He must have deliberated calmly for his voice was still and carrying. "The god is right—you must stay, nephews. We can't survive without you."

"Every hamlet needs its young men," Gamefly said: a simple statement of fact.

In the moment of silence that followed, Merce wrenched away from his father and pushed his way to the *auchresh* side of the fire pit. "You don't need *me*. *I'm* going."

"Nonsense," Reng said.

Reng's wife, Faith, laughed.

Merce's cheeks muddied, but he knew the firelight would disguise the color. He stood firm.

Gamefly opened his mouth, paused a minute, and then closed his hand on Merce's shoulder. He said to Cand, "But, Godsman, how can you disallow *this* volunteer? A twelve-year-old boy is not essential to the well-being of the hamlet. But he could be of infinite use to us!" His voice thickened, betraying real fervor. "Is it right for Humility Garden's family not to send a single representative to the Divinarch's banner? Can you permit *that*?"

There was a brief, shocked pause.

"Humi," Merce's aunt Faith croaked, "my *daughter*."

Her wrecked, beautiful face hung at Reng's shoulder. Her nails dimpled Reng's smock. Merce was a little afraid of her. Her face was haggard, her throat loose, but her fur and hair were a rich ruddy chestnut.

"Humi is in the best of health," Gamefly said to Faith. "And preparing to take back her throne. You are to be congratulated on the excellence of your bloodline, Godsie."

"Humi. Gods. Humi." Faith launched herself forward. "I must see her! I must tell her—that I was wrong—"

Reng seized the back of her dress. He held her at arm's

length, an expression of disgust on his face. Merce had heard from his older cousins that Reng and Faith had not lived as husband and wife since Faith allowed their daughter Humi to go to Delta City—worse, that they hated each other. Faith did not struggle in her husband's grasp. She began to cry softly.

"Humi is in Delta City, Godsie," Sion said gently. "But we will remember you to the Maiden General. And Hope is in constant communication with your daughter. Merce will convey the message himself, that Humi's family still cherishes her, and looks forward to her reinstatement on the Throne."

"I don't believe you," Faith cried quietly. She brought her ruined face up. "I don't believe you will let Merce near your precious Maiden General. In fact, I think it would be better he didn't go to Pirady. Do you hear me, Reng?" She turned to her husband. "I made that mistake once, but I shall not let it be made again. We will not lose another of our eldest children."

Reng's face twisted. With a kind of delighted dread, Merce saw what was coming. Reng would do *anything* if he thought it would hurt his wife. "On the contrary. Merce can go wherever he wants. You have no authority over him." Reng watched her reaction with detached sadism.

"As you say, my brother," Cand wheezed. Merce saw he was half-sitting against Prudence. "As long as—my sons— stay where they belong—"

"No!" Joy cried, a high predatorial shriek. "Nooo! Reng, you're abusing your authority! *Please,* Cand, don't let him!"

Oh, gods, Merce thought, *oh, gods!*

But it was too late for his mother to intervene. Gamefly evidently considered it fair and aboveboard to make his getaway now. Beaulieu vanished, and in the place of soot the wet green reek of bruised sphagnum filled Merce's nostrils, and it was morning.

"Now here you are." Preoccupiedly, Sion stuffed bundles into Merce's arms. "Your blanket, your kit. Your weapon."

Merce hitched the armful on his hip and tested the weight of the knife. He'd never had one before. It was long and curved like a Hand's blade—unwieldy for a boy his size, but so sharp. So cruel. He imagined it cutting through armor and flesh, and shivered and grinned.

"And these, I think, are the scouts?" Sion pulled a face. "I think so. I really have to get along. Merce—the Seventh Younger Cabal. Mode is the captain, so Gamefly says."

Mode was a friendly-seeming boy of sixteen or so, with gray Piradean fur and a catlike smoothness to his movements. He clasped Merce's forearms for a moment. "Welcome." He shot a glance in Sion's direction.

But the *auchresh* was gone. A puff of purple dispersed in the air.

He must really've *been in a hurry,* Merce thought. He had already noticed that as a rule, here, *auchresh* did not *teth*". Perhaps it was in order to conserve their extranatural energy for the coming battle.

The camp crouched still and low on the meadows. Mode laughed. "Dumped *you* quick, didn't he, Domesdean? How good are you with a knife?"

The billowing tents, raised out of the mud on wooden platforms, were novelties to Merce. Some of the soldiers dragged travois laden with wood or water; some carried game slung across their shoulders; some just wandered along, whetting their blades, carving arrows, batting short bursts of conversation from one to another. Voices echoed through the morning, sharp and loud. The air felt taut, as though the whole camp were being held like a bubble inside some huge creature's lungs. The air was colder, and calmer, than Merce had ever felt. He could feel the hum of the camp in his bones. *Auchresh* voices made up most of it.

He had never seen so many gods in one place. Gamefly's talk of thousands made sense now.

Gamefly, it proved, was the Maiden General's officer in charge of human recruits. When he had persuaded Merce to come, he was just doing his job. It had been a bit of a blow to find out that no one cared two farthings whose cousin Merce was. But all the same, now he'd got here, to this green, cold clime, he was *glad.* He might be the lowest of the low, nothing more than a go-see boy. But better a scout here than a shepherd at home!

The members of the Seventh Younger Cabal were all staring at him.

He would not look down.

"Not such good ground for a camp, is it?" Mode said. "It's all bog here. There's standing water in the hollows.

See the sphagnum round the edges of the tents? See the logs, how they're raised up out of the wet?"

"Why did the Maiden General camp here then?" Merce asked.

"We had to surround the city. Like this, we've got the Inviolate Ones penned in. They leave, and turn Grussels over to us, or they fight. We've got 'em!"

Merce shuddered. It was the cold.

"Hey." Mode was smiling. His eyes were kind, though so dark—all the boys were dauntingly foreign, not another Domesdean among them, mostly Piradeans with a few Veretreans, Calvarese, and Royallandics thrown in. "When it comes down to it, you won't have *time* to be scared. I know. I was in the fighting in Whitecliff last sixday." Mode turned Merce around and pushed him a couple of steps to the left. "Look through that gap. No, toward the forest. See that tent?"

"The one with the yellow flag on top?" Merce guessed.

"That's the Divinarch's banner. And *that's* the Maiden General's tent." His voice quivered with an unwonted tremor. "We can't go look now—we've gotta relieve the Fourth on fringe patrol—but I'll show you where to hide next time she reviews the spearmen. Then you'll see her. She's *beautiful*."

Groundswell

Hope pushed the parchments away from her until they fluttered off the other side of the camp desk. She sank forward until her head touched the wood, her arms stretched out before her, and breathed long, shallow breaths. The roof of the tent shivered above her. Outside, she could hear the sentinels chatting. Recently, whenever she tried to sleep, her tiredness evaporated as soon as her head touched the pillow, to be replaced by a kind of edgy supersensitivity. She found herself clenching her fists at small noises and irritations that had never used to be irritating. Because of this she was almost glad she was too valuable to lose, and therefore would not be fighting in the coming battle.

And at the same time that she despised her own cowardice, she was sneakily glad. She was an *iu*. Her place was not in the field.

Instead she sat here, the Maiden General, her presence and her dedication to Humi keeping the cause from being diluted with a thousand petty grievances. She had made the decision early on to sacrifice fanaticism for numbers. She knew it would mean a higher proportion of losses. But the recruits were coming in at such a rate she did not think it mattered. In Delta City, Humi had made the opposite choice: one of her dispatches had said, with the merest trace of self-satisfaction, "From Gold Dagger himself down to the youngest renegade, everyone in the Rats' Den is mine, body and soul." Hope feared she was not flattering herself when she went out on inspections and saw the same thing in the faces of her own followers.

It was like having a pot of water come to the boil while she held it in her bare fingers. All she could do was to try to keep them focused while they waited for the Hands in Grussels to break.

The same thing went for the other continents. To that end, she wrote countless letters and dispatches to her lieutenants in Domesdys, Calvary, and the Archipelago—Shine, Truth, and Whitenail, all of whom had started amassing their own armies. In her name. In Humi's.

They would be visiting the camp today. The *er-serbalim*. She had to prepare herself.

Their consent to give her an audience was perhaps the most significant thing she had achieved yet; after Divaring Below, she'd thought she had lost their confidence forever. She should not receive them when she was this tired!

Her nails dug into the parchments, splitting them. She got up. Her booted feet thudded with an unfamiliar noise on the planks as she crossed the tent. She sank down into one of the expensive armchairs she had had imported from Delta City and began to fill a pipe. It was thus they found her.

The tang of sulfur filled the tent. The space filled with overheated *auchresh* bodies. Hope stood up, mentally congratulating herself for having been found at her ease, and embraced Broken Bird and Bronze Water. "*Perich "him!*"

she exclaimed. Inside her head, something screamed, *Old ... they are so old ... look how heavy Bronze has let himself get* .. "My quarters are not large. Would it be too great an inconvenience for you to send your guards outside? I assure you, you are safe!"

She grinned at them.

"My dear, we did not mean to imply that we do not trust you!" Bronze rumbled. "Out!" He snapped fleshy fingers. "Disperse! Gather information! Report back!"

He winked at Hope.

She suppressed a sigh of relief.

When the *keres* were gone, Broken Bird sank into a chair and said, "We only brought them because ... well, let us say that *they* brought *us*. We have too many demands on our energy, now, to waste it *teth"ing* around the continents."

"I summoned you from Iceland!" Hope said. "I apologize."

"Think nothing of it." Bronze Water lowered himself with an exhalation into the largest armchair. Hope held her breath and wondered whether the springs would hold. It looked as though they would ... just.

They all smiled guardedly at each other. Hope felt the atmosphere was one of goodwill, and she experienced a surge of confidence.

"Beautiful work." Bronze traced the labyrinthine red swirl on the arms with a fat finger. "Must be human crafted."

"There are some extremely talented upholsterers in Leadentown," Hope agreed. "If you had come by sea, Leadentown is the port you would have landed at."

Broken Bird had wedged herself into a corner of her chair, knees drawn up to her chest. Her *urthriccim* covered her like a raveled blanket. She looked like a wizened child. "Well, Hope," she said in a suddenly brittle voice, "enough of this false informality. What do you want of us?"

Hope gasped. *The haugthirres,* she thought. "Ah ... it ... has been ... too long. I thought we would renew our friendship at our leisure—"

"Nonsense," Bird said. "Bronze, pour me some of that slop, will you? Hope, your agents have been reporting our movements to you for at least eighteen days. We've seen them. They find it difficult to hide in the Icelandic Heavens.

Three sixdays is quite long enough for you to have formed a detailed picture of our life. Nothing has changed since you saw us in Divaring Below, almost a year ago, except that we do not move from Heaven to Heaven as fast as we did. Nothing has changed."

What did she mean? Was this genuine hostility, or just intimidation tactics?

"Yellow Riestasis." Bronze placed a cup in Bird's hand. Then he turned to Hope. "We would have come to you before long, even had you not invited us. But this is better. Now we know that we all have a concurrence of purpose. And this little layout"—he waved a hand at the tea table and silverware, the small red glass lamp burning in the center of the table—"the milieu you have prepared to receive us in—tells us more about you than we could have learned if we came on you unawares."

Hope leaned forward and poured wine for Bronze Water and herself. She did not have the faintest idea what they really wanted. She had lost control already. She must not let it show. *Concurrence of purpose?*

That seemed impossible, too easy. Such neat circles of intentions were created only by slipping through the loopholes that destiny left—by outguessing the game a dozen moves ahead. Neither she, nor Broken Bird, nor Bronze Water, was *that* clever.

She had to reassert her primacy. *That* could very easily be what they were trying to put over on her: that, and no more. For them, it would be a diversion.

"I make no threats," she said. "No offers. No promises, beyond that of my lasting friendship. This, with my most humble respects, is what I suggest to you. Your ideology, your method, are failures." She paused, Neither of them blinked. "You *must* be aware that nothing has changed since you began preaching isolationism—except that more *auchresh* have left the salt, to join Pati or more recently, to join us. *War*—the one thing the salt cannot offer—is drawing them out. What have you got to hold against that? Theories."

She stopped. A drizzle was falling on the tent roof. *Plip plip plip* on the waterproofed spindlespun. A shadow had slipped over the afternoon; Broken Bird's and Bronze Water's cheeks appeared to sink even as their features pushed out from their skulls, until they looked as exaggeratedly *auchresh* as an effigy-maker's apprentice's practice pieces.

"Well," Bronze said testily, "it seems your spies are doing a good job. But there is one place they have not been able to see, and that is Broken Bird's and my hearts."

Broken Bird steepled her fingers. "Hope, we are aware of our failure. We have been aware of it for longer than we care to think. Isolationism is dead and buried. It was only ever useful as an antidote to Pati. I remain convinced that in the early days of his rule, our influence was the only thing that kept the tyranny from spinning utterly out of control. But now our medicine is no longer strong enough. The time for stagnancy has passed. We are waiting for you to provide an alternative ideology. So far we have seen no sign of one." She drank deeply of her wine. "We have come here to spy on *your* heart, Hope. We will weigh everything you say fairly."

"What a challenge!" Hope said. *And what an unsurpassed chance to win them over! I can't blow it!* "But you really need to talk to Humi. She's the one with the grand theories."

"But she is not *auchresh*," Bronze Water pointed out.

"That means nothing now. *There's* my ideology, if you want. I believe in the equality of the races. The fact that I am an *iu*, not a woman, is only a disappointment to me." She looked straight at Broken Bird. "*You* understand."

Broken Bird nodded imperceptibly. Hope's heart lifted.

"You will see I have taken to wearing boots." She lifted one of her feet. "It is a poor example. But I am ready to subordinate—or make use of—my *auchresh* nature in any way necessary. I do not discriminate." The words were flowing more freely now. "All I care for is Humi's cause."

"That troubles us," Bronze said gently. "You care so deeply for Humi's 'cause.' But we have been doing our own spying, and some of your followers feel that this war ought not to be a *cause*. They fight only for their own freedom. To you, *wrchrethru,* and to others steeped in the history of the Conversion, a war without a cause may sound like a paradox—but think of it in practical terms. Many of the older renegades are worried by your commitment to a mortal woman they have never seen. This commitment seems divorced from the concern you profess for their freedom."

"Why must the two things exclude each other?" Hope said impatiently. "We are all fighting Pati. *And* you would do well to remember that this is *my* army, not yours."

"No threats, mm?" Bronze hummed ruminatively.

"You have never given me anything. Why should I now start to accept your advice? Simply because you are my *elders?*"

There was a short, ringing silence. Then Bronze Water laughed. It sounded as if saucepans were banging together in his belly, as loud and sad as a gong. "There was a time"—he hiccuped—"there was a time—"

Broken Bird put her hand on his arm to quiet him. "But we are no longer idealistic enough to be driven away from the honey tree by our ideological differences with the bees, Hope."

Hope inclined her head graciously. Her insides were churning. Did this mean she had *won?* Did winning, in fact, mean she had now to make concessions? She knew she would never get any less abstruse an admission of defeat out of her *perich"him*. She had to seize the moment, had to gamble, pray she was right.

She shivered. Injecting as much fluty sweetness into her voice as she could, she called, "Blackash! A fire! It grows late!"

A human orderly scuttled in, head down, and started a fire in the metal brazier in the center of the tent. When he left, Hope settled herself more comfortably, and turning her unlit pipe between her fingers, stated (flatly, to hide her nerves): "As I said before, I offer no terms. Only opportunities."

Bronze Water sniffed the singeing pine logs. "There are some sensory experiences which only human country can offer. Of course, those are acquired pleasures—but then, human babies are not born with developed palates or discriminatory sensual tastes, either."

"At the moment, I cannot offer you riches or possessions," Hope said. "And anyhow I hardly think you want them."

"No," Bronze Water said. "We cannot slough our years."

"Then perhaps you will deign to accept some of my young humans into your retinue." She paused. So far, no explosions. "I know this may not seem appealing. But what I should also like you to do is to mention Humi's name in your speeches. I need you to speak of the—the cause. I need you to be inflammatory." She held her breath. If they promised, she could trust them.

Bronze Water shrugged. "We cannot adjust our rhetorical style. As I said—we are too old. The other seems easy enough. There is no need to be sincere, I hope. As for your young men, they are welcome, as long as they can adjust to *teth*"*tach ching* and keep out of fights."

"But there is something I must know." Broken Bird was suddenly, disconcertingly forthright. "Hope, are you really doing this for Humi? What are your own ambitions?"

Hope gasped, caught off guard. Astonishment washed hotly through her. How could they doubt the sincerity of her allegiance to Humi? It was the one thing she was sure of in a troubled world. The one expression of her beliefs that was not ambiguous. "I have no ambitions." Her face was burning. "Do the honeycats not love honey? They have no need to cut down the tree!"

Broken Bird smiled with a mouthful of pointed, feral teeth. "Just making sure."

"We should not want the bees to swarm without warning," Bronze explained ponderously.

The audience seemed to have come to a standstill. The fire crackled happily. Hope swallowed. She was no longer sure who was interrogating who. "Your metaphors are confused. I still do not understand—"

"Why we are here? For *you*." Broken Bird's lips scarcely moved. "For you, Hope."

She blinked.

"And perhaps for Arity. We used to like him, you know. Pati has ruined him. All one can do is dismiss it as a bad job—but one cannot help wanting to redress the evil. And we recognize now this is only possible at a personal level."

They stood up, and Hope followed suit, like a sleepwalker. One after another, they pressed her in their arms.

She had hardly extricated herself from their hugs when their Icelandic *auchresh* clattered into the tent. The *keres* studiedly did not look at her as they took their leave. She was left standing alone by the fire, coughing, her eyes running with the smoke of a dozen simultaneous *teth*"*tach chings*.

She had to believe in herself. Rightly or wrongly, she *had* to believe it was she who had put one over on them.

She had to believe in her ability to keep track of all the strands of the vast, tangledy net she found herself knotting with both hands.

And she had to believe in Humi. Humi was her groundswell.

Her head had started to ache. She picked up her neglected pipe. It was a means of comfort, a reflex, like a swallow of chocolate before bed—a habit of her youth she had never grown out of.

She put it down. Going to the camp table, she called for her orderly. "Blackash! Come here!"

He entered at a run, his dark, furry face set with devotion. She smiled at him and was rewarded with a frenzied leap that lifted him several inches off the floor and brought him down with a thud. He loved her insanely, considering she had never spoken a personal word to him.

"Set up my bed, please. Then you can go fetch Scribe Dryburn." For the benefit of the rumor mill, she said, "I am going to dictate a dispatch to Humi."

The Wall of the Chrumetown Granary

When the fighting rang out in Curentise Street, not two streets away, Gete realized they were backed into a dead end. Pressed against the heavy stone wall of a granary, with equally impenetrable walls on either side, in the hot clinch of a weeping, praying, cursing crowd of Chrumetowners, he tried to assess his chances rationally.

If he and Thani did not escape, they would die. Being on the wrong side of Chrumetown when the violence bubbled over this morning had marked them as devotees—whereas had they been a half-league to the south, they could have passed as atheists or apostates, friendly with the south-towners who had sheltered the renegades. As it was, when they fled the square where blood had first been spilled, they had run north, downhill, riverward. A renegade had yelled in his god's voice, "Hands' sheep! Devotees!" and hurled a knife that whickered past Gete's shoulder.

He had been right as it happened. Thani was as staunch a loyalist as anyone could imagine. But on the whole the killing was horrifyingly nonsectarian, while it pretended to be directed by ideology. Apostates, loyal flamens, foreigners, Deltans, and outcountry folk, some of them looking askance at each other, some openly hostile, were all crushed about Gete so close that he could taste their breath. There had been two stabbings. The dead men were held upright in a ghoulish semblance of life. But when the porous line of Hands—their ad hoc defenders—in Curentise Street gave way, *all* of them would die.

Predators, Gete thought, his fury and fear compounded by a sense of unfairness: the renegades should have recognized him, if anyone, as a sympathizer! They were slaughtering everyone they uncovered in their surge toward the river. With the blood lust in their veins, they seemed scarcely to distinguish between gods and men.

In the short sixdays since Gete and Thani reached Chrumetown, he had seen a few of them about. They had worn hoods to disguise their *auchresh* features; but that was only wise, in a town in the heart of human country heavily policed by Hands. One would *never* have guessed *this* was brewing.

Fear smelled sour, like turned milk.

Babies wailed. So did grown-ups.

Gete could hear the Hands' and rebels' war cries over the racket of the terrified crowd. A wonder they had any breath left to kill each other. But they did. Gete's boots were stained piebald with divine blood. There was some agent in the white stuff that took the tan out of leather.

Thani had a child in each arm which she was trying to soothe. People were looking at Gete with a kind of wild hope in their faces. He was a leman: he had to do something. Escape to the river was impossible, unless they could get *through* the granary ... He wriggled, scanning as much of the wall as he could see. No door. No opening. Thani had done so much already—could he ask her to break a hole in the granary wall? She would do it, of course, if he said she had to, but it might kill her. As a loyalist, almost all her miracles were worked on people, and she had told

him that inanimate objects were far more difficult to
"heal," let alone "injure." He would not ask her unless he
had no choice.

But it was beginning to look as if he did not.

The Hands had been outnumbered from the beginning.
A good many of them had left Chrumetown three days
ago. Maybe Gete should have guessed then trouble was
brewing. But Thani wouldn't have left anyhow ... Rumor
screamed silently that there was fighting in the capital.
Since the departure of the Hands, Chrumetowners had
gone about looking lost in their familiar streets. Thani had
healed a rash of sudden, severe illnesses.

A big old man with turquoise fur, near Gete, was fighting
to get out of the crowd. "Let me through! Let me out! I
am an apostate! I can help the Hands!"

The world is turned upside-down.

"Godsbrother!" Gete shouted. It was necessary to shout.
He caught the apostate's red old eye. "Listen a moment!
Can you use your powers to break through this wall?"

"Why?" the apostate shouted.

With dismay, Gete realized the old man was in the claws
of his own, obscure killing lust.

*Am I the only person here who is even trying to keep his
head?* "We have to break down the wall! Then even if we
can't escape, we won't trample ourselves to death!"

"Save us, Godsbrother!" a woman screamed. Others
took up the cry. Though it did not seem possible, they
squashed closer together, creating a little space around
the apostate.

He clenched his aqua-furred fists. Then the rage that had
seemed in danger of spilling over onto the Chrumetowners
evaporated. He dropped his chin to his chest as if he were
nodding off.

Gete dived under peoples' arms, pushed an old woman
out of his way, and caught the apostate as he began to
crumple.

He had expected to fetch up against the wall. But the
wall was gone. Before he apprehended this, the world
whirled sideways and he landed with the unconscious Godsbrother on a pile of rubble. The sky glowed at his feet.
Bodies blotted out its blueness. Instinctively he curled
around the apostate, trying to shield both their heads.
Boots hammered his hands, his arms, his legs. A corner of

stone dug into his kidneys. People were stampeding over them, fleeing like sheep before the slaughtermen's knives.

After an eternity, the pounding ceased. Footsteps rang on wooden stairs. Thani knelt over him, shaking him. "Gods! gods, you're bleeding ... your face ... oh, gods' breath, please wake up, Gete!"

He sat up, hugged her briefly. Then he felt his nose. The fur of his face was sticky with blood. The apostate did not look in very good shape either. He was breathing, but not moving.

Gete suddenly realized that he had failed to think of the most important thing of all. "Thani!" he said urgently. "Close the hole!"

"What hole?" She stood up, patting the air. She sniffed the breeze and made a face at the scent of bloodshed.

She thought she owed him anything he wanted, for taking care of her, when in fact it was he who owed her everything. He owed her the life she had given him that night on Qalma, when she woke him from the sleep that had been his life on Sarberra.

He guided her hands around the ragged edges of the stonework. The gap was slightly higher than he was tall, and as wide. The cobbles of the dead end shone with a scuffed patina of blood and dirt. Three bodies and some dropped possessions were the only things left in the dead end. He could not see how the crowd had fit in such a small space.

From the noise, the Hands must have been pressed back into the next alley. They had seconds, at most. He tried not to let urgency into his voice. "We're inside a building now. We have to seal this wall. When the renegades get here, they mustn't know where we went. If they can't see us they won't bother to look. The lust is on them. Use a miracle the way the apostate do. I know you never did it before, but it's our lives, Thani," and he was begging. "You *must* have it in you! I know you do!"

"To foil the enemies of the Divinarch," she whispered, and grabbing his hand, she screwed up her little blond face and stood as still as a column swathed in drab homespun, her feet planted firmly on the rubble beside the unconscious apostate.

He held her as she lurched, held her though the blue disorientation, the trembling strain that felt as though every muscle in the body were being pulled, the certainty that it was impossible—that this time, she would fall into the void instead of bridging it—

and the *twitch*.

In the days before her audience with the Divinarch, when she had told him everything, she had wept hours afterward with the remembered pain of healings. Nothing could make her cry except his sympathy.

The air felt different on his face. Stonework swept from the vaulted ceiling to the floor of the granary. The pile of rubble had changed shape to accommodate the new wall, but it had not diminished.

They were alone in the vast, empty space. Stairs zig-zagged up one wall. The wooden banisters showed yellow where they had recently been snapped by the herds of Chrumetowners. Kerneled wheat lay drifted in a corner. The air smelled musty. Gete bent to shake the apostate.

Above him, Thani smiled carefully. "We're safe now, aren't we?" Her lips cracked, dribbling dark blood down her chin.

When the noise of the fighting finally diminished toward the river, the Chrumetowners breathed again. Several times during the afternoon that ensued, renegades' footsteps rang below in the granary. Every man, woman, and child froze, aware that one creak, one cry . . . or if the renegades saw the broken banister . . .

There had not been a sound for several hours.

But no one in the attic moved. Families huddled together. Those who had been caught alone slumped in groups scattered through the vast, dusty crawl space, Deltans with Deltans, Veretreans with Veretreans, and so on. Gete supposed they drew some measure of succor from the default bond of ethnicity.

A man could not stand upright even in the middle of the attic. Piles and piles of ledgers (etched, in the old-fashioned way, on large wooden tablets) blocked Gete's view. He sat with the apostate Godsbrother's leman, a sly-looking Calvarese boy of ten or eleven, and Thani, and the old apostate himself. Two flamens, two winged souls encased in depleted, infirm bodies.

Gete had refused requests for Thani to heal that child's cut, this one's fever, examine that little girl who had not spoken since her mother was killed. "The Godsister has saved you once already today. Let her sleep. Please."

Perhaps because they knew that if Thani had been awake, she would have tended them all, squeezing the last drop of strength from her soul, they nodded and tiptoed away.

And Thani did sleep. Gete wrapped her in his cloak without waking her. The infinitesimal disturbances of dreams made her dirty face twitch; insect-sized motes of dust settled on her hair. As day faltered, stopped, and relinquished the field to night, they became invisible.

Gete was cold in his shirt sleeves, but in a way he enjoyed shivering, after all the horrors of the day. Enjoyed controlling it. The old apostate was "watching" him in that way Thani had—fingering him with all his senses. His leman slept, curled doglike around the apostate's legs, all the precocious stealth drained from his face by exhaustion. His dark-furred cheeks were as round as a baby's.

Periods of drifting marked that long night, when Gete felt as though his mind had come loose from his body and floated into the rafters. In one of the intervals between these delusions, the apostate started talking.

"My name is Godsbrother Quest." He touched the sleeping boy's head. "This is Avi. You are Gete? Let me guess. Your name is Regretfulness."

He asked about Gete's relationship with Thani, their history, how long they had traveled together, where they planned to go next.

"The Divinarch posted us here. I suppose we'll stay until he sends us somewhere else." Gete could not keep the bitterness out of his voice.

"Do you think he will remember to call for you in the middle of *this?*" The apostate gestured around the attic. "Mark me, Archipelagan, he has forgotten he ever saw you or your flamen. You should have stayed in the Archipelago! He has more urgent matters to deal with now. The Divinarchy is eroding out from under him faster than a sandbank in a flood. Have you heard about Pirady? Domesdys? Veretry?"

Gete shook his head.

"They are all in the hands of the rebels. The Divinarch will have to fight merely to hold on to what he still has. And anyhow, in my opinion, the flamens were never more than a pastime for him." Gete opened his mouth in outrage. "No. Perhaps that is not quite fair. You were part of a test he subjected himself to, to prove he still possessed whatever ability it is that he has."

"He brainwashed Thani!" It felt good to come out with it. For Gete to admit that he resented, no, *hated,* the Divinarch for the huge open spaces he had installed in Thani's soul.

"*That* is a mystery. Some of my own faith speculate, because of his unusual powers, that the traditional belief that we flamens draw our powers from the gods—is not altogether unfounded. But then—there are humans rumored to have this ability, too . . ."

"Who do you mean?"

"Humility Garden . . ."

"That's my flamen's sister." *Perhaps I shouldn't have told him that!* The apostate seemed to invite confidences. Gete bit his lip.

But all the apostate said was, "Really? I have never seen her, but I heard from a friend, an apostate in Delta City, one Godsbrother Phantasm, that she does have unusual powers. Phantasm was sent to offer the apostates' allegiance to her, back when we were still questioning where our political loyalty lay. He described her as 'coruscating.' Do you know what that means, Archipelagan?"

"That's how Thani talks about seeing gods."

"Precisely. I confess I felt a slight trepidation when Avi read Phantasm's letter. My brother flamen was shaken by his experience, which at the time was very recent—too shaken to have been impressed either favorably or unfavorably by the Divinarch. But I hazard a guess that that visit had a great deal to do with his subsequent suggestion that we all offer our allegiance to her."

"What is it?" Gete asked. "This 'seeing'?" Starlight came through a crack in the roof, painting a white streak across both their laps. Godsbrother Quest's hands lay interlaced, calm. With a conscious effort Gete stopped fidgeting with the frayed cuff of his breeches. He said, "I've talked to— I've talked to gods—who say that it is all nonsense. That they have no divine blood in their veins."

"Rebels, I suppose. But they are not flamens," Quest said crisply.

"That's blasphemy!"

"Inasmuch as?"

Gete rubbed the bridge of his nose "You're—you're saying you and Thani have powers gods don't!"

"Exactly. Boy . . . boy. Power has nothing to do with superiority. What do you think the prime doctrine of the apostate creed is? Do you know *nothing* about us?" Godsbrother Quest smiled. Perhaps it was meant to be reassuring, but his eyeteeth caught the starlight and his salt crystals glowed over them like a pair of white flames, and for a moment all Gete could see was the hollow, carved head of a god standing on his mother's table in the middle of the winter when the sun only rose for an hour. A head with a candle inside it. Flat planes and raw edges of stone.

"You think you are all-powerful," he said fearfully.

"Not in the *least*." The Godsbrother unlaced his hands and shaped the air emphatically with them as he talked. "We do not believe the gods are divine. We believe they are merely another race, whose oddities and weaknesses we have yet to discover. The renegade gods are working toward an acceptance of their own ordinariness; but the majority of them still, in their hearts, believe they are superior to us. The only way we can achieve equality is through years and years and years of the intermingling the renegades have started. And it is bound not to be so easy as it has been thus far. It may look to us, *now*, as though the numbers of gods in human country can increase illimitably, and mortals will only be pleased and flattered—but eventually the common saltsider will realize that his 'divine' guest is really no different from his own cousin. The fact that the god can do the work of ten men will certainly sweeten the cup—but eventually, there must be a backlash. I do not know if we will ever really live in peace." He leaned forward. "But to apostates the question is more or less irrelevant."

"What do you mean?" Gete frowned, mentally struggling to understand. "What difference does it make where the gods live?"

"No difference. That is what I say. The gods have nothing to do with miracles."

Gete laughed.

"And the power does not spring from within ourselves, Archipelagan! If it did, *you* would work miracles. Every street urchin would keep himself clothed and fed. *We* would be gods.

"It seems safe to say that the power comes from the salt pilgrimage. Perhaps miracles' source lies in the salt, in some deep locus of brilliance. Perhaps it is in the air, in the salt winds themselves, in a chemical reaction of that sodium with our vital fluids." Quest shifted, tilting his slablike chin, and the starlight died in his crystals. "If so, the gods know no more about it than we do."

"Then you aren't any cleverer than Thani," Gete said disgustedly. "You don't know what you're talking about, either. The only difference is that you *know* you don't know."

"You have hit upon it!" For the first time, the apostate laughed. "We are mystics, Gete. That is our creed." Merriment rolled out of him like hands hitting a bass drum. Unwillingly, Gete smiled. The other leman raised his head, blind with sleep, and felt clumsily for his knife.

The Godsbrother stopped laughing. "It's all right, Avi."

The boy nodded. Quite clearly, he said, "Good." Wrapping his arms securely around Quest's foot, he curled up in a ball. In minutes he was breathing regularly again.

Uncontrollable shivering, the kind that relieves excessive tension, was making Gete's teeth chatter. He shoved his knuckles into his mouth. Around his fist, he said, "What do you believe in, then, Godsbrother?"

"We give it a name." It was almost as if Quest had been waiting for this question. Quite suddenly, Gete realized that the purpose of this little disquisition was to try to convert him. He felt an overpowering, but brief, desire to laugh as the Godsbrother had done. "The Power. A translation of the word *Rigethe,* from the language of the gods. They use it like the name of a deity in their speech, but we cannot make out from the renegades, who are mostly antireligious, to what extent they actually worship it. To us, it is not something one prays to, anyhow. Reverence toward it signifies our belief in something greater, something beyond— something whose existence must be acknowledged, and which must be feared, as one fears the unknown, as one fears destiny."

Gete did not want to give these crazy ideas time to sink in. But he could not think of anything else to object to.

"The Power is a source. A reason. The future."

In the morning, this will all seem like nonsense. "Well—
but—what—" The minute Gete spoke, he knew it was absurdly irrelevant. "What does this all have to do with what
we were talking about? The Divinarch's powers?"

Godsbrother Quest laughed again, more softly this time.
"Aaah. We come full circle. It has *everything* to do with
it—it is the *proof* of all I have told you. In that it is nothing.
Gete, my dear boy, Pati's power is nothing more than an
excess of charisma. Such a human trait, to mistake imbal-
anced souls for geniuses—or divine entities."

Outside, far off, a cheer went up. *Auchresh* voices, laughing and shouting with pure abandon. Gete did not smile in
response. He was too afraid. He scrambled to his knees,
twisting his head sideways, and screwed his eyes into the
crack of the roof.

Yellow light showed over the roofs at the top of the
town. Rivers of fire flowed down one street, then another.
The topmost streets were glowing steadily now.

Arson.

"It's burning," he gulped, "they're burning the town, oh,
gods—"

Abruptly he stopped. The light did not leap with the
ravenous lack of inhibition that characterizes house fires.
There were no flames at all.

He could smell the river, which flung its muddy mists
over the whole town as it rolled by, leaving a dusty residue
of algae on stones and windows, sliming the streets when
it rained. He could not smell fire.

In Curentise Street, below one side of the granary, flame
leaped. And steadied. Gete saw the huge squares of light
swaying on walls, which meant lanterns.

Footsteps rang on cobbles, fading eastward.

The Hands were lighting the street lanterns, which had
been neglected all winter to save fuel, in celebration of
their victory. On the hill the cheering swelled, louder
than ever.

Gete sank back, disappointed.

City of Charity

There was no traffic on the Chrume. The devotees who had recovered enough from their ordeal in Chrumetown to notice such things muttered that they had never seen anything like it. For ten days, the barge swished down the river in a padded cell of fog. Only the cry of a heron, or the complaint of a hungry child, broke the silence. "Don't fret," mothers murmured distractedly. "When we get to the city there'll be food. Plenty of it. Hush. Hush."

After a four-hour shift, the blue-furred Veretrean sailor, Godsman Reedbloom, relieved Gete at the *Sunflower's* wheel. Gete sought out Thani. She perched on the prow of the barge, wrapped in woolen robes. "Regretfulness," she said dully.

He cast a worried eye over her. Her fur looked clumpy. The damp air on the river was doing nobody any good—but she had been squeezing far too many miracles out of herself these past few days, healing burn victims, stab victims, and those who had simply refused to move or speak after escaping Chrumetown.

"Ye're not all right."

"Yes, I am." She clutched her robe closer, her pale fingers like buckles on its folds. "Gete, they're all depending on me. I should never have brought them onto the river. I'm so afraid this is horribly wrong . . ."

He could not believe she had actually admitted her doubts. He had not known for so long what she was thinking. Only what she had decided to do. And for her, the decision-making had always been the most tortuous part. "Don't be a goose!" he said robustly. "We couldn't've stayed in Chrumetown. Renegades would've killed us all for some reason or other." Almost all the refugees on the barge were devotees who had risen to affluence under Pati's rule; they could adequately have been described as "Hands' sheep." "Ye *know* that. That's why we left."

"But would they have killed them? The sentinels on the docks didn't stop us casting off. Perhaps they really didn't

278

care one way or the other what faith people professed. Perhaps theirs is a new creed we are incapable of understanding."

Gete had sometimes wondered what happened to Godsbrother Quest, the old apostate with whom he talked all night in the granary attic when they were hiding from the Hands. Those crackling, brilliant ideas had looked so faint when day came and Thani needed him again. Out of politeness, Gete had offered the Godsbrother a place on the *Sunflower;* but Quest had gently reminded Gete that *he* was not a devotee, that he was in fact well known for his apostasy, and thus was in no more danger, now that the killing was over.

Were the renegades apostates, then?

It was all too confusing. But perhaps Thani would not have been in danger any more than Quest was. Gete remembered the renegade sentinels' hollow eyes, their gratitude when people sidled nervously out of their houses and offered them chairs to sit on. "They were *exhausted,* Thani," he said now. "That's why they let us take the barge. If we'd given them so much as one day to recover from the battle, they would've cracked down. We'd never've gotten away."

"It would be wonderful to believe you, Gete. But I *cannot* stop wondering what might have happened if we had not fled." She gestured behind him at the barge, the masts with their enormous, limp bundles of sails, the grilled hatches that opened into the hold. "They are all in my care! What if I have misled them?"

"Look"—he put a smile into his voice—"right now, they're all in Godsman Reedbloom's care. If he falls asleep at the tiller, in this fog we would plow right into the bank before anyone notices we've lost course."

She grinned thankfully, and for a moment she was the old Thani, the Thani he had known before their audience with the Divinarch. "You are right! I accord myself too much significance! That way lies vanity. They aren't my responsibility."

"*There's* the spirit!" Gete said pleasedly.

"They're the Divinarch's."

Gete closed his mouth.

"He *can't* turn them away! They are his people. His Hands died defending them. And I'm his flamen. *There's* my responsibility, if you like, Gete. Even if there were too many supplicants in Delta City for Pati to help our little flock, *I* could get them a hearing! He knows me. He loves me ..."

Gete stepped forward and took her in his arms, pulling her down off the rail. The veils of fog twined around them, drifting back along the barge, striping the white sails gray. There was a smell of mud. A seagull hooted. Gete held her close, pressing her face into his shoulder. They were almost to Delta City.

A pack of children materialized out of the jumbled riverfront and helped the refugees tie the *Sunflower* up at one of the jetties that jutted into the Chrume. In six dozen berths, there was not one other barge. Gete bit his lip. He remembered rumors of fighting in the capital. But perhaps everyone was just hiding in their houses—perhaps the rumors were exaggerated, and people were only frightened, not dead.

Or perhaps it was Dividay. The day of rest. He had lost track of the sixdays.

As the refugees clambered unsteadily up onto the jetty, the Deltan children jumped, froglike, around them, hissing demands for money. "Or sump'n t' eat! Give us sump'n nice, Godsmen, an' we'll let you go!"

By this time the refugees had barely enough provisions to make themselves one more meal. Some of the men cursed the children and told them to take themselves off. Thani protested, but the men ignored her, and drew their daggers.

The urchins broke their mandate of whispering and fled, screaming.

Each Chrumetowner family had knotted together, arms around waists, heads on shoulders. The journey from Chrumetown had started in a delirium of terror, and concluded in a near-coma—not a relief, but a distillation of that terror, induced by the silence, the fog, and the paucity of food. Delta City's silence seemed to have infected the Chrumetown children: not one was making a sound, not even the babies. Their eyes were wide, their fur stretched sparse over their delicate skulls. The little ones clutched big brothers' or sisters' hands. Quite unexpectedly, the sight rent Gete's heart: for the first time in months, he missed his own little sisters.

Godsmen Reedbloom, the Veretrean sailor, rolled up to them. "What now, Godsister?"

Thani shook herself. "The Palace, I suppose. Gete and I have been there before. He remembers where it is. He can lead us there ..."

Gete shook his head in helpless anguish. "No," he mouthed silently to the sailor. "No." Over Thani's shoulder, he could see something truly dreadful. Without looking at the flamen, without looking up from the ground, the Chrumetown families were slipping away. One by one, they sidled out of view between the shuttered houses.

Godsman Reedbloom's throat jumped. He glanced at Thani, then over his shoulder at the departing Chrumetowners. Finally, with obvious discomfort, he said, "Godsister ... will you excuse me? I see Widow Sevenna is alone. The city may be dangerous, is it? She may need—"

Gete answered quickly for Thani. "Yes. Go." He held up his fingers and moved them to and fro as if for a blessing. "Gods be with you, Kines."

Quickly, shocking Gete a little, Kines Reedbloom turned his head and spat on the boards of the jetty. Then he mumbled a courtesy to Thani and strode off. Gete watched him catch up with the widow and her little son and place his big hand on her shoulder. Together, they vanished into an alley.

Thani let out a long sigh. "Well," she said hopelessly. And again: "Well. They are gone, aren't they? They didn't trust us."

Gete certainly did not trust himself to say anything forgiving about the Chrumetowners. White flocks of seagulls pitched and tossed overhead. The Chrume churned around the piers of the jetty, sheeny brown, roiling seaward. A curtain of gray fog cut down after twenty feet, hiding the sea, hiding even the last jetties. Thani stood like a badly constructed scarecrow, unmoving, head tipped, no more intelligent than a machine in repose, and seemingly as incapable of thinking for herself. Their knapsack of possessions sat lopsided at their feet.

"You and I must go to the Divinarch, anyhow," she said. She pulled herself upright. "We must tell him that we are here, and will serve him. It is obvious *something* is wrong: the city is far too quiet. We must help in any way we can."

But what kind of machine?

Regardless of the months they had spent together, regardless of the ever-increasing esteem in which he held her, not until that moment did Gete fully appreciate her strength.

One thing of which there was no shortage in the capital was corpses. They lay undisturbed in corners, intersections, doorways, human and divine bodies both. Nearly all of them wore some kind of emblem. The Hands had bright silky uniforms rucked around their immobile limbs, and the rest, men and renegades, sported the white-and-gray patches Gete had come to recognize as the badge of Humility Garden's followers. Some of the Chrumetown renegades had had those, some not. They gave even corpses a dreadful air of officiousness. Gete shuddered. This was all becoming so organized!

So many bodies. Few of them showed signs of having been looted. The Deltans must be afraid.

But the common people of the city scurried along the streets as briskly as they had the last time Gete was here. In some places they had spilled stone dust over the bloodstains. They looked behind them more often then rabbits on an open hillside, but at least they had not all disappeared into thin air. The shop doors stood open, though few people carried any purchases. The relative liveliness of the city surprised Gete. But then he thought, *How else could it be? These people have nowhere else to go. They're already in what we thought was a refuge.*

He did not shrink from describing the carnage to Thani, but he left out the badges. She did not want to hear of anything connected with her sister, although that was growing increasingly more difficult to manage.

Some of the sprawled dead were flamens. If the faces were hidden, or the salt crystals gone, he knew them anyway from the way little and big corpses clung together, faithful to the last. Would that be required of *him?* No pilgrimages for these children. Would the world feel their loss? After this was over (and he knew in his bones it must end soon, it could not go on, could not, this silent scream which was the city), how many flamens would be left?

Death was a loud, rich note in the air.

Everyone avoided Thani as industriously as if she were six feet tall and wielding a fiery knife. He knew she sensed it: an expression of pain grew on her face as they passed along the broad concourses, so that he was relieved when they reached the palace district and there was no one to stare at them and run. Here, many houses were blackened shells. In some places the sides of mansions lay in rubble all over the streets, as if they had been demolished by battering rams. A little way to the east, Gete heard shouts and cries. He quickened his pace, wondering how to avoid the confrontation.

A knife whizzed by his head, seemingly out of nowhere. "Gods!"

A few paces in front of them, a Hand appeared in a puff of brimstone. Gete staggered back. "Where are you going?" the Hand shouted. "Where are your colors? Quick!"

"We come to serve," Thani said simply, while Gete retrieved the Hand's knife.

"Who?" The Hand took the proffered knife in a way that was almost an insult.

"The Divinarch!"

"Thought you were creeping up on our flank, and making a damn poor job of it at that." He eyed Thani scornfully. "But I can see you're upcountry. Good, that's good. We need you. Right over there, in fact. Wait—" He raised his sleeve to his mouth and ripped the silk with his fangs. It shrieked thinly as it parted. Glancing thoughtfully toward the noise of the battle, he came forward and handed Gete two burnt-orange strips. "Tie this around your arm. And have her wear it somewhere it's visible." He shook his head tiredly. "You wouldn't believe how many of the deaths— on *both* sides—have been caused by overzealousness."

Overzealousness! Gete thought. *That's what killed half of Chrumetown.*

"Now get moving!" the Hand shouted. "Go on! Get over there!"

When Thani did not move, he cursed impatiently, and pulled her toward him.

She let out a squeak of fear. Gete made a grab for her,

alarms clanging in his mind, but he caught an armful of
nothing.

Sulfur shimmered in his eyes. He reeled back, tears wet-
ting his cheek fur. He was alone.

Gods' blood. Damn!

The worst possible eventuality, the thing every leman
feared. In all his months with Thani this had not happened.

Without pausing to get his bearings, he flung himself
down a side street, toward the noise of the fighting.

But it was farther away by foot than by *teth*". The streets
of the palace district lay treacherously coiled one upon the
other, linked by alleys that looked like service doors, rife
with dead ends. To one whose sense of direction was already blunted by desperation, the maze was impenetrable.
Gete was beside himself, a stitch biting into his side, by the
time he located the battle.

And by then, it was over. Cold air rang with the note of
death. Gete could smell the sea. The wounded and the
dead—all *auchresh* except for one flamen and leman—
sprawled in the windows of a mansion with a good-sized
front garden, which must have looked very fine before it
was burned to soot-streaked stone. A strip of bright blue
silk twisted from a chimney pot. Rivulets of lurid crimson
trickled in the gutter. After a minute of incomprehension,
Gete realized the strange color resulted from the mingling
of human and divine blood.

The Divinarch's forces had apparently taken the day. The
Hands glanced up to see who had arrived, and then paid
no attention to Gete. *Where was she?* The Hands were
winding their way among the casualties, cold-bloodedly slit-
ting the throats of wounded enemies, doing the same for
their friends if they were beyond help, *teth*"ing away with
the wounded *auchresh* if there seemed to be any hope at
all. They paid no attention whatsoever to Gete's wild inquiries, speaking when necessary to their fellows in weary
undertones which ill matched their quick, graceful
movements.

A little way off, several ragged flamens and lemans stood
in a dejected group. They were *not* prisoners, but the
Hands' allies. And there—*there* she was! Not standing with
the rest, but slumped on the cobbles, her back against a
wall.

Dead.

He dashed to her side and chafed her hands, kissed her face, whispered into her hair.

She stirred. Light moved in the depths of her salt crystals.

"First fight?" said the girl leman, a Piradean of about fifteen.

Gete nodded.

"Thought so. She was blooming terrified."

"What'd she have to do?"

"Only what my Godsbrother does. What they all do. Miracle spears. Fire in the eyes. Fire in the guts. Twist the guts. Things like that."

"Did she? Did she kill anyone?" He felt like a cad, going behind Thani's back. She hadn't returned to full consciousness yet. "Or is she no good at this? Should I take her away?"

"No, no! We can use her!" A tall Piradean man—the girl's Godsbrother?—took an interest for the first time, swinging his head with its heavy crystals toward Gete. "At first she was too frightened to move. I had to show her what to do, so that she did not hurt herself. But she understood quite quickly. Before it was over, I would guess she dispatched half a dozen of them. I could hardly believe she had not fought before."

"At least ten," his leman said admiringly.

"We faced no apostates today." The Piradean flamen was silent a moment. "Lucky for her we did not. She knows nothing of self-defense. That is more difficult. But if she can master it, I daresay she will be a great asset to us. She is not afraid to use her strength."

Oh, gods, Gete thought. *Poor Thani.* "But she's exhausted, Godsbrother. She won't be any use if she doesn't get some rest." It irked him to appeal to these loyalists. "She needs a bed, and good food, and a fire—" But if Thani had to fight again ... *gods, gods* ... maybe these flamens could help him keep her alive. Maybe they knew tricks. He would take the brunt of the fighting himself, if that would do any good. "We just got here today, from Chrumetown," he said desperately. "I don't think—"

"Ah. I heard that Chrumetown was burned."

Rumor travels fast! "No, it wasn't. But the renegades have it."

The Piradean flamen shook his head in pious disapproval. For a moment he looked ludicrously refined: far too gentrified to be standing out on a gray winter's day with no cloak, and soot stains on his face, and obscenely red blood trickling past his feet.

"The renegades have Domesdys and Calvary too," the other leman murmured in Gete's ear. "And Pirady. Me and my Godsbrother can't ever go home again. Unless the Divinarch wins it back."

"I will show you myself where you are to stay," the Piradean flamen said abruptly, almost as if he did not want to hear what his leman had said. "The Inviolate Ones have no need of us at the moment. The Divinarch has offered his hospitality to all whom the city has refused it to. The soup is hot, and there is a floor to sleep on; a flamen needs no more."

Gete winced. He knew it was a gentle reproof for begging luxuries for Thani.

In her slumped position, she shifted. She said in a clear, dignified voice: "Thank you very much, Tranquillity, for your kind offer. We are pleased to accept. Now, Gete, if you will assist me to my feet ..."

The Hands barely looked up as their allies straggled off. The chilly air had a bite to it that took the smell of blood to Gete's nostrils. His feet remembered the turnings that led to the Palace. Before long, he found himself leading the motley band.

Loyalty is the blindest so-called virtue on the face of this earth.

He had got a bad scare. Losing Thani ...! He gripped her arm tighter. Her flesh was cold through her robe. It was then he knew for the first time that they were both going to die, and that there was nothing he could do to stop it, and that he was terrified.

The air seemed to tingle. A vast, shimmering maw hung overhead, greedy to swallow the roofs of the houses, to consume them until its heavy swollen grayness sunk to the earth and nothing was left but a few inches of air between the dirt and the sky.

Is this what we know as prophecy?

No symptoms. He kept walking. He might even have been talking to the Piradean leman; he wasn't sure. No shaking, or foaming at the mouth, or loss of control over his limbs. But he could think of nothing except death. Her death, and his own. He had not know he was such a coward.

The energy of fear galvanized his step.

This is for you, he thought, looking sideways at the girlish, set face of the Piradean leman. *This is for everyone in Chrumetown, for everyone in this hateful city. I don't think I ever did anything really disinterested before. So this is for all the times I failed in my duty to humankind. All the times I acted out of love for myself. Or love for her. Atonement.*

I understand now.

That had probably been his worst crime. Loving her.

That, at any rate, was what that made it hardest to reconcile himself to a swift, ugly end to everything.

Conquering Passion

Arity and Pati balanced on the ancient Ellipse chamber chairs, one at either end of the council table. It had been a sixday since either of them had a full night's sleep. Deep within the Palace, they couldn't hear the noise of the fighting that drew constantly closer to the fortress. But they were not safe even here. Right now, guards stood three-deep outside the Ellipse door. On one occasion a scruffy little assassin trying to earn glory had burst in while they sat in session. That was when *lesh kervayim-serbalim* had still been here. He had been crucified on the east turret.

Pati played with the old voting stones, spinning them like dice. Sacrilege, none of the stones was ever supposed to "meet" each other. Arity sat bolt upright, concealing his restlessness.

All the *ex-kervayim* had gone to the continents to conduct campaigns against Humi's lieutenants. Some of them were dead. Glass Mountain. Crooked Moon. Unani. Pati's coup had not dissolved *lesh kervayim,* but the war seemed likely to put an end to them once and for all.

"Why are you unwilling?" Pati said. "Because we have not got a full council to vote on the motion?"

"Well, it *is* technically illicit."

Pati sneered, "Don't be absurd. This is war."

"I know."

"Some things are necessary evils! With its head cut off, the beast of rebellion must die—or at least sicken. We have to roust her out before the damage spreads any further!"

He was right about one thing, Arity thought. This ploy would bring Humi out of hiding, if anything could. They were pretty sure she was in Shimorning; but since the whole district was tacitly on the renegades' side, not even *auchresh* willing to die for their Divinarch could find out where the rebel headquarters were. Or if they could, they were invariably silenced before they could pass the information back. Humi had some method of spotting traitors which was extremely effective. Every agent Pati sent to try to infiltrate the Shimorning network was returned to him, dripping, in a little gold lamé bag. Suicidal attacks had been no more successful.

At last, even Pati's tolerance for needless death was strained. That was when he had come up with the idea of using the ghostiers—not to find out where Humi was hiding, but to bring her out.

"It's destroying the Crescent I am averse to." Arity steepled his fingers, aware he was stalling. "The ghostiers are one of the most valuable bargaining chips we have."

"And at any moment they may decide to flee overseas."

"I hardly think they will do *that* . . . they are too strongly bound to the city. And Delta City would not be Delta City without them. Aren't you sacrificing them too readily?"

"I would not sacrifice them at all, had I the choice! But if you think you can manage to spare them while preserving the verisimilitude of the ambush . . . you have my blessing!"

Humi was cleverer than that, Arity knew. She would not come near the Crescent if she smelled the least whiff of trickery. Reluctantly, he realized he would have to go through with it.

Better that than give Pati cause to doubt him. False though such doubts would be, they could prove fatal. Arity was painfully aware he was not immune to Pati's suspicious rages. Poor blameless Val had died in one such. He sighed.

"How many Hands do you think it wise for me to take?"

"By all means take as many as you can without making yourselves a target. Marshtown is not neutral territory! *Don't* take any unnecessary chances. I cannot afford to throw *you* away."

Pati met Arity's eyes. His mouth shaped other words. Arity closed his eyes. Heat spread from his ears to his cheeks. Thank the Power they were alone!

There was a sudden stink of *teth "tach ching*. His eyes flew open. Pati's face pressed close to his; steel pricked his throat. He overbalanced, and his chair crashed to the floor. By windmilling his arms he managed to keep his feet. "Power! Don't *do* that!"

"Every now and then, I have to make sure you *really* trust me," Pati said. He jammed his knife into its sheath. His eyes were stars.

"Power! I'm going to murder the *ghostiers* for you! How can you suppose I don't trust you?"

"Perhaps you merely agreed so that you could get a chance to see . . . *her.*"

Arity was angry now. *Let* Pati think that if he wanted. It was untrue! All he wanted was to get the abominable task over, so that he would never have to see her or think of her again.

He slapped his hip knife. "I'm off. Anon."

Pati let him walk a few paces toward the door. Then he *teth "d* again—wasting precious energy, when so many were starving!—and clamped his hand down on Arity's shoulder.

Arity stood stock-still, staring at the intricate fruit-and-vine carvings on the door of the Chamber.

"Don't get killed," Pati hissed in his ear. "Why do you think I sent all the others to the continents rather than send you? Some would call if favoritism: they would be right." Hot breath on Arity's ear, and for an instant teeth nipped the lobe. "I *love* you."

Arity let out an angry sigh. Why did those three words always make him so impatient to be free of him? It was unbecoming. Unbecoming. He wrenched away and walked to the door.

"When next I see you," he said, "I'll have her head in one of those little gold bags she favors. Perhaps you'll trust me then? Mmm. I always have valued trust over love. Couldn't tell you why, but I believe it has something to do with being *auchresh.*"

The door thumped shut behind him, and the faces of the guards swam in his vision. Pale, tan, black, country-boy flowers, with strange mutated petals. *Wrchrethrim* all, loyal unto death, most of them both stupid and immature. Arity straightened his back. It was not difficult to feel taller than them, though several were over six feet. *Take the stupidest ones.* "You," he said, pointing, "I want *you* on detail right now, for a strike. And you. And you."

While the Hands outfitted themselves, Arity paid a visit to the human quarter of the Palace, where fanatical devotees willing to carry out suicide missions could always be found. He picked a starved-looking adolescent and told him to run to Shimorning and spread the word that the Hands were planning an attack on Tellury Crescent. The boy was not to try to convey this intelligence to Humi herself; that would be risky. She might smell a rat, and torture the boy until he squealed. He was merely to drop significant phrases in certain taverns known as hotbeds of rebellion. "That way," Arity said kindly, placing his hand on the boy's neck, ruffling the fur, "you'll live to serve us another day."

Shuddering with joy, overwhelmed to be chosen, the boy seized Arity's hand and planted a kiss on it. Then he ran off.

The squad made their way quickly through the palace district, circling the Folly (empty now and staffed by Hands), and concealed themselves in a dead end just outside Tellury Crescent, wrapped in drab rags, like a band of immigrants with nowhere to go. Two of them strolled openly down the street, masquerading as an ordinary patrol. The locals scurried out of their way. At the end of the street, they faced about and returned to Arity. In whispers they reported that they had glanced in the windows of the Chalice and seen the ghostiers relaxing after their midday meal.

"What luck!" said Arity cheerfully.

The sky hung low and fleecy, like a sheep's belly, over the city. A mean wind was screeching higher and higher. Scraps of cloud tore off and blew underneath the mass, pale on dark gray, fleeing landward.

With a gloved hand Arity secured his cap more firmly on his head. "All right. On my word."

The squad stormed the Chalice with all the hullaballoo they had been careful to avoid as they slid through the palace district. Arity ordered the ground floor torched immediately. Flattening himself against the wall of the anteroom (where so often he had listened with Humi while the

ghostiers talked of him and her) he heard screams from
the street, and running footsteps. Within minutes, Tellury
Crescent would be empty of men, beasts, and valuables.
That did not matter. The ghostiers couldn't escape. Hands
ringed the Chalice and Albien House, up the stairs of which
the ghostiers had been seen hurrying when the first win-
dowpane shattered on the ground floor. Hands combed
each floor, covering all possible bolt holes. The ghostiers
would be caught on the top floor, in Humi and Erene's
old apartments.

Wiping smoke out of his eyes, a single guard at his side,
Arity waited for her. The wave of fleeing civilians would
convince her that the strike was for real, even if the informant had not succeeded.

She had better come! How despicable this strike would
be if it had been all for nothing!

Fire giggled inhumanly on the other side of the wall.

Arity dug his elbow into the guard. The Carelastrian
jumped to attention. "Upstairs!" Arity shouted over the
sound of the flames. "Tell Night Dog not to kill the
ghostiers—not yet! Take them prisoner! Wait—until she
comes!" He yelled out the message again to make sure the
Hand had it. The little yellow Carelastrian nodded, and
teth "d. The sulfur of his departure was no fouler than the
smoke bulging around the ill-fitting Chalice door.

What could be burning in there? Paintings? Silverware?
Arity knew better than to open the door. He moved away
from the wall. It was getting hot.

The Chalice was all stone, but for its roof, floorboards,
and furnishings. But Albien House was of antique wood—
and so was part of the connecting wall. If they weren't
careful, the conflagration might spread, and the Hands
would die along with their victims.

He yelled at the top of his lungs for his sergeant, Night
Dog. When the tall, black-skinned fellow appeared, Arity
ordered, his voice cracking, "Have six men draw water
from the kitchen and stand by to douse the fire when it's
done its work! See it doesn't spread to the roofs!"

"The fire is in the kitchen, *perich "hi*," Night Dog
volunteered.

Power! He should have thought of that. "Have them
draw the water anyway! Fire be damned! They can cover
their faces with wet cloths."

He knew that the Hands considered him soft. It pleased him to watch Night Dog's esteem for him rising visibly. "Yes, *perich "hi!*" The sergeant executed a minimal bow, stamped his booted feet (all the Hands, in their fight against a movement composed largely of humans, had taken to wearing hobnailed boots; they gave better purchase), and *teth "d.*

Arity stood, listening. The flames crackled closer to the wooden wall.

Sweat ran in rivulets down his face, down inside his uniform. The smoky air was nearly unbreathable. By sheer strength of will, he held himself still.

Then, almost simultaneously, he heard a ripping, splintering discord from overhead, and something hit the floor of the Chalice, shaking Albien House like a battering ram.

With unbelievable speed, the smoke was sucked back around the door. Arity pulled off one glove, wrapped it around his other hand, and used that hand to throw open the door.

The whole section of wall surrounding the door gave way and tumbled into the Chalice.

Roiling billows of smoke showed him: glimpses of blackened rafters fallen in crazy configurations, some of them reaching from floor to ceiling, making a dead jungle out of the hall; Hands popping in and out of sight, rags wrapped around their heads; glittering sloshes of water heeling through the air. A sour stink rose from the remaining section of the wall. The Hands nodded to him and kept on sloshing, except for one who ceased his duties in order to beat out the flames that had caught the shoulders of another.

He yelled to get their attention. When they had all solidified where they were, he said, "Enough. Get upstairs! The ghostiers are more subtle than you think!"

"Yes, *perich "hi!*"

"I'll cover the ground floor. Listen for my summons."

Some of them shot him uncertain looks. But they all vanished.

Alone, Arity coughed and spat phlegm. Almost all the flames were out. The walls of the kitchen and library were stone; they still stood, though unquestionably all the books and tablets (thousands of years old, some of them in *auchraug*) were ash. Little puffs of smoke curled around the

fallen rafters, giving the scene a look of steaming comple-
tion, like the frame of a second, inner building designed
by an eccentric architect. Outside the shattered windows,
nothing moved. Even the larks that usually flocked around
the eaves of the Crescent (as he remembered from days
of another life, memories of another self) had decamped.
Somewhere, a woman was sobbing. How much longer could
he keep from going up there and having Night Dog replace
him on lookout? He ought to be there. The execution was
his assigned task. *Must* the ghostiers be executed? If she
wasn't coming—

If he did not go upstairs, the Hands' blood lust, which
surely must be lapping at the backs of their throats, after
all this destruction—would cause them to kill the
ghostiers regardless.

At the library door, somebody stepped on a red-hot
ember and said, "Damn."

Arity went rigid. Without breathing, carefully he turned.
She was alone.

In all his hastily dismissed dreams of this moment, he
had never dared to hope she would come *alone*.

She wore an old-fashioned, beautifully embroidered dress
of green silk, cut on the bias so that it lapped the curves
of her hips. She wore tiny green slippers. Soot already
blackened their toes and streaked the dress. Her hair
fanned electrically about her face. She advanced with halting steps, hands patting the air ahead of her. When one
hand encountered a rafter, she brushed her fingertips along
the wood, then raised them to her mouth. She grimaced
as she tasted the soot. "Too late," she said aloud. "Too
late. Gods!"

No time to think (*don't think*) no time to plan (*don't
plan*) just *do* it.

He *teth*'d behind her and jammed his arm under her
chin, forcing her head back, pinning her arms, drawing his
knife from the sheath slowly, so that she could hear the
rasp of leather. "Don't struggle," he whispered. "You'll
only make it worse. It'll be over in a moment."

Actually, he doubted his ability to finish it quickly *or*
slowly. But then he could not get enough breath to shout
for the others. She was struggling, of course; how stupid to
imagine she would not struggle just because he told her not
to. Only she'd never been a match for him.

Power, enable me to get this over with.

"It's me. I wouldn't have let anyone else do this. That's scanty comfort but—I want you to know I still hold you in the highest esteem."

"You have become like Pati," she breathed. "Trickster. Heartless trickster. You sacrificed Emni and Zin and the rest of them, all to get at me. I did not believe it could be true. I was sure it was a double blind."

His voice would not come. His hands would not obey him. Touching her, protecting her from the chilly wind (for her bodice left most of her beautiful breasts bare), tasting her hair in his mouth, he found it difficult to remember exactly how they had both come to be here. All he knew was that it was wrong. The configuration was all skewed, the knife was in the wrong place, the wrong hand, its blue-black sway razoring the air as if it were silk, carving a distinction between the reality that was and the reality that would have been had he not drawn it; that distinction finer, ever finer.

Indifference was the real trickster. Indifference blunted the blade, numbed the agony of bifurcation, that splitting of the soul which Pati prompted in all his creatures. Indifference had corroded Arity faster than anything that preceded it. He had done more atrocities as a lieutenant than he had in all his months as an ordinary Hand.

Now there was no other option for him but to turn. Turn away. Open his eyes to this changed Humi of the arrogant, halting carriage, the dead eyes, the vicious whisper. Place himself on one side of the blade.

"You always had that gift"—he whispered to her—"of making one see oneself more clearly. I know it sounds ironic to say that to you now. But I can't . . . I can't—" With the thumb of his knife hand, he touched the poor useless eyelids.

She shuddered, shook, and started to whisper abuse at him. A continuous stream of highly charged obscenities. Her voice sounded more and more like crying every minute. But at least she was not indifferent to him. At least she wasn't laughing!

"I wish I knew what to do," he told the swearing girl helplessly. "But you see, I have been a hypocrite for so long now—"

"And you still are!" she hissed, practically in tears. Then

she sidestepped quickly, neatly, and wrenched away. He had not been ready. Belatedly, he cursed himself for watching her face instead of her feet. But then as she edged rapidly away, the end of a charred beam caught her in the lower back and bent her double.

Arity was terrified of approaching her again. She straightened up, coughing, with tears running down her face. One of her false-ribs, cracked, protruded whitely through her bodice. "Do you know what's changed, Arity, why you are going to kill me now? We have become conscious of ourselves. We know ourselves. And when you know yourself you know the unreality, the lethal transcience of faith. In *anyone.*"

Her nose was running. She wiped it with her sleeve, a gesture that made him want to sweep her into his arms.

He must have made some small noise. She stiffened, and on her face was masterfully controlled fear. "Do you still love me, Ari? Drop that knife, then! Drop it!"

He let it fall. It bounced, ringing dully on the flags.

"Oh, hell," she whispered wretchedly.

And warned by some instinct passed down to him by his predator parents, Arity realized what was happening. Just as he spun around, someone snarled a mad-cat noise behind him and slammed a powerful arm across his neck.

Caught, just the way he had caught Humi!

And now *genuinely* unable to call out. A blade traced spider tracks under his jaw. White blood coursed down his captor's arm.

"Got him!" the man breathed.

Upstairs, all was silent. Or perhaps Arity just couldn't hear over the blood in his ears. What were they *doing* up there? (*The treacherous daughter of a predator.*)

"Hume," the man said, "are they—Emni—Zin—"

"I expect so," Humi said. "I didn't think they really would massacre them, Sol. I'm sorry."

It was Sol. Sol Southwind, the ghostier who had refused to make Arity into a ghost, a lifetime ago, in the nightmarish days before he learned the secret.

"I was wrong."

Sol gave a great gasp, and clamped Arity's neck until Arity could not breathe. Did Sol remember him? "So what now?" he said roughly. "Have you thought through to this eventuality? Or were you so sure it wasn't true—"

"Of course I have thought it through!" Humi said. She slumped against the rafter, smiling, soot staining her sleeves. "I always think things out, don't I. But Ari says— he says he will turn. Much good that it does now ... The bastard!" She laughed hoarsely. "Anyhow, I don't believe it. He betrayed me once before, and he will do so again ... he has already done so ... he is a hypocrite of the yellowest dye. Unless I mistake myself, killing him is the order of the day. It will end this war. The Hands will be thrown into disarray. Pati will be devastated." She flapped one hand, as if to say, Go ahead.

Sol's arm tensed. His breath quickened. Arity could tell through the bloody throbbing in his brain that demoralized though he might be, the ghostier did not want to do it. Whatever principles he had, they forbade him to kill a god without the justification of making a ghost.

But though Sol had rebelled against Pati rather than kill Arity for him, he would do it for Humi.

She had always had that knack, too: the knack of getting men to do what she wanted.

"Get on with it," she said. Her voice was almost a sneer. What were the relations between these two? Why was Arity wondering that now? "What are you waiting for? You don't suppose he's here *alone,* do you? I tell you, that boy we captured wasn't exaggerating when he babbled about death squads. The Hands never do things by halves. Perhaps we should learn their lesson."

"Humi, for the gods' sake," Sol said. "If you're doing this for *love,* you'll be sorry—*I* know—"

"He's *Arity,* isn't he! First Lieutenant to the Divinarch! Do it!"

And a piercing *auchraug* call split the air. Sol's body vibrated. Arity staggered free and sprawled on his hands and knees, retching. Blood from his throat dripped on his hands. When Sol was hit from behind, the knife had gone in deep. Sweat stung in the cut.

Then hands took hold of him, strong Hands, friendly Hands, helping him up. "Master! *Perich"hi!* What happened? Are you—"

Later he would discover that—just as he had feared— the Hands' impatience had been too much for them. To pass the time while they waited for the ambush to be sprung, they had slaughtered all the ghostiers in various, intriguing ways, first jamming rags into their throats so that they should not scream. It was a source of hilarity among the Hands how easily and involuntarily mortals gave way to pain.

Only when that amusement was no more, they took it into their heads to wonder what had become of Arity. Having heard no noise, they presumed there had been no developments, but nonetheless Night Dog took every caution as he slunk downstairs to investigate. He saw what looked like his lieutenant in danger of his life. Luckily for Arity, he did not stop to wonder if the situation was what it seemed. He just *teth* "*d* into the air, letting out an ululating yell, and brought both hobnailed boots down on Sol's head.

But after that, his concern was all for Arity's life. In the minutes it took for the other Hands to hear his shouts, and straggle down from the scene of their carnage—which they had arranged as artistically as any of the dead ghostiers could have, and in which they took as much pride as a child takes in his pickled frog collection—Sol had recovered and fled with Humi out into the street. The two of them were alone, and they knew Marshtown inside-out and up-side-down. There was no trail to follow. But Night Dog assured Arity they could not get far. The whole city was still the Divinarch's territory; they could not *teth* "*;* the whole pack of Hands had set off in pursuit.

For maybe one minute Arity gave in to despair, dropping his face into his hands. Then he ordered Night Dog to report back to the Palace while he, Arity, organized a city-wide hunt for her.

The Face of Treachery

Emni.
  Ziniquel.
  Tan.
  Suret.
  Yste.
  Lighte.
  Algia.
  Eternelipizaran.
  He was not able to keep from her the fact that they are
dead. Add them to the roster, *she thinks as Sol drags her
through the darkness that conceals the Marshtown alleys,
stumbling wet palm in wet palm, turning, starting to jog.
Several times he curses and wishes they were in Christon,
where they could lose themselves in the maze of the roof
roads. He wants to bang on a door and beg for shelter, but
she keeps saying,* No, No, No. *Any door would open to
them here, but it would mean death for their hosts. The
Hands would discover the work of a few minutes and a
seditious heart, and would string the hapless family (father,
mother, and even the baby) from the Palace's turrets, new
beads for the grisly necklace it already wears.*
  She hisses again at him. "Our only hope is to get back
to Shimorning!"

  *Throw their bodies on top of Hem's and Leasa's, on top
of the little corpses of Meri and Ensi, the children. I am
amassing quite a heap here in my heart, aren't I? They are
rotting, too. How will I feel when I have managed to clamber
onto the top of it? Revenged. Satiated, I hope.*
  Victorious. Content.
  *Maybe Hope could tell me how to rescue someone in time,
before rescue is useless, before there is nothing to do except
revenge. She rescued me, four years ago, though I'm not so
sure her actions were for the best. Why didn't I realize she
was my dearest friend until I sent her away? Hope. I miss*

*her sweet and oh so obvious flattery. I miss the spicy warmth
of her embraces.*

*I hear she is fighting in the front lines now, with her troop
in Calvary. If she falls, too, I think I shall destroy myself,
as a service to my friends.*

*Or perhaps I'll just turn myself over to Ari. We can make
love once more, for old times' sake, and then I'm sure he
will hand me to Pati.*

*But that would mean giving the world also to Pati in a
gold napkin, the way the Hangman packages their spies (I
hate it that I have become so indispensable; my having let it
happen reveals my own weakness). Giving the world to Pati,
its corners all tied up with the old, strong thread.*

She cannot forget that when he embraced her, a fearful
passion flared up inside her. She was afraid she would crumble and cave in like the burned Chalice. Nothing mattered
in that moment. Not the loss of her imrchim. Not death. For
if he killed her, she knew she held onto his heart so tightly
they would both perish. His arms around her made her forget all the hard bargains and points of honor and boredom
she cherished as ammunition against him and Pati. His arms
came very close to making it all worthwhile.

But there was a knife in his hand and everything was wrong.

Conquering that passion is something she believes she will
count, in the future, among her greatest achievements.

(That is, if she can truly be said to have achieved anything;
if the very notion of achievement must not now be classified
as an irony with this rank of murdered friends behind her, this
mute army of watchers following her with lidless eyes—and
how is it that with death those who in life were just flawed
mortals grow into giants, withering the significance out of all
our deeds with their dark breath, their complacent possession
of the Answer before which all of us can only flinch?)

She hardly hears Sol whisper: "It's no use. They've got
ahead of us. We shall have to hide, and pray. We have no
choice."

The breath rips painfully through her lungs as she sinks down.

She felt as if she were flattened into a corner. Dampness
touched her through her dress. She smelled mold. The
Hands' voices echoed through the streets, circling, closing
in. She smelled a faint waft of sulfur.

Sol wrapped his arm around her, caressing her shoulder. His touch was absent, repetitive. Although she was too numb to be afraid, she felt the familiar, rote apprehension that a reader feels, flipping the limp pages of a book toward the denouement.

She could no longer lean heavily on him. She prayed they got out of this before she had to make any more demands on his loyalty. They *should* have taken shelter! The sacrifice of one Marshtown family would not have weighed so heavily in the Balance—so many more would die, if she died ... That rankled, like an imposition of her freedom. Too hard that she must try her utmost to live, when the odds were stacked against her!

But she must try. And without Sol's help. The attack on Arity had exhausted the limits of what Sol would do for her. He had just lost a sister—no, more than a sister, a twin, a lover, a friend, for whatever Emni had been to Humi, she had been a thousand times more to him—and that not unjustly, he blamed it on Humi.

And grief did strange things to people. She remembered how she herself had wept when Erene eloped with Elicit—as if she'd been genuinely bereft. The only thing that eased the pain had been taking control of her new position as senior ghostier.

Likewise, while Sol mourned Emni's death, other things might swell large to fill the place she had occupied in his hopes and dreams.

What possibilities might he see on a Conversion board suddenly swept clean of half its major pieces?

His touch on her arm grew intensely irritating. She brushed him away.

Booted footsteps rang almost over their heads.

"Where are we?" she breathed.

"Storage bin. Underground. Behind a bakery." His body was rigid with tension. *"Shush."*

Twice, at least, now, she had made the mistake of interpreting ambition, disguised with a superficial affection for herself, as loyalty. Self-interest was in Sol's very character: he could almost be forgiven for the crime he had not yet committed. At a stretch, it was even possible to think of him as innocent.

The Hangman was the other one, Humi knew now, who had betrayed her. Evita: sly, calculating, cold-blooded. The

knowledge. Evita was a traitor: she had had the Lakestones
killed in order to bind Humi, who believed Pati had done
the murders, closer to her, and incense her more thoroughly against Pati (as if that were necessary!). Humi's lingering softness had refused to accept that possibility then.
But now she had done away with softness. Now she knew
that Evita was a snake in the grass. And the snake would
be extirpated.

In order to do *that,* at least, she must escape. She must
go on living.

Her fur stood on end. She prepared for Sol's shout.
"Here! She's here! Take her—but let me go free! I was
always faithful to your master!"

She smelled Sol's human sweat, and her own. The tiny
cut Arity had opened in her neck ached. The wall of the
storage bin pressed grittily into her back. *Auchresh* voices
resounded through her bones, seemingly in the very pit
where they crouched.

It came as a rude, painful surprise when, although Sol
had not made a sound, iron slammed back along its grooves
and a loud cry split her ears. She felt herself grabbed and
yanked up out of the bin, thrown face first against a wall.
The impact brought tears to her eyes. Blood streamed from
her nose.

She straightened up, lifting her head, holding her sleeve
to her face. Her ears tintinnabulated. Somewhere in front
of her, a fight was going on. At first she did not understand;
then it hit her like a blast of cold wind through a door.

Sol was fighting to get near her.

To save her?

Wrong? Could she have been *wrong*?

Fists connected with flesh. The Hands chattered in *auchraug,* congratulating themselves. Sol hit the wall beside her.
He slumped against her side. His breath whuffled.

She could not forgive him his loyalty, could not feel any
gratitude. She wanted to jerk away and let him slide to the
dirt. She hated him for deceiving her.

Pure, unthinking loathing suffused her. She lifted her
head. "Kill us then! You have us where you want us! Do
it!"

"Oh, no, milady. Beloved Superior has more things than
a few to say to you. You cannot remove yourself from our
inflicting of punishment," one of the Hands said happily.

"Speak *auchraug*!" she said in that language. "I would understand you better."

They jostled and muttered. "How does the lady come to know our tongue?" a different Hand asked.

"I have been a frequent visitor at the Heavens."

"Might this humble servant ask which ones?"

She sighed. "Mostly Wind Gully Heaven, in Kithrilindu, by the side of the *Writh aes Haraules* . . ."

"I'm from Red-tongued Bird Heaven!" another Hand said delightedly. "Did you ever—"

"Yes. The *mainrauim* and I visited the Red Tongue frequently. We always walked instead of *teth"ing*. Those are pleasant hills." A knife of memory pierced her. Silky salt grass swishing about her legs, trees low and pale in the distance, the vast purple arc of the twight sky. *Sight.* Early morning, for the *auchresh.* Arity's arm about her shoulders—

"Oh, they are!" the Hand agreed. "We used to—"

"Enough!" snarled another Hand. "Silver Eye, I shall have you disciplined for insubordination. You too, Ordi!"

"Oh, no, you won't!" Humi straightened her back. The wind was drying the blood on her face.

Emni. Zin. Hem. Lease. Lighte. Algia. Suret. Yste. Meri. Ensi. Eterneli. Tan. Sol. Ari. Evita.

She put them all aside, to be finished at her leisure. Took a deep breath. Putting more into her words than she had ever done before, she started to speak.

Not until he was moving fast through Marshtown, jostling close beside Humi in the knot of Hands, his wrists untied, his face wiped clean of blood, did Sol realize exactly what had happened. The Hands behaved as if they had just awakened from a dream. They were looking forward to meeting old friends in the rebel stronghold. All eighteen were boisterous, joyful, forgetting again and again to modulate their voices, until Humi had to remind them they were no longer in friendly streets.

Everyone gawked as the party filed down into the Rats' Den. The Hands held their heads high. Sol could see the pride gleaming off them, as if they had just been polished.

Humi dismissed them to Gold Dagger's underground apartments, to receive badges and destroy their loyalist uniforms. Then she beckoned an errand girl. "Bring me the Hangman."

"Yes, milady!" squeaked the cringing child.

"In manacles."

The child's eyes popped. "Yes, milady!"

When the Hangman was escorted into Humi's presence, in the little cave that served as a temporary audience chamber, she was bound only with ropes. Sol supposed they hadn't dared to manacle her, on the off chance that the errand girl had been wrong. She wasn't. Neither was Humi. And Sol had a pretty good idea what Humi was doing: she had finally realized the truth about Evita, realized the woman's obsessive near insanity, and she was losing no time in acting on it.

Humi's jaw was locked, her fingers steady on the reed-bundle arms of her makeshift throne. Difficult to remember that she had just had as devastating a loss as he had. But maybe that was what had brought this on. The massacre of the *imrchim* had caused her to see her own actions anew, perhaps; had scrubbed the glory off the war.

The Hangman's mousy head rose proudly out of her cowl. Sol found it hard now to see how anyone had ever mistaken her for a man.

Humi seemed to stare at her for a long moment. "I accuse you of murdering the family of Hem Lakestone, Evita," she said finally. "Four crimes against innocents, and *allies*. Treachery."

"I did not," Evita said steadily.

"You had a motive. Political. Self-ingratiation by elimination of rivals. Rivals who didn't even know you existed." Humi tok a deep breath. "And it *worked*. Oh, yes, you are *richly* deserving of punishment."

Sol looked down at his feet. He stood with his back to the wall in a corner of the audience room. Poor-quality reed torches flared dimly around the walls, dying and being replaced by servants. Flames flickered as fast as Emni had died. As she would be replaced.

He would be the one to replace her. When the time came, whether Humi fell, despite her visibly mushrooming abilities as commandante, or she triumphed, the victor in this war would still ordain Sol as senior ghostier. He was the only candidate. Mory and Tries were too far gone into rhapsodies of pain, too far off the normal aesthetic map. They didn't know the things about popular appeal that he did. And no matter what it cost, he would take the post that would allow him to use that knowledge—to do the only job he was really trained for. This business of war was not only grueling and painful, but *boring.* He missed his art. Missed ghosting. As soon as this was over—no matter how it turned out—he would sever the links that tied him to the new regime, chaining himself into the antiquated set of rules he knew so well, that hierarchy custom-fitted to a system of government as dead as she was. He had wanted command of Tellury Crescent for as long as he could remember.

But strangely enough, the prospect gave him little joy. His resolve sat bitterly in his mouth, like a pellet he could not swallow.

Emni. Sister. Lover. Enemy. His reason for living.

Smeary light, smeary soot stains on the rock walls, smeared vision.

The Hangman stared at Humi. At last, Humi sighed and said shortly, "You're executed for treachery. Take her away."

That jolted the Hangman into speech. She railed at Humi, first denying that she had ever betrayed her, and then cursing her for a bloodless bitch and avowing she would have killed twice as many if she could once have seen Humi weep.

"For your insolence," Humi said, "burial in the marshes. And there will be no flamen to consecrate your body to the gods."

The Hangman's face muddied in horror. Sol remembered she was pious: an unconsecrated burial, for her, was probably more frightening than death itself.

The guards dragged her backwards out of the room. She fought grimly against their strength until one of them drove his knuckles together under her ears. Then her head flopped.

Her thin, pale, foxy face was vacant. But Sol knew she was not dead. They wouldn't kill her for several days. Execution for treachery took an especially ugly form here in Shimorning. It was the only type of execution Humi sanctioned that was not merciful.

Later, in bed, he said, "Why did you execute her? You realize what this means to Gold. He'll be chortling. You may actually have endangered your authority."

She lay on her back beside him, hands folded behind her head. Their underground chamber was tiny, only a cubbyhole, but out of reach of the noise of the forges and the newly excavated barracks. And it enjoyed access to all the major escape routes.

They had burned candles earlier while they made love. The scent of lavender still lingered in the darkness.

"She was a traitor," Humi said. "I don't have to justify my decisions to you, or anyone."

"Do you mean she *did* kill the Lakestones?"

She started. "Did you think I executed her out of paranoia?"

"I thought you did it because you'd come to see who she was."

"I *liked* her, Sol!"

"I know you did. Too much. Mory and Tris and I thought she might have done it, for the very reason you said. Even Aneisneida had an inkling. But we didn't suggest the possibility to you because we didn't think you would believe us."

"I would at least have considered it."

Sol swallowed. "Perhaps we didn't want you to." He remembered those conversations, most of them held in the apostate ghostiers' workshop. The comforting safety of bitchery about other *imrchim*—safe because it was based on unshakeable affection. "We found it sweet that you refused to see. That you still needed to place absolute trust in *someone*." He smiled. "At heart, you were still our little Humi who loved Erene so deeply and absolutely."

Her voice went chilly. "I placed absolute trust in too many people. Now I know that you and Mory and Tris were among them. What if she had killed me? What would you have said then? Keeping your suspicions to yourselves was indirect treachery!" Her voice shook. "Trust is the most misbegotten of emotions!"

"What absolute crap," Sol said. "That's rotten fish guts."

She turned on her side. Cool air rushed down the gap between them, under the bedclothes. "I realize that you are not everything I thought you were."

"Because my sister was murdered? Because I was half mad with anguish and I couldn't manage to hide it?"

"No," she said sadly. "No. That's not it at all."

She curled up, pulling the covers around her like a little girl. Sol flopped back on the mattress, stiff with fury, waiting for her to qualify her rejection, to apologize. He was aware that his limbs were relaxing. Waves of tiredness washed over him: tiredness like an abnegation of the world, the inevitable result of extreme grief. *I have to ... have to ... she'll come around, I know she will, she's only a girl ...*

At last he could stay awake no longer.

Sword-lizard-winter

The war in the city had been going on for almost a season. Guerilla attacks and bloody ambushes had worn down both forces. But the rebels and the loyalists had not yet met in a full, pitched battle: an event that Humi held would end the excruciation of the city once and for all. Hope's dispatches, written in a hand that grew less hurried and more fluid every day, said that her lieutenants, renegades every one, now controlled all the continents except Calvary. In reply, Humi dictated instructions to the lieutenants as to how their new possessions were to be managed. Hope herself was still in the northernmost land. Pati had consolidated the remnants of all his defeated armies in Samaal—determined, Sol thought, to hold onto "the land of the pious" both out of pride and because, should the war drag out much longer, Calvary was home to the metal mines.

He sat beside Humi, watching the faces of the people he sometimes, jokingly, called his new *imrchim* while the renegade who had brought the latest dispatch read it out. The messenger was still sweaty from the northern sun. Hope had amassed her forces outside Samaal; they planned to attack within the sixday.

"Excellent!" Gold Dagger chuckled when the *auchresh* finished. "Victory is ours, eh? Eh, Hume?"

He seemed to have gained weight every day of the war. Mory had said, cattily, that his gold-plated waistcoat showed signs of having been let out. She noticed things like that. Sol didn't. But he took a particular interest in Gold Dagger. It was his self-claimed duty to guard Humi's back. And Gold was the most obvious threat to that tawny pelt. He stared at the fat Deltan, and kept staring, his face blank. That had always worked on the ghostiers. Sure enough, it silenced Gold Dagger's laughter. "We 'ave to make a move," he grumbled. "We've been sittin' on our arses too long. Gotta finish it. Men are gettin' tired. Impatient."

Humi blinked, lizardlike. "Yes," she said. "I know this: without Delta City, we are not victorious. And the danger

that we will be burned in our beds increases the longer
we stay here. Pati knows where we are. Somehow, he has
found out."

Nobody mentioned the possibility that it had been the
Hangman's vigilant eye for spies which had kept the location of the Rats' Den a secret for so long. Nobody looked
at the chair beside Humi's—still empty after months. Gold
Dagger muttered something in a voice too low for anyone
to hear, and his eyebrows met and shook hands, ominously.

"But there is a reason why he hasn't attacked us," Mory
said, and supplied it, looking please with herself. "He is
afraid."

"His forces are inferior," Tris said. "He doesn't want to
fight in Shimorning, where the people are on our side. He
thinks to force us to carry the battle to him."

"Then perhaps we ought to do just that," Sol said.

"Nope," Gold Dagger said. " 'Be a bad move. I've
heard—never mind *ow*—that 'e's been callin' more and
more Hands back from Calvary to bulk up the forces in
the Palace. We'd be squashed like soggy lentils. Gotta wait
till 'e's off his guard."

The rumor about the Hands, at least, Sol knew to be
true. For the past few days, when the wind was right, the
smell of sulfur had blown steadily from the Palace, a foul
exhalation. For many Deltans who had remained stoic in
the face of civil war and the ravaging of their homes, this
was the last straw. They knew it for the demons' wind, the
devil's breath, the yawning of the gates of purgatory, where
all the atheists who had been arrested in the early years of
the tyranny hung screaming. The core population of the city
had started to break down. Bargeloads of Deltans sailed for
the mainland every night—until the Chrumecountry folk,
weary of the uninvited burden on their hospitality, started
forcing them back across the river with arrows. Devotees
who came to Delta City from farther up the river, supposing it a last haven of safety, found themselves mired in
suspicion, hostility, and petty crime. Food supplies having
been almost completely cut off, the islanders were killing
each other for bread and pork.

As a result, a counterrevolutionary swell had begun to
rise under the poorest districts of the city. Pati had started
offering food and lodgings to any human who would fight
for him; previously, only Hands had been allowed into pa-

trols and battle squadrons. A thin, but not insignificant, trickle of Deltans was flowing daily into the palace district. The edge that Humi would have enjoyed in a pitched battle there—the advantage of not having to worry about injuring human civilians—was disappearing.

The apostates were no help. Never better than provisionally allied with Humi, they had started to preach against all Divinarches, all uprisings, and all gods, be they Hands or renegades. Mory and Tris tried to apologize for them; so did the harried Godsbrother Phantasm, who, having fallen absolutely under Humi's spell, was a pathetically divided man. Humi could not stand their moral double-dealing, and often said so in Phantasm's presence. But Phantasm's fellow flamens seemed not to see anything wrong with working dark miracles against the Hands one day, and preaching Humi's redundancy in the Marshtown streets the next. Their audiences were motley, and fervent.

The conspirators, as happened so often, had got themselves mired in arguments and counterarguments. Sol had not been listening. He interrrupted brusquely. "*I* think Gold Dagger is both right and wrong. We have to finish this war before it's too late. But in order to do that, we *have* to carry the battle to Pati. There's just no other way."

He sat back.

"Thank you, Sol," Humi said. "I have been trying to make these people agree to that for the last fifteen minutes. But I don't blame you for rationing your attention. There is nothing less interesting than listening to five intelligent men and women try not to look like cowards."

"But *I'm* for it," Mory said hastily. "With the apostates in our front lines, we can hardly lose, no matter where we fight!"

Tris pursed his dark lips.

Soderingal glanced at his wife. Aneisneida gave a tiny nod. "If the Divinarch is for it, so are we," Soderingal said reluctantly.

"It seems we have a majority, then! Are you with us, Gold?" Humi's voice carried a hint of menace.

Gold Dagger beamed. He had evidently decided to make the best of being outnumbered. His cheeks bulged like green plums. Sol marveled at how innocuous he seemed. You would never think, to look at him, that here was the most dangerous man in Delta City. He was an amazing dissembler, better

than any of them, even than Humi. Soderingal remained a
pale copy of him, brooding, vicious, cowardly.

Aneisneida, on the other hand, resembled *her* father
more markedly every day—except that she remained slender, as Belstem Summer had never been. Recently Sol had
found himself looking at her with new eyes, marveling at
the ingenuous, instictive, not quite conscious artistry with
which she played her husband on a string.

"Of course I'm with yer!" Gold Dagger boomed. He
slapped his hands flat on the table and, slavering, did a
realistic imitation of a wild dog about to attack. Then he
let loose a boom of laughter.

Tris flinched backward, then made a face of disgust. *That
boy's really been spoiled by piety,* Sol thought. *He used to
be up for a laugh anytime, though he was so shy—and you
could depend on him.*

Aneisneida giggled.

"What else 'ave I been waiting fer you pigheads to agree
on?" Gold Dagger heaved himself to his feet and offered Humi
his arm. She accepted it, beckoning behind her back for Sol to
lead the way. He resented the way she ordered him about,
but he knew she was grateful for his protection; it was only
that she would not admit to it herself. "Come, milady Divinarch, soon ta be enthroned!" Gold Dagger bellowed.

Sol was intimately familiar with the Rats' Den barracks,
but he did not like them. To his fine-tuned ghostier's sensibilities, they were impossibly wretched. Dirty, steamy tunnels, newly hollowed out; some sections dug in antiquity,
but unused for generations, for a good reason—they were
cramped and labyrinthine. Several times he lost his sense
of direction, and had to fight to remember if they should
climb up or down the next flight of slimy, twisting stone
stairs. He was supposed to be leader, and if he had deserted
the others, they would have had to apply to the soldiers
themselves to be let out. That would have been an unthinkable humiliation. As Gold Dagger and Humi progressed
from squad room to squad room, announcing that the end
was approaching, cheers followed them, echoing off the
walls of the maze.

The Rats' Den had never in its history been so crowded.
Only tallow candles lit the tunnels. The smell of frying hung
heavy in the air. Only the inadequate fans, which shifts of

skivvy children cranked day and night, ventilated the low-ceilinged squad rooms. These same rooms were used for sleeping, relaxation, some drilling, elimination, and food preparation. How did the human soldiers bear it? *Auchresh* were naturally hardier, but even they had soot-blackened faces, and looked weary and underfed. There was not the least sign of organization in the whole giant honeycomb. The thing that held them all here was no longer their love for Humi and her cause but the fact they had burned their bridges behind them when they came.

Gods and mortals mingled indiscriminately here, as they did everywhere in the Den. Sol and the rest came on most of them in the act of honing or testing their weapons. They leaped to their feet and fell instantly silent, bowing to the ground. But they never sheathed their blades. As soon as Gold Dagger steered Humi out again, Sol would hear the bubble of silence pop, and the buzz of talk jump to a feverish pitch.

That was how they bore it, he supposed. Dreams of blood. Pathetic.

But then, *he* hadn't had enough contact with foulness in his life to know what it was really like, had he? His sunny, pristine Archipelagan childhood. His years as an apprentice, a ghostier, a councillor, cloistered—*in* Marshstown but never of it. And in Westpoint, he had commonly passed whole weeks without speaking to a soul except the woman from whom he bought his bread and the landlord who took his rent.

Foulness took many forms, though!

In one squad room, they came on an able-bodied Deltan soldier and a Carelastrian *auchresh* making the beast on the floor, while the rest of the squad cheered them on. When Humi stepped through the doorway and stood silent, waiting, the whole crew bounced to attention, their faces muddy or dark with shame; they made more fervent obeisances than any others had done before them. But after the party moved back out into the corridor, Sol heard the fun start up again, more quietly.

Aneisneida asked in a small voice, "Humi, is it really necessary for us to do this ourselves? Your lieutenants—"

"I have to reassure them that I have faith in them," Humi said. "That I am depending on them. That I need them. I have to do this in person, or it would be pointless." She turned as if to look over her shoulder at Aneisneida. "*You* can go, if you want."

Aneisneida shuddered, and clenched her teeth. Gamely, she said, "No. I suppose I shall have to get used to—this. When we are victorious, I shall have responsibilities. My father was never afraid to walk the streets where he grew up. I will not be, either."

Humi sounded surprised as she said, "Excellent! Anei, I am proud of you!"

By the time they reached the lowest levels of the barracks, the news of their advent had traveled ahead of them. Communication between the squad rooms, beth *teth* "*tach ching* and ordinary, never ceased. In the great mess hall (where the sword lizards had first been discovered, before they were chased lower yet, to Humi's private cavern) a sea of men and gods waited for them. Sol boosted Humi up on a table and climbed after her. Gold Dagger heaved himself up and stood on Humi's other side, flanking her.

Erect and beautiful in her simple gown, she bathed in the noise of adulation. Sol felt her hand clenching into a fist. He was slightly shocked to see tears sparkling on her cheek fur. Her artifice extended even to details no one except he and Gold Dagger could see. Or was it artifice? Did she really believe they all still loved her? She couldn't see, but surely she heard the sour notes in the hullabaloo?

"You ought to be cheering for yourselves!" Sol heard her whisper. She sounded unutterably miserable. "Not for me!"

He shot an appalled glance her way. The tears were *real*. She cleared her throat. She shouted, "Thank you!"

The Red Haze

Arity stopped the messenger *kere* at the door of the royal bedroom and put his finger to his lips. Pati was sleeping for the first time in many nights.

Closing the door behind the uniformed *kere*, Arity rubbed his nose thoughtfully.

The cold tile floor and glass and bone furniture of the royal bedroom took on a soft, misty aspect in the gray light rising off the starlit sea.

The prospect of waking Pati up with *this* news had a certain masochistic appeal.

But not yet!

He had no patience. He *teth*"*d* from the floor where he stood to the foot of the great bed. Golden Antelope had always had it in the middle of the room, but Pati and Arity had shoved it against one wall. Late in Golden Antelope's life, when he spent all his time in bed, he had often had himself wheeled out onto the balcony. The Old One had, Arity thought, enjoyed being afraid. Of attack, of oblivion, of the five-hundred foot drop to the gnashing sea.

He sat on the footboard of the bed with his elbows on his knees and watched Pati sleeping. The sight had never ceased to entrance him. Only when Pati slept could you see how young that wolfish, delicate face still was. Responsibility had left no physical marks on him. His nacreous hair spread like fine straw across the pillow.

Did he feel Arity's stare?

Did he dream?

I could do it right now. This moment . . .

Panic took hold of Arity, freezing him in its iron-clawed grip. The ability to imagine more than one possible course of action was surely the worst feature of intelligence! Unable to bear it, he *teth*"*d* again, outside to the sea balcony. An unexpectedly freezing wind greeted him: in seconds, his body was the same temperature as the air, and as liquid. Salt water. *The wind—*

Below the sea, a haze of freezing spray misted the waves that lapped grayly to the horizon. Strange bright quality to the night. Almost like it was in the salt just before a blizzard. Perhaps it was going to snow.

He knew what he had to do.

But whenever he thought about *doing* it, the indifference that carried him so smoothly without trouble day and night quailed and trickled out of his brain. The trouble was that he could envision the act so well! And that picture cast a red haze over everything that might possibly occur afterward, so that he had no way of guessing which course of action was best.

And according to the messenger, it would soon be too late to choose either one.

The cold iron railing pressed into his forehead. He straightened up. The trench in his skin burned as he went inside. Getting Pati awake was a task for a predator. He flailed and groaned, and finally Arity lost patience and slapped him.

Huge eyes, one brown, one blue, blinked up from the snow-colored drained mask. Power, he was beautiful. That look would have melted anyone's soul. Arity bent down and kissed him. "Get up," he murmured. "It's started."

The Folly stood like a rock in a river of blood, parting the sweep of the devastated gardens. Gete had backed up against one of the wrought-iron perimeter fences. His feet slipped on bloody swathes of chopped-down greenery. The sword slice in his leg kept trying to intrude on his attention, but he had to concentrate on keeping Thani safe in the circle of his left arm, and moving, wielding his knife, weaving a net of clear space in front of them. Aeons ago, when the whole company waited tense and silent beneath the base of the Folly, he had felt so keenly the weight of the blocky, refractive mass hanging over them that he thought he must move out from under it. Move, move, move, *move,* or the breath would be driven out of him by the weight of it. Poised there it compressed the air into something liquid. Sublime. Leather-clad loyalists shifted and fingered their weapons in three painful dimensions. The smells of fresh-forged metal and unwashed flesh scorched his nostrils. Smiles glinted like stars. The crushed grass beneath the Divinarch's army's feet was a carpet of razor-edged oxidized knives.

Flamens stood motionless, heads tilted to catch the whispering of the lemans at their sides. Loyalist girls and boys too young to be here rolled their eyes, more frightened than they would admit, and made dirty jokes. Grown men stared into space, caressing the knobs of their hilts. Only the Hands seemed perfectly at their ease: smiling, feet planted wide, rocking slightly back and forth. Blood lust crackled tangibly around them. Within the tight squad formations, the mortals gave them as much space as possible.

Gete and Thani's squad comprised both Hands and civilians. Thani herself was supposedly its prime weapon. Gete had taken up a position in the front center of the wedge: she would not take the brunt of the attack, but he could see enemies, pick them out for her.

And she had proved her virtuosity. Oh, she had. She

killed neatly, by reaching within her enemies' bodies and
stopping their hearts. Unlike the apostates on the other
side, she did not mangle her victims, nor make them drown
in their blood, or claw at the entrails wrapping around their
throats. Some of the human soldiers bawled hysterically,
"She's not doin' nothin'! Make her use her powers, leman!"

"She is!" Gete yelled back. " 'Tweren't for her ye'd be
dead already!"

Gete himself wasn't a killer. He was a fisherman, a sailor,
crofter, leman. Yet now that the necessity presented itself,
he found himself quite capable of hacking necks and limbs,
stabbing eyes, slicing faces into bloody messes. It had surprised him a little that he was not desperately outclassed.

But he quickly realized nobody on this battlefield except
the Hands, and some of the criminals, knew how to do
what they were doing. They had only the weapons and the
instinct, like tame beasts who have never had to fight for
survival. And like animals, they killed without regard for
the suffering of others. Gete had never before realized just
how much pain people were capable of. The dead and the
dying fell like snow on the gardens: they hindered the feet
of those who fought, sometimes maliciously, with their last
gasp of strength, and sometimes insentiently, like briars. He
stepped on still-living bodies as the squad retreated by
painful inches to the fence.

Thani, like precious few other flamens, operated in a
more humanistic style. Her way took more finesse. But she
was determined to keep to her standards as long as she
could. She inflicted mercy, not pain.

Though they had retreated as far as possible, she kept
on destroying targets with mechanical economy, barely killing one victim before moving to the next. No more than a
quarter of their squad remained alive for her to defend.
The battle had degenerated into a panting struggle for life.
Blood and mud misted Gete's vision. Everything seemed
to have gone dull, devoid of reality, as if the gray sky had
slumped down onto the battle and enveloped it, like the
roof of a tent collapsing. The only color was the wet magenta haze hanging in the air, the reaction of human and
divine blood. Its fetid, chemical smell filled his nostrils. Its
redness was both the mark of death and the stamp of
unreality.

"They're 'xhausted," panted Godsman Freebird, on Thani's left, leaning on his sword.

Bodies lay in drifts around the few trees that Pati had not had cut down. Each heap was soaked with that unholy crimson—as if the bodies were gradually coming apart, disintegrating into each other, like bread soaked in milk. *If only we could all melt into the ground,* Gete thought with sudden, maniacal sentimentality. And the sky would come down and cover the earth like a blanket, and there'd be no more scurrying and sticking pins.

Oh Thani Thani.

He rememered making love to her, in the days before K'Fier. An obscenely malapropos gust of sweetness.

melting.

"They're comin' on again!" Godsman Freebird cried.

And indeed, there seemed no end to the stars flashing in the magenta dusk. Fresh forces? Could it be? No. It was the onslaught. Gete felt the remains of the squad gather about him. A physical drawing up. A tightening as of the strings of a little bag. He and Thani were the jewel. He felt an exquisite gratitude. Cowardice: that was what it was; a craven hope that the deaths of the rest of the squad could keep him from dying. But cowardice would do him no good. Retreat was not an option. They had nowhere to go. The squads stationed behind them, in the palace district, had orders not to move, but to slay any deserters from the front lines. Each division of squads was another wall of defense around the Palace. The Divinarch's plan, as far as Gete understood it, was that somewhere between that first clash on the borders of Christon, and the Palace, the rebels would exhaust their forces. They would die on the spiked wall of the loyalists who had not yet fought, who were fresh, and dying for blood.

But who knew how large the rebel army had been to start out with, how far back into Christon it had extended? The squads who took the brunt of the first attack had known they would be crushed. That was why the first division had consisted solely of Hands, who could *teth*" away when they were wounded, before they were annihilated. The burning question was, how much farther could the rebels press before they exhausted themselves?

The lines on the far side of the Folly must have disintegrated, letting the rebels flow over them *en masse*. It was

now Gete's and Thani's turn to try to stem the momentum
of the slavering atheists and apostates.

Gete's sergeant, Chequered Moon, gave a hoarse yell.
The attack was upon them.

"Here, Godsister, in front of us!"

"Ten paces before you, in front of Moon, Godsister!"

It was necessary to sustain two levels of consciousness at
once—the bodyguard and the leman, the knife hand and
the tongue.

Flash, stab, hack.

Chequered Moon went down in front of them, the top
of his skull gouting blood. Gete brought his knife across,
parrying the blow of a faceless, hurtling assailant. The god's
superior strength and speed were his undoing: he knocked
Gete's blow so far aside, and his lunge carried him so far
into Gete's reach, that it was a simple matter to slash sideways and open his guts. He wore no armor. None of the
gods did. They were too proud.

Thani finished one rebel. Then another. And another.

Gete defended her desperately.

Then he heard Godsman Freebird's death rattle. Emptiness blew cold on his left arm.

He felt Thani quiver, and become a dead weight, dragging on his shoulder.

Gods no! He lost his balance. His left foot skidded out
from under him, and his knees buckled. A star flashed in
his right eye. For a moment he saw the battlefield starkly
reversed, white on black, the whole thing canted, so that
people were fighting at an angle, like dolls with their feet
nailed to a board. Simultaneously, he experienced a powerful physical memory. He was on board a sailboat. Not an
intercontinental clipper like the *Foam Rider,* but one of the
little fishing boats he had grown up in. He must be very
small, for he wasn't holding the shrouds but sprawling in
the prow, his chin on the bulwark, gripping the sun-warmed
wood, tasting the spray. When the boat listed, he listed with
it, so that the shore

became a black silhouette as the sun exploded behind
Sarberra peak

Bright, incredibly bright, darkening everything that had
happened to Gete to mere cloudy memories, nightmares
for which there was no room anymore. The sun hurt his
head as it expanded, bulging out and out and out, losing

its sharp snowflake edges, until it grew bigger than his head
could hold and it burst free.

Reality's needled jaws closed on him, and would not let
him go back to sleep.

Far across the field, broken edges of windows glimmered
in the lower stories of the Folly. All about that great black
shape, stars peeped guiltily through the clouds. Trees
slumped haplessly, branches half severed. Most of the
fences had been rooted up and cast down.

The smell of death hung in the air.

All the living had gone, leaving behind them a terrible
silence. In their battle lust, they had rolled over their refuse
like the sea churning over rocks. He knew they were pressing on to the Palace, inexorably to the Palace. But he had
not breath to worry about what was happening anywhere
except right here. The dusk took the color out of everything. Thank the gods for that. He felt as if he would not
be able to look at anything red ever again.

*Don't thank the gods! They are lying flat all around, piti-
ful dead things like I nearly was, like Thani! Thank the
Power it's dark and I can't see her!* "Thank the Power for
night," he whispered aloud.

Vague, ambiguous. Good enough.

The power of night.

Good enough.

He raised himself up on one elbow. He could just see
her beside him. Her lips, normally thin, were swollen with
blood. Her robe was torn. The sharp edges had been broken off her salt crystals, leaving a grainy mess in one eye
socket and a clot of blood in the other.

But her chest rose and fell ever so slightly—

He let out a hoarse, desperate cry of thanks and gathered
her to him. Never mind the pain, never mind the dizziness,
kneel upright, cradle her, *tenderly!* The wound was in her
back and shoulder, a hideous wet gash. Oh, Power. It must
almost have bled her dry before her blood clotted. *Remember all you know about healing, don't reopen it, moving her
might finish it—* "Thani!" he whispered urgently. "It's me!
Are you all right?"

Did she hear?

She moved her head, infinitesimally.

Grief crashed down on him like a weight of water, knocking his breath out of his lungs.

She would know if she was all right!

A chilly wind fingered his hair, tossed a filthy lock into his face. It stung. His eyes filled with tears.

His red hair. She had chosen him for it. Because of it he had come halfway across the world with her, only to watch her die.

He was crying on her neck. *Oh, Power, no, wipe her fur—*

She reached up and touched his lips. Her hand fell back on her chest. Her mouth formed slurred words, but no sound came out. He had to bend close to catch even the ghostliest whisper. "Gete: love ... you."

"And I you! Oh, Godsister—"

"Gete ... there is something you do not know." The facial expression was hardly anything at all, a mere twitch of the lips, but his familiarity with her face showed him a self-mocking smile. No humor in it. None at all. She breathed: "Do not ... grieve. I am not worthy of it. I was born ... evil. So that I could fulfill ... the task ... which I prophesied. I had to kill a god. A ... renegade ... but still a god ... someone utterly evil was needed to destroy him. So that no one's soul should be contaminated. That was my task. After that ... we came to the Archipelago. And every minute I lived ... was a gift from the gods. From *him*."

Her hand was cold in his. It exerted no pressure. A night wind blew through the garden, rattling the remaining twigs of the trees, stripping the last vestiges of warmth from the limbs of the corpses.

"I was steeped in evil ... Gete ... when we met. But you did not know ... it was not a girl ... who you seduced with your red hair. It was evil ... in human form. Evil. And *he* ... he is evil, too. *He* made me what I am. The gods cause all of us to exist ... if they caused evil, then they must be evil. Do not look at them for succor ... Gete."

"You can't believe this! Thani! No!" He did not know what to say. In the deserted battlefield it was hard to have faith that she was deluded. She could be visionary.

She turned her head to one side, as if to refuse argument. He did not doubt the truth of the first part—that she had

killed a god. Unbelievable though it sounded, she was in
no state to lie. That meant—that the rest of it—

Unbelievable. Could pain alone have brought this on?
There was already so much pain in her day-to-day life. And
as blindly as a child trusting in its mother's goodness, he
had thought it could never taint her compassion, her belief
in human and divine goodness. She forgave flaws in others
and in herself, even as she aimed for perfection.

Apparently this battle had managed what nothing else
had been able to.

Was it the battle? Or was it that she was *dying*?

Could dying confer a clear-sightedness life, with its cares,
never had?

She *wasn't* dying! She could live!

"You mustn't!" he hissed at her. "D'you hear me? You
mustn't talk this way! It's a sacrilege! The—the—the Divinarch wouldn't want you to say these things!"

As if she had merely been gathering her strength, she
resumed.

"But I failed to kill the god. And my evil . . . was consolidated. Evil thwarted . . . feeds on itself. I did not know I
had failed until . . . I met the dark one face to face. Face
. . . to face . . . when you and I returned to Delta City. Do
you . . . remember? I spoke kind words to him. The renegade. *I did not know him!*"

She hissed this so loudly that Gete flinched.

"*You* . . . you are good all the way through. You must
not . . ."

She paused, blindly gulping air.

"Evil . . . is useless. Violence focused . . . toward no goal.
I am the tool . . . the gods are the sources . . . renegades or
no, they are the sources . . ."

"You don't have to explain *evil* away! The gods aren't
evil! Neither are you! Do you think you can cleanse the
world by *dying*?" Tears boiled in his eyes. "You're kind.
You're generous. Compassionate. Selfless. You're *good*!"
He was shouting into her face. "You're the goodest person
I ever *knew*!"

She made no reply. Perhaps she did not hear. The wind
whistled. In his anguish he must have gripped her too
tightly: the wound reopened, and wetness trickled over his
arm. The pain must have momentarily restored her faculties. She jerked as if she had been hit. Her free arm lifted,

and her hand, hitting his, seized it with remarkable strength.

Half out of his mind with grief, he shouted, "You were always good! Do you remember those children? Do you remember—I could tell you a thousand stories about your goodness! You're compassion *itself*!"

The clots of blood in her eye sockets had begun to trickle darkly again. The wild jerking ceased. He heard her whisper, hoarsely, quickly, as if she were trying not to let her pain overhear her, "What was that? Good? D'you think so? Really?"

"With all my heart! Oh, *Power,* Godsister—"

"Heh. You'll learn, Gete. You'll learn." She smiled almost kindly. The old Thani's smile. And she snuggled impatiently into his embrace, tugging at his clothing like an infant hungry for its mother's milk.

But no matter how close he held her, he could not protect her from the cold wind. Could not prevent the blood from flowing out of her, soaking his knees. And all at once she shivered, a violent shiver that made her spine arch and her neck twist, as if she were trying to see something behind her.

Slow Time in the Eye of the Tiger

Nobody had ever seen the Old Palace as a fortress. But a fortress it had become. The wooden ramp was winched up; it fitted into the cavernous gateway that had led into the calm, tree-scattered courtyard. The dirt and rot of thousands of years, clinging darkly to its underside, contrasted with the smoothly weathered walls. "But no less solid for that," Soderingal muttered.

A day and night had passed since the battle started. Aneisneida and Soder were standing in the sixth-floor window of a town house which, in the days of the atheist court, had been unfashionable because of its proximity to the Old Palace. They could see the army seething outside the gate of the fortress. Humi had invited the Nearclouds to the front with none of her usual ambiguity; through her *auch-*

resh messenger, she had assured them that her men had
scoured the town house for lurking loyalists, that there
were decayed but luxurious armchairs for them to sit in,
and chilled wine to refresh them. For some reason, right in
the middle of a battle which looked like being decisive, she
had started to treat them like the nobility they were. It
gave Aneisneida a comfortable feeling of safety. Fia was
back in Shimorning with her nurses: out of sight, out of
mind. Six *auchresh* guards stood in a row at the back of
the room, ready to *teth*" her and Soder away, should an
unexpected reversal sweep the army back. But that hardly
seemed likely.

When they first arrived, Aneisneida had stepped right up
to the window. Before Soderingal yanked her back, she had
glimpsed the topmost turrets of the Palace, sparkling with
the metal shields that had been slid across the windows.
On three sides the keep was deeply ensconced within the
courtyard; on the fourth, it rose sheer from the sea. Humi
had no way of assailing it save by taking the courtyard.
Fire had been ruled out. Her consideration there, Anei
thought, had been not so much a reluctance to sink to the
level of the Hands, as an unwillingness to gamble with the
seat of her future majesty.

Majestic the Palace certainly was, like an old man taking
up his sword in time of duress. No one can deny the razor-
edge of the sword he has kept sharp for decades. Flattened
mansard roofs topped the outer walls of the courtyard; the
shadows under their eaves sparkled with blades. Now and
then, a crossbow bolt darted out of the darkness, down into
the seething mass of the army. Roars arose where these
arrows fell, and flocks of bolts lofted back into the air,
almost slowly it seemed, like pigeons. Some crested the
walls and descended out of sight; some stuck quivering in
the mansard roofs. The window at which Aneisneida and
Soderingal stood was on a level with the shadows under
the eaves. The distance across the street was no more than
twenty yards. That the two sides of a street could belong
to opposing armies—the very idea was fantastic! Aneisneida knew she was safe. She could not discern the Hands
themselves, and therefore, they could not discern her. Here
and there metal caught the daylight, or a flame glowed as
a Hand lit a pipe. It had become something of a waiting
game.

And Aneisneida could see into the enemy's territory! It terrified and exhilarated her.

Soderingal's arm around her waist was a fleshy rope. She wanted to shake him off and soar out the window, as free as a crossbow bolt, as impossible to harm.

Her legs quivered. She wanted to step closer to the window. But there was her father's memory. Belstem would not have stepped closer to the window. *You could be* killed! And there was Fiamorina. And there were her responsibilities as a Summer.

This morning she had been afraid to go right down into the battle. But she had admitted it. She had said, "I'll stay behind. I'll follow at a safe distance."

Humi had nodded, preoccupied. "But someone must guard you. You make an excellent target for an assassin, you know."

With alacrity, Soderingal had volunteered to stay. He was afraid to go into the battle *and* afraid to admit it. Aneisneida felt glad Fia was safe in the Hangman's old residence, which Humi had given them when Evita was executed; the child's new nurses would take care of her. Anei did not even trust Soder to care for their baby! *That* was how much she despised him!

From below, she heard a monstrous sound, halfway between a cheer and a roar. A mortal woman's voice lifted above it, ragged but piercing. Aneisneida could not make out the words. She quivered violently, poised on her tiptoes, desperate to run to the window, terrified of feeling the bolt bite into her breast. She whirled to the *auchresh*. "What did Humi say? Did you hear her?"

The renegades were shifting in place, plainly cursing their lot. Impassivity was not the forte of those gods who chose to march under Humi's banner; on their faces, Aneisneida saw clearly that they wanted to go down and join in. Well, that was too bad. A Summer's wish must be obeyed, and Aneisneida wished for more protection, here, than her beloved husband would or could give her. "What did she *say*?"

"We are storming the courtyard, milady," one of the guards said. "We are going to break down the gate."

But at that point it was hardly necessary to explain. The first *thump* went through Aneisneida's very skeleton.

The army kept growling, a liquid, ugly, low-pitched, incessant noise.

Shaking Soderingal off, Aneisneida ran to the window and pressed herself against the wall beside it. Rolling her eyes sideways, she saw the packed flesh surge in waves, as if Humi had told her soldiers to hurl their very bodies against the barricade. The actual ram was invisible. Where had they got it?

Something *wheeted* past her face. For a minute, she was so caught up in the spectacle below that she did not see the crossbow bolt trembling in the floorboards. Then she gasped, "Gods!" she flattened herself against the wall.

It was black and crude and unexpectedly tiny. It had shot in through the glassless windowpanes without touching the lead.

"They don't know we're here!" one of the guards was saying urgently to Soderingal. "It's a stray bolt, milord! Please be calm!"

Aneisneida felt herself shaking. Her whole body vibrated, like the bolt quivering in the floor.

Life can be no sweeter than this.

Had Humi ever experienced this exhilaration? Anei was inclined to think not. Her voice was always cold with irony—she was like a fisherman, ripping the pride out of everyone she talked to with words like gutting knives. No matter how kindhearted they were, she could put it in their heads to do murder, on the off chance that it might please her. Sometimes Aneisneida looked at her and thought with a curious sentiment that was almost pity: *She has started retching up the wine she brewed. She is gritting her teeth, trying to hold on until the end.*

How I pity her!

Aneisneida, for her part, never wanted it to end. The terror, the giddiness. *This* was being *alive*! Hate for the Hands on the other side of the street (new, but not unpleasant) bulged inside her like a new muscle. She felt like a Veretrean tree cat. She stretched her claws.

The logic of it was simple.

Arity sighted along the stock of his crossbow and released. The shock vibrated down his arms.

Outside noises: that was an *auchresh* dying. That was a battle yell. That was the battering ram hitting the gate.

How long would it take the timbers to give way? From the west turret, he and his cabal had a stunning view of Humi's army surging around the gate. Due to the shields that left only slits of the windows open, the rebels did not have a stunning view of the cabal. The square walkway that ran all around the rooms inside the tower echoed with the eerie music of bows being loaded, wound back, and fired. Yells of fear and delight. Arity wondered if they realized how lucky they were that the rebels had bowed to pressure and initiated battle sooner rather than later: as it was, defector Hands constituted only a tiny percentage of Humi's army, but in a couple of sixdays there would have been more—and *they* would have been able to *teth*" into the Palace. A few renegades had tried, presumably from pictures, but Arity had taken the precautions of having human workers knock down some walls, and build others in unexpected places, and then the infiltrators died instantly, their bodies in neat pieces.

He shouted an order, then stepped back to let another Hand into his place. He was thinking about dying. Did it enter the minds of the others? He doubted it. They were good soldiers, unlike him! Their minds were focused upon the single slice of the world that included crossbow and target.

What would the consequences be?

In the salt, *auchresh* could and did *teth*" away from natural dangers and overwhelming odds. But fights, showdowns, duels, were a different matter. When faced with an inferior enemy (as the *auchresh,* with their traditional arrogance, judged all enemies) *teth*"*ing* dealt a crippling blow to the pride. Not to mention the loss of status it provoked. One's *ghauthijim* would cast one off, one's *breideim* would be disappointed, one would set a terrible example for one's Foundlings. The same went for any fight conducted in human country. In the dense, subtly warped world of the Hands, the respect of one's grand set of *kervayim* was even more fragile and desirable than life.

Arity picked up the water-skin lying dribbling on the wooden floor and took a swig. "Pathetic," he muttered.

What it came down to was this: like the rest of the *auchresh,* once confronted with a challenge, he just could not back down.

*   *   *

The extent to which he despised his own race amazed him. It was nothing new. He had felt it to one degree or another, consciously or unconsciously, all his civilized life. He even remembered (dimly, as in a series of faded tableaux) the time before he was Found, when the childish uncouth beast he had been scarcely knew it could think, let alone talk. In his shambling roamings through the salt forest, he had once come on another of his kind. The first *auchresh* he ever saw. An *iu*, a pale night spirit grubbing for termites in the ground, slurping them off her twisted fingernails.

The young mutant Arity had attacked her, mindlessly flying at her with fangs and talons. He had driven her away crying.

It had not even been his termite patch. He had hated her instinctively, desperately. Deep down in his being he had understood that they were the same, and denied that he could be like *that*.

In later life the incident had swum up from the mists of forgetfulness. And he had realized with wonder that if he met that *iu* now, he would be struck by her beauty.

An emaciated being with a form like a woman's and a face like a predator's, and no wings! Absolutely breathtaking!

(The whir and scream of arrow music; the grind of death below; the sulky thump of the ram. A Hand fell frothing on Arity's feet and his bow skittered across the walkway as if it were light as a feather.)

Time to find Pati!

The corridors were empty and dark. The smell of stale brimstone hung in the air. They hadn't torches to spare to light the inside of the Palace. Not anymore. Pati's habit of keeping the upstairs corridors as bright as day, as previous Divinarches had done, had been just that—a habit—and a feeling, Arity thought, of obligation: if he skimped on any tradition, he was not living up to the title he claimed.

The few Hands Arity encountered had not the temerity to look at Arity with reproach. They'd probably been hearing stories about his marvelous exploits with the crossbow. But he did hear notes of surprise in their voices as they murmured, "*Perich* "*hi*, Arity." Why wasn't he on the walls where he belonged?

He ran up the spiral stairs in the eastern turret, the one that topped the facade over the great doors.

The heartbeats of the battering ram had slowed down. A sense of urgency began to prickle under his skin.

The tower culminated in a large unfurnished room like a pagoda, with weathered wood-paneled walls and octagonal cutout windows. It always put Arity in mind of the inside of a tiger's-eye gemstone. Pati sat alone on the window seat, staring out. When Arity climbed through the central trapdoor, his face lit up. He swung his legs off the window ledge and came toward Arity, hands out. "I'm so glad you're here! I was going to send for you. We have to make some strategic decisions." The words were delivered with no hint of urgency: no awareness that his Divinarchy was in immediate danger of destruction. He was clearly far gone. He kissed Arity on the mouth: a brisk kiss of greeting, which lingered just long enough to intimate that he would have liked to do more.

For just a second Arity felt the old weakness. A numbness in his fingertips, a blurring of his vision. Pati exercised his power even when he did not mean to.

But Arity was no longer susceptible. Pati had made him kill the ghostiers. He had put that blood on Arity's hands. He had corrupted Humi, the only person Arity ever truly cared about: Arity had seen the result of that corruption firsthand. And the months stretched back, dim with clouds, shot through with lightning, and Arity could not even count the numbers of other times Pati had compelled him to his will.

And these were his offenses against one person only! The world teemed with mortals and *auchresh* who, in Arity's place, would lose no time in seizing their chance.

That was why he had to do it.

And in some twisted way he did not understand, it was also for *her.*

"Selflessness is the province of the emotionally destitute," he said to Pati. "Don't you think? Sacrificing oneself—surely that is the last pleasure of all?"

Outside, the screams and cries of the battle rose louder. "Hmm." Pati leaned against the wall, brows furrowed in thought. Arity himself knew what he had meant; he was rather shocked how obvious he had made it. Was some part of him trying to *warn* Pati? *Imbecile!* he told himself. *Seize every advantage!*

The wind blowing through the windows smelled of snow. It rushed over the roof with a sound like the grass on the Veretrean plains. The day outside was bright gray, as if the sun had dissolved, saturating the sky. Thousands of loyalists and rebels lay dead in the forsaken districts of Christon and Marshtown.

"I'm not sure you're right," Pati said. "I've always tended to think selflessness is a deficiency of self-awareness. An inability to see what's important. Of course, for all sentient beings, that *is* the self."

"But true selflessness comes after one's illusions are gone," Arity said with some annoyance. "And that includes the illusion that one's self is at *all* important."

"My dear Ari"—Pati shook his head indulgently—"there is no such thing as true selflessness. It's always a pose of one kind or another. The most common pose being that of the mortal who believes that giving things to people for free will force them to see how magnanimous and brilliant he is, when in fact it makes them resent him."

Disgust warmed Arity to the fingertips, welcome as a hot mug to clasp his hands around. "Is that why you never fell prey to the vice of benevolence?" he asked scornfully.

Either Pati had not heard his sarcasm, or he chose to ignore it. "The masses' perception of me has never affected my policies. The wheels and pulleys of the world are set in place, and they are as solid as diamondine."

"There was a time when you would have told me you carved those wheels yourself," Arity said.

Pati looked at him with unreadable eyes. "Why are you baiting me?"

For a minute Arity could not speak. Finally he said: "Look out the window and maybe you'll understand."

Pati glanced out. "They have penetrated the courtyard."

"It's insupportable! I may have stood behind you this far, but now I cannot but condemn your—*strategy.* Do you know how many of your Hands are dying down there? Not to mention the mortals?"

"I think I pity those with the illusion that they're going to Heaven more than the others." Leaning against the wall, Pati spoke to a point somewhere outside the window. "At times like this one *has* to pity them. Born so ignorant, into a society that can do nothing to redeem their ignorance.

To be shoveled into the machine." His voice hardened.
"But then there are the others. The apostates. Who are not
to be pitied at all. Wanton blasphemers! And the so-called
gods who have corrupted them—*haugthirres* of the blackest
dye! I would sacrifice the whole human population of Delta
City if I could wipe *them* off the face of the earth!"

He shook his head. His eyes were big and shocked. His
pale curls danced, turned to flames in the daylight.

"I think you've gone completely blind," Arity said hard.
"Those powers of yours go on at full strength to try and
subdue me, and you still refuse to admit to yourself that I
am a danger to you. You really are remarkable."

The roar of the fight swelled. He spoke louder. "Do you
realize what you've done? You've singlehandedly destroyed
the Divinarchy. And you've destroyed—or irreversibly altered—a whole generation of our race."

"I suppose I have." Pati nodded. "Of course, I had a
great many helpers. You haven't done so badly yourself."

Arity stared at him. "You know—don't you? You *must*
... I've given you enough clues ..."

His voice trailed off. There seemed nothing more to say.
He drew his knife and sprang forward, knocking Pati back
onto the floorboards, and slit his throat. Not deep enough
to sever the jugular, but the white blood flowed, flowed
like milk, almost as profusely as it had on that day when
the leman from Calvary half killed Ari. The curve of Pati's
white neck fit the curve of the blade perfectly. It was a
standard Hand's knife, but it might have been forged for
the job. Arity upbraided himself for not fitting the puzzle
together sooner.

Pati did not speak. The bicolored eyes glowered up at
Arity, brilliant with rage and fear. The dust and silt of the
tower room tarnished the silver-white hair. Arity's heart
was thudding. He took a deep breath. It did not help.

"Your only mistake," he told Pati, "was when you admitted to me that you didn't believe you were a god. Until
then, I was still guessing, so I respected you, I feared you,
just like everyone else. But you didn't want me to respect
you. You wanted something else. So you told me your secret. You should never have told it to anyone. Because
maybe there's something in your theory of not giving people things for free, because I hated you for doing it."

He heard the contempt in his own voice. "You're not
flawless. You're not self-sufficient. You're just a near-per-

fect example of an *auchresh*! And just like the rest of us,
you're terrified of being alone! We are a race with a dread
of primitive things, and a craving for them, a craving we
are so embarrassed by we hide it behind stone walls! And
the most horrible part of it is that to us *love* is a primitive
thing! In Rimmear it carries a taint of absurdity. My *elpechim* considered it laughably quaint. You saw what loneliness had done to Golden Antelope, and you thought I
could save you from that. But the sordidity of the thing
ruined it."

Pati jerked urgently.

He deserved to speak. He deserved that. Arity lifted the
knife blade out of the blood-spiderwebbed skin.

Pati coughed and coughed, his eyes running, his throat
pumping blood into a little pool under his head. Arity
watched. After a while, he wiped Pati's eyes with the corner
of his sleeve.

"You thought . . . I wanted to be saved . . . ?" Pati whispered. "You are wrong. I didn't need saving. *You* did.
Maybe it was vulgar of me . . . but I was content living
alone in what you're pleased to call"—one corner of his
mouth twitched—"my overcivilized world."

*He knows he is trapped. He thinks he has a hope if he
comes clean—or pretends to.* Arity thought, *I will not be
touched. I will not be deterred.*

Pati continued in the same rather abashed explanatory
tone:

"Golden Antelope was alone, too. He had his schemes,
his philosophies, his mad theories. He was his own companion. He wasn't lonely. He lasted so long, the dear scrawny
old *haugthule,* because he cared so passionately about living. Likewise, I was always driven by passion! My love for
you, through those years when we were apart, was a reward
in and of itself. I didn't *want* to consummate it. Like
Golden Antelope, I was full of other things to do, I had
plans and projects that consumed my energy. And I had
my *ghauthijim.* They satisfied me."

He sighed, and abruptly his face darkened. "But I felt
sorry for you. In fact, I couldn't stop thinking about you.
You were alone in Rimmear, ripping yourself to pieces,
with only your ghosts for company. I wanted to save you."

Arity swallowed. He shifted off Pati, knelt on the floor,
and jammed his knife back into its scabbard without bothering to wipe it.

"Oh, don't give up *now*!" Pati said. "I thought you were really going to ... You disappoint me." He rolled over, slowly, painfully, clutching his throat, and sat up. "I think now that when I went to find you, I was setting foot on a ship I had been harboring for a long time." Eyes like suns. "Bring it into port, Ari. We've traveled all the way around the world. Bring it into port."

Arity shook his head wordlessly. This was not the larger-than-life Pati of the Throne Room, nor the urbane, rapidly disintegrating Pati whose madness Arity had condemned out of hand. This was a Pati he had never seen clearly before, though he had always sensed he was there.

Pati laughed. "You won't, will you! Your idea of civilized conduct is more human than you realize!"

We are keres, *not men,* Arity thought through the snow of confusion in his head. Had they been mortals, they would never have been lovers, and everything might be different. But they were *keres:* by human standards, *keres* were both pompously, exaggeratedly male and effeminate. And therefore their friendship had become love, and their love had had to be a uniquely *auchresh* compound of feminine sentiment and masculine power play—saturated with sexual tension, violently combustible.

But *love*? It could never have been love unless—

"You are *wrchrethre,"* he said to Pati. As if that was a revelation. "More than any other *auchresh* I know, you are *wrchrethre.* Do you know how much"—he stopped, and let out a small, mirthless gasp—"do you know how much you are *like her*?"

"There you have it. The whole, sordid tragedy of this story. You made me like this," Pati told him softly. "You enabled me to see the hollowness of my claim to godhead."

"What on earth do you mean?"

The wind blew keenly through the tower room. Time had slowed and almost stopped. Minutes dripped by as slowly as bubbles moving in oil.

Pati pushed himself into a half-sitting position. He massaged his throat gingerly, the long knuckly fingers splayed down one side of his neck. His wings awkwardly open behind him, crushed against the wall, made him look like an injured seagull. "Before you and I were reunited, I believed completely, wholeheartedly in myself. After we were reunited"—he smiled crookedly—"less so."

"Don't blame me for your failure," Arity said. "It's not worthy of you."

"I am not blaming you. Not in the least. My *fascination* with you is the intangible villain in this drama. Gradually I found it overcoming me. I could no longer exert myself singlemindedly in the cause of the Divinarchy." He shifted, and looked sidelong at Arity. "I should have killed you then. But you were a project to me, too, no less important than any of the others. I was interested in you. I came to be obsessed by you. At first there was a balance. Then the balance tipped."

Arity hitched himself back against the wall. The weight descended like a yoke on his shoulders. Of course it was his fault; it was both their faults! Carrying the weight of it had worn Pati down to this nubbin.

Weathered. Wise.

But still Pati.

Still capable of deceit, to save his own skin.

"You're spinning stories!" Arity broke out. "You're convincing! You almost had me! But it won't do any good."

He shifted, sliding one hand under him, feeling for his knife. The belt had got twisted in the scuffle.

Pati smiled. A sweet, heart-stoppingly immediate smile. "And bring the boat into port."

Arity froze, his hand on the hilt.

"I don't like calling it love. We are *keres,* after all. But I can't think of a better word for it. It is an evil thing, and it is everything."

"Obsession," Arity said, and readied himself to spring.

"No. More than that. Much more. And you didn't have very much to do with it, strange as that may seem. You only had to be your sweet, indecisive self. You were the instrument—as you are the instrument now.

"Arity. If we spend our meager hoard of days in the pursuit of intellectual triumph, like Golden Antelope, we crumble to dust and are laughed at by posterity. If we throw ourselves against the walls that surround us—not metaphorical walls, but real walls, the boundaries of the world: the Chrume, the edge of the salt, the sea that stretches to the end of the world, the boundary between the races—if we hurl ourselves at them, thinking to break them with faith, then when we die we have accomplished no more than our *breideim* before us.

"But if we climb those walls!" Pati half smiled. "*That,* my *irissi,* is the true quest. That is the only noble way to spend a life, to waste a life, or give a life. I did all three."

Arity blinked.

And rubbed his palm across the hilt of his knife, to keep himself anchored in the real world.

"You are not noble," he insisted. "Evil! You're evil!"

Pati's powers were many. And he was so subtle ...

And yet he had loved Arity. Despite his predisposition to violence, he had not killed him, as he had killed those other *keres* when they threatened his singlemindedness.

Instead, he had confronted that (oh so human!) love, and accepted it. He had smashed all the bonds with which tradition bound the *auchresh* race, and saved Arity's life.

Saved his life. That job had not been completed until this moment, at the top of this tower, with the battle snarling below.

The degree of *selflessness* required in doing what you know is bad for you, the right thing, the only thing you can do ...

Nothing had been an illusion. Not a moment of the past two seasons had been an illusion. It had all been real.

Now it was over.

And the tragedy was that even though Arity understood now, no other course of action lay open to him besides the one he had already decided on.

"We've reached the top of the walls, haven't we?" he said. "We can't climb any higher."

"Want to jump off with me?" Pati smiled. "I never expected we would conclude our little drama against such a melodramatic backdrop. Did you? But I suppose it happens to the best of us. No, don't jump, Ari. That would make all of this a waste."

An earthquake shook the Palace. The battering ram must be at the great doors. The shouts and the ring of metal crashed into Arity's ears.

He stood up and brushed off his hands.

A crossbow bolt whizzed past his head. He dropped to the floor. "Damn!"

Pati's face was very close to his. It looked angelic. From the slim, well-defined lips came calm words. "I'm going to die, Ari. They're battering down the doors. But if you do it now, *you* don't have to die." His wings, tightly thrumming, scraped over the unpolished wooden wall with a sound like sheets of parchment being crumpled. "Do it!"

Arity moved his hand to his dagger. But Pati did not see. His voice rose. "Do you imagine I don't know how she will *kill* me? I have my pride! I know when it is time to bow out, and I mean to do it gracefully!"

A flash of the old Pati, gone as quickly as it came. Fear sharpened the smoothest tongues. And Arity felt Pati's fear as if it were his own. If Pati were captured, he would be chained to a choice of slow death by their tortures, or slower death somewhere in exile, through the festering of his own mortally injured pride.

Auchresh did not commit suicide. It was beneath their pride. It was too easy.

Twilight drifted across the sky huge and blue and gray like monstrous wings.

The cacophony of human noises from the battle, which seemed almost tasteful now, jumped from key to key, punctuated by the drumbeats of the battering ram.

Arity sighed, and squatted up on his heels, careful to keep his head down. He could not keep a corner of his mouth from quirking as he pulled out his knife. Here a bit of flash, there a bit of flair! All Hands were showmen.

Something zinged loudly off the blade as he tossed it in midair. When the hilt thunked into his palm again, the steel bore a dent the length of his thumb.

Pati squinted up at him, laughing silently. The bright, still quality of his eyes seemed to prevent him from seeing Arity. But it was not tears. It was something else altogether. "Take care how you cut now!" His voice was light, bantering. "Whatever you do, don't make me jangle like a mortal! I want to look my best when she hangs me on the gates." He shook his hair back, baring his throat.

Swordfish

Sol threw his weight into the blow, felt steel grind bone as his sword sank through the old Deltan woman's heart and out of her back. The woman, who had not known how to defend herself, crumpled to the flagstones. Black blood spurted out along Sol's blade. *Nineteen.* He was keeping count, in a rather delirious way. He kicked the corpse away and whirled, staggering slightly.

Someone grabbed him from behind, shaking him with *auchresh* strength. He flinched, spun, and stabbed at air. The enemy had got behind him again. *Gods—gods—*

"It's over!" a voice shouted deafeningly in his ear. "Look up! Look *up*, man!"

The voice did not belong to an enemy.

There were no more enemies in the vicinity.

This fact took some time to seep into his consciousness. In the meantime, he swayed away from a blow that was not there, blinked, and lunged rather halfheartedly at a shadow. He felt as weak as if he had vomited. His muscles twitched, urging him to lash out at the figures around him, although they had mostly stopped moving and he sensed they were his friends. After an interminable delay, the real world, the world made of sights and sounds and people who had fallen still, coagulated about him. Twilight was gathering. He could not hear the sea, or the wind, much less any birds, but that could be the ringing in his ears. For hours he had been an unthinking fragment of the bloody chiaroscuro of the battle, as a bird is part of a formation winging across the sky, constantly changing place with other fragments, blocking, parrying and stabbing, communicating (when there was time to communicate) in the terse, expletive-laden language of necessity.

It all seemed to dissolve very quickly.

Someone close to him let off a crossbow bolt. It whirred into the sky, and a ragged shout went up from the rebels all over the courtyard. "Stop him!" "Cease fire!" "Stick the bastard!"

Men and *auchresh* were craning their necks, peering up into the bluish-gray dusk. The sky was soft, near, the color of a pigeon's neck. Sol tried to make out what the misguided crossbowman had been aiming at.

On the battlements of the turret that reared above the splintered wreck of the great doors, a lone figure stood. An *auchresh,* from his fearless stance on the parapet. Unharmed. The marksman had missed.

His voice floated faintly, but distinctly, down into the courtyard.

"Listen to me! I am on your side! Put down your weapons! I—say—throw down your blades! The Divinarch is dead! The Palace surrenders!"

Wasn't the voice familiar somehow? Sol could not conjure up the memory from his leaking mind.

Then he realized what the fellow had said.

Whispers darted like fish through the disarrayed army.

"*What* did 'e say?"

"Oo is it?"

Not even *auchresh* lungs could make themselves heard perfectly down a drop of two hundred windy feet.

"We've won," Sol said. "And I know who that is."

"Won, 'ave we? Wivout even stickin' all of 'em? Ho well, I like *that*!"

Humi had done her job well before the battle. The speaker sounded disappointed, angry even, at the prospect of not getting to plant a banner in a bloody heap of Hands' bodies on the highest tower of the Palace.

In the shadow of the ruined doors of the Palace, the remnants of the loyalist army clustered, looking lost. They had not dropped their weapons, but they had dropped their guard. Sol watched without pity or hate as they turned to each other, blankly questioning. It was as if the possibility of their Divinarch's betrayal had driven everything else from their heads.

"It's the Heir!"

"Arity!"

" 'E's turned 'is coat!"

The figure on the turret stood silhouetted against the dusk. Some of the whisperers condemned him for his treachery; some praised him for his integrity.

"But there was no *point*," Sol said aloud.

The Hands were nearly all dead. He doubted there was one Deltan loyalist in ten left alive. Half an hour ago, perhaps, surrendering might have done some good.

Bitterness filled his throat. His sword shone with wet blood. It dragged at his hand, like a lead ball. He had gripped it for so long that he could not make his fingers uncurl.

Arity hasn't changed, he thought, staring at the small, slim figure with disgust. *He still makes an effect by being ineffectual.*

The renegades, apostates, and Shimorningers did not move. They stood leaning on their swords, whispering un-

easily. Sol fought the force that drew his eyes again and
again toward the bemused loyalists in the ruined doors.

A flock of cold wind birds swooped into the courtyard,
invisible predators grabbing the souls of the dead in their
claws. The sea roared, as if it were rising up over the island,
a hallucinatory deluge of black that drenched Sol's eyes
and ears with momentary blindness and deafness as night
usurped twilight's throne on the peak of the sky. It came
to him that somehow, in one of those cracks of his perception, Humi had entered the Palace with her bodyguards.
Perhaps the wind had carried her in. That was what they
were all waiting for. Waiting for her to replace the Heir on
the parapet, signaling a *real* victory. Waiting for that white
and gray flag to flap out, so that they could toss their hel-
mets in the air and hear their own yells rain comfortably
down on them.

Victory

Humi had told Hope she would find Arity outside. She left
the Palace through the ragged maw that had been the great
doors. The sheer amount of damage that had been done to
Delta City while she was fighting overseas still shocked her;
and the Palace had not been spared. The ramp into the
courtyard was a mass of twisted timbers. People had to
clamber over it, as if up a giant stairway. Crossbow bolts
bristled in the eaves of the roofs that topped the outside
walls.

Her dagger banged gently against her thigh as she
walked. She was aware of the smooth play of muscles from
her toes to her shoulders. The soldier's walk. I have a soldier's body. Not a lady's, not an *iu's*. Try that one on for
size.

She had got quite used to fighting in the lines; even
started enjoying it, in a terrified way.

The winter sun flooded over her. It wasn't as bright as
it had been in Calvary. But the light had a freezing clarity.
No one was left to light fires in Delta City; no smoke sullied
the air. They were returning: Humi had told her of the

barges ferrying refugees back to the Marshtown jetties. Mothers and fathers and children and craftsmen and immigrants, fearfully venturing throughout the city, returning to plundered, scorched houses. Law and order, supposedly, had been reestablished. But privately, Humi had said she anticipated a good many skirmishes and petty vengeance killings before the city settled back into any semblance of normality.

Then she had said, *But that will be for Aneisneida and Gold Dagger to worry about.*

It had taken Hope a while to understand. In the end, Humi had had to tell her straight out. She had presented it clearly, sanely, and in the end Hope had not been able to deny that she was right. That it was everyone's fault, and no one's. Hope's fault, for being so desperately loved by her soldiers. Humi's fault for being blind, for not being able to *teth*", for being tied to Delta City. Shine's fault. Whitenail's. Truth's.

Hope stepped aside to let a family of nervous Deltans shuffle past her. A woman and an old man, with three small children. They gazed aimlessly about; eventually they attached themselves to the end of a queue that snaked around the courtyard, spiraling in toward the spot where Aneisneida, along with several women volunteers she had rooted up from the remnants of the merchant class, was serving hot stew and bread.

Hope had forgotten to ask Humi where Aneisneida found the food. Even as she wondered how the Summer girl had managed it, in a starving city, the conundrum solved itself. A delicious whiff of new-baked bread blew into her nostrils. She jumped out of the way just in time to avoid a crew of *keres* hurrying out of the dark Palace. They bore trays of new-baked loaves on their shoulders. Their faces glistened with useful sweat.

So she had *auchresh* importing food from the provinces. An absurdly labor-intensive enterprise. Nobody would dream of going to such extremes, except a woman like Aneisneida, who had no conception of what *teth*"ing really was. And even *she,* Hope thought, giving her the benefit of the doubt, would have to have been convinced this was really an emergency.

Things had changed. The Palace's great underground kitchens had been put back into operation. Had the first

Divinarch, their architect, ever envisaged their use for such a project? That ancient *er-serbali's* shade must be restless.

Laudable of Aneisneida. Laudable. Of course it is. Power—how that girl has improved.

Hope's mouth watered as the breeze wafted the scent her way. How long since she had eaten? Not since returning from Calvary yesterday. She had been too sick at heart, choked with the duty of telling Humi that a cousin of hers had been scouting in the army since before the first battle for Grussels, and that he had died after the battle for Samaal. Hope had apparently been supposed to find out about him, but someone had forgotten to inform her, and the boy had had too much pride (or been too intimidated) to come to her. At times like that she hated the power she wielded—will-she, nill-she—over her followers. It was too much like Pati's power over the Hands! It was during the mop-up of Samaal that a scout of one of the Younger Cabals had approached her, hop-skipping sideways, paralyzed by bashfulness. In tones of terror, he squeaked something at her about a child named Merce—Humi's cousin, and almost dead.

With her bodyguards, Hope had followed him to the rocks of the Eastern Rim, where the other survivors of the cabal had carried the boy. The dust kicked up by the battle thickened the air into a solid substance, through which the boys moved as awkwardly and agilely as salt herons in the morning mist. The sun was going down in a blaze on the desert. Hope was still in full battle gear; her metal-reinforced shirt clinked as she knelt by the boy's side. "Are you our true Divinarch's cousin?" she asked him gently.

He didn't look twelve. He looked a stunted twenty-five, what with the lines on his face and the scars on his thin forearms and the tobacco stains on his teeth when his lips parted. If he had been anything like Humi was when she first came to Delta City, three months in the army had changed him a good deal. "I . . . my name . . . Merce Garden."

She could hear the Domesdean accent even in those few words. The wound in his thigh was killing him fast. The black arterial blood seeped through the bandages, redolent of hot metal. There were no flamens left alive who could have helped him.

"Then why didn't you come to me?" she asked. "I would

have made sure this didn't happen! I would have sent you to Humi in the city—you would have been safe with her, and having you by her side would certainly have made a difference to her!"

"It ... doesn't matter ... what you would of ... milady Maiden ..." he whispered. "I couldn't ... of left the Seventh!" He threw up an arm, as if begging his friends to agree. One of them seized the chapped fingertips and held them. The rest of them hovered around: children with patchy fur, gangly and scarred, the very flesh of Hope's army.

"I wish my little sister ..." Merce turned to the boy who was holding his hand. "Tell her ... tell her I asked for her .. not for Humi ... tell her ..."

With a quiver, he died.

Hope clenched her fists.

"Bury him," she said coldly to the Seventh Younger Cabal. "Don't leave him for the hyenas. That is beneath the standards of this army."

When she told Humi the little tale, she had left out the most painful details. The tattoo on Merce's arm, in a patch of burned off fur, which matched those on the other boys' arms. The impossible loneliness of the sunset, the silence of that place above the cauldron of life and slaughter. What she, Hope, had thought that night, tossing on her camp bed, when she could not get the child out of her mind, and she felt cold sweat on her back and her forehead, and she knew that—even had it not officially been over—it was over for her.

The news of the cousin's death had shaken Humi. That surprised Hope. Muddy-faced, looking quite unlike the serene conqueror into whose presence Hope had been ushered, she clutched the arms of the Throne.

Hope had muttered something in an unmodulated voice and fled out into the sunlight.

She looked around the courtyard. There was Arity, unobserved and unobserving in a corner, his face shaded by the hood of an *auchresh* tunic too big for him. His head was tipped back; the sunlight shone on the apple-green skin of his throat.

She *teth* " up to him. He started upright, fumbling at his side for a knife that was not there. She stepped back.

"Hope!" He moved to embrace her. She slid aside. Hurt, he stopped. She stared at him, trying to see *through* him.

How was he different? How had he changed? She would not have it that he had not changed at all.

"*Is* it you, Ari? Is it really you?"

He leaned back against the wall, picking at a splinter. The weathered, perfectly fitted planks, undamaged but for a few blade marks, soared twenty feet over his head. "Forever picking at half-healed scabs," he said sadly. "You are a true *auchresh,* Hopie."

"You know what I mean," she said.

"I suppose I do. I had hoped that you, of all people, wouldn't harp on it."

"Have other people?"

"No." His mouth quirked. A smile, almost. "That's what makes it worst of all! No one has mentioned it, although I half expected to be executed. No one except Humi, who *had* to. And she just offered a few cut-and-dried words of thanks."

Hope drew a deep breath. "Don't take this the wrong way, Ari. But I didn't think you were capable of it."

He sighed. He tugged his hood down, revealing that same vulnerably handsome face that had always tugged at her heart strings. A small cluster of brown circles shone on his neck, in the shade of the hood. He was still clipping his thorns. He was not going to revert to the state in which she had left him in Rimmear.

His expression was philosophical; he looked tired. "When you last met me, I wouldn't have been capable of it. But while you were away—a lot happened ..." He smiled wearily. "I think Pati knew all along, deep inside, that I was dangerous to him. Maybe he even knew I would be his death. So he tried to control me. And by trying, he made me able to break free."

"Which came first," Hope said, "the flower or the seedpod?"

Arity's nose wrinkled. "I'm through with paradoxes now."

"So am I." She shifted. "We are equals now, Ari: I think. We both stood up to him, each in our own way."

His eyes sparkled, but he did not respond. She felt slightly disappointed. In her interactions with other *auchresh,* she seldom admitted equals. That was not the *iu* way.

But then, both of them had left such finicky, obsolete standards behind in the old world. She said, "Of course, your gesture was far more dramatic."

He flung his arms out. "I am Drama!" Then he dropped his hands, and swept his eyes up and down her. "But I don't know! You have become rather dramatic yourself— everything from the way you smile to the way you stand! That's what soldiering does to you, isn't it? It makes you feel that the world is a dramatic place, worth giving yourself to, body and heart." He sobered. "And you gave yourself to it. I did too. *That* was the thing, wasn't it?"

"Yes." Hope thought of splitting Calvarese teenagers on the end of her sword, of sleeping with a human soldier twice her size whose passion had briefly been able to overcome his urge to worship her. She thought of Humi's cousin dying at her touch on Samaal's Eastern Rim. "That was the thing."

He nodded. "You *do* understand. You are the only one. Perhaps there's something in this business of blood."

"Doesn't Humi understand?" She had to ask. It was all over now. Nothing more stood between the two of them. Surely . . . surely . . .

"She is blind," Arity said with unexpected vehemence. "She didn't *see* the battle. In just the way that Pati, in his turret, didn't see the suffering. She did not see. She still does not see."

"Give her credit where credit is due, Arity! She's changed, too!"

"Fig juice! She still believes all this is *glorious*."

Hope did not know what to say. Behind them, the queue of Deltans shuffled slowly around and around the courtyard. More supplicants came all the time, even while those who had completed their circular pilgrimage shouldered out through the queue and plopped themselves down by the walls, wolfing their bowls of stew. They spoke in whispers, as if they had not yet realized that it was safe to raise their voices. Aneisneida's recognizable treble rang out in laughter for a moment. *There* was a woman whose energy had scarcely been tapped. *She,* Hope was willing to bet, still saw a possibility of deriving glory from this mess.

Humi was beyond that. Hope knew she was.

"It's absurd that *I* have to defend her when *you* were

here," Hope said. "But I can see you're biased. So I'll do it."

She had to remind him, although she herself did not like to remember. The wound was still raw.

"I have talked to her. It was the assassination of the ghostiers, I think, which convinced her once and for all that there is no glory in this war."

"Do you know what part I had in that?"

She nodded. "But that hardly matters now, does it? Not after—what you did. I meant that she has lost as many friends as anyone else. She is to be pitied."

Arity was staring at the soup queue. "And if she has not had her fair share of suffering," he said viciously, "she will."

"Not here, though. This act is over. For her." Hope took a deep breath. "She is abdicating."

"*What?*"

"She hasn't announced it yet. But she is quite set on her plan."

"She—she *what*? She *can't*!"

"She is Divinarch. She sits on the Throne. Or haven't you realized that yet? She can do whatever she wants to."

Arity stiffened. He looked searchingly into her eyes. Puzzled, she didn't respond. Finally, he relaxed. "Thank the Power! For a moment, there, I was afraid you—had suggested it to her!"

"No," Hope said ruffled. "I have no ambitions of that sort. All I meant was that it is completely within her scope, if she wants to. She is supreme."

Arity's face softened, green wax in the sun. He smiled broadly, and then he hugged her. "I love you," he said into her ear. "You understand everybody. Power . . . ! Saying that makes me feel like a Foundling again! But I mean it."

"Oh, Ari." Overcoming astonishment, she extracted her arms from the cinch and hugged him back. They stood pressed together for a long moment. She closed her eyes. His clothes were warm from his body heat. His breath thawed the chilly point of her ear. He smelled faintly of salt mangoes: she guessed he had been for a visit to Wind Gully Heaven. It was a comforting smell of Heaven, of home, of long-ago Foundlinghood. But he had come back here again, to the city.

"I love you, too, Ari," she whispered. "I always have. But now . . . now I can depend on you."

"Whatever is within my power, Hope."

"I only ask one thing of you. Survive, and keep on surviving."

"That's a lot to ask."

"I ask it anyway. You will do it. For me."

He let out a deep breath. After a moment, he said in *auchraug,* with a smile in his voice, "All right! All right, female one, you have your way!" In *auchraug, female* meant *powerful* and *manipulative,* and at the same time "weak in a way which makes one want to aid her." Hope in her turn felt small and young and loved. He gave her a last squeeze and then let go. "Now I had better go speak to Humi. This decision of hers changes things."

Oh! Oh . . . but Ari, don't be a fool! She won't thank you for coming to her when she is at her weakest! She closed her mouth on the words. *Perhaps what she needs is foolishness.* "What are you going to say?"

"I don't know."

"You'll probably do more harm than good."

"I know that."

His eyes were narrow. He was no longer smiling. He drove his hands decisively into the pockets of his tunic.

"Go then," she said, and moved to the wall and leaned against it as he started toward the doors. She was no longer the Maiden General, whose followers, after the battle of Samaal, when she officially disbanded the army, when she expected them to throw stones, had shocked her by opening their throats and letting out a yell of adoration that would ring in her ears forever. For love of her, they had died. For love of her, the rest of their lives would be pale. Her authority sickened her; she had not been sorry to cast it off. She was no longer the Maiden General, or a maiden, or even, she thought, possessed of any qualities one might term general. No virtues. Only tiredness. *Cold wood hold me, hold me up.*

Humi had taken up residence in a suite high up in the Palace. Ari had been told she wished to emphasize her break with the old regime. He understood that—especially if her resolution were only tentative, and she feared that the shades in the royal suite might whisper in her ears and convince her she was really meant to be Divinarch, after all. He nodded to the *auchresh* sentinels who stood on either side of the heavy blue-glass door, jaws jutting at the ceiling. They studied him from the corners of their eyes.

From inside, he heard voices. A human woman and a human man. In another minute he identified them as Humi and Sol.

"What is the layout of the suite?" he asked the sentinels softly.

"Lieutenant?" one questioned, finally. The fellow must be an ex-Hand. None of the renegades conceded any title to Arity except *perich "hi*—and that grudgingly.

"Is there an anteroom, or does this door open directly into the reception room?"

"Oh," the ex-Hand said. "Yes, there is an anteroom!" He grinned. This kind of thing was, of course, familiar to him from the days when the *kervayim*-councillors plotted and schemed against each other. Arity remembered those night and days of eavesdropping with a flush of shame. "It has heavy drapes, Lieutenant! And this door makes no noise!"

"If I were still Pati's lieutenant," Arity said as he pushed the door open and slid through, "I would have you executed for that." The slab of opaque glass closed behind him. It was a small room, and it felt as if it were underwater. Heavy blue velvet curtains hooked back to reveal aquarelles, and a blue frescoed ceiling gave an impression of the surface of the pond. Flaking, ancient ghosts, most of them Deltan or Veretrean (in accordance with the color scheme) struck old-fashioned poses.

He stepped to the far door and pressed his eye to the crack.

Diffused sunlight filled the reception room beyond, rippling on the ceiling, bouncing off various refractive *objets*. Piradean glass sculptures, a silver incense burner, a glass table. One wall of this room, like the royal bedroom several stories below, was completely glass, offering a panoramic view of the sea. Humi sat in a hard chair with a solid back that had probably been crafted for someone three times her size. She faced the sea and her back was to the door. Her feet rested flat on the floor, her hands rested flat on the claw arms of the chair. Her mint-colored dress lapped over the green handkerchief points of the seat drape, blending with it, as if she were sewn in place. "I tell you, my mind is made up," she said flatly. "You might as well leave. Do you understand? I am speaking the truth."

Sol paced up and down behind her chair. His skin showed dark and muddy through his white fur; his mouth twisted. "I do not think you have *ever* told me the truth," he said in a controlled tone. "Not in all our years as *imrchim,* and not afterward. I see no reason for you to have straightened your tongue now."

"But I have changed."

"Yes! You *have* changed! You've become *weak!*" Sol swung to face the armchair, gesturing—pointlessly, of course, for all Humi's victories had not given her back her sight. "How can you give up the Divinarchy, now that you have it in your very *hands*? How can you have lost your ambition? You used to glitter with intent! We loved you for your energy! It was like—like drinking wine!"

"I *told* you. I have *changed!*" She laughed mirthlessly. "Sometimes I think Emni's death affected me more deeply than it did you. Do you understand? Are you listening to me?"

"You certainly weren't listening to *me* the day she died," Sol muttered, too low for Humi to hear; but Arity's sharp ears picked it up.

"And my—loss of ambition, as you call it—is compounded by the state in which I find the world." Humi sighed exhaustedly. "I've already explained this once today, to Hope, but I'll do it again. Think, Sol. Really, I have already lost the Divinarchy. Despite all our efforts, we did not make the war cohesive enough. It was too ragged. How did we put it? 'Sacrificing dedication for numbers.' Well, we might not have won if we had done otherwise. Our losses were staggering, even though our armies were ten times the size of Pati's. But from the point of view of keeping the Divinarchy unified, it was a terrible mistake."

"I don't follow," Sol said angrily.

"Each continent was freed by one of my *auchresh* lieutenants, through the exertions of soldiers who adored that lieutenant. Each continent *freed itself from Pati.* It did not *deliver itself to me.* My name was no more than a symbol for freedom. My goal was to end Pati's tyranny. It seems I succeeded too well.

"In four short years, Pati created a miracle. By taking the flamens for his own, and spreading his Hands throughout the world, he made the structure of local and continental government so thoroughly *his* that the only way to take it back was to destroy the structure. And so we did. And now the continents are all spinning off in different directions. Domesdys follows Shine. Iceland follows Whitenail. Veretry follows Truth. The Archipelago is sliding into quiet anarchy. And Power knows what will happen to the continents Hope won by herself, because unlike the other lieutenants, she has absolutely no wish to govern. Other renegades may try to fill her shoes. But more likely, quarreling human upstarts will shove them out, and there will be civil war again. Pirady and Calvary may even split into separately governed countries."

Sol had stood still through this monologue. Finally, as Humi halted for breath, he interrupted. "And like Hope, you have *absolutely no wish* to try to stop this projection of yours from coming true? What about *duty*? Don't you consider it your *duty* to hold the Divinarchy together—"

"Honestly, Sol, even leaving my personal indisposition to ruling out of it, looking at the situation objectively, there is no hope. Holding the Divinarchy together for five more years, or ten, would simply make things worse when it finally breaks up." She paused—"Or else—and this is a possibility I'm afraid even to speak of—I would turn into another tyrant. Then it would break up at my death."

"You think you have the ability to be like Pati? After all you've said about your lack of ambition, and so forth, and what I remember from your first reign—your indecisiveness, your *chronic* indecisiveness that forced us finally to ask you to step down—you expect me to believe that you fear becoming a *tyrant*?"

"Yes."

On the other side of the door, Arity understood. Intuitively, like a flash of pain.

Sol evidently did not. He let out an exasperated puff of breath. He began to pace again, three steps and whirl, three steps, whirl. "But you can't give up the Divinarchy because you think you would make a bad Divinarch! That is pure cowardice."

"Haven't I made myself clear by now? I do not think there *can be* another Divinarch."

"Delta City is yours! You can't argue with that! Royalland is yours! And Delta City *is* the Divinarchy!"

Humi let out a mirthless little noise. "*Was*. Royalland was damaged too badly in the war for it to worry about anything now except getting back on its feet. And the city. What is it now? A tiny island awash in starving refugees, whose oldest and most beautiful districts have been burned out. The intercontinental ships have stopped coming here. The city can recuperate. But I would hinder its recovery, rather than help it."

"Who will have the city, then? You haven't thought about *that*!"

"Do you want to have it?" Arity could not hear a glimmer of humor in her voice, yet this time, he could not believe she meant what she was saying. "You can, if you do. And Royalland, as far as I am able to give it to you. I was planning to hand the reins to Gold Dagger, Soderingal, and Aneisneida—I like the idea of creating a new Royallandic dynasty, only human this time—but the strongest contender will come out on top, no matter what I dictate. And you're stronger than two, anyway, out of those three, so I might as well forestall the infighting by giving it to you."

"No," Sol said in a strangled voice. "I have no ambitions in that direction." Arity heard Hope, in his head, echoing those words almost exactly: her voice which had been like a length of silk hoarsened to burlap by years of tobacco and months of open air. He blinked. For the first time, he felt the pinch of his scruples. This was an intensely private scene he was witnessing: was it the breakdown of an old understanding—or the start of a new one? The cause he had come here to plead, continents and monarchs regardless, could pivot on the next few moments.

He couldn't *not* watch. He glued his eye to the crack again. The incense burner in the other room exhaled a musky twist of smoke, marbling the air.

"There is only one thing you could give me that I would care for," Sol said in a careful voice, higher pitched than usual. "Tellury Crescent."

Humi's hand jerked. It was the first movement he had seen from her since he began to watch. "Tellury Crescent? Sol, are you *mad*! Nothing in the world could make me go back there! The Chalice is a shell! Soot and rain puddles! Nobody has—nobody has removed the bodies—"

Arity gritted his teeth, closed his eyes.

Sol said, "But *imrchu*, *I* would go back. *I* would rebuild the ruin."

"Take it, then!" The arm resting on the chair vanished; Arity guessed she had muffled her face in her hands. "Take it. Make the ghostiers a power again. Be senior ghostier. Enlist Mory and Tris to help you. What a different institution it will be when *they* have a hand in its shaping!" She yelped laughter, unstably. "You *do* have a nose for the unworthiest of all our unworthy problems!"

"What have I done?" Sol said. "Is it a crime now to yearn for beauty?"

"It—Sol, have you *forgotten*? I am no longer a ghostier! I am *blind*!"

"But *I* am a ghostier! You are so incurably self-absorbed! I sometimes think your heart was never in ghosting at all. But me—it's in me. I always have been a ghostier. I was born yearning for beauty."

Her voice was small, not like Humi's voice at all. "I think you are stronger than I am."

"But I'm a very simple man, really." Sol clasped his hands behind him. His back was to the door, his face to the sun's glare and the sparkling black sea. Arity wanted to look away. "I need something on which to fix myself. Then I circle around that center, snapping. Like a dog on a lead."

"Emni!" Humi breathed.

"You," Sol said brutally.

"Did you ever . . . I have to know, Sol. Did you ever think about betraying me?"

"I wish I could say I never thought about it. But that isn't . . . isn't my nature. I thought about it many times. But I couldn't betray you. In the end, I didn't want to." He paused. "I didn't know that *you* would betray *me*."

"Gods . . . !" Humi was, Arity thought, close to tears. The idea shook him strangely; made his stomach churn.

"You've let a great many people down," Sol said. "But to me, personally, you have made everything up. Giving me Tellury Crescent has erased any debt there ever was between us!" His voice was brisk now, businesslike. He walked to the door, saying over his shoulder, "Come visit me there before you leave. If you can overcome your horror of the place."

"How—how did you know I was leaving?"

.Arity hastily scrabbled his mind into order for *teth"tach ching.* Sol stopped with his hand almost literally on the doorknob. "Doesn't everybody know? You're going with *him.*"

Arity's mind reeled. He did not manage to *teth"* until Sol strode out of the room. But Sol did not see him. The Archipelagan was walking fast toward the door, gripping some kind of a glass ornament, twisting it in both hands. Purplish blood ran down his wrist. His jaw was set. Just as Arity finally *teth"d,* and the other whirled toward the shrinking light, Arity saw the tears spill out of Sol's eyes.

By some meaningless quirk of image memory he found himself in the Sea Garden, in the cliff below the Palace. Winter gave it a bluish-white beauty: the salt shrubs, leafless and stark, looked their best. The sea threw sequins of light up into the watery shadows of the rock grotto. Somehow his *teth"* had gone slightly wrong and he had got sulfur in his throat. He slumped against the side wall, coughing. He was exhausted; he had not been able to sleep in over two sixdays. Not, in fact, since that twilit evening.

The smell of salt rejuvenated him like a quick glass of *morothe.* For five minutes he let himself dwell on the memory of those last, terrible moments.

Then he gathered himself and *teth"d* back to Humi's subaqueous reception room, where he found her sitting in the same place Sol had left her, weeping softly. She was beautiful; she was blind; she was twenty-three; she was tall, and too thin; she was the Divinarch. Her cheeks were rumpled and wet.

Decent Bones

"It's me." He squatted at her feet and took her hands in his. "I heard everything."

She did not resist his grip. "Heh. I should have guessed." She appeared to be staring out over his head, at the sea.

Didn't she feel the tension in the air? Didn't she remember everything that lay between them? Did she plan *ever* to let down her mask? Could she?

At last she said, "I know now why Sol is more of a ghostier than I ever was."

"Why is that?"

"Historically we—they—have taken murder lightly. It is a requirement of being a ghostier. And Sol still does. Being a ghostier made him immune even to his own twin sister's death, I think. I—I have always been different. I killed ghosts with a clean conscience—"

"Not your first. I was there. Don't you remember?"

"Ari." Her voice was raw—as though the reminder had peeled away a protective rind. "I'm trying to *confess*! Aren't you going to listen?"

He squeezed her hands. "Go on," he murmured, modulating his voice.

"I never entered all the way into the *imrchim* bond. I never killed another ghostier. I always held back, living half the time in Tellury Crescent and half the time in Antiprophet Square. Sol, on the other hand, has been *imrchi* right to the bone for years. He killed Beisa. And that's what's keeping him going. That strength."

She paused.

"Emni was his only weak point. Now she's gone, and he is invulnerable."

Arity thought of Sol striding out of the reception room with tears spilling from his eyes. But he didn't mention that. Instead, he argued: "You're equating strength with the ability to do murder!"

"Oh, you mistake me! I mean the ability to *recover* from the death of your loved ones. Whether you caused it, or someone else did, death is fair, no matter how unjust it seems, and one person is essentially like another. And there are always others to love." She stopped, and finished in a half whisper. "I think at the end, Sol was glad to be free of her. I, on the other hand, have always been unnaturally afraid of losing the people who make me weak."

Oh, Power. Arity's restraint almost crumbled. He wanted to take her in his arms and tell her that in his eyes, her weakness made her beautiful. But he could not bridge the gap. The incense smoke stung his skin. He said, "I think you are wrong. I believe that real strength is the ability to

not lose people. To hold onto them. Even if they made
you weak."

"Ari, Ari, Ari!" She smiled faintly, shook her head.
"You were always so marvelously impractical. It's nice to
know *somebody* hasn't changed."

He bowed his head. With that one remark of hers, the
gulf between them had widened, yawning.

For a moment there, we were close . . . !

*But it was an illusion. She doesn't, can't understand where
I have come back from!*

His thighs were starting to quiver. His head spun. He
knelt down on the floor, still holding her hands, and leaned
carefully against her knee. Touching her, even through the
folds of green satin, soothed his body, soothed his nerves.

"What are you—I can't see! Ari, get away from me!"

He shifted away, clamped his palms onto his cheeks,
rested his elbows on his knees.

She breathed harshly. A wind was getting up. Far below,
far away, white horses the size of cats frolicked on the tops
of the waves.

All around him, the abyss whistled.

And Pati stood in the abyss, barefoot, his toes mucky
with the slime at its bottom, looking at Arity with mournful
inscrutability. A hollow-eyed enigma.

Sadness gripped Arity like a rage.

"There have been moments," he said, "when I think you
and I can be again as we were. Companions in weakness.
Trusting. *Loving.* And at those moments, it seems to me
that this ghastly deluge of racial enmity, the toppling of
false gods, the arising of real ones, the destruction of the
Divinarchy, your abdication, my—my killing Pati—*everything*—has all been organized by I don't know what—*Rigethe,* perhaps! to lead to one thing: our better
understanding of each other."

"What appalling arrogance," Humi said.

Of course I don't really believe that is the truth!—The
cold wind. Withering all arguments, withering all impulses.

"You are as arrogant as every other *auchresh,*" she said.
"You think the world turns around you. I used to think
the same—but I've been cured of it."

"And this is one of those other moments," he said
loudly, "when I know you no longer understand me at all.
And I no longer understand you. I think I never did."

The sides of the abyss creaked farther apart. The wind

gathered speed, a lightless wind from nowhere, howling. In the darkness Pati laughed self-deprecatingly. Arity squeezed his head in his hands and shook it in a vain attempt to dislodge the sound. With the progression of the afternoon, the sun had ceased to come into the room: all the little reflective *objets* were dulled. Humi's fur held none of the reddish glints the sun habitually gave it. Her dress didn't flatter her. That was one of the most crippling blows she had ever taken, he thought. The loss of her fashion sense. And she didn't even know about it.

"Love is a sideshow," she said harshly. "The war was ugly, but it was necessary, and for a long time it was everything. We were all caught up in it. You and I weren't the only ones whose sideshow got trampled."

It sounded as if she might be making an effort to explain. Arity put his fingers to his temples again, pressing, as if he could press out the other voices in his head.

"And now it's finished with us. It isn't over. It won't be over until everyone alive now is dead, and new babies have grown up—and probably not even then. But it's finished with *us*. We can go."

"You're trying to avoid responsibility for the part you played in it! That's not worthy of you!"

"Everyone keeps telling me that this or that or the other isn't *worthy* of me!" Anger flared. It made her momentarily beautiful. Arity wished he could appreciate it with all his being. "All I can say is what Erene said once to me. *Nothing is unworthy of me.*" She stopped, and chuckled morosely. "Make sure they write that in the histories. If there are any more histories."

"Why don't you write it in them yourself?"

"I shan't be here. I am going to visit Erene and Elicit, in Pirady. Did you know that was where they are living now? Hope is coming with me." She bowed her head.

She was so sad. So young. And completely hollowed out. He wondered if there were anything left inside her apart from theories and enmities and justifications rattling around loosely. Did she *ever* dwell on her memories?

If you have pulled a plant up and shaken it bone-clean, scraped the last traces of dirt from the crack where it grew off its roots . . .

The cruel, the terrible thing was that he, Arity, was no better than that himself. When he killed Pati, he had killed so much of himself that he could not even sum it up yet.

The gulf closed. Its vanishing left the room bright and quiet and still.

He sighed. Getting up, he sat on the arm of her chair. He slipped an arm companionably around her shoulders. "Skin and bones. You're just a satin bag of bones."

"I know I haven't—haven't been eating."

"I'm coming with you to Pirady, you know. We'll fatten you up—Erene and I between us. She's a mother now, after all."

If it had been a different kind of moment, they might both have started crying. As it was, she just rested her head against his hip. She sighed, tremblingly. "*You're* skinny, too," she said, tracing the protruding bone of his hip. "I never liked skinny men."

"Doesn't matter. I have decent bones."

She smiled: a hopeless little twitch of the lip. "If you really want to come. I don't care."

Outside and far below, afternoon was expiring gently. White horses glowed in the half light. Night seemed to sink to touch the sea, not so much a curtain as a mist: the world's thankful retreat into amnesia.

Sideshow

Watching Humi say her farewells, Arity thought her manner unnecessarily regal. This, after all, was not a formal abdication; *that* had gone past half a sixday ago, in a blur of wine and improvised finery.

Humi stooped and kissed Fiamonina's little furry cheek. She straightened up and moved her hand across the air like a benediction. "Power be with you," she said to the group assembled on the newly built stairs into the Palace courtyard.

From now on, Aneisneida had said to Arity as they watched the workers hammer pegs into the joists of the steps, *the sedans will have to enter the stables through the Hare Gate. I will construct an arched walkway from the stables to the Palace doors, so my ladies don't get their hair wet if they arrive when it is raining. But the courtyard itself*

*will be a plaza with a fountain and a performing space for
public use.* Her face shone.

She doesn't understand, Arity thought. *Her business won't
be with building fountains. It will be winning more of the
people than her husband or her father-in-law can. It'll be
about promising the people the good things they used to take
for granted, and slithering out of the promises when the ships
don't come.*

But maybe his guesses were too dark. Maybe there would
be no infighting. One could not forget Sol, stewing away in
the Crescent with Mory and Tris; already there were rumors of rebuilding the Chalice, and screams in the dead of
night. But these things had been run of the mill for the old
Crescent. And Arity had never found Sol as objectionable
as other people seemed to. Especially now there was that
double link between them. A life spared, a woman shared.
They had never spoken plainly of it, and they probably
never would. But the point was that Arity knew Sol had
scruples. It was quite possible that that *look* of his, the look
that could chill the blood in your veins, was merely
technique.

So Arity hoped. And a few huge flakes of snow sparkled
in the sunlight as they tumbled out of the sky. One landed
on Fiamorina's head. She giggled and patted at it.

Aneisneida came down from the steps, bringing her child
with her. While Fia squatted, one arm stretched over her
head, and scraped industriously at the cobbles, Aneisneida
talked to Humi. Her teeth glowed, offset by her light green
fur. On the steps, Hope was speaking with Gold Dagger,
Soderingal, and a newly washed trio of young Deltans—
Gold Dagger's henchmen. By Aneisneida's grace, the crime
lord had been made a *real* lord. Lord Dagger! It sounded
like a tavern singer's stage name.

Hope still wore *kere* clothes, and like Arity, she still carried her knife. She leaned back and stuck her hands in her
pockets as Soderingal expressed himself eloquently into her
face. Wrinkling her nose, she dragged one hand out of her
pocket and indicated the cobblestones. She was modulating
her voice well, so that Arity couldn't hear what she was
saying; but from the way Gold Dagger mimed scrubbing a
window, he guessed they were talking about getting the
bloodstains off the street.

This was where the second biggest clash of the battle had

taken place, of course. Was there anything in the *breideiim* tale which said that where blood had been spilled nothing would grow for a hundred years? The blood still blackened the cracks between the cobbles, and stained the dented walls of the courtyard. The sprigs of grass around the bases of the walls were brown. But then, it had not rained. Winter, and no rain. Was that usual? He could not remember.

He turned to survey the mansions on the other side of the street. Somebody had hung brocade curtains in a downstairs window. Could it be Aneisneida's ladies?

Humi could feel Anei's closeness like the heat from a bonfire. Somewhere along the road, she had become as sensitive to humans as if they were *auchresh*. She fought the urge to lean back.

"I feel so *free*," Aneisneida was saying intensely.

"What do you mean?" Humi put everything she had into her smile.

"I don't know!" Aneisneida laughed. "No, Fia, don't eat that! Stand up straight! Gods, Humi, this child. A fine Divinarch she'll make if she can't keep her hands to herself!"

Humi laughed. "Don't worry about Fia! She's both precocious and well-mannered—and that's rare in a child so young!"

"Do you really think so?" In Anei's voice, Humi heard a mother's pride—and fear that her pride might stop her from seeing her child clearly. Silently, Humi congratulated her for understanding her own instincts.

"I do. But please school her well. An all-around education is so important."

"Ah." Humi could almost hear Anei's false-ribs squeaking as she swelled up like an excited cat. "Do you know what I have arranged, Humi? We finalized it just this morning. I am going to apprentice her to Sol. She'll live at home, but she will be trained as a ghostier. I remember existing in the shadow of the ghostiers, when I was a councillor ... gods, I was miserable! And thoroughly aware of my own incompetence. I am convinced now that there is no better school for a diplomat than Tellury Crescent. It will cement the ties between Marshtown and the Palace—which your lovely Erene, gods rest her soul, instituted—and Fia will avoid potential enemies by growing up alongside the future

ghostiers. What did Sol say they would be? There is a word
for it ..."

"*Imrchim,*" Humi murmured.

"Yes, that was it! Sol and Lady Glissade and Lord Sepal
and I spoke frankly about these things! None of us want
to destroy the little that we have left through ...
misunderstandings."

Humi felt a smile cracking her impassive mask. She had
almost forgotten what it felt like, having someone out think
her. "Anei, you're a marvel. It's a masterstroke. I would
never have thought of it."

"Oooh," Aneisneida said. She embraced Humi tightly. Fia
didn't make a sound. Humi guessed she was eating dirt. Her
mother smelled overpoweringly of old perfume—probably the
last she had been able to dig out from the last old trinket
box in the city. "I *shall* miss you, Humi!" she sputtered. "Isn't
it odd how we never used to be friends?"

A snowflake fell on Humi's exposed nape, below the
knob of her pulled-back hair. No colder than her skin, no
drier than her eyeballs. "Terribly strange!" she said. "But
I'm sure we had our reasons at the time—"

The apostate flamen spoke eloquently. Hope had heard
all his sentiments before, and so probably had the ragged
audience but they were hanging on every word. Hope stood
beside Ari and Humi at the back of the little crowd, in the
shade of a mansion with high, broken cornices. The apostate had set up his podium in the open, at a crossroads of
the palace district streets. A month ago, he would not have
lasted ten minutes here. His voice had been faintly audible
as they walked away from the Palace. They had wandered
over to hear what kind of thing an apostate would say in
public—whether it would be inflammatory, or at the very
least thought-provoking. The patchwork beast of the crowd
swayed and writhed. Whenever the flamen paused to make
a dramatic point, they hummed:

"Speak aright, Godsbrother."

"In the name of the Power."

The Godsbrother smote the air constantly with his heavy
hands as he spoke. His words were unpolished, unpremedi-
tated, and occasionally embarrassing; but they carried a certain heartfelt conviction.

"All given to melodrama, these apostates," Hope
muttered.

"And trusting in the ineffable correctness of the Power! We may forgive our old masters for their atrocities against us. We may open our hearts to our new masters, and fairly ... *fairly* ...! reward their benevolence toward us with trust or punish their hubris with uprising. For now that the rule of the *serbalim* is over—"

"*Serbalim?*" Arity hissed, advancing his lips to her ear. "How does he know ... ?"

Hope shook her head. "An ex-Hand. A renegade. Anyone. I don't doubt that one thing we *will* have to resign ourselves to, now, is the loss of *auchraug* as a private language."

"Maybe we can come up with a new one."

The flamèn was in full spate. " ... I say, now that the rules of the *auchresh* is over, it will be possible to divide the rule of the body from the rule of the spirit. The task of governing belongs to those who lust after *secular* power. Be they *auchresh* or mortal! And this is all it has *ever* been. But the rule of the spirit belongs to the Power. And *the Power is unknowable.*"

"Say on, Godsbrother."

"All we can know is its attributes. It creates the Balance anew every day. And the Balance will *ever* weigh down on the side of benevolence, goodness, sympathy, and renewal. Yea! And death!"

"Yea," murmured the crowd. "And death."

Most of them had sunk into a kind of exalted reverie, stilled by the flamèn's words. Just like every generation of Hands' sheep since the Wanderer, Hope thought. For them, the apostate's theology, though it might subvert every precept of religion—falsely or enduringly, who could tell?—need do no more than justify the immense changes in their lives. All they wanted was to be assured that the deaths of their loved ones had not been meaningless. They *wanted* to be dragged from the side of the grave of "If only." They wanted to be exhorted not to give in to apathy, now that the streets were rusty with blood and parched grass straggled along the doorsteps of the palace district where maids had once scrubbed twice a day.

And no traditional flamens, with their insistence on gods who had proved undependable, could have met their need. Only the apostates would be listened to now. This man altered old formulas enough that his listeners did not intellectually recognize them; yet his concepts were not in fact provocative. He dared not leave out the Balance. *That* was

essential even to Hope's conception of existence. Without
the necessity not just of momentous actions but of slight
ones, what point was there to *anything*? The people needed
desperately to be reassured of that necessity.

Taking that into account, Hope knew she would have
been churlish to criticize apostasy. But she *felt* churlish.
Ghastly images drifted just under the surface of the day.
Blood was seeping from the old sword slice on her ribs:
she could feel it trickling down her side. Her stomach felt
sour with cynicism.

The trouble was that once the flamen admitted divine
justice—even if he called it something else—his doctrine
was the same as that with which everyone here had grown
up. Only its focus was altered, from the *auchresh* to the
Power. And after all, most *auchresh* had always denied they
were the judges in the divine court. At most, its watchdogs.

"*Rigethe*," she said to Arity. "Do you think it can satisfy
them for long?"

"The mortals?"

"I don't think they are disaffected enough to keep from
trying to embrace it. And of course you can't embrace *Rigethe*. It slips away. You have to hate and distrust and
revere it—the idea of it—all at once. And I don't think
they will be able to keep their distance from it, the way we
can. They need a headier belief."

Arity rubbed his chin. "But hatred, distrust, reverence
. . . isn't that what they used to feel for us?"

"Mmm . . ." She hadn't thought of it that way. "The
more *awake* mortals, perhaps. The nobles. The councillors.
But not these!" She gestured at the backs of the crowd.
Most of them looked like refugees. A few wore soldier's
garb. Some wore the more countrified dress of Marshtown.
"They *loved* us! That's why they need this playacting Godsbrother so badly now."

"Well then, perhaps the pursuit of apostasy will force
every last mortal to wake up," Arity said. His mouth
quirked, but his eyes were tired. "Awareness. Investigation
and comprehension of the impulses. That would be a noble
goal for any religion, wouldn't it? As a matter of fact I
could do with some of that comprehension right now."

She looked more closely at him, and modulated her voice
until her lips scarcely moved. "Do you mean—" She jerked
her chin toward Humi.

Ari nodded, and grimaced. "Do you see? I think that if

one completely understands one's impulses, one ceases to
feel them."

"Power, Ari."

Whetted beams of sunlight drove down the street. Blood
trickled from windows, dripping off the sills onto the Deltans' heads. Blood everywhere. Hope's eyes hurt.

"And let us keep this in mind"—the Godsbrother brayed
suddenly, at top volume—"as we turn and go forth to rebuild our city! To the delight of the Power and the appease-
ment of the Balance!"

The crowd had been growing more and more restless.
When he finally released them, throwing up his arms and
then dropping them by his sides, bowing his head (a marvelous bit of stage business, Hope noted), the moans of
approval swelled to a crescendo, then broke in a cheer.

"Praise the Power!" the Godsbrother shouted. "No mortal is worthy of your adulation—least of all, your ignorant
servant! Praise the Power!"

Arity's hand rested protectively on Humi's neck. She
slumped loosely against him. Throughout the sermon, Hope
had noticed she was as still as a stone, and that her eyes
gleamed. Tears of rage, or real feeling? Or just artifice,
triggered by years of crying at the proper events?

She leaned over and touched the girl's arm. Ari seemed
ambivalent about their reconciliation—but her own reaction to the news had astonished her. She was saddened just
as much as she was overjoyed. And in the black depths of
that sadness, she sensed selfish, wrong emotions, not to be
touched even with the tip of a finger.

"Shall we go?" she said. "You wanted to come and listen, but I think we've heard all there is to hear. There are
clouds coming up."

Humi shook herself. "I would like to talk to the Godsbrother," she said clearly.

"Hume—" Arity expostulated irritatedly, then cut himself short.

"Would you lead me, Hopie?" Humi placed one hand on
Hope's arm and walked fearlessly out of the shadow of the
building where they had stood. Hope, skipping to get ahead
of her, tried not to flinch in the sunlight. The crowd had
dispersed, but the ripe stench generated by the gathering of
Deltans still hung in the air. She and Humi attached themselves to a short queue of men and women. People stared at

her full-size wings, their golden tips brushing her boots. She
had sickened of cloaks, so today she let her wings poke
through slits in her tunic. Already she wished she hadn't.
Though there had been a couple of renegades in the crowd,
none of them looked as obviously *auchresh* as she.

Finally their turn came to speak. The flamen sat on the
edge of the overturned fish crate that had served as a podium.
Close up, he was not a large man. His jowls rested meatily
on his collarbone, and his arms were eel-like—all muscle and
no bone. His face hung down from his salt crystals, vertically
creased with tiredness. He had pale blue fur. He could have
been Veretrean, Icelandic, or even Piradean. The leman holding a metal cup of water to his hand, waiting patiently for
him to take hold of it, was unusually mature—a young man
of at least twenty-two or -three, with arms like a sailor's.

A strange pair!

The flamen smiled up at Humi. He appeared not to *sense*
Hope; or at least, not to *sense* her as anything more than
mortal. "Why didn't you have them gather in a circle?"
Humi said bluntly.

The flamen's face registered surprise; then he laughed.
"There wasn't room. I do agree it's more communal. And
more traditional. Next time. Any more questions, my dear?"

Hope's heart hurt when she saw how Humi softened—
like stale bread under a drop of water. Then Humi shook
herself. "No," she said in the same hard, jagged voice, "I
liked your sermon. That is what I wanted to tell you."

"Any merit my words may have is that which they pro-
duce in your heart. But remember the rule, child: No living
thing, be it mortal, *auchresh,* or flamen, is infallible. Everything I've told you today may be wrong. But this is how
the Power chooses to inspire me. And *that* is all that matters." The flamen shrugged engagingly. "If you are inspired
too, then speak accordingly. There is nothing that separates
us, you and I, except the miracles. And *those* I will only
employ insofar as they benefit you."

"A well-rehearsed disclaimer," Humi said. "You cover
all eventualities."

The flamen gave a puzzled smile. Somehow Humi's tone
of voice had made the observation into a compliment. But
he was too clever not to see that it was really an insult.

The leman stared at Hope. His honest, snubby features
were covered with white Archipelagun fur, but he had blaz-

ing red hair such as Hope had never seen, not on the battle-
fields nor in the cities. She shifted under his scrutiny.

"I am Godsbrother Quest, my children," the Godsbrother said. "And who are you, that I may address you
by your names when we meet next?"

"We won't—" Humi was replying stiffly, when Hope interrupted. Giving Humi a little shove, she said:

"I am the erstwhile Maiden, Godsbrother. And this is
the erstwhile Divinarch."

Humi muddied painfully. Hope almost wished she could
allow the girl to hide her identity. But that wouldn't be
good for her—not in the long run.

"Humility Garden."

"Ohhhh!" the leman exclaimed. With a quick, careful
movement he put down the cup of water and sprang upright.
Hope felt his hostility. She yanked Humi backwards, keeping
a mask of pleasantness in place. The leman stopped at the
sight of her divine inscrutability. Grudgingly, he bowed. "My
flamen . . ." he said. "My *last* flamen was her sister."

"Oh, Power," Humi said. "It's not true. It's not. Tell me
what her name was!" Her hand seemed to press into
Hope's elbow like a brand. "Describe her to me!"

The young man narrowed his eyes at Humi. "I don't
think you *want* to believe me, Divinarch. But it's true. You
killed her, indirectly. So you ought to know the truth. Then
you can choose whether to believe me, or not. Her name
was Thankfulness. I called her Thani. She was the de-
voutest loyalist you could ever hope to see. I loved her for
it. I loved her for her strength."

He could have been any commoner with a grudge against
Humi, some scraps of inside information, and a flair for
cruelty. But Hope understood in a flash that the brittleness
of his voice was not designed to hurt Humi, but to stop his
own pain from breaking him open. This *Thani* . . . she was
real. She was that sister of Humi's who—how cruel the
Balance could be!—had tried to kill Arity five years ago.
Humi had helped her to escape, then.

"Describe her," Humi rattled. Brimstone swelled into the
air, melting the falling snowflakes, so that for a second it
appeared to be raining, and Arity materialized at her other
side, taking her arm as if to hold her. She shook him off.
"Describe her, I say, Archipelagan!"

"She . . ." The boy closed his eyes. He was not as old as

he looked, Hope saw. Probably only seventeen or eighteen. His Archipelagan accent was muted, but still recognizable. "She had very light hair. Sunbleached, not natural. And blond fur that looked so rich, when she was healthy, because of its dark roots."

Humi pushed her fingers into the thick fur on her neck. The ends were tawny, like the backs of her fingers, the roots were darker.

"I can't remember her eyes. I saw them just once before her salt pilgrimage. But I think they were gray. Maybe black. Like yours, blind woman." He sighed. "She was generous, and loving. More than her calling asked, I mean. She was as thin as a thread. She pushed herself and pushed herself until she didn't even have the strength to eat. Then she would get ill and not eat anyhow. Gods." He shook his red-tousled head angrily. "The struggles I used to go through to get a little food down her—"

"She was always a stocky child," Humi said.

"You haven't *known* her since she was a child!" The boy shook his head. "I don't even know why I am telling you this! I shouldn't have started!"

"You are speaking aright, Gete," the apostate Godsbrother Quest murmured. "You are evening the Balance. No need to stop."

"Yes, *indeed* I thank you!" Humi said. "You will never know how much it means to me to know—"

The Archipelagan turned on them, red hair blazing. "To know *what*? That she is *dead*?"

Hope flinched from the full frontal blaze of his grief. Arity flinched too—she saw him physically pull back, as if he were going to be attacked.

Such unwieldy, devastating emotions mortals fermented in their hearts!

Razors of passion, cutting them apart inside.

One could only profess flippant incomprehension.

Because the other possibility was to envy them.

Humi spoke in a measured voice. "To know that my last hope of even a little good surviving this year's inferno was an illusion. For that, I can only thank you."

"*Power,* Humi," Arity wailed softly. He tried again to pull her against him, but she resisted. Godsbrother Quest got to his feet. He was the most obvious figure of authority in this muddle, from the spectacle of which the Deltans had fled, like servants slipping out of the room when milord and milady have a tiff. Hope noted that the flamen kept clear of his trembling leman as he reminded them, "Humility, remember ... the Balance. The good which survives the 'inferno,' as you called it, the good which *stems* from it, doesn't have to be restricted to you. Thani's death fulfilled some other necessity."

Humi said, not to him in particular, "Fuck off. My sister is *dead.*"

"She died in my arms," the leman said. If Hope had not been able to see otherwise, she would have been convinced he was trying to hurt Humi as much as possible. "In the battle for the Folly. At the end, she recanted everything. Everything. Though I can't be sure"—he bared his teeth—"I couldn't even keep her alive. long enough ... long enough—"

"She saw the truth," Humi whispered.

"I couldn't even convince her that I *loved* her!" For a moment he looked a great deal like Godsbrother Quest as he rocked on the balls of his feet. "There has to be something beyond. That was when I went to look for Godsbrother Quest. I had met him before. He had a leman then. Avi was killed in Chrumetown."

"You," Humi hissed. "My sister's leman. An apostate."

"I plan to go home to the Archipelago to make my pilgrimage. I have a friend there who will care for me, and he may even want to join me on my travels. Though not as a leman." His eyes rested on Arity. Then he looked at Hope, with the same air of seeing *past* her—as if the very core of her being was not enough to distract his attention from the distance. His fury was concentrated, contained. She felt her heart stop as she saw the future in his eyes. Bluer than the sky.

Humi was shaking, leaning heavily on Hope and Arity. "Did she speak of me at all?" Her voice was hoarse. "Did she hate me?"

"I could never tell. I know she thought of you. You were one of the burdens she could never shake off. The other— the other was her conviction that she was responsible for her Godsbrother's death."

Humi moaned. Arity snapped at the leman, "You could have spared her *that.*"

The leman turned and looked at him. His clear blue eyes held all the anger in the world, compressed into two points.

Hope had to take control of the situation. She had to

stop this. It was turning into torture. "I agree with Ari. That's enough! When we stopped to listen to your sermon we were on our way ... on our way! It would have been better if we'd never come!"

Humi lifted her face. Tears were coursing down her cheeks. Hope was frankly appalled at how completely she seemed to have lost control of herself. Arity hissed through his fangs. "Sister or no sister, we have to get her away, or the tales will never stop circulating."

Distancing oneself from them was the only way
The only way

"What's your name?" she asked the leman.

"Gete," he allowed.

"And you can call me Hope, and this is Arity." She turned on her heel, pulling the others around with her. "Good-bye."

Humi twisted her face over her shoulder. "Don't ever go near the Crescent without your flamen, redhead!" She smiled horribly. "My friend Sol would make a ghost out of you ... just as quick as *that*!" She snapped her fingers. "So would Mory ... so would Tris ..."

"On the count of three," Arity whispered, rather desperately. "Around the corner. Anywhere. The Folly! Just outside the gate—"

Only as they *teth"d,* in the instant of nothingness, did it occur to Hope to wonder how Humi had guessed Gete had such red, red hair. Humi was no ordinary blind woman; Hope had known that for a long time; but what had made the boy visible to her extrasensual perception?

Elpechim

They ended up, by some fluke of Hope's imaging, just outside the fences of the Folly's grounds. Beyond the twisted fences, the gardens rolled downhill, denuded humps and hillocks. In many places island rock showed through the soil. The barrenness of it insulted the senses. Every time Arity thought he had gotten used to it, it slapped him in the eyes again, forcing him to look.

"Let's get out of here," Hope said abruptly.

"No," Humi said. "Are we near the Folly? Good. I want
..." She shivered, and brought her head up proudly. "I
want to walk in the gardens."

Hope looked at Arity. He shrugged. They counted to
each other and *teth"d* over the flattened fence, into the
devastation.

The snow fluttered silently onto the brown earth. The
sky was clouding over. Arity envisioned the thin, huge, icy-
lipped maw of winter sinking its fangs into the ground.
Icelandic weather in Royalland.

But Pati had chopped down all the trees. And maybe the
breideim tale about the spilling of blood accounted for the
parching and withering of what scraps of greenery were left.

Scraps of cloth fluttered from the twigs of the broken
saplings. The Folly loomed silently. The huge windows of
the lower stories gaped with broken glass. Many of the
upper windows had been broken, too.

"Looters," Hope said.

From outside, the broken windows gave the Folly an appearance of having succumbed to some dreadful pock-
marking disease which had crept upward from the ground.
Hope walked with her hand through Humi's arm, lips
pursed, holding her wings at a fastidious angle above the
ground. This must be worse for her, Arity thought, than
for him or Humi. Humi was walking with her eyes half
closed and a look of intense concentration on her face.
Arity attempted not to glance at her every other moment.
He knew she could feel it.

He stepped over a fallen log and his foot sank into a
partially decayed *auchresh* corpse. It lay curled in a fetal
position. Since he had stepped on its face, it was no longer
grinning. He just managed not to yell. "Damn it," he said
softly, and pulled away from the females, trying to wipe
the foul stuff off his boot on the earth.

"What a revolting smell," Hope said, wrinkling her nose.

Humi sniffed. "Why don't you just take your boots off?
Leave them here. It's not as though you need them."

She was right. A short distance away, a wooden half tub
stood bottom up. Must have held water for Humi's troops.
How had she managed the frentic planning, the ability to
think of a dozen things at once, all that was necessary to
organize a war more or less singlehanded? He sat down on

the tub to unbuckle his clumsy footgear. "Just as long as I don't step in anything else," he joked. The gesture seemed all too significant.

The dusty-damp earth, with its tiny cold wet patches, felt uncommonly good under his toes. Resilient. His heel talons dug in, providing a satisfying *connection* with the ground. The cold traveled up through his body, clearing his head.

A little later, without a word, Hope took her boots off and left them standing.

They circumabulated the Folly.

Nothing moved except a few stray blades of grass. The snowflakes fell a long way apart, slowly.

"I went to such expense to have those windows put in," Hope said regretfully. "A Power-damned expense."

"I never even went inside," Humi said. "After all the times you said we'd go."

"Do you want me to show you around?" Hope brightened. "It's probably been looted more thoroughly than any other building in the city! But the structure of the place is really the thing. Some of the inner chambers—"

"No," Humi said. "Thank you, but I don't think I could appreciate it as you meant it to be appreciated."

"I didn't forget you were *blind,*" Hope said. "I meant you could touch the walls, feel the ghosts and the furnishings and ornaments! If there are any left—"

"I know!" Humi faced her across Arity. There was something unnerving in the way her eyes remained wide and blank. Unhuman, un*auchresh,* in fact rather animal. "I meant that the *circumstances* under which I would have to *enter* your monument to the old days, namely my sister's being *dead,* and my having failed in what I tried to do, would keep me from concentrating on the architectural merits of the edifice! Am I not allowed to *mean* what I *say*?"

No, Arity thought. *Not anymore.*

"The privilege of unpleasant memories is not yours alone!" Hope said angrily. "Why did you want to come here, then? Why are you putting us all through this?"

Humi wrenched her hands out of Arity's and Hope's arms and hugged herself. "If you must know, I was hoping to find my sister's body!"

"Morbidity doesn't help anyone!" Arity interrupted.

"Oh, Humi," Hope said. She pulled Humi across Arity, and wrapped her arms around her.

They swayed to and fro in the middle of the empty battlefield, and Humi started crying.

"She was my responsibility," Arity heard her sob into Hope's shoulder. "She was my baby sister. I wish I had cared for her better—then she might have married and had children! She might have been allowed to stay at home! I know that damned man Transcendence chose her because he thought she looked as though she wasn't loved! Power, Hope, do you realize how *badly* all of us Gardens who dared to venture out of the saltside have ended up? Our story could be the stuff of a bad joke! A punch line! A ghost . . . a slain soldier . . . a dead flamen . . . and a broken-down diplomat!"

"Don't sell yourself so short," Arity said in irritation, but neither of them listened.

"My mother must have learned I was still alive. I can't hope *that* kind of news failed to reach Westshine. But there's a real chance she'll never know Thani died. I pray she never finds out. Oh, Power!" Tears drowned her voice.

Arity had seldom heard her speak of her mother. It put his mind to rest on one thing, anyhow: she did not contemplate going home to Domesdys.

Where *did* she contemplate going?

Did she have any idea?

It looked increasingly as if *he* would have to make that decision.

Hope patted Humi's back and whispered endearments. The golden fringes of the *iu's* lashes were wet.

Arity folded his arms. The snow was falling more thickly now. He gazed up at the top of the Folly, where it opened into the sky like a flower. The ridiculous little cupola was invisible from here. This huge building wasn't going to last forever: Hope had built for effect, not endurance. He could see the early signs of deterioration in the way the overhanging floors of the topmost stories bellied downward.

The Return of the Good Things

"The balls at Divaring Below have been delightful," Broken Bird said. "Sugar Bird's Foundling Uali has returned from human country and set up house. He has brought a most eclectic entourage with him, and he seems likely to be a natural host."

The last time Arity had seen Broken Bird, at Rose Eye's estate in Rimmear, with Pati, she had seemed tired of existence itself. Now the very wrinkles in her shriveled blue face danced with animation. She sat on Bronze Water's lap, her little legs swinging as she turned her benevolent regard on one member of the party after another. "You really should consider coming to Divaring with us, Hope! You would be quite a celebrity. Arity—well, perhaps it would not be so advisable for you to return! Not just yet. There is a little ill will fomenting around your name—at the best houses you would be, if not *endangered,* certainly not an honored guest."

"*Someone* has to be blamed for everything," Arity said without rancor. "And after all, I did kill him!" He laughed, turning the stark statement into an outrageous sally. "No, I don't contemplate returning to Divaring—or to the salt at all—anytime soon."

Bronze Water stroked Broken Bird's thigh indulgently. "Just as well. If you were assassinated, you would upstage us all!" He turned to Hope. His demeanor was genial, but he was evidently getting down to brass tacks. "What about it, Maiden?"

Hope sat in the corner of the hearth, holding Erene and Elicit's little daughter Artle. The fire's red glow danced over her. Since Broken Bird and Bronze Water arrived that afternoon, somehow having learned where Hope, Arity, and Humi had hidden, the *iu* had been unusually reserved. Arity hoped she knew she did not have to respond. The atmosphere was social, not political.

But she did answer. "Bird, I'm sorry. Humi and I appreciate the work you did on our behalf during the war."

("We do," Humi murmured from her seat in the shadows.)
"I *should* oblige you. I know. But I can't."

"Can't—*why*?" Bronze Water said. "Are you afraid of
finding Heaven changed, my dear? It *has* changed, with the
return of so many Hands, and the influx of young men and
women from human country—but this has all led to a sort
of *reawakening,* which means Divaring is more itself than
ever before! Old Divaring Peak glitters at night like a girl
in a new set of jewels. Heterogeneity is the craze; you'll
hardly see a couple on the lakeshore who aren't of different races."

"And if the rebels are so celebrated now—aren't you
two rather on the outs for misleading your people before
the war?" Elicit asked.

Elicit did not comprehend the issue of status among the
auchresh, Arity thought. He did not understand how the
title of *er-serbalim* protected Broken Bird and Bronze
Water from anything that might befall them. Even from
ridicule. The ex-ghostier sat beside Erene on the floor, in
the shadows, holding their son Xib on his lap. Erene had
one arm around him and one around Humi. A slack-furred
woman with a discernible belly, well into middle age, she
might easily have been the mother of the lanky girl leaning
against her side.

It had been about six years since Arity last saw Erene,
but motherhood seemed to have aged her twenty. The
beautiful, forcefully urbane senior ghostier of Golden Antelope's court could have been a different woman. Yet she
evidently felt at ease with herself. She had exhibited more
kindness in a sixday than in all the years Arity had sparred
with her in Ellipse. When the trio arrived in the clearing
in the woods, tired and wet with snow, even before Erene
greeted Humi she had thrown her arms around Arity, whispering, "I thought we would never see you again,
dearheart."

He had almost wept. Shocking.

And the children were adorable, of course. Like all children. Hope was hardly able to keep her hands off them,
hugging, petting, spoiling them with games and indulgences.
They melted her. Erene said she would make herself indispensable if she didn't watch out. In the last sixday, Erene
herself had got three times as much weaving done as usual;

she said she had time to make things instead of just mending them.

Make what?

Arity observed her covertly. Pine-needle baskets. Festival clothes. Little, pretty, useless *objets* of yarn and wood. There was not a ghost in the house. Except, of course, the ghost Humi had brought, that white seagull with its charge of murky emotion that could knock you down at a touch. Erene had said she could not keep it in the house because it would chill the rooms too much. Elicit ignored her, installing it high over the head of the big bed in the third room. Arity had made a point of going to him afterward and thanking him.

Resin-flavored smoke bulged into the room as a puff of wind came down the chimney. Bronze Water was considering Elicit's question, but not seriously. Smiling, he rubbed his jowls. "No one can accuse us of hypocrisy, Elicit! *We* do not think we were wrong to promote isolationism. We only changed sides for the sake of political expediency."

"*Oh,*" Hope whispered.

"Let us just say, events have not yet proved that those who disagreed with us were right. We stand by our theories."

"And I think that our steadfastness earns us admiration, rather than disapproval," Broken Bird said immodestly. "We maintain that isolation would also have been a viable alternative. And at the same time, we accept defeat with grace, and maintain a perfectly—*perfectly*! courteous demeanor toward the humans who have moved to Divaring." She expected her explanation to be taken in good faith, Arity saw. It was only now that she introduced a note of humor. "Why, some of those boys are quite delicious. Even the older ones ... mmm! Don't you agree with me, Bronze? And once we have taught them how to dress properly ..."

"But you're lying," Hope said. She sounded really upset. *Why oh why now, Hopie?* Arity thought wearily. "You did *not* flip-flop for the sake of political expediency! You *knew* your beliefs were wrong! You affect unpopular attitudes now, because your status protects you, and you think it gives you an interesting reputation! You will do *anything* not to get left behind by the quickly moving chariot of society!"

Everyone, including the three humans, turned shocked stares on her. Hope put her hand to her face. The little girl, Artle, reached up and tried to pull it down.

"Well, I'm sorry if I told the truth!" Hope said.

Humi said, "But aren't you going back to Divaring Below, Hope? And won't you, too, be just as much of a social hypocrite?"

"No. I'm not going back. I'm sick of glitter and games." Hope pulled Artle fiercely to her. The little girl wriggled. But she must have felt the tension in the air, for she didn't make a sound.

"I'm staying with Erene and Elicit. For the time being. Since Shine is quite firmly entrenched in Domesdys . . . and they will need help . . . when the spring comes . . ."

Artle looked around the gathering. "I'm *glad,*" she squeaked.

Bronze Water laughed, then stopped when he saw no one else was.

Arity caught a movement in the shadows. Elicit disengaged himself from Erene. He brushed past Arity's chair, his coattails releasing a waft of the scent of the dried flowers Erene kept in the clothes chest, and gently put his daughter aside. He lifted Hope to her feet. She was more than three times Elicit's age in years, but with her smooth face and slender form she could have been his daughter as easily as Humi could have been. Gold shadows rippled in the folds of her wings. Elicit said, ostensibly to her, but really to the whole gathering: "I asked you to stay, and I'll stand by it. Erene agrees with me. When you came, we realized how empty our house has been since our gods left us. Of the two who used to live here, Keef is dead, and Shine is the governor of Domesdys. *You,* on the other hand, are alive. You are a reminder of everything we did not remember we had lost."

Broken Bird resettled herself in Bronze's arms. "Well, *elpechu,* I do hope you will reconsider," she said in *auchraug.* She sounded ruffled. "It may be congenial here, but nobody can make such beautiful gowns as they do in Fewarauw! I should be surprised if there is even a decent beautician within a hundred leagues!" Her voice took on a vicious edge. "Soon you will look like a perfect *salthirre.*"

Arity and Humi walked through the trickling woods. The evergreens fluttered in the darkness. Birds hummed frag-

ments of melodies which, had they been completed, would
have shattered the world like glass.

Arity was barefoot. His breeches were soaked to the
knees. Water dripped down his neck. Humi's shoulders
were cold under his arm. He had asked her to come walking with specific things in mind, but he could not broach
the subject.

They climbed another of the many slopes that comprised
the forest. Above, a faint light slipped through the trees.

"Surely it can't be dawn already?" Arity said.

"We're coming to a cliff. I can feel it in the air. Look
out," Humi said sharply.

And indeed, the trees fell away, and they found themselves on the top of a precipice.

Arity took a deep breath, then guided her slowly to the
grassy edge.

Impossible to tell how far down the sea was. Little white
curls broke in stately motion on a scrap of beach. The dawn
would come, eventually, from behind the trees; but the sky
was paler over the sea than anywhere else. Starlight shone
through the thin cloud cover, down onto the water. Humi's
face looked ghostly and stiff, like the stretched mask of an
dead animal.

He turned from her to gaze out at the ocean. Thousands
of leagues of it. Royalland did not extend this far south.
The closest land in this direction was the South Reach of
the Archipelago. "Where are we going to go?"

She let out a long sigh, as if she had been waiting for
him to ask. "I have given it some thought. But I don't
know. I can't seem to imagine any farther ahead than this."

"We can't stay here. Not now that Hope has declared
she's going to. It would look mean for us to try to share
Erene and Elicit's hospitality—and their lives—when it's
her who has claimed them!"

"I know. I know. And it will be best if we go soon. Erene
and I love each other—but it'd be fatal for us to try to live
together. We have discovered that very quickly. In no time,
it would be Tellury Crescent all over again."

"Well, then"—he sliced the grass with his toe talons—
"there are other places we'd be welcome."

"I can't go—"

"Back to the city? I didn't ask you to. At least, not now."
He nudged her, trying to make her smile.

"Not ever!"

"What about the salt?" He dropped into *auchraug* without thinking about it. "I know that in most Heavens I would be an outcast. It'd be a miserable existence. But I shouldn't mind going back to Wind Gully. I'm pretty sure Cheris and Oak would take us in. Pati wasn't really popular there, the *ruthyalim* envied him too much—and they have longer memories there than they do in Rimmear, or Tearka, or Divaring—"

"No! I couldn't bear that!" The gutturals and trills of *auchraug,* on her lips, sent unexpected shivers down his back. "I used so much to love the ghostly way the salt forest looks at night. And the storms boiling up the gully. And your *ruthyalim* themselves, with their horns and wings and tattery clothes. Wind Gully Heaven *was* heaven for me, Ari, did you never notice that? An escape from reality into strangeness so ... so complete ... I could understand nothing about it except that it was beautiful. I don't want to ruin those memories. If I go back, *blind*—"

"Your last illusions would crumble." *You would have to learn the hard way that there is very little underneath the beauty. That* auchresh *treat profundity like a dead enemy— a corpse to be shredded and then laughed at.*

Is that *why I want to go back?*

The very idea chilled him.

"But you must go!" she said in a cold little voice, still speaking *auchraug.* "I shan't have you sacrificing yourself for me."

Rain began to fall, fat droplets oozing from the clouds, tumbling down and splatting on the ground, on their faces.

Arity squeezed her tighter.

"*Irissu,*" he said quietly, "if I went without you, I would be miserable. And if I went with you, I would lose you. The salt isn't part of me anymore, and I can't get it back. Let's not speak of it again."

"Oh, Power," she muttered. The rain plastered her fur to her skull. She stared straight ahead, blindly. "Why do you love me? Why, why, why?"

A soft, pervasive, susurrating roar identified itself as the sound of the rain on the sea. The ground exuded a wet, earthwormy smell.

"I want to know. I fail to—to understand it."

"Do you understand *me*?"

"N-no. And I don't think I ever will. But I'm *trying*— I'm *trying*—" She was close to tears.

At one time an admission like that would have sent him wheeling away from her. But that had been too soon after Pati. He had rocked for a long time in the waves of that passion which had grown all the more terrible as it atrophied. Now, despair just shivered briefly through him and vanished. He kissed her on the mouth. It was the first time he had touched her since their reunion. Her lips were soft and icy. "You have to stop trying to understand. Give up. That's my conclusion, my dear. Just stop understanding."

"Ohhh. Oh, Power!" She shuddered as if it did not bear thinking about. Quickly, she said in a caressing voice: "Do you remember how we used to *teth*" to Veretry, to have some time to ourselves, and it would always be raining? I came to love the rain. It meant something like Wind Gully Heaven meant to me. This rain is different—but it brings those days back. I remember . . ."

He kissed her again. This time she kissed him back, hesitantly. They moved closer together and she shut her eyes, pressing herself against him. Momentarily she drew back. "Gods, Ari, you're all covered in scars."

"So are you." He pulled her close again. Either through heat transferral or excitement, her flesh was warming up.

She giggled. She actually giggled. "But yours are on the outside."

"Wait till you see me naked." He cursed. "Damn! I didn't mean that!"

"I know you didn't," she said. "Anyhow, I'm used to it. It just means you aren't guarding your tongue around me—which is a measure of trust I don't get from many other people."

Her movements as she rubbed against him became languid. After a minute, in a half-wondering voice, she said, "I shouldn't mind going back *there*."

"Where?"

"Veretry."

"Veretry?"

"Can you take us there?"

"Not now." He kissed her eyelashes, her cheeks, tasting the salt on her fur.

"Yes, now!" She pulled away, keeping hold of his tunic. "It's important. It's raining, Ari. We can come back later for our things. *Please*—"

The rain had thudded so loudly on those vast expanses of grass. You could see nothing in those storms. You could hardly breathe. It was like a warm perforated sea.

And there were the jungles. Arity had never been there, but he had heard countless accounts of them, as everyone in the civilized lands had. Steamy green labyrinths that never turned brown, even in the depths of winter. Crystalline streams trickling by knotted tree roots, and moss monkeys kneeling on their banks, chattering. The tree cats never came down from the tree cover. They drank from the hollows high up, where the rain collected.

Humi launched herself forward again and wrapped around Arity like a skinny little beast. She was almost warm all over now, except for the ends of her fingers and her knees. "It's coming back, Ari. I don't know exactly what it is, but I think maybe it's what I felt, all those awful nights in Hem's house in Temeriton—before the war got in the way—the stuff of my dreams of you. But it's so—so tenuous—I don't want to lose it—I think—I think if we go *now*, I might be able to love you again—"

I might be able to love you again

"Hold on," he said. He wrapped his arms securely around her and stepped off the edge of the cliff.

The air screams past their ears. They tumble with their fingers locked in each other's clothing, curving farther and farther from the gray rock. Her mouth stretches in a soundless scream. Their wet clothes clap loudly.

Falling

Into the red blackness where there are no heartbeats, no noise, no air, where it is like being underwater in a sea the consistency of sand.

In Human Country

Humi wore the heat like a second coat of fur now. The damp tepid air; the daily rainstorms; the rare, freezing winds that blew at high speed through the forest, tearing leaves and branches and small animals from the trees, leaving great gaps in the tree cover, disarranging, destroying, *cleansing*. She loved them. The currents in the air, the wafts of sweet and sharp and disgusting scents, the prickle of dead twigs and the squish of ground-runner liana under her feet as she walked. These were her world.

But it had taken her much longer than she had anticipated to get used to them. For at least a month, she and Arity had been absolutely miserable. They had caught a southern chill and spent days stretched coughing by the side of a stream. Finally they had realized that the atmosphere in the forest was too strong for them. That was why nobody lived here. One day in twelve, on the average, they had to breathe fresh air. So they *teth"d* to the pampas plains, where no mortal ever went except for the bands of blue-furred nomads. And field mice as big as her fist. Their flesh was tough but it had a subtle smoky flavor. Ari spitted them, and she cooked them over a fire, basting them with pijreed juice. They had to clear their blackened fire circle anew each visit, the grass invaded so fast. It was manual labor of a sheer relentlessness she had not experienced since the long-gone days in Beaulieu.

The wind blew constantly on the pampas, fresh and sweet. At night they had to cuddle together for warmth. Not that they wouldn't have slept curled together, anyhow. "But it *would* be nice to live like people instead of animals," Arity said wistfully.

In the vine-hung clearing which they had chosen for their own, deep in the forest, stood a one-room cabin they had built with their own four hands. They began to consider setting up a tent on the pampas, too, with materials they could obtain from the nomads.

Barter capital would not pose a problem. They could *teth"* to any one of a number of places—Shulage province, Delta City, even Wind Gully Heaven—and whatever they wanted would be given to them.

But so far they had not gone back. Not even to get their things from Erene and Elicit's house.

No one knew they were here. Power knew what people thought.

Humi did not care.

It had been almost two years.

They lived on an *auchresh* schedule now, like the forest animals. To Humi, it made no difference: her ruined corneas perceived only a slightly redder darkness during the day than they did at night. And *wrchrethre* or not, Ari tangibly gained energy when the jungle was cool and the screams of the night monkeys echoed from tree to tree. So she was happy to go along with his wishes. She found it more difficult to get to sleep, true, when birds were singing outside the cabin and the sun fell on her back—in the clearing, the trees couldn't obstruct it, and she *felt* the rough-cut shape of the window Arity had chopped in the wall, hot on her fur—but she never told him. She liked to lie beside him when he was sleeping, anyhow. Times like this, right now. Honey bubbles of euphoria. Heaven in human country.

She curled inside a warm, gently pulsating envelope. The sun warmed her back and the heat that radiated off Arity's poor, scarred body warmed her breasts and stomach. She turned her face to him. with one finger she touched a budding thorn at his hairline. His thorns were so sensitive; she teased him about it!

He shuddered. She let her hand fall, and wriggled closer until their noses touched. He smelled of sweat and wood-shavings. Covertly she shared his breath.

They shared everything. More often than not, she did not need to speak more than one word for him to know what she meant, and the same went for him.

Not that they no longer talked. Almost every night after supper, as dawn drew near and the forest quieted, they held long, rambling coversations. They talked of grudges and murders and pederasty and poisonings. Dark and unpleasant, but comfortingly familiar. If they were in the pampas, Humi felt glad she could not *see* the vast, rustling darkness outside the circle of their fire. Ari could keep watch for both of them.

But of course, to him, night was not dark. The pampas was a rippling, endlessly shaded chiaroscuro of starlight. Once, he had described to her how he could *see* the breeze sweeping across the grass, the glider bats riding on the breast of the wind like gulls riding the sea. It had made her want to claw her useless eyes out of her head.

Quite often, now, she grew frustrated enough with her own particular darkness to weep. It usually happened on her rare escapades into daylight—her indulgences in mortality. When she was with Ari they were not woman and *auchresh,* but differently evolved beings, the only two of a race of their own: forest dwellers, hunters, gatherers; Charity and Humility. But sometimes she needed to be alone. And then, when she sat by the side of a brook in broad day with her tiger spear beside her, her toes in the warm water, or when she roosted in the crutch of a tree, the bark dust tickling her nostrils, the tears came. She had no more control over them than she did over the running brook. She was reminded of those nights in Hem's house when she cried uncontrollably, confused by a weakness she had not suspected in herself.

Then, she had thought she was crying for Ari. Now—

Thani was dead. Pati was dead. Hope was presumably far gone on her quest for humanity. Sol, Humi only remembered in the same vague nightmarish way one remembers a fever. There would not be another end to her and Arity's togetherness.

Then what was she crying for?

Ari always knew after it happened, and he took special care to make absurd jokes, or tickle her, or surprise her—anything to get her laughing. That was when she loved him most of all. No. *Most* of all were the times *she* found *him* alone, when he said he was going hunting, or woodcutting, and she (sitting outside the cabin plaiting lianas, or pounding leaves for cloth) lifted her head with a sudden knowledge that he was just standing there, somewhere deep in the forest, gazing into the greenness. She had not his self-control. She would drop whatever she was doing and run to find him, and seize both his hands and kiss that strange, dazed expression off his face. That look . . . ! She could picture it so clearly it was almost as if she had *seen* it.

She still thought in terms of images. Even though she had not made a ghost in well over a year, that tendency of the visual artist was embedded in her. But at least she was no longer stuck in a world she could not see. She had developed a sort of sixth sense, a forest sense that let her walk through the undergrowth at a normal pace, putting a hand up to ward off branches just before they caught her in the face. When she heard a wild pig in the brush, she could spit it cleanly through the eye with her tiger spear before it even attacked.

Nostalgia, crying fits, fresh tropical fruit, the best water she had ever tasted, long lazy days making love and dozing.

Was this what she had yearned for, all those dark days in Temeriton?

She thought of the last, miserable days at Erene and Elicit's when everyone had been so kind to her. She had not really wanted anything at all, then. So cloyingly kind they had been. Tiptoeing around her with soft-shod feet, touching her with careful hands, trying to make her feel at home with "*imrchu*" and "my little Humi"! And it was all wrong. She had scarcely been able to think for disappointment. But she had known it wasn't what she wanted.

They were still *afraid* of her.

All she wanted was to be with *him,* to talk with him, to sleep curled up with him, to char to ashes with him if that was what it came down to.

In that last half a minute, she had been pretty sure that was what it *had* come down to. On the top of the cliff in Pirady, as it started to rain, she had forced herself to say what she meant. She had torn down the walls of stone around herself by force, and clutched him with her bleeding hands. And it had somehow been too much. He meant to kill them both. She had pushed him quite literally over the edge.

There was nothing she could do about it, and she didn't care. As they hurtled downward, doubling their speed by the split second, and the air whistled around them, cold and hard as a stone tube, they were *together.* The whistling vacuum stre-e-e-etched into a long, freezing silence and she heard her scream die away.

She had time to think, exultantly: *How superb that it should end like this! It is like a flamen's precautionary tale: the wanton lovers, offenders against rectitude, falling to their deaths in each other's arms!*

The waves roared louder and louder. She was falling facedown. Tears streamed up over her temples. The surf breaking on the beach was much stormier than it had sounded from up above. Hungry, violent waves. She wouldn't have been surprised if they were twenty feet high.

And
then
—

Damp grass under her palms, and warmth. And heavy scented air filling her lungs like water.

                                    *   *   *

"We can't stay here forever, you know," Arity said.

They were perched on their log-stump stools, warming their feet at a fire they didn't really need. In a baza tree at the edge of the clearing, a dawnflute sang his piercing good-morning song. But for Arity and Humi, it was the end of a sweetly tiring night. They had decided to build their tent in the pampas without approaching the nomads; they had spent the day transporting piles of the huge, fibrous kibre leaves they used to make cloth to the campsite. Ari had had to do all the *tech "tach ching;* Humi had only done the fetching and carrying. He was weary to the bone. *That* was why he had said something so unexpected.

But was it really unexpected? That strange little frown she sensed more and more often in his voice—

"We can't go on, and on, and on like this."

She moved to him and put her arm around his shoulders, stroking the packed muscle on his chest. "Of course we can't. But do we have to talk about it? I'd rather not."

He sighed, and shook his head. "Power," he said, admiringly, "you moved like a sighted person just then."

She knew her "forest sense" worked best when she wasn't concentrating on it. But she was flattered all the same. She smiled. "I can fake it well enough to fool everyone except myself!"

"And me."

"Mmm?"

"Everyone except me. You still wear the sapphire necklace with the ruby earrings."

"They feel the same!" She laughed. "And does it really matter what color they are, when I'm wearing them both with dresses made of *leaves*?"

"They're very nice leaf dresses. Especially the patchwork one. Our *er-serbalu* would be envious. I wish you'd make me a tunic like that."

"Make it yourself!" She nudged him.

He pretended to think about it. "Only if you kill that tiger that's been leaving tracks over by the Chrume"—this was the title they had bestowed on the largest of the local trickles—"for me."

"Oh, you!" In fact it was quite possible that he would take it into his head to make a tunic. He was nearly as proficient with a needle as she. It had rather surprised her when she first found out: he said he had had to learn, in Rimmear. After she discovered *why* he had had to learn, she had worked extra hard at acquiring the *mainraui* skill of the spear, as a kind of compensation for the horrors he had put himself through in that shadowy *auchresh* city.

It had all been for her sake. If she ever felt herself getting annoyed with him, she convinced herself of that all over again.

He shifted in her arm, and she felt him grow serious. "But doesn't it make you want to find out if you really *could* fool someone who doesn't know you? Doesn't it make you want to go back to Delta City and try out your skills on the court? I'm sure Aneisneida has a fine new flock of courtiers and nobles scuttling around the palace district by now, plump and ready to be skewered."

"You aren't really suggesting it!"

He shrugged. "Am I?"

"You're assuming Delta City has grown soft in our absence," she pointed out. "I think that if those fat nobles exist, they probably have fangs that even you should take into account. Humans have learned two lessons they won't forget in a hurry."

"What are those, then?"

"Never trust an *auchresh*." She was warming to her subject. It was not exactly an unfamiliar one, although neither she nor Ari had ever placed themselves in the hypothetical picture before. "Of course, that doesn't mean there aren't any *auchresh* in positions of power. I should guess that whoever is left of the *ex-kervayim* has worked his way to the top, or close to it."

"And what's the other lesson?"

"Believe in *nothing*. In other words—never let your guard down."

He pulled her down beside him. She knelt up on the ground. The gathering dew soaked into the knees of her skirt—the old, tattered one she had brought from Pirady, her "work clothes." "We *auchresh* used to secretly worship your people for your ability to trust others. I shouldn't think even Lady Summer, Lord Nearecloud, and Lord Dagger can entirely purge themselves of that ability! There are some people who will be simply beyond suspicion—who will have been transformed into legend. And I'm not talk-

ing about the flamens, either. Or the apostates. I suspect
they play a very active role in the court."

"Then who *are* you talking about?" she said, although
she thought she knew.

"Us," he said, his mouth close to her ear, his voice intense. "They wouldn't be prepared for us."

"Ari!" She pulled away. "What are you thinking?" But
the pictures had flashed through her mind, of course. The
possibilities. The flattery and the delightful hypocrisy of politeness to a mortal enemy, and the far more visceral sense
of triumph when someone creeps up behind you intending
to stab you (it had happened to her twice during the war)
and you let him get close, secretly tensing your muscles,
and then whirl around and get him with the pearl-handled
stiletto you keep in your bodice as a brooch before he gets
you. Straight in through the eye. Spurt.

"Never," she said. "Never!"

"You've thought about it, though. Haven't you? I know
you, my love."

She kissed him and pulled him to his feet. "You know
me too well. You're really tired. We need to damp this fire
and get to bed. And we should spend tomorrow on the
pampas. We can work on the tent. Today was the first time
in a couple of sixdays we've been out of the forest; I think
it's getting to you."

"Do you still keep track of the sixdays?" he asked, sling-
ing his arm around her waist. They padded barefoot toward
the cabin. The grass licked her legs, a thousand sharp, wet
little tongues. No matter how much they walked over it, it
sprang back up every day.

"More or less."

"I have been, too, recently."

"Oh, don't say that. Stop it!" She spun around and threw
herself against him. She clasped her hand over the back of
his skull, burying her fingers in the soft curls. Their lips
met. His hands worked down over her hips, squeezing her
buttocks, and she slid her other hand inside his shirt, fingering the closed mouths of the scars on his back. Some of
those were erogenous. What a bizarre and wonderful beast
her lover was! She delighted in the streamlined shapes of
his shoulder blades: she imagined baby wings folded wetly
inside, stillborn.

His breathing quickened. His body heat increased. She

felt her heart responding to the excitement, too, thud a *thud,* thud a *thud.* He probed her mouth rhythmically with his tongue. Pride in her new flesh, her repossessed curves, flickered through her. Power, how she loved satisfying him. She writhed against him, pushing her hips against the lump of his erection. They were exactly the same height. She had always liked that.

"*Irissu,*" he growled. "*Power—*" The flowers of human country scented his breath. Lilies of the valley, honeysuckle, roses. It was the scent of predators, of every last saltborn creature, no matter how mean or foul. It exuded through his very pores when he was most aroused. "Love. You," he whispered. "Love. You. Love. You."

Her lips were seared when he took his away. His hands left branded marks on her hips. The dawn air flowed down her throat like some freezing acid drink. "Come on!" He took her hand and pulled her across the clearing at a run.